I0674877

Trust I Seek

Laura Gates

Copyright © 2020 Laura Gates All rights reserved

The characters and events portrayed in this book are fictitious. Any similarity to real persons, living or dead, is coincidental and not intended by the author.

No part of this book may be reproduced, or stored in a retrieval system, or transmitted in any form or by any means, electronic, mechanical, photocopying, recording, or otherwise, without express written permission of the publisher.

ISBN: 978-1-7352839-1-3

Cover design by: Mary Hatton
Edited by: Jessica Smith
Library of Congress Control Number: 2018675309
Printed in the United States of America

Introduction

Metallica is the original artist who wrote the song titles named in this book. Feel free to purchase a Metallica album and follow along for an amazing journey of two people who have been through a lot of trauma who grow in friendship, love, and trust. I would recommend the following records: The Black Album, Ride the Lightning, Reload, and St. Anger. The following characters and stories are loosely based on members, family members, and associates of the heavy metal band, Metallica. Any similarities are strictly coincidental. I got the idea while watching the documentary Some Kind of Monster. At the same time, a bunch of my friends were going through or went through various divorces mostly because their husbands mistreated and abused them. It broke my heart watching them struggle. This book was also an opportunity to combine various passions of mine: Metallica, music, the performing arts, fitness, Zumba, and Strong Nation.

Chapter 1

Relapse

Beau stared at the three coffins in front of him. One was an adult coffin, and the other two were for children. Inside the adult casket was his wife, Phoebe, and the children's caskets contained his two children, Chloe and Cordell. The minister recited the famous Psalm 23 as Beau reflected on the last day his family was alive.

Phoebe loaded Cordell into the car seat just as Beau kissed Chloe on the cheek before she climbed into the car to buckle herself up. It was Tuesday, Library Day, where the kids would enjoy dancing, storytime, and a craft at the library. Phoebe would then take them to go check out some books so they would be able to have new stories to read for the week. Even though Beau was a member of Death Toll, the most successful metal band in the world, he and his wife decided to raise their kids as normal as possible giving them chores, library days, trips to children's museums, and the occasional meal prep when Phoebe cooked. Beau baked cakes for everyone on their birthday and even decorated.

Beau stood between 6'1 and 6'2, towering over his band mates, Luke, Kade, and Rick. He had blond hair, hooded almond shaped blue eyes, and very broad shoulders and chest. Down-picking on the guitar had something to do with that. He also had sleeve tattoos up and down his arms, representing major events in his life and beliefs. He also had a neck tattoo of a flying skull singing. He had tattoos going across his clavicle with his kids' names on them as well as a spot reserved for a third name. "Carpe Diem" was tattooed on his arm with flames around it, representing a pyrotechnic accident that happened about four years before that nearly killed him, but the only evidence of the accident was a few scars on the right side of his face. He had the bass solo played by the original bassist of Death Toll and his friend, Nole Bradshaw, tattooed on his arm shortly after Nole died. He had the words "Riff Life" tattooed on his knuckles. Even though he abandoned the religion of his childhood, Christian Science, Beau considered himself Christian, still.

Just before she climbed into the Subaru, Phoebe walked back to Beau and kissed him. "We will be back in about an hour and a half. Lunch afterward?" she asked. "Yes. Let me know where to meet you," he said before giving her one last kiss. "Will do. I also have some news for you and the kids," Phoebe said. "Oh, did you get your acceptance letter yet?" Beau asked, hoping Phoebe had received her letter to the Academy of Art to receive her Master's in Fashion. "No, not yet. It's something different," Phoebe said, "Bye, Baby." Phoebe leaned in for one more kiss. "Bye, Babe," Beau said, kissing her back, opening her door for her, and watching his sweet family drive away.

Everything from there on seemed hazy, from the time he got a phone call that his family had been in a car accident, killing Cordell instantly and putting Phoebe and Chloe in the ICU. Both died within the hour. Phoebe was ten weeks pregnant with their third child. The very next day, the acceptance letter for Phoebe arrived in the mail.

Beau watched as his family was lowered into the ground. The minister had asked him to say something, but Beau forgot. The minister nudged him before Beau pulled out a piece of paper.

"Phoebe was Argentinian by birth, but you would never have guessed because of her blonde hair and blue eyes. She wasn't the typical-looking Latina, but she was beautiful inside and out. I met her on our Thrash Tour where she worked as a costume designer for us. She always had a good eye for Fashion. Phoebe was an avid dancer, especially Latin music. She obtained her BFA in Fashion all while dealing with a husband battling alcoholism. Rather than abandon him, Phoebe stuck with him but gave him an ultimatum. She was so loving and kind. Phoebe devoted her time as a wife and mother to making sure her kids were ready to take care of themselves in adulthood. Before she died, she was accepted to get her Master's in Fashion, a dream she had had since Cordell was born. Phoebe Halstead will be missed tremendously, but may we all remember her devotion to her family and friends," Beau concluded.

Beau wondered what he did to deserve this as fellow bandmates, Luke, Kade, and Rick, approached him with their families. They each offered their condolences and offered to open their homes to him if he wanted a change of scenery. He declined the offer because he wanted to be alone. Soon, his in-laws came to give him a hug, as well as his sister, Dinah. His older half-brothers, Edward and Ethan, were also there to offer their support at the funeral. His siblings had been staying with him in preparation for the funeral as well as helping him out. "Are you sure you don't want us to stay with you another week?" Ethan asked. "No, I'll be fine," Beau reassured. One by one as everyone approached him and Phoebe's parents to offer their condolences, they said goodbye.

Soon, Beau was all alone in his 11,000 square foot home. He sat down in his favorite armchair, feeling empty inside. Suddenly, all of the awful thoughts came into his head; *she finally abandoned you, and she took the kids with her. Everybody leaves you. First, your dad, then your mom, Nole, Jacob, and now your family.*

Beau had ignored that voice for five years since he got home from rehab, but it was louder this time around. You have nothing. Soon, everyone else you love and care about will leave you. *There's only one thing that can help you get through this, the voice said.* Beau couldn't take it anymore. The scenery around him became hazy again, and he soon found himself in a cab on his way to some place he hadn't been in five years; a bar.

Beau, still wearing his suit, sat at the bar drinking his drink of choice, Jagermeister. "Hey, man. Can I have another one of these?" Beau asked the bartender holding up the glass. He looked up at Beau and realized, "You're Beau Halstead from Death Toll. So sorry to hear about your family." Beau winced a smile and nodded. The bartender set another bottle down in front of Beau, and he began sipping it slowly.

"Hold on, haven't you claimed to be straight-edge?" the bartender asked.

"Are you my mother? I'm a damn paying customer. What else matters?" Beau said, starting to slur. The bartender held up his hands, giving up the argument.

What now, he thought to himself again watching the bartender work to fill other customer's drinks. He only knew of two lifestyles, and he gave the other one up for his family. *There is no family, so why bother*, the negative voice in his head said.

Beau drank a bottle of Jagermeister from the early evening clear until Last Call. He soon ordered a beer, watching the place go from being mostly dead to hopping with lots of people. There were all sorts of people, including some captivating girls. One had very long blonde hair just like Phoebe, another had short black hair that sat on her shoulders, and the other had very long brown hair. They sat at a booth not too far from the bar where Beau sat at.

Eventually, the three girls were joined by another group of girls. They all looked like they were happy, which was something Beau missed being for the past week and a half. He kept sipping his beer and watching the group of girls. Whenever one would stand up to get another round of drinks for the booth, which was usually the pretty blondee, some idiot guy would hit on her, but the blonde kept blowing the guy off. Beau tried remembering some of the things he used to say during his crazy days. He knew he didn't have to work that hard considering he was the frontman for one of the biggest metal bands in the world.

Beau decided he was going home with one of those girls, preferably the blonde because of her long hair like Phoebe's. He grabbed his beer and stood up. Beau stumbled a little but managed to balance himself. He walked over to the group of girls and said, "I could not help but notice you guys having the most fun in this bar. May I join you?" The girls were at first, a little taken aback because of his appearance. However, the blonde he had his eye on asked him, "Are you Beau Halstead of Death Toll?" Beau smiled and thought to himself, *Nailed i*t. "Yes, I am," he said. The blonde scooted over and made room for Beau to sit down.

All of the girls started to talk to him about what he was doing at the bar, showing sympathy for the loss of his family, asking what they could do to make him feel better, and offering to pay his tab. "You know," said the blonde to everyone, "let's get out of here. There is a club down the street. Let's show Beau a good time." The girls and Beau started climbing out of the booth. The girls took turns throwing down dollar bills, and Beau threw down $50.00.

They all stumbled down the street towards the nightclub. The group of girls and Beau walked towards the front of the line knowing that Beau would get them in. When the bouncer saw Beau, he immediately let him and the girls in. Beau hadn't been to a club for a long time, so Beau wasn't sure what to expect. When they got inside, he regretted not having earplugs. The lights flashed, and the music was EDM, which was not his favorite. He watched the blonde girl dance to the music as they made their way to the dance floor, so he decided to make an exception.

The girls proved to be quite loose as they all danced with each other, ground with other guys, and ground in Beau's lap. He had bought a beer to sip on while dancing to make the evening more tolerable. The room began to spin as he stumbled while dancing. The blonde girl soon started to dance closer to Beau. Their faces got incredibly close before she made a move. They kissed, danced, and kissed some more. Beau's head kept spinning and pounding in pain.

Everything inside of him was telling him to stop this erratic behavior, but then the negative voice inside his head kept saying, *Why bother?* He eventually ended up in the blonde's apartment. They went at it all night long until they fell asleep in her bed.

The next morning, Beau woke up to the biggest headache of his life fighting the urge to throw up. The previous night was a little hazy. Beau looked around to see if he recognized where he was, which he didn't. He didn't remember the girl in bed with him. Beau quietly slipped out of bed, grabbed his clothes with his phone, slipped his boxers back on, and proceeded to leave the apartment very quietly. He descended the stairs while getting dressed.

As Beau put his shirt on, he walked outside onto the street. The light stung his eyes, and he covered them up with his hand. As his eyes adjusted, Beau looked at his surroundings, trying to figure out where he was. Once he became familiar with the street he was on, he hailed a cab to take him back to his house in Novato. He paid the cabby as he climbed out of the car. He walked up the driveway to his house.

Beau opened his front door and walked in. The house felt very lonely as he walked into the kitchen to get something to eat. For the past few days, he had been living off of cereal, toast, and energy drinks while his relatives stayed with him.

The previous night was the first night he had touched alcohol in about 5 years. He felt dirty inside, but the emptiness he felt was even stronger. The void needed to be filled somehow, and he only knew of one other way to fill it. He checked the time, and he realized he had to get to the studio in less than an hour. He quickly showered and cleaned up to get rid of the stench and memories of the previous day. Beau brushed his teeth twice to ensure the alcohol smell was gone. He put on new clothes, and he slicked his blonde hair back. Beau trimmed his goatee.

Beau looked down at the P tattooed on his left hand. He missed his wife so badly. The irony in all of this was that she would know how to help him feel better. Fighting his demons, he ran downstairs, grabbed his helmet, walked out to his garage, climbed on his favorite chopper, and drove off to the studio. He stopped at a coffee shop on the way to help combat the hangover and headache.

When he got to the studio, Beau walked inside the equipment room and picked up his white ESP Explorer. He proceeded to walk into the recording room. Beau started noodling on his guitar. He could not help but feel sad, angry, depressed, and frantic, which appeared in his guitar playing. He went along with it and began writing everything down that he did. Everything became louder, more agitated, and angrier.

Soon, Luke, Kade, and Rick joined Beau in the recording room. Luke sat at the drums, Kade plugged his guitar into his amp, and Rick plugged his bass into his amp. Soon, the other bandmates began noodling along with Beau. They matched the anger he felt, and they began to empathize with him. The bandmates hadn't seen Beau this angry since before he met Phoebe.

Luke Jeppsen stood a little over 5'5, the shortest member of Death Toll, and the only member born outside of the US. He was born and raised in Copenhagen, Denmark. He did not look like the stereotypical Dane, though. Luke inherited the Jewish traits from his paternal grandmother, so he had dark brown hair like a Jew, but because of the Scandinavian blood in him, he ended up with green eyes. He was considered very slender, almost feminine looking. Beau often teased him about that. Whether it was this reason or some other reason, Beau and Luke often butted heads.

Kade Hansen, the lead guitarist, stood about 5'7, had black curly hair that sat on his shoulders, and dark brown eyes. He was the only member of the band that had Filipino ancestry, which showed in his physical features. He was also considered very slim, but that's because he was a vegetarian just like Luke. Kade often tried to keep his ego in check, especially during the early days when Beau and Luke argued a lot.

Even though Rick stood 5'9, he was the strongest out of them all. It was mainly due to all of the surfing and skateboarding he did with his two kids. He was the third bassist in Death Toll after the second one, Jacob, quit. Rick was of Mexican and Native American descent with the longest full name of the band; Ricardo Angel Manuel Eduardo Diego Sebastian Torres Vasquez. His black hair went all the way down to the middle of his back. His wife, Kaylee, often braided his hair in four braids during concerts. His eyes were dark brown. Of all the band members, Rick was the happiest and most laid back.

Luke stopped playing, got Beau's attention, and asked, "Do we need to take some time off? I mean, your family's funeral was yesterday. Maybe we can resume in about a month or two when you've had time to process."

"I need to stay busy," Beau replied.

"Are you sure?" Kade asked.

"If I don't stay busy, I will fall apart. We need to finish this album," Beau said irritably. The guys decided to back off.

"Okay, let's get to work," Luke said.

The band ended up writing about five songs that day with this crazy edge that Beau brought into his playing. Plus, they went back to their old thrash metal rhythms, which made Luke very happy. When they were done, it was about 6:00 PM. They were all hungry and went into the kitchen where they had ordered food for the week. Beau watched his friends begin digging into their food.

"You know what? I'm going to take off. I have some things I need to do before tomorrow," Beau said, imagining the taste of Jagermeister in his mouth and the thrill of going home with another woman that evening. Luke, Kade, and Rick turned to look at Beau.

"You sure, man?" Luke asked.

Beau nodded. "Yep, I'm good. Just need some more alone time."

"All right, see ya, Beau!" the band said each one by one.

Beau's night ended up just like the previous except he went to a different bar this time where he felt the girls would appreciate tasteful music. He woke up the next morning in another apartment in a different bed with a new girl. As he slipped out of the apartment, he got a phone call. Luke's name and picture appeared. "Hey, man. What's up?"

"Have you looked at the time? Fans are showing up for the tour of the studio we promised!" Luke snapped.

Beau looked at his watch and realized it was almost 9, which was the time of the tour. "Sorry, got caught up with something. I'm on my way," Beau said.

"Did you go to a bar?" Luke asked.

Beau hesitated to answer, trying to think of a lie. "No. I'm just at home. I will be there in 10 minutes."

"Are you sure you don't need time off?" Luke asked.

"No. Stop asking me that. I'm fine."

"Did you hook up with someone last night?" Luke asked again.

Beau hesitated again. "I've been staying in hotels at night because it still feels weird to be in the house by myself. I've been eating at home, though." Beau could feel the trench he was digging getting bigger.

Luke felt very suspicious of Beau's words, but all he could do was take his word for it. "All right, see you in 10."

"See ya, man!" Beau hung up his phone.

The weeks started to blur together, and Beau's days and nights remained the same. He started going to different clubs and raves throughout San Francisco to avoid running into the same girls. His targets were usually in their early 20's because they didn't know who he was, and he found that appealing. He would always sneak out of the girl's apartment and head to the studio the next morning.

The other band members would be inspired in their writing, and Beau went through Writer's Block. There was only one additional time in his life where he felt like this, and he ended up going to rehab. As his thoughts wandered, Beau wondered what would happen if Luke, Kade, and Rob found out he was living his old lifestyle and going against the straight-edge lifestyle he firmly represented in the past. Beau knew he could stop if he wanted to because he already had rehab. He knew he didn't need to go back.

Death Toll's new album was coming along rather slowly mainly because Beau lacked the inspiration he felt during previous albums. Luke, Kade, and Rick tried to help him, but the Writers' Block kept getting worse. Beau tried watching the news, going to a park, at times tried talking to a girl instead of just kissing her, hanging out with Luke and his family, but nothing was working. The band began to notice Beau's erratic behavior as the weeks progressed. Whenever they suggested taking a break, Beau snapped at them, and the snaps would get harsher and harsher. Luke was especially getting frustrated with Beau because he thought Beau would have moved past this behavior. One particular evening, Luke decided that he would follow Beau around to see what the deal was.

Luke excused himself early after practice only to hide his car just a block away from where he had a clear visual of the studio exit. Beau left shortly after, trying to figure out which bar or lounge to go to that night. He climbed into his Rover and drove off, not realizing that Luke was following him.

Luke followed about a car length behind Beau as they drove towards downtown San Francisco and parked in front of some hip lounge or bar. Luke couldn't tell what it was. Luke parked across the street and watched Beau walk past the bouncer assuming the bouncer knew who he was. Luke got out of his car and walked across the road to the bouncer.

"Hey! Luke Jeppsen! Are you here with Beau?" the bouncer asked.

"Yes. I am meeting him here. Did he walk in already?" Luke asked, trying to sound casual.

"You just missed him," the bouncer said, "but go ahead and go in."

"Thanks," Luke said, sighing in relief.

The lounge was very loud and full of young people in their early 20's. The EDM gave Luke a little spring in his step as well as motivation to find his friend. He surveyed the crowd trying to find his friend and bandmate. Finally, he found Beau sitting at the bar sipping on a bottle of Jack Daniels. Luke's worst fear had come true.

Suddenly, Luke had flashbacks to that awful time right before Beau checked himself into rehab. Their bassist had just quit, Beau drank heavily every night while they were on tour and often cheated on Phoebe while she was pregnant with Chloe. A therapist was helping the band cope with their bassist quitting, but Beau transferred all of his abandonment issues onto other members of the group. That was when Beau went to rehab.

Luke continued to watch Beau drink his beer, go talk to a girl, kiss that girl, walk into the bathroom with her, come out looking like a mess, and leave the lounge with her. Luke followed Beau and the girl to her apartment where Luke stood outside to make sure his hunch was correct. Sure enough, he heard his friend moaning along with the girl who couldn't have been more than 22.

Luke walked back outside to his car, climbed in, and drove back to the studio. He had sent a text to Kade, Rick, and their former therapist, Dr. Peter Bennett, to have an emergency band meeting in 20 minutes. When they all arrived and met in the living room of the studio, Luke conveyed every detail of what he saw to the others. Kade's face matched the terror Luke felt inside, Rick processed the information, and Dr. Bennet thought about a solution. They sat in silence for about two minutes.

Dr. Bennet finally chimed, "He needs to go back to rehab. Clearly, those issues have resurfaced and possibly more because of the deaths of Phoebe and his kids."

Kade nodded his head. "I agree. Something has snapped with him lately. He has been a pain to work with, and he hasn't been like this in five years," he said.

Luke also nodded his head. "All right, so the question is, how do we tell him?" Luke asked.

Rick said, "We might need to trick him. We know how stubborn he can be. He's not going to go easily or willingly."

"I will do some research on facilities, find the best one, make a reservation, and drop Beau off without him realizing it," Dr. Bennet said.

"Okay. I just don't want to go down this road again. The band almost broke up last time Beau lost control, and I'm not sure if I can take it all again," Luke said.

"I understand, but right now, we need to focus on Beau overcoming this weakness of his," Dr. Bennet said.

A week later, Beau walked into the studio entirely clueless of what the band and Dr. Bennett planned. He noticed the band being extremely kind to him, and he thought that was weird. Luke kept checking his phone every five minutes, which was very unusual. Little did he know that Luke was texting Dr. Bennet about Beau's reservation at a facility in San Francisco that would allow Beau to continue working on their album and live there for six to twelve months depending on his progress. Dr. Bennet would be involved in the counseling side of things to ensure Beau made a full recovery. They also included some counseling on grieving.

After band practice, Luke walked up to Beau. "Want to go out for some barbeque?" he asked Beau. Beau shrugged. "Why not? I've got some time," Beau said. Luke followed Beau to his roadster, where Beau tossed Luke the keys. Luke felt pleased about this, considering he knew how much Beau would be yelling at him later. As they climbed in, Luke nodded at Kade and Rick signaling them to let the bodyguards know that they were on their way. Everyone knew that Beau would fight this decision and get physical, but they all knew this was the best thing for him.

They drove across the Golden Gate Bridge into San Francisco. Luke felt very tense with what was about to happen once they got into the city, but he had to stay calm so Beau wouldn't suspect anything. Beau looked around him, trying to figure out what bar, club, or lounge to go to that night. He pulled out his phone to look up some of the bars and clubs near the barbeque joint they were going to.

Luke parked on the street in front of the facility. Beau put his phone away and looked around, realizing where he was. Beau turned to look at Luke. "Why are we in front of a rehab facility?" he asked. "Consider this your intervention," Luke replied as he waved his arms.

Beau turned around to look behind him and saw these two huge guys walking towards him. His eyes grew three sizes when he realized what they were there for. Suddenly, he saw Dr. Bennet walking behind them. "You think I need rehab?" Beau snapped at Luke.

"I followed you yesterday to the lounge and to that one girl's apartment. You've been drinking and sleeping around again. This behavior is what almost killed the band last time. Do you really want that to happen again?" Luke asked.

"I don't need to go back. I know the tools. I can stop at any time."

"Can you? Do you want to? Look, I know how much you miss Phoebe, but..."

"I don't want to talk about this!" Beau yelled.

"I understand you're mad, but I don't want to go down this road, again. Whether you like it or not, you're being checked in," Luke said just as the bodyguards opened the doors and put their hands on Beau's shoulders.

Beau shook the hands off his shoulders, but they grabbed him a little firmer. "Don't make this harder than it needs to be," Luke said, "they are not afraid to use physical force if they have to."

Beau was so mad at Luke and the whole band for their betrayal, but he also felt the bodyguards squeezed his shoulders even tighter, warning him of their abilities. He climbed out of the roadster and walked with them without fighting. Dr. Bennett followed behind them. "Beau," Dr. Bennett greeted. "Pete," Beau responded. "I will be coordinating with the counselors here." "Awesome," Beau said sarcastically.

Chapter 2

Divorce

Evie came home from work early. The PLC meeting she had to go to ended earlier than anticipated, and she was excited to spend the day with Jude, Levi, and Harper. Jude and Evie had been going through a dry spell ever since Harper was born, which Evie hoped would end tonight by coming home early, putting dinner on the table, getting the kids in bed, giving Jude his favorite shoulder massage, and hoping they could have some more quality intimate time.

She recalled a happier time when she and Jude were first married. In spite of his somewhat rocky upbringing, Jude was very devoted to Evie. They both attended school until Evie graduated with her BS in Music Education, while Jude continued with his MBA. He knew how much Evie loved the acoustic guitar, so he learned how to play for her. Once the kids came along, Jude became a partner for a big brokerage company in Baltimore after graduating with his MBA uprooting his family from Annapolis. He began spending more and more time working, leaving Evie with the kids during the holidays.

Jude stood about 6'0 with brown hair and dazzling blue eyes. He was about average size with no true muscle definition, but he was still a handsome guy. His blue eyes were what got Evie's attention at first. He wore a suit every single day.

Evie, herself, had dark brown hair, the most intense blue eyes a man had ever seen, slenderly athletic body, and stood about 5'5. Levi inherited his father's eyes, which were hooded and light blue, but had dirty blonde hair, and was considered tall for a 5-year-old. Harper inherited her mom's blue eyes. Despite being opinionated, stubborn, and sassy, Harper was the sweetest little 2-year-old with the curliest blonde hair. She was considered very petite for her age, just like her mom.

Evie went looking for her kids in the house. She found them outside playing with the nanny in the backyard. Evie quickly rushed outside, and her kids ran to her, giving her the biggest hug. She loved and adored her children, and her children adored her. Their mom was their whole world, because their dad was hardly ever home.

While holding Levi and Harper's hands, Evie led them back into the house where the smell of sweet pork burritos filled her nose. Evie loved crock pots ever since she got married. She was always hoping for an Instapot someday for Mother's Day or her birthday, but Jude never seemed to listen or even care about celebrating holidays with his family for the past four years.

She put a movie on for her kids, said goodbye to the nanny, and decided to do some housework to surprise Jude hoping he would want to spend some time with her. The one neglected place in dusting was his office, so Evie grabbed the dust cleaner and paper towels. She walked into his office and began wiping down every surface that had dust on it. Evie wiped his desk, monitor, keyboard, leather chair, and the bookshelves. Evie noticed that his office desk was a little disorderly, so she decided to straighten it up a bit.

As she began to stack some papers, she noticed a business card for a divorce attorney's firm sitting mixed in with the pile. She grabbed it and stared at it for the longest time. She hoped it was a joke or for one of his friends. Evie decided to put the stack of papers in his top desk drawer and opened it up. Before she could set them inside, she noticed divorce papers sitting on top in the drawer. She pulled them out, looked at them very carefully, and saw Jude's and her name on it. Her heart sank. She read over reasonings, and the overall impression was irreconcilable differences. Evie grabbed the papers and put them in the kitchen.

Tears streamed down Evie's face as she continued to declutter and straighten up her house. What did I do, she thought to herself, what about the kids? Why would he choose to spend time at work than here with us? She had zero answers to her questions, but she was determined to get them out of Jude tonight and possibly resolve the matter.

She thought back to the last time they had quality intimacy, which was six weeks after Harper was born, which wasn't as good as it had been in the past because of the episiotomy that had to happen for Harper to emerge into the world. Jude had just acquired the big account he hoped for, so Evie assumed his excellent mood would lead to titillation. That night, Jude pushed her away right in the middle of it and went to his home office to work. After that, the limited time Jude spent at home became less and less. Evie immediately began to blame herself for Jude falling out of love.

When 5 PM came rolling around, the dishes were placed on the table just like when she stayed home with the kids, dinner was ready to be consumed, and the house was spotless for once. She hoped that Jude would change his mind, but deep down, she knew it might not. Jude walked through the door at 5:30.

"Daddy!" both kids yelled, jumped off the couch, and ran to their dad to hug him.

"Shhh! Why are you guys so loud?!" Jude yelled and pushed the kids away from him. Jude had a bad day at work and brought a bad attitude home with him. Evie was not looking forward to the conversation at that point because somehow, he would make his problem her fault, and often she would concede because she just wanted peace in their home. Jude walked right past the kids and Evie into his office. Evie heard him shuffle a few things inside before there was stillness. Movement from the office started again when she heard Jude start going through his desk.

"Evie!" he shouted, sounding very angry. She swallowed a lump in her throat, grabbed the divorce papers, and walked into his office.

"Yes, Jude?" she said as calmly as possible, hiding the papers behind her back. "Have you been in here? Nothing is where I left it, and I seem to have misplaced some important papers," Jude said without even looking up at her. He was still searching through his desk.

"Looking for these?" she said as she pulled the papers out from behind her. Jude froze and looked up at his wife. He became a little rigid.

"You weren't supposed to see those for another week or so," he said.

"Oh, so that makes it okay?" she said calmly.

Jude began to get angry. "Well, you were the one who decided to go back to work instead of raising our children!" he shouted.

"To help you pay off debt for your schooling, hospital bills, and my group fitness things!" Evie said.

"But it wasn't supposed to be full time! You never communicated with me when it would change!"

"Really? All of this is my fault? Where were you when I told you I had some important things to discuss with you, and when we finally discussed them, you were too busy even to pay attention? So you just said, 'Do what you want. I don't even care.' Is that my fault?"

"All of this is your fault. You never wanted me to pursue my dreams! All you have ever wanted is to teach and go to the gym. You have no respect for me or my decisions."

Tears flew down Evie's cheeks. "I loved you more than I have loved anyone, Jude. When have I ever given you the impression that I didn't support you? I got my job to help relieve some of the financial burdens you complained about, which are gone. My schooling has been paid off, Harper's hospital bills from when she was born have been paid off, and I have contributed to major savings accounts for you and myself. I have $40,000 saved in that bank account."

"Well, after we sign those," Jude said pointing to the papers, "the $40,000 will be all yours, you get to keep the Kia, and I get to keep the house since I bought it. You will get primary custody of the kids, and I will have partial custody."

"I read them. I saw what we each get. I can live anywhere within the country as long as you have visitation of our children, and I will receive alimony; $4,000 per child into my bank account. Are you sure you want to go through with this?" she asked.

"Can we get this over with?" he asked impatiently. She laid the papers down on Jude's desk, grabbed a pen, and signed everywhere that required her signature. She suddenly felt black and hollow inside. Jude also grabbed a pen and signed his name.

"Thank you. I will take these to the courthouse tomorrow. You have about two weeks before you, and the kids need to get out."

"Why are you punishing the kids? They need a father. I cannot be their mom and their dad."

"I will contact them once things settle down," Jude grumbled.

Evie nodded her head assuming he wouldn't. "Fine."

Evie's whole world that she had known for eight years crumbled. She had worked so hard to keep her marriage from falling apart in spite of all the neglect, mind games, verbal, and emotional abuse she had put up with since Jude started business school. Evie knew her soon-to-be ex-husband would still be working in his office for a while. There was a pull-out bed, so she determined that Jude would sleep on that.

Evie went through her entire house collecting all of the keys that would unlock the bedroom doors from the outside including hers, gathered sleep stuff for Levi and Harper to sleep in her room, and began preparing for the big move. She would call her parents in the morning telling them that Jude filed for divorce and see if she could move back home, tell her school she would not be coming back the following year, and begin job hunting.

When she went into Levi's room, Levi and Harper were curled up on Levi's bed crying. Evie rushed to them. "Hey, guys, what's wrong?" she asked.

"Daddy doesn't love us anymore," Levi said bawling.

Evie's tears streamed down her face again as she held both children in her arms. "Would you guys like to sleep in my room tonight?" she asked them.

Both of them nodded. "All right. Let's go downstairs and have some dinner. Then shall we get ready for bed?" Evie asked. Levi sniffled and nodded his head. "All right. I will finish taking your stuff to my room, and I will meet you downstairs for dinner. Okay?"

"Okay," both kids said, still sounding sad.

Evie took the keys into her room besides one that she kept in her pants pocket. She prepared a burrito for Jude and took it to his office. She set the plate down away from his computer. "Here is dinner for you. I figured you would want to eat in here?" she asked. Jude nodded his head without looking up from his computer. "All right. I will have the kids come to say goodnight to you before they go to bed." Jude acted like he didn't hear that last part. Or not, she thought to herself.

Evie felt sorry for this man who was the father of her children because he uninvolved himself from his family. The kids met her in the kitchen, and they ate sweet pork burritos. Somehow, all three of them left the table smiling with some of the funny things that happened at preschool to Levi and Harper's stories about the pretty butterflies she and the nanny caught. After Levi and Harper helped their mom clean the kitchen, bath time started. Evie washed them up and helped them get ready for bed all dressed in pajamas.

"Do you guys want to go say goodnight to Daddy?" Evie asked. Harper shook her head, and Levi said firmly, "No."

Evie's heart sank even more. "All right. How about we go to bed in my room, I turn a movie on, and we watch it?" she asked.

"Yeah!" the kids said enthusiastically. Evie knew that it was a lot of TV watching that day, but it was just one of those days. They went into her room, positioned themselves on the bed, and Evie turned on *Coco* for them.

As the movie started, she changed into a large tee shirt she had had since college and some joggers she bought at the store. Evie brushed her teeth and washed her face hoping to wash the day away. Before climbing into bed with her kids, she made sure her bedroom door was locked.

Just as the kids were about to nod off, three loud thuds sounded at the door, causing everyone to jump. "I thought you said they would say goodnight to me!" Jude shouted.

"They chose not to," Evie responded calmly but scared.

"Yeah, right. You are keeping them from me!" he shouted.

"Go away, Daddy!" Levi shouted.

"Levi, shh!" Evie scolded.

"He hates you, and doesn't love me and Harper!" he said, trying not to cry again.

"What makes you think that, Buddy?" Jude said, trying to sound calm.

"You pushed us down, and yelled at Mommy," Levi yelled before finally starting to cry causing Harper to cry, too.

"Son, I..."

"Jude, go away! You wanted the clean break. It starts now!" Evie raised her voice a little.

"Nowhere does it say I cannot sleep in my bed."

"You haven't slept in your bed in months, almost years, actually; so why does it matter now?"

"Because it's my house!"

"You're right, it is your house, but nowhere does it say that the belongings are yours except your office. You could have new papers drawn up that say so, but it would take longer for the divorce to process. So it's either have the house with nothing but your office furniture and belongings while I get everything else, or you wait longer to divorce me." Jude grumbled and stormed off.

Just as the movie ended, Levi and Harper were sound asleep. Evie decided to peruse her library on Netflix. She found a fascinating documentary about a heavy metal band she admired throughout high school and college, Death Toll. Since her kids were deep sleepers, Evie could watch it without the kids waking up.

She always found their life interesting since they no longer lived as wild and crazy as they used to. The lead singer turned his whole life around for his wife and kids. She admired this band for making their careers all about the music rather than the lifestyle.

By the time the documentary was over, it was time for Evie to go to bed. She quickly made a to-do list of all the things she needed to get done like finding a hotel for her and the kids to stay in until the school year was over, find a storage unit to store all her belongings, pack up the kids' rooms and clothes, pack her belongings, and look for a new job somewhere else.

The next morning when Evie's alarm went off, she startled awake. She remembered the events of the previous day and hoped it wasn't real. She went downstairs into Jude's office. He was already gone, but the divorce attorney's business card was sitting on his desk as were the carbon copies of the divorce papers. She quickly got ready for work, went through to see if she had her to-do list, updated the nanny on what was going on, and left for work. She did her best to hide what was going on in her personal life from her students.

During her prep, she called her parents letting them know what was going on to see if she could move home for a while until she found a new job. Her parents showed her so much support for her during this tough time in her life. She went and told the administration that she would be moving to Annapolis, Evie's hometown. The administration said they would miss her, and she said she would miss them. She quickly prepared lesson plans for the next two days for all classes. She then found a hotel she and the kids could check into that evening that was relatively close to work and where the nanny lived. She also called movers to come that Friday to move her belongings, including furniture, TVs, and pictures into the storage unit.

That night after her kids fell asleep in the big king size bed at the hotel, she was looking up jobs. Evie was determined to get as far away from Maryland as humanly possible, so she began searching for any job on the West Coast. In her social media feed, she noticed that Death Toll's lead singer had been checked back into rehab, and their tour manager had quit. They had a link to apply for the position. The requirements were a Bachelor's degree, but any Music degree was preferred. As she read more information, the lead singer, Beau Halstead, was expected to be in rehab for the next four months and then spending the next ten months in therapy giving the new tour manager and the band a chance to put together an album and set up a tour. The job would require her to relocate to San Francisco. Evie had always wanted to see the West Coast. She applied for the job giving her availability date, which was one month. It was precisely the day she was needed. It would give her time for her parents to spend time with her kids, spend time with her sister's family, find an apartment, and enroll Levi in kindergarten.

She wondered why the lead singer had relapsed. She quickly found an article. His sweet little family was killed in a car accident on their way to the library. Evie felt very empathetic towards Beau because just like her life, everything changed overnight, and things would continue to change for her.

The last two weeks of school ran smoothly, and the last day of working at the high school had approached. Evie chaperoned the students as they signed yearbooks and gave hugs to all her band and orchestra students who kept telling her things like, "We will miss you, Ms. Long." "You are the best teacher ever!" "I don't know what we will do without you."

All of these statements broke Evie's heart. She wished with all of her heart that things didn't have to change, but they did. Her students had been such an important part in her life besides her own kids. The students soon went home, and Evie checked out with her team. They all said goodbye to her as well as her principal.

Evie drove to Levi's preschool and picked him up. The car was packed and ready for the drive to Annapolis. After picking up Levi, Evie went to the nanny's house to pick up Harper. Soon, the journey to Annapolis began. Suddenly, Evie felt like she needed to take the kids to say goodbye to their father, so Evie took a little detour to Jude's office building. After getting her kids out of the car, they walked inside, waved to the security guards, and got on the elevator up to Jude's office. They walked down the hallway, and Evie opened the door.

To her utter horror, Evie saw Jude sitting in his office chair with his pants undone, shirt opened, and a woman with dark hair, and olive skin in lingerie straddling him. They immediately stopped when Jude saw his family. Evie quickly covered her children's eyes.

Very calmly keeping his cool, Jude said, "In all fairness, you were supposed to be on your way to Annapolis," Jude said. Evie could not believe he was defending his behavior. "Well, then, by all means, continue!" Evie said sarcastically, "Don't let me or your children stop you!" she said with chagrin.

She led the kids out the door down the hall to the elevator. As they were waiting, Levi kept asking all sorts of questions. "Why was Daddy kissing that lady? Was she wearing underwear? Was Daddy's....?" "Levi, not now," Evie snapped. Soon, Evie saw a put-together Jude come running down the hallway. She seriously considered taking the stairs to get away from him.

"You weren't supposed to see that," Jude said.

"How long has that been going on?" Evie scolded.

"About six months," Jude said.

Evie was flabbergasted. "Is she the first one, or have there been others?"

"... No, she's not the first one."

"How long has this been going on?"

"On and off for the past four years."

Tears streamed down Evie's face. "I know I'm going to regret asking this, but why? Why in the hell would you cheat on me repeatedly for the past four years when you had a family?!" Evie's voice was practically supersonic.

"Because I watched you push our kids out of you. That is something I wish I could erase from my brain, but I can't. You were so sexy and free when I met you, but becoming a mom has changed you. Carmen is more of what I am looking for, sexy and free-spirited."

"I had to grow up because of the kids, though. Why can't you understand that? We wanted kids, remember?"

"That just proves how naive I was, and how naive you are, still. How could a man find you attractive after they've seen what I've seen? They will only see you as an unattractive mom, not a sexy, free-spirited, adventurous, and independent woman like you used to be."

Jude's words cut Evie to the very core as she began to tremble. Just then, the elevator doors opened. Evie robotically walked inside, holding her kids' hands. She watched as the doors closed on Jude. Suddenly, she slipped down onto the floor and curled into the fetal position. "Mom? Mom!" Levi shouted. Harper began crying even harder. Evie became unresponsive. Levi quickly grabbed his mom's phone and made an emergency call.

"911, how can I help you?" a female voice said. "We are inside an elevator, and my mom is not moving," Levi said frantically. "Okay, honey, calm down. Where are you at?" she asked. Luckily, Levi knew his dad's company and address. Evie taught him those things just in case.

"All right, honey. Stay calm. Help is on the way. Want me to stay on the phone with you?" she asked. "Yes, please. I'm scared and so is my sister," Levi said, beginning to cry.

"What happened to your mom?"

"My dad."

The 911 operator paused fearing the worst. "Did he hit her?"

"No, he was naked with another woman in his office, and we walked in on him" Levi said.

The operator was not only very impressed with Levi's speaking abilities, but she made note of the indescretion of the father. "What's your name, honey?"

"Levi Long."

"What's your sister's name?"

"Harper Long."

"How old are you?"

"Almost six."

"How old is she?"

"Two."

"You are a smart boy. Do you know that?"

"My mom tells me all the time. I don't always listen to her, though."

"Well, maybe when she wakes up, you can listen to her better."

The sweet 911 operator continued to talk to Levi until the paramedics showed up. They immediately called Evie's parents who drove to Baltimore as fast as they could to meet an unconscious Evie and their terrified grandchildren at the hospital.

When Evie woke up, her dad was sitting in the chair by her side. "Evs," he said. "Hi, Daddy," Evie responded, "What happened?" "You suffered a major panic attack and passed out."

"Where are the kids?"

"Your mom has them. Evs, I'm so sorry you are going through so much."

Evie began to cry a little again. "I want to go home," she said.

"Annapolis?"

"Yes."

"All right. I will work on that."

Richard West, Evie's father, and powerful insurance man, immediately stood up and went looking for a doctor. After arguing for about a half-hour with one, Richard had his daughter discharged from the hospital. Her mom, Karen West, drove Evie's car with the kids to Annapolis while Richard drove his car with his daughter. Evie confided in him about what

Jude had been doing ever since Levi was born, and her dad listened. He tried not to express his rage to his daughter.

Once they arrived at her childhood home, Jennifer, Evie's older and only sibling, along with her family, greeted Evie and the kids with open arms. Despite being sick from pregnancy, Jennifer wanted to see her baby sister and hug her extra tight. While Levi and Harper played with their three cousins, Evie's parents and sister led her upstairs to her old room. Evie, still feeling dazed and confused, laid back down on her bed and slept the day away.

Chapter 3

Evie

Beau sat down in his group session with a couple of guys he had become friends with, Dr. Bennett, and two counselors from the rehab center. It had only been two months since the band checked him into rehab, and yet he wasn't ready to admit his insecurities in the sessions.

His rock, foundation, and what kept him grounded died in a car accident. Phoebe was always supportive, helpful, kind, and brutally honest with Beau. He listened to his buddies start talking about how they found console in drinking just like he did and how they were searching for other outlets to replace their addictions. Beau found himself noodling on the acoustic guitar that Luke brought in for him to help distract him.

Beau often played some of their ballads to soothe him, but yet he had the hardest time finding inspiration for their new album.

One day, Beau decided to write a sequel to another song he wrote for the band. The original had heavy verses and a soft chorus, so he thought it was only appropriate to do the opposite. Beau still couldn't think of lyrics. He wanted to use a lot of the same words from the original song, but he kept drawing a blank. He kept thinking about Phoebe wishing she and the kids were the ones still alive and he was the one who died in the car accident.

Chloe and Cordell had such bright futures ahead of them. Phoebe could have lived off of Beau's earnings and life insurance. She was pretty enough to marry again. He recalled some of the things Phoebe went through in her life and began incorporating them into his lyrics. He remembered laying in a field on tour looking up at the stars and exchanging life experiences with Phoebe. She spent a lot of time comforting Beau to encourage him to be better. As Beau and Phoebe continued dating for three years, he remembered letting his guard down so she could fully be in his life. They fell in love over their mutual understanding of one another.

He decided to repeat some of the same lyrics from the first song, but he changed them up a little to accommodate the mutual understanding between Phoebe and himself. Despite only having a verse and the chorus written, Beau played those parts of the song every day for two weeks finding comfort in them. Then he would start playing the original song to give himself even more peace.

Luke, Kade, and Rick would visit Beau a few times a week to check up on him, maybe write some songs, have a meeting, and discuss what to do about hiring another tour manager. The album was halfway done, but Beau's visit to rehab pushed the release date back quite a bit, but everyone except Beau was content with the repercussions of the decision.

"I am interviewing a couple of candidates today for the tour manager position. One person is from the Bay area and has been following us from the beginning. He has a certification in Music Therapy and plays the guitar, so I thought that might help you," Luke said, pointing to Beau. Beau acknowledged the statement but dozed off a little.

"Then there is another candidate who has a degree in teaching Music, top of her class at the University of Maryland..." Luke began, but Beau interrupted, "Her?" That word got his attention. Beau hadn't heard of very many female tour managers. "Is that a problem? 'Cause if it is, we could get sued," Kade said. Beau shook his head. "No, not a problem. Tell us more about her," Beau said. "She is a superb musician herself, helped produce various concerts while attending school, taught music for three years at a high school, produced those concerts, and she sounds like she has excellent organizational skills, which would help us stay on track," Luke concluded.

All the band nodded their heads. "That is an impressive resume from the teacher," Rick said, "Where is she from?" "Annapolis," Luke said, "so this will be a video interview." "Cool. I am already impressed with the teacher, but we will see how the interviews go," Beau said.

The next day, Luke called a band meeting at the rehab center. They all sat in Beau's room in a circle. "I interviewed both of them, and I have decided to hire the teacher. She will need to relocate from Maryland with her two kids, but she has no problem doing that. What should her salary be?" Luke asked. "$84,000? If she has two kids, that should be enough for her to live in the Bay area and provide for them, unless she is married. Is she married?" Beau asked.

"Single mother, so I think we should offer her $100,000 to help cover some extra expenses," Luke said. Death Toll nodded their heads. "All right, it's settled. The teacher it is. What is her name?" Beau asked. "Evie Long." "How old are she and her kids?" "She says she is 30, but the girl looks like she is in her early 20's. I believe her son is 5, and her daughter is 2." "Cool. Go call her." The meeting adjourned, Beau picked up his guitar while everyone walked out of his room, and Luke made the phone call and called Evie. He offered her the job, and she accepted immediately.

Evie celebrated in her old room with the kids at her parents' house. Despite her divorce, soon-to-be ex-husband's infidelity, and fatal panic attack she encountered a month previously, things were beginning to look up again. After Evie put the kids to bed, she immediately began searching for apartments near San Rafael where Death Toll's studio was as well as band members' houses.

The cost of living in the Bay area exceeded any city in Maryland. The least costly place Evie found was a condo for $3500 a month, three bedrooms, two and a half bathrooms, 1361 sq ft, and reserved parking in Larkspur, which was a ten minutes away from the studio. *The commute isn't as terrible as it could be*, she thought to herself. Evie quickly applied to get the condo and began calling around for schools within good school districts to sign Levi up for kindergarten. She made arrangements to have all of her big items in her storage unit in Annapolis, including her car shipped to the studio. Luke Jeppsen, the drummer, said that her family could live at the studio for a while until they found a place to live. Evie would start work the following Monday.

Luke made all the arrangements to fly Evie and her kids out to San Francisco, what time he would come to pick them up at the airport, and a storage unit for her belongings just in case she would be living at the studio longer than anticipated. The flight would leave early in the morning so they could arrive before the band meeting to meet everyone before heading to the rehab center. Evie was very nervous about meeting a band she idolized in college. Her and her roommates followed Death Toll on their East Coast tour during her sophomore year of college to the point where they thought they followed the band to a bar, but they ended up having way too much to drink and doing a topless dance on the actual bar. That next morning, Evie woke up in a stranger's bed with lots of ones and twenties in her shorts. All she saw of the stranger was a tall, skinny guy with long, thick red hair.

She resolved to be as professional as possible with her employer. The fact that she now worked for one of the biggest heavy metal bands in the world excited her beyond anything she could imagine.

Evie, Levi, and Harper slept on their flight from Annapolis to San Francisco. She wore a wide-brimmed hat to hide the fact that she woke up without doing her hair to help Levi and Harper get ready to leave. They were still in their pajamas, but Evie had carried them to the car while they were sleeping. Evie wore a graphic tee, skinny jeans, and sandals so that she would be comfortable on the flight.

About an hour before the plane descended, all three went to the bathroom, and Evie helped the kids change their clothes. She gathered her belongings and made sure her seatbelt and the kids' seatbelts were secured. Both of them started to doze off again as the plane began its descent. Evie closed her eyes for a moment as well. The aircraft touched down and pulled up to the terminal. All three of them woke up and stood when prompted.

Evie found a cart for the carry-ons, put her backpack purse on, and carried Harper to baggage claim while Levi held on to one of the straps on his mom's backpack. As she got to baggage claim, she saw three big guys wearing black suits and sunglasses and a short guy about 5'5 with a receding hairline, green eyes, and average build standing in the middle of the big guys. One of the big guys held a sign with her name on it. She walked up to them. "That's me," she said.

Luke could not help but find Evie very attractive. Plus, he recalled the early years in Death Toll seeing this pretty girl, but he wasn't sure when or where. She was about an inch shorter than the Death Toll drummer with shoulder-length brown hair styled in waves, very intense blue eyes, and a slender build. He soon saw a little boy with dirty blonde hair and blue eyes.

Luke assumed this boy was Levi. Then Luke saw the adorable little toddler with blonde curly hair and blue eyes that matched her mom's eyes in Evie's arms. Harper was an absolute doll.

Luke and Evie shook hands. "It's nice to meet you in person," Luke said. Evie, trying to maintain her professionalism all while fangirling on the inside, replied, "You too, Mr. Jeppsen." Luke laughed. "Call me, Luke. I hope you understand we aren't that formal," he said, still chuckling to himself. Evie blushed a little. "Sorry," she said. "It's all good. We are very excited your family could join us," Luke said. "Thanks."

Luke helped Evie grab her luggage and take it out to the car. The bodyguards helped out as well. They walked out to the car, loaded up, had car seats for the kids, and started heading to the studio. When they got there, Kade Hansen and Richard Torres were standing outside waiting for them to arrive. Evie had the hardest time containing herself. When the car parked, Evie unbuckled her kids and helped them climb out. Kade and Rick introduced themselves shaking Evie's hand, Levi's hand, and Harper's hand. So far, everyone was super accommodating and kind. Harper even began flirting with the band a little, wrapping them around her finger.

The band helped Evie carry all of her luggage to the spare room with beds inside the studio. When they tried showing the different rooms for the kids, Levi chimed in and said, "I want to sleep in my mom's room. She cries in her sleep when she's alone." Evie blushed. "It you want to share a room with me, Bub, that's fine," Evie said. "Me too," said Harper.

Luke, Kade, and Rick looked at the little family with puzzled looks. "Is everything all right?" Kade asked. "Yeah," Evie said, trying to cover up the hardships she and her kids have been going through for the past few weeks. "With all the changes going on in our lives, we have been sharing a bedroom," Evie said, trying to explain.

"Hey, your business is your own. I hope that we didn't aid a possible fugitive from the law," Luke said, trying to pass a joke. Evie smiled and laughed a little. "No, you are not harboring a fugitive, although that would be very rock n' roll," Evie joked, "we just need a fresh start." The band laughed at her joke and nodded. "All right. Once you guys get settled in your room, we will head on over to the rehab center so you can meet Beau," Luke said.

Evie's heart began racing. Today was the day she looked forward to since college; meeting the frontman of Death Toll. "Sounds like a plan," she said, trying to stay calm. After they unpacked, they loaded back up into the car and drove to Beau's rehab center.

They climbed out of the car just as they pulled up into a parking spot. The facility looked very rustic and soothing. Evie could see Beau getting the right kind of help here considering she knew how much he appreciated the outdoors. They walked up the path and inside the doors. Evie followed the band into the sitting area of the lobby.

Sitting on the couch playing an acoustic guitar was the man Evie hoped to meet someday with his tattooed arms and hands, short blonde hair coming to a point in front, a flying skull tattoo on his neck, short goatee, and sweet almond shaped hooded blue eyes. The tattooed arms made him look a little intimidating, but the eyes softened his demeanor. He had a few scars on his face from a pyrotechnic accident that happened a few years ago during a concert, but Beau Halstead indeed looked like a king while playing the guitar.

Beau heard all sorts of footsteps approaching him when he looked up. He greeted his bandmates, but then the new faces caught his eye. Beau saw the cute little girl with blonde curly hair and vibrant blue eyes. He saw the little boy with similar blue eyes who would eventually grow up to be a handsome executive, or so Beau thought about him.

Then he looked at the woman. The little girl's eyes didn't do justice to this woman's intense blue eyes. She had shoulder-length brown hair, and her body was very slender and fit. She wore a maroon hat, a v-neck graphic tee, skinny jeans, and sandals. The resume said she was thirty, but she looked like she was in her early 20's. Beau couldn't believe this woman was a mom.

"This must be our new tour manager. Nice to meet you, Miss Long," Beau said, holding out his tattooed right hand. Evie grabbed it and shook his hand. "Please, call me Evie," she said. "Nice to meet you, Evie," Beau said. They smiled at each other. "And who's this?" Beau asked, turning to look at the kids. Levi hid his face at first, and Harper began hiding her face from Beau, teasing him. "This is Harper," Evie said, touching Harper's shoulder, "and this is Levi," she concluded, reaching behind her leg to run her fingers through Levi's hair. "Nice to meet both of you," he said.

They all sat down and began having a meeting about Beau's plans of how long he would be in rehab, estimated date of completion for the new album, and approximated tour dates. Levi and Harper ran around the room all while a bodyguard tried to keep them close and quiet. Evie planned to make something for that bodyguard later.

Beau felt he would be in rehab for another three months, the album would be complete in December, and the band could start touring next

March or April. Beau and Luke made suggestions to Evie what stadiums to call with contact information. She put the information down on her phone, so she would have it when the time came. Evie asked the band if there was anything else she could do for the group considering her job description was to ensure everyone's happiness. They all shook their heads.

The band meeting concluded, and everyone stood up to leave. "Hey, Luke, could you put my kids in the car for me? I need to talk to Beau for a minute," Evie said. "Sure. We will be outside," Luke said. Evie assured her kids that they would be fine as they walked out with the men. Evie trusted them considering all of them were married and had families of their own.

Once they were out the door, Evie turned to Beau. He looked at her eagerly. "What's up?" he asked her. "How serious are you about your recovery?" she asked him. "Excuse me?" "Are you going to let your band and crew down, or are we going to be back here two months after your release? I am just trying to anticipate a pattern." Beau looked at Evie in disbelief.

"We just met. Isn't it a little early for you to judge me? Do you already think I'm a failure?"

"On the contrary, I don't think you're a failure, but I think you need the reassurance of that fact. It is not in your nature, but I think after these past six months since your family died, you have lost perspective on who you are. How serious are you about fixing your alcoholism?"

Beau wasn't sure how to answer that because he wasn't sure how dedicated he was to this.

"Your silence is very reassuring," Evie said sarcastically before walking out the door.

Beau could not believe how stubborn and blunt Evie was. The only other person he knew who was like that was Phoebe. As weekly meetings started up, Beau could not help but get annoyed at this woman. He could not put his finger on it other than she acted too much like his late wife, and he still missed her.

Beau began to be tardy to meetings not really wanting to face the new tour manager, and there were days that Evie let him know what time meetings were. There was one particular day that he decided to throw her off with his charm and charisma. Beau knew Evie would wait for the others to leave before talking to him, so he decided to say, "Is that what all of this is about, or are you sure you don't wait for everyone else to leave just so that we could have some alone time together?" He touched her shoulder in hopes it distracted her.

Beau's plan blew up in his face when she brushed his hand off her shoulder rather hard and responded very loudly, "Are you really that full of yourself and cocky?" Beau froze because he didn't know how to react.

Evie's brutal honesty flipped on, and she just let her mouth go. "I did not move all the way here to watch my favorite band implode because their frontman refuses to change. Clean up your act, or else I will replace you with any imbecile who can sing and play guitar. If I have to do it, I will. You have been through too much already to back-peddle now. Don't let your family die in vain." That hit a major nerve inside Beau as he watched Evie walk out of the rehab center, climb in her car, and drive away.

Beau, feeling angry, stormed back to his room, picked up his guitar, and began playing to help him process what he just heard. Even though he was too proud to admit it, Beau knew Evie was right. It took a couple of weeks, but he decided to change his life again since he had come so far. His family couldn't die in vain because they all believed in him. Beau just needed to believe in himself.

When he went down to his group session, he finally opened up about his feelings, why alcohol brought him solace and trying to find different coping mechanisms to dissipate the pain. "Losing my family kills me every day, especially Phoebe. My foundation, my stabilizer, is gone. My children are gone. I will never see their faces again as long as I live. The pain hurts too much, but when I drink, the alcohol numbs the pain. I only know two ways of living. The first is a raving alcoholic, and the second one is a straight-edge rockstar with a family. I don't know how to be just a regular guy," Beau concluded.

Dr. Bennett chimed in with some advice. "Try taking an interest in other people's lives and realize you are not the only person with major problems. It may surprise you how many others struggle with issues."

Beau listened to his therapist before the counselor decided to speak up. "There are some amazing opportunities for you to serve other patients. Some listen to you play your guitar while you are in your room. Maybe visit their rooms and play for them, start up conversations, show interest in their lives, and I bet your problems will begin to seem smaller," she concluded. Beau listened to his therapist and counselors absorbing their advice.

One month passed, and everyone saw a massive improvement in Beau's behavior and lifestyle. For the first time in months, Luke saw a real smile from his friend. Evie noticed how reliable he became to the band following through with what he said. Kade and Rick often brought ideas for songs to Beau, and he was open to their artistry rather than yelling at them. The producers found it very easy to work with Beau again. His professional demeanor returned with a sense of humor before his family died.

One day, everyone heard Beau laughing at a joke. He hadn't laughed with his infectious laugh in months. Evie remembered hearing him laugh in movies and videos, but it was much better in person. Two months later, Beau was cleared to go home and return to his routine. Dr. Bennett wrote up a schedule for him to follow as well as suggestions to help him stay on the wagon.

Beau was packing his room up when all of a sudden, Levi burst through the door. "Hi, Beau! My mom is coming!" Levi yelled before running out again. Beau laughed as he continued to put clothes in his suitcase.

Suddenly, he heard a very stern female voice in the hallway, "Levi Richard Long, if you ignore me again, you will spend all day in your room tomorrow. No playing with friends!" Beau knew Evie was scolding her son.

"I was just trying to…" Levi tried rationalizing.

"I don't care what you were trying to do. When I say walk by me, you do it! Do you want to end up 'here' someday?" Evie asked.

Beau felt a little weird hearing his tour manager discipline her son. Beau guessed Evie told her son what rehabilitation was and meant.

There was a long pause before Levi answered, "No."

"That's good because if you continue to ignore Mommy, your choices could lead you here," Evie concluded.

"I don't want that," Levi said, crying.

"So what do you need to do, Bub?"

"Obey you."

"Good job. Now, I need you to take your sister out to the playground in the back while I talk to Mr. Halstead. Will you do that for me?"

"Yes."

"Thank you. Have fun, guys!"

After Beau heard little feet running down the hall, there was a knock on his open door. Sure enough, Evie poked her head inside the room. "May I come in?" she asked. "Sure, be my guest," Beau said motioning for her to take a seat in the chair. "Do you need any help with your stuff?" she asked as she sat down. "I don't think so. I didn't bring a whole lot with me," Beau said.

Evie smiled before staring at the floor. Beau could see the wheels in her head turning. "Something on your mind?" he asked. Evie finally stood up. "I am proud of your efforts here, and I am glad you are doing so well. Thank you for thinking about the bigger picture for Death Toll." "Well, a lot of the things you said influenced me, so I should be thanking you." "You're welcome."

Chapter 4

First Day Back

Since he left rehab, Beau stayed at the studio to avoid vulnerability. He had not entered the equipment room out of fear. Last time he went to rehab, he wasn't sure if playing guitar brought him joy until that first day. History was just repeating itself. Even though he played guitar at rehab, it was different playing with three other people than by himself. Luke decided to stay there for a while until Beau felt comfortable enough to go home. Luke checked in with his wife, Jetta, every night.

"Beau, when do you think you'll be ready to pick up a guitar again?" Luke asked. Beau scratched the back of his head. "I was actually thinking about it in two days," he responded. Never before had Beau seen Luke excited about anything. "Awesome!" Luke exclaimed, "Want me to go contact everyone?" Beau smiled. "Yeah, go do it," he said. Luke ran out of the room faster than a cartoon character, which made Beau laugh. Luke's short stature made it even funnier.

Beau walked out of his room into the hallway where he could hear some singing. He followed the voices only to find Evie and the kids singing some silly songs using actions with their arms, hands, and legs. Harper imitated her mother's singing and actions, which made Beau laugh. He knew Evie's family had been staying at the studio, too, while Evie looked for a place to live. He still wasn't sure how long they would be there. When Evie was done, she tucked Levi and Harper in bed. She sang the sweetest lullaby to her children, which made Beau smile. "Goodnight, my sweet girl. I love you. Good night, my sweet boy. I love you," Beau heard Evie say to each of her kids. "Good night, Mommy. Love you," each kid responded. Evie walked out of the room closing the door behind her.

In her peripheral, Evie saw Beau. "Hey!" she said. "Hey," Beau said back, "do you do that every night with your kids?"

"Yes. I've been singing that same lullaby to both of them since they were born. I like to think that the lullaby helped sleep-train my kids, although who knows? They've always been good sleepers. I got lucky," Evie said. Beau nodded his head in fascination.

Suddenly, he remembered what he needed to talk to her about. "Oh, we are going back into the studio in two days," Beau said.

"Really?" Evie asked, "Are you ready?"

"As ready as ever. I'm a little nervous," Beau responded.

"Well, were you nervous the first time?" Evie asked, referring to Beau's first spat with recovery.

Beau nodded his head. "But then I fell in love with music all over again," he said.

"Well, remember that feeling, and I bet you will have the same experience. Maybe it will be better," Evie said before walking into the kitchen.

Beau watched her walk, finding her insights very helpful. He soon followed. "What time will you be available in two days?" he asked.

"A little after noon. I have a meeting with Levi's teachers," Evie said after turning back around.

"Is he okay?" Beau asked.

"Just needs a little extra support that his teachers are offering," Evie said.

"Okay. How much longer are you going to be here at the studio? Not that we don't mind having you, just wondering," Beau said.

"I don't know. I'm trying to find a place close to the studio, but everything is just so expensive," Evie said.

"Well, I know some people around here who could give you a fair price on rent. What's your budget?" Beau asked.

Evie hesitated to answer, but eventually she said, "$3,000."

The number surprised Beau. "That's all you can afford? That would get you two bedrooms at the most! Do we need to pay you more?" Beau asked, a little shocked.

"No, I'll be fine. I just suddenly got slammed with a bunch of debt as a result of my divorce, so I need to make some compromises on housing for right now," Evie said.

"But you shouldn't have to. I can help you, and we can give you a raise so you can pay off your debt and live comfortably. We don't want you to have to share a studio apartment with your kids," Beau said.

"That's okay. I need to figure this out on my own. Thanks, though," Evie said.

"Why won't you let me help you?" Beau asked.

"Because I'm not a charity case. I'm perfectly capable of being the nurturer and provider for my children," Evie said with gusto before walking past Beau towards the second living room.

Beau began to be a little annoyed. *She is stubborn*, he thought. He thought about pursuing the conversation more, but Beau remembered what it was like dealing with a stubborn girl. Phoebe's determination often turned into stubbornness, and Beau dealt with it throughout his marriage. Even though it was annoying, stubbornness was a quality he admired about Phoebe. He walked into the bathroom to brush his teeth. On his way back to the audio room, he overheard someone talking in the kitchen. "What do you mean there's an outstanding balance? I paid for it last week!" Evie said, sounding defeated. *She must have gone back to the kitchen*, Beau thought. "No, please. Don't do that. I'll just have to figure something out."

Beau peered around the corner and watched Evie set her phone down. Sitting in a chair, she rested her head into her hands and began to cry. Beau continued to watch her cry, wipe her face, pick her phone back up, and make another phone call. "Hey, Mr. Cho! It's Evie Long. I was wondering if you received...." She paused and listened to her phone. "Oh, I didn't get it? All right. Thank you. Maybe next time," Evie said, hanging up her phone and crying again. This time, Evie laid her head down on the table and continued to cry.

After what seemed like five minutes of crying, Beau finally saw Evie stop moving and crying. He realized she had fallen asleep. He walked into the kitchen, picked the woman up, and laid her on one of the couches in the first living room by the kitchen. He found a blanket and laid it over her. Evie stayed asleep the entire time, impressing Beau. *She needs help*, Beau said. He could see her drowning. Beau resolved to help her out in any way he could.

Two days later, Luke, Kade, and Rick were looking forward to the day when Beau Halstead felt well enough to come back to work. Beau looked forward to the day as well. He walked into the equipment room of the studio and picked up his ESP EXplorer custom-made chrome guitar.

Beau remembered the first time back at the studio five years ago picking up that guitar after a ten-month absence from working.

Just like it did then, playing that guitar while it was set to his settings on the amp was the happiest he had felt in a long time. Luke went back to sit on his throne, Kade picked up his guitar, and Rick started to pedal a note supporting the riff Beau was playing. Luke began an accompanying beat as Death Toll continued their songwriting. After that, Kade joined in. All four of them looked across the room at each other with big smiles on their faces.

Meanwhile, Evie was on her way back from an IEP meeting with Levi's teachers about his behavior, some goals they all had set for him, and words of encouragement that she really was doing a fantastic job raising Levi despite all the changes he was going through with moving to a new city and the negative effect his absent father had on him. Jude made it clear that his only role in his son's life was a financial one, and Evie had a feeling Levi knew that. Harper was with Evie at the meeting because she still didn't know anyone well enough to ask for help to watch Harper, and she missed half of the meeting mentally because she was trying to get her sassy toddler to sit still so she could focus on the teachers.

Evie held back tears as she drove towards San Rafael over the Richmond-San Rafael Bridge. After the IEP, she needed to go run an errand in Oakland before heading back to the studio. Suddenly, traffic stopped. Evie figured it was a car accident. She watched a lot of drivers climb out of their cars to see what was going on, so Evie did the same. She quickly walked over to the railing side to see if she could see how devastating the accident was. All she saw were emergency lights flashing ten to fifteen cars ahead.

She looked out over the water admiring the glassy effect and reflection all the way to the other side of the bay, and a horrible thought came to her head as she looked down; *You are a terrible mother. You should jump off this bridge.* More tears came down her cheeks as she walked closer to the railing, but she could not stop staring at the water. She was hemorrhaging failure at every corner. She couldn't find a balance between working and motherhood. She was sinking, much like if she were to jump off the bridge.

As she got even closer to the railing, Levi's and Harper's faces came to her head, but then that awful voice in her head came back again; *Those kids are better off without you. They should be with their father.* Evie was now sobbing at the ridiculous thought, but she still couldn't stop staring at the water. *What is bringing on these awful thoughts*, she asked herself, but she already knew the answer.

Jude had called the previous night again, reminding her that she had lost who she really was. He taunted her and said, "So, have you met anyone, yet? Of course you haven't. You're a mom, not the free-spirited girl I knew when we first met. Plus, when was the last time you got all dolled up and sexy? Who would find you sexy after knowing you pushed two kids out of your body? Your body is wrecked."

Evie cried as she remembered the deep wound the words left inside her. But as she kept on picturing Levi and Harper's faces, Evie ran away from the railing and climbed back into her car, buckling her seatbelt, ensuring more barriers between her and her suicidal thoughts. "You okay, Mommy?" Levi asked. "I'm fine, Bub. I thought I saw something in the water," she quickly responded.

After sitting in a stand-still traffic jam for ten minutes, cars finally started moving, and Evie proceeded to San Rafael with both kids in the back of her Kia Optima. *As The Wheels On the Bus* played in the background, Evie continued pondering her life choices and her kids' well-being. What would Jude do if the kids were with him, she thought. He seemed preoccupied with his life at the moment, so Evie assumed he would have hired another nanny to raise and possibly copulate with once the kids were in bed.

Never before had Evie's confidence been so shaken than when she walked in on Jude and Carmen with both kids at her side. She quickly shoved that memory down inside her. She hated how Jude made her feel. Evie knew she had to figure out solutions and healthier behaviors, or else she would eventually jump off that bridge.

Meanwhile, Beau began playing another riff he came up with in rehab. It was in the key of Eb, and the notes sounded very bluesy. The others began freaking out at the sound and loved it. Luke started fiddling with his drum set to see if he could make it sound different, but he couldn't think of anything.

As the band revered the new riff, Evie set the kids up in the toy room. Evie grabbed some toys for Harper and the table and chairs for Levi to sit at to do a writing assignment. "Bub, where's your homework?" Evie asked. "I don't know," Levi replied.

"Okay, where was the last place you remember having it?"

"Over my shoulders."

"Okay, what room?" Evie was getting frustrated with her kid. *Why must you lose everything*, she yelled in her head at Levi.

Levi paused and began thinking. "I think I left it in the kitchen," he responded.

"All right. I will go get it. Can I trust you to stay here with your sister?"

"Yes." Levi rolled his eyes. "Bub, let's try to have a better attitude today. I'm frustrated with how today went as well, but we can try to have a good day, still."

"Okay." Levi didn't sound convinced.

On her way to the kitchen, Evie went into her room to take a deep breath. *Okay, everyone is having a bad day. Just get through it, and it will be fine*, she thought to herself. She took a few more deep breaths before leaving her room.

Suddenly, Evie's brain went blank. *Why did I walk down this hallway*, Evie yelled at herself, *what did I come this way for?* Because of the previous night's sleep, Evie had a hard time thinking straight. *Did I need a snack? Did Harper need a drink? Did Levi... Levi left his homework in the kitchen! Ugh, stupid Mom Brain*, Evie exclaimed in her head as she rushed towards the kitchen.

As Evie walked past the equipment room, she overheard the band jamming as well as this snappy bluesy riff. She really liked it, but she could tell there was some controversy between Luke, Beau, Kade, and Rick about the drum set. "It just sounds so stale," Luke said. Evie agreed. She understood that today was a big day for everyone with Beau being back, and Luke wanted to change up the drum set sound to celebrate the big day. *They want to remember his first day back on the record*, she thought.

She walked into the equipment room as the band continued to discuss what they could do differently to make this song pop. "I can't figure it out," Luke said, pointing to his drum set, "how can we make this song stand out?" Beau, Luke, Rick, and Kade gathered around one of Beau's amps to discuss what they could do differently for this song. Evie walked over to the drum set without anyone noticing, and she turned the snares off on the snare drum. The snares made a loud crash, causing everyone to jump and look at her.

"Try that," she said, standing up. Luke walked back to his drum set and sat down. He played a few paradiddles, and he heard the difference. It wasn't the traditional sound the band was accustomed to, but he really liked it. Beau thought it was original. The snare drum had a hollow sound to it. "You just turned off the snares?" Luke asked. "Yep, and I think the song will sound the way you want it to," Evie said. Beau began playing the riff again, and Luke soon joined him playing lots of flams on the snare and offbeats on the hi-hat.

Both men smiled at each other before turning to Evie. She smiled back at them. "This is awe-inspiring. Thank you," Beau said. "You're welcome. When I taught band in Baltimore, I often had my drummers turn off the snares for a more hollow sound. I could tell that's what you wanted," Evie grinned. "Thanks again. Go ahead and go back to what you were doing," Luke said. "Crap, what was I doing?" Evie vocalized, not realizing she said her thought out loud. They all looked at her. "What were you doing?" Rick asked. "I don't know! I was walking towards the kitchen for something, and I overheard you guys playing, and..." Evie stammered through her words, trying to figure out what she was doing in the first place.

Suddenly, she exclaimed, "Homework! Levi left his homework in the kitchen. All right, I'm good," Evie reassured everyone in the room, including herself. Death Toll just stared at her, wondering if she was a little crazy. "Are you okay?" Beau finally asked. "Yeah, I'm fine. When I don't get a lot of sleep, my Mom Brain gets really bad," Evie said. "Mom Brain?" Kade asked. "Hey, all women have it including Laila. You try keeping up with children all day and a full-time job on about four hours of sleep. Not easy," Evie defended as she walked out of the audio room. Death Toll laughed and resumed playing the song, writing down the notes and the form and solidified the sound. Once their foundation was built, they sat their instruments down again, and they grabbed notepads and pens.

After grabbing Levi's homework from the kitchen, Evie walked back into the toy room where the kids were at, resolving to get some work done. She juggled phone calls to venues and radio stations all while trying to give her kids attention. Levi had been acting out all day because he knew his negative behavior was receiving attention from everyone around him. Harper wanted her mom to hold her, read her books, and cuddle with her blankie. Evie was feeling stretched out particularly thin this day. Breaking point had come and gone once already, but it was approaching again. It was about 2:30, and Harper missed her nap because of the IEP meeting. Evie prayed for 4:00 when the workday would be over. Her kids were going to bed at 6 PM that night, she resolved.

Meanwhile, Death Toll moved into the audio room and began jotting down some thoughts on lyrics. Kade used some of his own free spirit zen beliefs of dukkha as he wrote down his thoughts; birth is pain, life is pain, death is pain, and it's all the same.

The axioms jarred a bunch of ideas and thoughts Beau had over the past few months about his old lifestyle. He remembered all the days he wasted in the past and even months ago being drunk, hungover, waking up in a stranger's bed, playing the music he loves, and holding the band back from completing their album. Suddenly, words began flowing to his brain, and Beau wrote them down. In his lyrics, he talked about if he had a chance to relive the past few months again, would he do it differently? Or would he continue to live the same old mundane, repetitive, boring, self-destructive lifestyle he knew?

While in rehab, he often wondered if Karma was a real thing because everything terrible he did would come back to bite him. It happened as well when he would do something good, but rather than bite him, those good deeds would benefit him. More lyrics started flowing, and he questioned if he had enough faith in himself to stay away from alcohol and other abusive substances as well as deal with the abandonment issues he had throughout his whole life. Then the answer became clear; you either do or don't.

A crazy catchy word-turned-into-a-phrase came to mind because he remembered feeling this way when he was drunk, hungover, in a stranger's bed, and wasting his valuable time alive. He quickly wrote it down and knew it would be incorporated into the title of the song. Finally, when the band members began sharing lyric ideas, Beau read Kade's, which inspired some more lyrics that came to mind, which reminded him he had to keep on bettering himself and finding ways to live more healthily. All four of them began piecing together the lyrics to form verses and choruses, but they noticed they needed one more verse, but everyone was coming up blank. They at least had a name for the song, *Frantic*.

Just as Beau was about to suggest taking a five-minute break, the door to the audio room swung open, and Levi and Harper came running inside like wild hyenas. Beau's instant reflex was to catch Levi. Kade snatched Harper. "Hey there, little man! Whatcha doing?" Beau asked in a playful way, "Where's your mom?" Beau began tickling and wrestling with Levi as Kade showed Harper that his fingernails were painted black. She oohed and awed. "Do to me!" Harper said before the whole band burst into laughter with how cute that sounded. Suddenly, Evie appeared with fumes coming out of her nose and ears.

Death Toll suddenly became very afraid of this mother. "Levi," Evie said very quietly, but extremely terrifying, "I need to talk to you." Beau suddenly felt bad for the kid. "Hey, Levi, let's follow your mom into the living room," he said, hoping he could help out. Levi grabbed Beau's hand and walked with him into the first living room. Evie followed behind, hoping whatever Beau had to say would help her son.

"Levi, you are such a good kid, but it seems like your mom needs you to stay in the living room while we're working," Beau said very kindly but firm. "Why?" Levi asked. "Because your mom asked you to. That's all that matters. You need to make sure you listen to your parents, especially when they love you as much as your mom loves you," Beau said with a smile. "Does that mean I need to listen to my dad, too?" Levi asked. The question stumped Beau. "Yes," Evie chimed in, "because he loves you, too." "No, he doesn't," Levi mumbled before going off to play.

Beau found Levi's attitude towards his dad peculiar. "What did he mean, 'No, he doesn't?' Has Jude mistreated them?" he asked. Evie shook her head. "It's nothing, really," Evie said, trying to keep her cool. The last thing she wanted was to lose her cool in front of Beau. "What's going on with Levi? I know he is a smart kid. We've heard him practice his math problems on our breaks in the kitchen. Did I do anything wrong? Have you been crying?" Beau asked a million questions.

"I'm fine, and no, you didn't do anything wrong. For the longest time, he has been having major behavioral problems at school even before we moved here. His dad would often just yell at him and blame me for his bad behavior rather than step up to be a father and follow through with discipline. Levi has been diagnosed with ADHD and ODD recently, and I had to go to an IEP meeting this morning to ensure his goals for the school year were set in place," Evie said holding back more tears. She felt like she could unload this problem on Beau.

"Whoah, that's a lot of acronyms. What's an IEP?" Beau asked. "An individualized education plan usually for SPED kids who need extra help."

"SPED?" Beau asked not quite sure what the terminology was.

"Special Education. Levi does great academically, but his teachers tell me he needs some extra help and support behavior-wise," Evie said.

Beau began to sympathize with her. "I had no idea. I'm sorry," he said, "Remind me again, what is ADHD and ODD?" Beau asked.

"Attention Deficit Hyperactive Disorder and Oppositional Defiance Disorder," Evie said.

"Okay, I know what ADHD is. I think I had it as a kid. What exactly does ODD mean?" Beau asked.

"Levi has a tendency to defy authority like teachers, parents, or any adult who tells him they are in charge more than a regular child, and it's been causing lots of problems."

Beau couldn't believe that such a smart kid could have all those problems. "Well, what can we do to help?" Beau asked.

"Well, offering to help him is huge. Thank you. I will accept your help in this area. When you see any bad behavior, ride Levi's butt. Follow through with what you said to him because he knows when you are serious or not. His father never followed through with his consequences, and Levi knew he wouldn't," Evie said.

"All right, I can do that. Do you want the band and crew involved in this as well?" Beau asked.

"Might as well. It takes a whole village to raise children, and it seems to me that Death Toll is our village," Evie said. Beau smiled at that thought.

"Well, when we are healthy, we are a powerful village," Beau said.

"I just wish I was more focused on the meeting today than on Harper," Evie said.

"I will talk to the guys to see if any of their wives can watch your kids when you need to go to important meetings or anywhere else you need to go," Beau said.

"Thank you. That would relieve some stress," Evie said.

Beau was afraid to tell Evie what he had been up to since he last talked to her. He had gone apartment hunting and found a townhouse with three bedrooms, two bathrooms, and a pool about a mile away from the studio. Beau also made sure that the Master suite would be a relaxing place for Evie to unwind after working all day, taking care of the kids and Death Toll. The townhouse was relatively close to Levi's school as well. Since he knew the complex manager, Beau was able to negotiate Evie's rent down from $3500 to $2800, saving her $200 a month. Beau also spoke with Luke about the phone calls Evie made. They both agreed to give Evie a raise from $100,000 to $150,000, alleviating some of the financial stress in her life.

"Well, speaking of relieving stress," Beau said, reaching into his back pocket and pulling out a lease agreement, "I was able to find a place for you to live. I had to cosign the lease, but it just needs your signature, and I will go turn it in for you. Rent is $2800, so under budget. The townhouse is close to Levi's school as well as the studio. Also, I talked with Luke as well as some of our lawyers, and we agreed to raise your pay to $150,000 a year. We want you to feel like you're a part of the family, which you are."

Evie had no idea what to say as she listened to Beau telling her he solved all of her problems. "I didn't ask you to do any of that," she finally said, feeling stunned, grateful, and put out all at the same time.

"I know, but I overheard you talking on the phone a couple nights ago, and..." Beau was soon interrupted.

"Why are you interfering with my life?" Evie asked, sounding angry.

"Are you seriously getting mad at me for helping you? If you want, I can undo all of this, and..."

"Fire me?!" Evie said in terror.

"What!? No! We would never let you go. You're the best manager we've ever had. I just meant undo all the help," Beau said.

Evie started crying again. Beau had no idea what to do. "You're right. I'm sorry. You've actually saved me from a ton of financial stress. I hate asking for help. I don't want to be a charity case to anyone," Evie said.

"You're not. You've been trying to handle all of this on your own, but we are here to help you. You can count on us," Beau said.

Evie wiped away the tears and said, "Thank you so much."

Beau smiled. "You're welcome. Now, when the day is done, shall we drop off that application so that you can start moving in?" Beau asked.

"Yes," Evie said as Beau handed her the application. She signed it, and Beau folded it back up and put the application in his pocket.

When 4:00 hit, Evie followed Beau to the complex she would be living at. It was in a fairly safe area of San Rafael. There was a large pool, a spacious living room and kitchen, large rooms for the kids, and a nice bathroom for the kids with a tub. She was completely blown away by the Master suite. It had a fireplace, patio overlooking the canyon, a waterfall shower, and a separate soaker tub. After she and Beau signed the lease agreement, the complex manager handed Evie keys.

"All right. The band and crew are at the storage unit waiting to move your belongings into the townhouse," Beau said. Evie was completely blown away by Beau's kindness. "Thank you so much for doing this for me," she said. "You're welcome," Beau responded.

Chapter 5

The Park

Five months had passed since Beau checked into rehab. He had been out for a month. Beau sat in the first living room with Dr. Peter Bennett. "I am very impressed with how dedicated you were in rehab for the last four months and how you're following the program I made for you. What happened that made you change?" Dr. Bennett asked Beau during a session in therapy.

"It was something that the new tour manager said that pulled at my heartstrings. She said, 'Don't let your family die in vain.' I suddenly started thinking about what Phoebe would have thought about all of this. I realized I would have been kicked out of my house for good, I would never see my kids again, never see my unborn baby at the time. Death Toll, my friends, all of it would be gone.

"I remembered Phoebe's threats after I went on that hunting trip in Alaska after Cordell's birthday when my erratic behavior spun out of control. I knew this was all too familiar. I realized that even though they are not here anymore, they still love me. I didn't want to explain to Phoebe why I was being cast down to Hell while she and the kids were in Heaven. I also prayed that somehow, Phoebe would guide me or send angels to help me. I've told you I've always felt like there have been angels protecting me from all the stupid stuff I've done. I asked if Phoebe could be one of them."

Dr. Bennett took notes while Beau talked. "I am very proud of you. You have made way more progress this time around than I expected. Take pride in that. So, what have you been doing to help manage your addictions?" Dr. Bennett asked.

"I mainly just stay here at night until I know I'm ready for bed. My house feels too empty right now. I feel like if I went somewhere, I would be tempted to go back to the bar. I can't do that, and I don't want to do that," Beau responded.

Dr. Bennett listened and thought of a solution. "Have you thought about spending time with other people not at a bar?" he asked.

"The only other people I know are my band and roadies," Beau said, "and they all drink on occasion. I am too scared to be around that temptation, right now."

"What about the tour manager and her family?" Dr. Bennett asked. Beau shook his head. "I've spent time with them while they stayed here, and I co-signed Evie's lease. Other than that, no."

"It seems like they are your only option right now. Since she is with her kids, I bet she stays clear of alcohol around them. I would say try spending time with them. Aren't the kids around the same age as your kids?" Dr. Bennett asked. "Yeah, they are." "Okay. I bet it will do you some good."

Dr. Bennett began loading up his briefcase while Beau sat down, picking at the hole in his jeans on the knee. He thought about what Pete had said. Beau had never seen Evie touch a sip of alcohol. Even when she lived at the studio while he stayed there, she didn't go near the whiskey Luke brought to share with Kade and Rick. Evie was also kind enough to ask the three of them to keep their alcohol at home as a way of keeping Beau safe. Now that she found an apartment, he had no idea what her habits were.

Suddenly, Evie walked in. "Sorry to interrupt, but Luke needs to talk to you, Beau," she said, breaking his trance. "All right, thanks," he said. Dr. Bennett walked past her as well before turning around and asking, "How are you adjusting?"

Evie shrugged. "Fine, I guess. Every day is a new adventure," she replied. "Do you need anything?" Dr. Bennett asked, sensing some unresolved issues she was holding onto.. Evie hesitated to answer.

"I understand if you're not ready. Separation and divorce are hard to process," Dr. Bennett said. "How do you know I'm divorced? I could just be a single mom who has no idea who the father of her kids is," she said.

"You keep reaching for your wedding ring with your thumb out of habit. It must have been a huge ring. Plus, word travels fast around here about the hot new tour manager with two adorable children," Dr. Bennett concluded quoting one of the roadies. Evie was taken aback by his comment. "Not my words," Dr. Bennett said, holding up his hands. "They're probably saying that because I'm the only woman here. A man doesn't want to date a mom who pushed two humans out of her body and lost all of her adventurous nature," Evie said.

Dr. Bennett started to get more of a feel about Evie's self-image and worth. "Why would you think that about yourself?" Dr. Bennett asked. Evie shrugged. "A friend of mine told me," Evie said. "Whoever is saying that is not your friend. Look, whenever you're ready to talk, I'm here," Dr. Bennett concluded before walking out of the living room.

Evie hadn't addressed her demons at all since she moved away. She tried very hard not to go to the awful place the demons hid where her thoughts of disappearing were. Her thoughts wandered to that terrible day she caught Jude with Carmen and the double-edged sword of words he used to cut Evie down.

Jude's words still messed with her head and self-esteem, and the whole incident caused her children to lose respect for their dad. Since then, she tried helping her kids build trust with their father again. He would talk on the phone with them about once a week, but Jude would always ask Levi to hand the phone back to his mom, and Jude would proceed to yell at Evie for many different reasons whether it was moving so far away, taking all of their belongings, and for getting a job as a tour manager where she would be vulnerable to rejection. She would often end the day hiding her tears from the kids while they went on adventures throughout the Bay area, tucking them in bed, crying and screaming herself to sleep in her room.

Evie quickly stopped her thoughts before they got worse. She went into the second living room where all of the kid toys, comfy couch, and large TV was. Levi and Harper were playing with all of the toys. "Hey, guys! What do you want to do when I get off work?" she asked. "Can we go to that park again?" Levi asked. Evie nodded her head. Evie did a lot of research on parks and things to do with the kids in case they got restless or bored as well as giving her healthy outlets to release her negative thoughts. She found a park less than a mile away.

"Absolutely," Evie said enthusiastically. The kids ran towards the front door before Evie could get a handle on the situation, but she had figured out a way to get their attention. "Everybody freeze!" Evie yelled as she got outside. Both kids stood still frozen in place. They looked up at their mom. "We need to put shoes on. I also need to get the stroller, remember," Evie concluded. Both kids walked to the shoe covey Jetta, Luke's wife, had installed for all of the kids to put shoes, backpacks in case they needed to do homework, toys, etc. Levi took his shoes and put them on while Evie helped Harper put hers on. They walked outside to the Kia, and Evie pulled the stroller out from the trunk and unfolded it. She placed Harper in the seat and buckled her. There was a spot on the stroller for Levi to ride just in case he got tired.

Evie began pushing the stroller and walking when suddenly she heard a deep voice behind her. She turned around and realized Beau was calling after her. He overheard them leaving just as he finished his session, and he wanted to avoid temptation. He rushed over to her and asked, "Can I join you? We are done for the day, and I need some fresh air." "Sure. We are just going to Gerstle Park to play. Nothing too exciting over here," Evie said. "Sounds perfect," Beau said. All four of them started on the journey to the park.

Evie looked around at all the trees. It was the middle of August, and the leaves were very green. She noticed the colors were more vibrant than back home. The air was drier than she expected, but she knew monsoon season was approaching. The sound of occasional leaves on the sidewalk crunched underneath shoes and the stroller wheels as she pushed. Despite being from the East Coast where there was more humidity, she loved the weather and climate in the Bay area.

Every now and then, Levi would begin to wander too far from the group, so Evie occasionally reminded him to stay close. Beau observed this cute little family interaction and decided to help out. "Hey, Levi, how about you hold my hand to help your mom keep track of you," Beau said, holding out his hand to Levi. "Why?" the little boy asked, challenging Beau's authority. "Well, do you want to be safe?" he asked the 5-year-old. "Yeah,"

Levi responded. "Okay, hold my hand, please. I can help you be safe," Beau said kindly but firm.

Levi hesitated but grabbed Beau's left hand, which was covered in tattoos of letters. "Why do you have letters on your hands?" Levi asked innocently. "They each represent some stuff that has happened in my life," Beau responded.

"What do they mean?" Levi asked again.

"Well, if you look at my knuckles," Beau said as he stopped walking, kneeled down, and began pointing at the letter tattoos on his hands, "My right-hand spells the word 'riff.' Do you see that?"

Levi started saying the letters out loud pointing at each of Beau's knuckles. "'Riff,'" Levi sounded out.

"Now," Beau continued, "I have the word 'life' tattooed on my left hand. Can you spell that word?"

Levi kept pointing at each letter and knuckle, "L-I-F-E."

"Good job, Buddy," Beau praised, "that spells 'life.' Now, when you combine both hands together, what does it say?"

Levi watched Beau put them together. He focused very hard reading the words on Beau's knuckles. "'Riff Life,'" Levi said.

"Good job, Buddy! You are a good reader!" Beau said, giving Levi a high five.

Levi beamed from ear to ear with pride. Then he asked, "What does it mean?"

"I play guitar, and we tend to call sections of music on a guitar, 'riffs.' So, I play a lot of riffs as a guitarist, so I live a 'riff life,'" Beau explained.

Levi laughed. "Is that kind of like a run in orchestra music, Mom?" Levi asked Evie.

"That is exactly right. You are learning so much, Bub," Evie said.

Levi proceeded to ask about the letters D and T with the number 98 on his right hand between his index finger and thumb. "The DT stands for 'Death Toll,' and the 98 is the year Luke and I started the band," Beau responded. Levi absorbed the information like a sponge.

"And what's that one?" Levi asked, pointing to the fancy letter P on his left hand between the index finger and thumb. "That one stands for 'Phoebe,' my wife who died in the car accident," Beau said very somberly. "I'm sorry," Levi said hugging Beau's leg.

Beau was surprised at the affection, but he smiled anyway as he rubbed Levi's back. "Hey, I'm fine. You are doing a great job cheering me up. Now, how about you grab my hand, and we walk to the park so that you and Harper can play?" Beau asked enthusiastically. Levi gasped with excitement. "Okay!" he said. Levi grabbed Beau's hand, and everyone resumed walking to the park.

Evie had never been more grateful for any human than she was at that moment for Beau being so kind and firm with her spirited son. Beau, himself, was unsure how he felt about explaining some of his tattoos to his tour manager's son, and he was uncertain if she would approve.

"If I crossed some sort of line..." he began to explain, but she continued, "No. It's fine. It was kind of interesting to hear the stories behind your tattoos. Plus, you were so kind to him. I don't know very many people who explain those things to an inquisitive little boy."

"Do you think he will ask you for a tattoo?" Beau joked.

Evie responded, "If he does, he's not getting one until he's 18, on his own, and earning his own money."

"Fair enough," Beau said.

They smiled at each other for a moment before glancing down. Beau looked at the ground while Evie looked down at the stroller. "Harper, you okay, Sweetie?" Evie asked. "Yeah," they heard Harper's sweet voice. They continued walking to the park.

When they got there, Levi immediately ran for the playground. Evie pulled Harper out of the stroller, and she ran after her brother. "Levi," Evie called out, "keep an eye on your sister, please." "I will," Levi called back.

Evie sat down on the bench closest to the playground, and Beau sat down next to her. Evie pulled out her phone, ready to document their adventure. Beau noticed. "Do you take lots of pictures of your kids?" he asked.

"I try to. Since my family lives so far away, I use social media to let them see my kids. I try to tag my ex-husband in the photos as well so that he can see them, too," she said.

"So, what's his name?" he asked.

"Jude."

"What does he do for a living?"

"He is a partner for a huge corporate real estate company."

"Wow, he sounds important."

"He is."

"What does he look like? Does he have curly hair like Harper? Blonde hair? Blue eyes?"

"He has thick brown wavy hair and blue eyes. He looks kind of like a young William Shatner from the original *Star Trek*," Evie said.

"You watch *Star Trek*?" Beau said, trying not to laugh.

"Don't mock. My parents did. I just remember the face of Captain Kirk." Evie smirked but laughed.

"Where did the blonde hair come from?"

"Jude's brothers have blonde hair. Harper has the same texture of hair as Jude's, and Levi looks like a blonde version of his dad with straight hair." Beau listened and nodded.

Beau and Evie began talking about lighter subjects. He could sense she was uneasy talking about her ex-husband. "What's your favorite music?" he asked her.

"Obviously, Metal, but I also like Latin, Classical, and Jazz. I also like some of the other genres in Rock like Hard Rock, Southern Rock, Blues, that sort of thing."

"No country?" Beau teased.

"There are only three places where country music is appropriate," Evie began, "The first one is a rodeo, the second one is line-dancing in a country bar, and the third is riding in a truck to go do one of those things or go do something outdoors."

Beau laughed. "Do you listen to the music of today?"

"Not really. I only hear today's music at the gym. Why listen to a song by Beyonce that nine people wrote when I could listen to *Bohemian Rhapsody* written by one person?" Evie posed a crucial question to Beau.

"Okay, that was probably the best thing I have ever heard a girl say," he said, *not to mention the hottest thing a girl could say*, he thought to himself. He could feel a little crush developing, but soon shoved those feelings deep down as Evie blushed and laughed, causing the crush to resurface a little.

"Do you have any tattoos?" Beau asked.

"No. I am too chicken," she said.

"It doesn't hurt that bad," Beau said.

Evie looked at him in disbelief. "Says the man who cried on social media when you got a tattoo on your arm. Admit that they hurt," she said.

"Fine, they hurt," Beau admitted with a chuckle.

Evie's attention went back to watching Levi and Harper play together. She stood up off the bench and took pictures of the cute things they did. She loved watching them play together.

Suddenly, Levi shouted, "I'm gonna get you, Mom!" He ran to his mother. She fake-screamed and began running away, Levi laughing. Harper began chasing after both her mother and brother. Finally, Evie said, "Now I'm gonna get you!" She began chasing her children before grabbing both of them in one arm. Evie lost her balance and fell on the grass, trying to adjust. As Evie laid on her back, her kids tackled her. All three of them laughed and giggled. This adventure cheered Evie up, and she no longer felt like a loser mom.

Beau sat and watched this little family, and his heart swelled up inside of him. He saw how much Levi and Harper loved their mom. He observed the way Evie looked at her children, and he could tell how much she loved them. She loved being a mom. Beau knew he needed to spend more time with this little family.

Evie soon got tired wrestling with her kids and sat back down on the bench. She picked up her phone and started snapping more pictures. She pointed her phone at Beau and took a picture, which caught him off guard.

"What was that for?" he asked.

"Just letting my family know that we had a guest accompany us. Don't worry about me selling it," Evie joked. "I know. It's in your contract," Beau joked back. "In fact," Evie began, "could I get a picture of you showing your tattoos to Levi again? My family will find the story interesting," Evie said. "Sure. Not a problem," Beau said as he stood up off of the bench.

Beau called Levi back over as Evie stayed with Harper for a minute. Beau started showing Levi his tattoos again, and Evie took a few pictures. As she watched the frontman of her favorite band spend quality time with her son, Evie could feel a crush developing also, which scared her. *Really, the frontman of Death Toll? Could you be any more of a cliche groupie? No, not going to happen*, Evie thought to herself before shoving her feelings down, remembering Jude's words.

Evie then took a couple of selfies with Harper. After watching her brother interact with Beau, Harper walked over to him and even began telling him stories about her toys, baby dolls, and her blankie. Beau just smiled at Harper, and she eventually ended up sitting in his lap. Evie smiled and captured the moment on her phone.

All four of them had an enjoyable time at the park. Evie looked at her smartwatch and realized it was 5:15. They needed to get back home and have dinner. She put Harper back in the stroller, and Levi grabbed Beau's hand again. They walked the mile back to the studio. Beau helped Evie load the kids and stroller back in her car.

"Thank you for letting me come with you," Beau said.

"You're welcome. Anytime you want to join us on our adventures, you can. You actually have no idea how much you helped out with Levi today. Thank you," Evie said.

"You're welcome. I'm sure your ex-husband used to help out a lot of the time on outings with his kids."

Evie felt a little rigid. "Actually, Jude never did stuff like this with us at all. Today was the first day I have had more than one adult at the park with me besides my mom, my sister, or a nanny," Evie said.

Beau suddenly felt stupid. "Sorry about that," he said.

"How could you know? It's okay. Anyways, see ya tomorrow!" Evie said as she climbed into her car and closed the door. Beau watched her drive off and felt like he triggered her anxiety. He hoped to eradicate the problem the following day.

After everyone had dinner at home, Evie got the kids ready for bed. She got on her phone and proceeded to upload the pictures to her various social media accounts. She looked at the pictures of her kids, and then she looked at the images of Beau with her kids. Despite his hard exterior, he had such a kind heart to accompany a single mom and her two kids on a dull outing to the park. He really was as down-to-earth, goofy, and genuine as she imagined. For the first time, Evie felt giddy.

The giddiness was short-lived. Jude called. "How could you let such a man near our kids? You know the type of person he is!" Jude scolded.

"Do you really think I am the type of mother who lets any weirdo around our kids? I have been working closely with Beau for the past three months, and he has changed. No need to freak out. He is fine," Evie said.

"How close are we talking here?"

"Why do you care?"

"I just don't want some rocker showing my son tattoos," Jude noted with disgust.

"I am trying to teach our children substance over materialism. It's not like he offered Levi a beer. Beau volunteered to come."

"Now why would the frontman of Death Toll hang out with a single mother and her two kids?"

"Maybe because he is a nice guy who saw a mother in need."

"Oh, good. You're learning that men only see you as a mother"

"Jude, drop it. I know, I'm not as adventurous, free-spirited, and sexy as I used to be, so you can just save that speech for next time."

"Also, shouldn't the father be the one going on these outings with his children?"

"Kinda hard to do when he decided to divorce the mother so that he could upgrade his model." Evie hadn't been that blunt with Jude in a very long time, but something about today seemed like the perfect time to do it.

"Just because I divorced you doesn't mean I wanted the three of you to move across the country."

"What happened to your clean break?"

"I only expected you to move back to Annapolis with your parents, find a teaching job there, and eventually get an apartment. Not have you move cross-country to be a tour manager for a rock band."

"Well, I needed a fresh start, too. And a part of me longed for ..." Evie hesitated, wondering how Jude would react to what she was going to say. "I wanted to be adventurous, again," she finally said.

Jude laughed. "This wasn't adventurous. This was irresponsible," Jude argued, reminding her that Levi hated change, calling her hypocritical, and threatening to take the kids away to bring some normalcy back into Levi's life.

Evie countered Jude and said, "If we keep moving Levi back and forth, that will mess him up even more. Plus, we both know you'll just hire a nanny. Levi is in a better situation here."

"With a bunch of rockstars?"

"They all have kids or have had kids. Beau was amazing with Levi today. The others are good with our kids, too."

"I don't want my family to be seen with a man who has been to rehab recently," Jude tried to defend, but Evie wasn't going to put up with it.

"I work for the guy. We're going to be seen with him. You have no control over who I can and cannot be seen with male, female, or hermaphrodite."

"Well, I should be the one going on outings with you and the kids."

"I agree. You should be, but you waived that right when you slept with Carmen, Kara, Crystal, Lana, and half the city of Baltimore. Plus, you never came with us to the park in the first place when we were married. I am trying to understand what your point of calling me is other than to tear me down."

"How did you find out all of the women's...?"

"It doesn't matter how I found out. Again, you were the one who needed the upgrade."

"Well, I am still Levi and Harper's father, not that gorilla, Beau Halstead."

"Beau asked to come along on his employee's outing with her kids to get some fresh air. He took an interest in his employee's life and her kids' lives. What's the harm in that?" Evie asked.

"Just remember, no one will love you the way I loved you. He will not know the amazing version of you that I fell in love with," Jude said, shoving that double-edged sword further into Evie's interior.

"That's one thing you won't have to worry about," Evie said with a mousy voice, "Now, I am sure Carmen, Kara, Shaniqua, or whatever slut is breathing in your direction is waiting for you. Goodbye." Evie hit the end button on her phone and threw it on the couch.

Just when Evie thought he couldn't possibly make her feel any worse about herself, Jude managed to accomplish that goal. He continued sending awful texts to Evie telling her what a horrible mother she was and possibly involving his lawyers to take the kids away. She eventually put the phone on silent and cried herself to sleep again. She was losing count how many times she did that.

The next morning, Evie woke up early with a pounding headache. She reached for her phone. There were a ton of text messages from Jude repeating the same old things he had been telling her since their divorce. It was starting to lose its potency.

After scrolling through all of the missed texts, Evie came across a message from Beau. She opened it instantly and read, "Thanks for letting me come with you and your family to the park. You have no idea how much it meant to me. You have two good kids, and you are a great mom."

Evie smiled after reading it feeling a bit better from her melancholy mood. She responded, "Thanks," with a smiley face.

She soon got a reply. "I hope I didn't cross any lines with our conversation before you left the studio," Beau typed.

"No, not at all," Evie typed back, "It was fun having you there. It meant a lot to us, especially Levi."

"Anytime he needs me, I will be there," Beau wrote.

Chapter 6

The Gym

For the next few weeks, Evie started settling down into a routine with her kids as well as her job. She would drop off Levi at school, take Harper with her to the studio, pick Levi up, take the kids back to the studio where they would have lunch, Harper would take a nap in the room they stayed in, and Levi would either work on his sight words, reading, math, or watch a movie on the couch sometimes falling asleep when his homework was all done. Evie began to work effortlessly with the routine in place.

Levi made friends at school as well as improved his behavior, and Harper would play with the bandmates' kids when they came to the studio. Evie thought about putting Harper in ballet when she turned three not only to help build her skills as a dancer but for the social skills. Evie even began to make friends with Jetta, Luke's wife, Laila, Kade's wife, and Kaylee, Rick's wife. Jetta was very tall and supermodel-esque, and Evie felt like they didn't have much in common other than their taste in music, but her boys were the same age as Levi and Harper. Laila had a hilarious, sarcastic sense of humor and personality similar to Evie's best friend and roommate from college, Abella. Evie admired how bold and eccentric Kaylee was because of her artwork, but she lived the farthest away in Santa Monica, so hanging out with her was sometimes hard. Death Toll soon became like brothers to her, but there was this chemistry with Beau that she couldn't put her finger on.

One day towards the end of August, Evie climbed into her car dressed in a black athletic tank top with a high neckline, green athletic leggings, and black Nikes. She looked forward to going to her Zumba class. Evie listened in on the band's session with Dr. Bennett a couple of weeks ago, and the doctor recommended Beau find something active to do to replace the urge to drink.

Evie thought about what he said and how it could apply to her. She began attending Zumba classes again after that day to replace her self-destructive thoughts, making friends with some of the ladies at the gym and the instructor. The depression she fought so hard to overcome had grown as well as the negative voice in her head, so she decided to take Dr. Bennett's advice and go to Zumba. Jude called the night before to talk to the kids and tear Evie down, so she needed a Zumba class to help her feel better. She called Laila to watch her kids saving a little bit of money on childcare.

After Evie shut the car door, there was a knock at the window. She jumped when she saw Beau standing outside, dressed in gym clothes. Quickly rolling down the window, she asked Beau, "What's up?" "Are you headed to the gym?" he asked. "Yeah, I have a class that starts in about 15 minutes at the Body Kinetics Health Club," she said. Evie was too scared to tell him it was a Zumba class because she didn't want to scare him off.

"Can I come with you? I am just trying to follow Peter's advice of replacing healthy habits with unhealthy ones," Beau said.

Evie looked up at Beau perplexed. "You want to come with me to my class?" she asked.

"Sure, why not? It's not like it's yoga… You're not going to yoga, are you?" Beau said.

"No, I am not much of a yogi," Evie chuckled. Beau nodded his head.

"All right," he said before walking to the other side of the car, opening the door, climbing in, and putting his seatbelt on.

Evie drove down 3rd Street in San Rafael to get to the gym. She knew 2nd Street was a one-way street that she needed to go around. Beau turned on the radio and found a rock station blasting the AC/DC song, *It's A Long Way To the Top*. Evie knew this was one of Beau's favorite songs. He bobbed his head to the music while Evie did the same thing. He turned his head towards Evie when he noticed the movement. "Really? You like AC/DC?" he asked her. "There is a reason I came to work for you," she said. Beau remembered some of the early conversations when they went to the park. "I forgot. Sorry," he said. "It's all good," Evie said, smiling, "Push the media button to my stereo. I think you will appreciate this," she told him.

Beau pushed the button, and to his surprise, *YYZ* by Rush blared through her speakers. "Huh, I am impressed. Excellent taste. I like Rush, but Geddy always sang too high for my taste."

"Whatever! He sings wonderfully. His vocal folds are thinner than yours."

"How do you know what my vocal folds look like?" Beau asked, feeling a little creeped out.

"I taught music for three years. I had to learn the basics of voice types. You are a baritone. The pitch of our speaking voices and singing voices are determined by the thickness of vocal folds."

Beau was blown away with her knowledge. "Were you an honor student in high school?" Beau asked, joking.

Evie laughed. "Yes, I was."

"What about in college?"

"I graduated Cum Laude, but I was still somewhat of a party girl."

"Wow, I'm impressed. So, what's your voice type?" Beau asked curiously.

"I'm a contralto. I have very thick vocal folds compared to most women. There aren't a lot of contraltos in the world," Evie said.

"Who would I know that's a contralto?"

Evie thought about it for a minute. "Amy Winehouse was one, Joni Mitchell, Stevie Nicks, Patti Smith, Courtney Love, and your friend, Lady Gaga," Evie responded.

"You all have low voices," he said.

"We sing best in the lower range where our voice sounds the richest, but we can get as high as a soprano and as low as a baritone," Evie smiled.

"Even still, you are teaching things."

"I will always be a teacher. That's also part of my job description as a mom," Evie said. Beau agreed.

They pulled into the gym parking lot. Evie felt a little awkward as she walked into the gym with this tall, handsome, rugged, slightly intimidating man next to her. She felt guilty, not telling him they were going to a Zumba class. Finally, Evie couldn't take it anymore.

"Beau, I need to be straight with you," she said, turning to him. Beau paused. "You are taking me to yoga, aren't you?" he said, looking nervous.

She shook her head. "No. This is a dance fitness class called Zumba. It is mostly Latin music, some hip hop, pop music, and a few rock song remixes if we are lucky. It requires a lot of hip movement," Evie spilled very fast, "If you want to go lift weights, walk a treadmill, or even go do the ropes and cables, that is fine with me."

Beau stared away into nothing processing what he just heard. He was familiar with some Latin music because of Phoebe, and he always liked what he heard. He thought it might be interesting to see what all the fuss was about. "I appreciate your honesty, but I will try it. If I don't like it, I will do something else next time."

"Okay. Now I am a diehard metalhead, but I also love Latin music. I hope you will understand."

"It's okay. We all have different interests." They kept talking until they walked into the Aerobics room and set their stuff down.

Evie took her place on the front row, and Beau stood about four feet away from her. "Why the front row?" he asked.

"Because I have a hard time seeing the instructor from where you are," she said, "In fact, I would stand by me if I were you so that you can see what to do better."

"I'm 6' 1. I can see fine."

"Okay, you can stand where you are if you want. People might recognize you as they walk in, though. At least if you're in front, your back is to them, and they are too far to see you in the mirror."

Good point, Beau thought. "Okay, I will come up front," he said before walking to Evie's left side and standing there.

The instructor walked in front of the class and began getting the stereo working. She turned on a song with a slow dragging beat, but the song sounded happy. Beau remembered Richard and Kade messing around one day with a rhythm like this before they started working. He also recalled his first date with Phoebe watching her dance to something similar. He couldn't remember what the style was called, but he turned to his right to look at Evie. Her face lit up when she heard the song. The instructor approached Evie and gave her a hug. "Hey, Evie! How are you?" she asked.

Evie smiled. "I'm good. Thanks."

"Will you want to teach a song or two today?" the instructor asked. "If you want me to," Evie said, cheeks turning pink, and looking up at Beau. Evie forgot to tell Beau she used to teach a couple of Zumba classes back in Baltimore.

The instructor turned to him, as well. "Is this who I think it is?" the instructor asked, recognizing him.

"This is Beau Halstead; my boss," Evie said. "Oh, my husband is a huge fan. I will have to tell him you were in class today. He might not even believe me," the instructor said. Beau felt a little stuck and turned to look at Evie. She looked up at him and mouthed, "Sorry."

"All right, everyone! Let's get started! I am Pam. If you are new to Zumba, just watch my feet, smile, and have fun," Pam, the Zumba instructor, shouted at the class. She turned on the music and soon led the class in some clapping and touch steps. Beau did his best to follow Pam. He looked down at Evie, and she had the biggest smile on her face as she moved her hips and raised her arms in the air one by one. She was even singing along to the words.

There was a lot of clapping and yelling. Beau wasn't sure what to think about the first song they did. He noticed that there were a lot of attractive women in the class. Beau did not complain, and he observed they all moved very well. He felt very intimidated at first, but he committed to trying the whole class. The first song turned out to be better once he figured out what he was supposed to do. The next song had a very distinct rhythm and beat. This song was more toning than anything with lots of ab work, coordination, and sumo squats. It was pretty simple to follow once he figured out the 6-count move. He occasionally looked at Evie to make sure he was doing what she was doing. Her dancing and technique were perfect, and sexy, he had to admit. He suddenly realized that she was probably an instructor at some point. Beau saw the passion she had for Zumba.

Evie kept looking up at Beau to make sure he wasn't throwing daggers at her with his stare for putting him through the class. The glances were short-lived because Zumba always put Evie in a better mood. The music, the moves, and how Zumba made her feel is what kept her coming back and eventually led to her becoming an instructor herself. She hadn't taught a class since she moved to San Francisco, and Evie figured she wouldn't be able to since she would be on the road a lot. She missed teaching a lot.

During class, Evie and Beau would look at each other and smile. She had no idea what he thought of her, but she thought he was doing a good job keeping up even for a beginner. Being a musician had its perks when she started Zumba herself, so Evie was able to stay with the beat. She also thought Beau danced very smooth and silly at times, which made her laugh.

Beau's favorite part of the class was when Pam asked Evie to teach a song. The song started out with some salsa side steps and salsa rock backs. He watched Evie and realized she communicated with the class nonverbally what was next very well. He started to listen to the song and realized the dancing complemented the song very well. Evie also took the energy in the class and amped it up even more. The heat reminded him when he was on stage looking at all the faces in the crowd only this time, Beau was surrounded by beautiful women being led by another beautiful woman.

Beau noticed everyone smiling in response to her infectious personality. There were even a couple of times he sang along to the song. Beau decided Zumba was an excellent way to help him in his recovery. Once the song, *Fun* by Pitbull and Chris Brown, was over, Pam took over, and finished out the class. Other students praised Evie for her teaching. The crush emerged again, but this time, Beau didn't fight so hard to push it down.

The cooldown began with a flugelhorn playing, and Evie suddenly started to freak out once she realized what song was playing; *Tumbao*. This particular cooldown was very provocative because of the full-body rolls the class would do very close to each other. Beau had no idea what was coming. It was a simple Bachata at the beginning with stretching, but the body rolls were next during the chorus. When the time came, Evie held back, but the other girl on Beau's left did not.

Evie soon regretted bringing Beau because she didn't want to give him the wrong idea about Zumba, and she got a little jealous of the girl. Not to mention, she thought Beau was a handsome man with his eyes and his kind smile. The tattoos on his arms added character whether some people would have viewed them as intimidating. The other girl must have figured out who Beau was because she wasn't holding back at all.

Jealousy filled Evie, and she didn't know what to do about it. Plus, Evie had a little crush on her boss. She knew there were some more body rolls, so she decided to go all out. The final leg of stretching came, and Evie prepared for the body roll section mentally.

Evie stepped forward following the music, turned when she was supposed to, and bent over down to her toes rolling her body up as slowly and sensually as possible. Beau's eyes suddenly went to Evie's body roll, and he forgot what he was doing. The move sent Beau to a flashback when Phoebe took him dancing on their first date. Phoebe moved just like Evie did. That date led to their first night of intimacy and their relationship. He couldn't think about anything else because his hormones were getting the best of him as he continued to watch his tour manager dance so provocatively.

Beau soon realized he was just staring at Evie, not moving a muscle. When she began walking away from him, he realized he needed to walk towards her so that the other girl wouldn't run into him. When his back was to Evie, Beau body-rolled a little more dramatically than before, responding to Evie's movements. She laughed, staring at his butt thinking how nice it looked. Soon, they locked eyes and felt some sort of electricity in their dancing. For the remainder of the song, he faced the right and focused only on Evie. When the song ended, they were both dancing very close to each other with Beau inches away from Evie that she felt him breathe on her neck.

Pam noticed the chemistry they shared and smiled. She sensed Evie's lack of self-esteem and figured this would boost it. When Pam gave her final bow, she clapped, and the rest of the class applauded, breaking the trance Beau and Evie were in. Blinking really fast trying to get a grip, Evie walked to her water bottle and got a drink.

After talking with lots of people, Evie and Beau walked back to the car. Beau had way more fun than he thought, and he made sure to tell Pam that. He even said he would be happy to meet her husband. They climbed into the car, and Evie pulled out of the parking lot heading back to the studio.

"That was way fun. Thank you," Beau said again. "You're welcome. So, what do you think of Latin music?" Evie asked.

"I like it. It has a lot of energy in it like our music. What are all of the different styles called?"

"The four basic Zumba styles are Merengue, Salsa, Cumbia, and Reggaeton. However, some others we did today are Moombahton, Soca, Dembow, Bhangra, and Bachata. I really like the last two styles."

"Which ones were those?"

"You would know one as Bollywood, and Bachata was the cooldown." "Oh, got it. The songs with all the Bom Diggy's, and the body rolls?"

"Yes."

"And I thought I was a music guru."

"You know way more about the B sides of metal albums than I do. Sure, I know a lot about different styles of music, but I wish I knew what you know."

"Well, I can always teach you."

"Sounds good. So, do they have any rock songs in the Zumba music world?"

Evie smiled. "Well, Zumba released a routine to *Another One Bites the Dust* by Queen, and *We're Not Gonna Take It* by Twisted Sister. I know a routine to *Pretty Fly*," Evie said, laughing.

"Can I request those songs for next time?"

"Yes, I will let Pam know." Beau pumped his arm and shouted, "Yes!" Evie laughed.

"So, are you a Zumba instructor? You seemed way more confident and aware of everything in the class," he said.

"I taught in Annapolis before I took the job here. I haven't tried to pursue anything because we will be going on tour soon."

"Why not? You are really good."

"I don't have time. There's a tour to finish booking, two little humans who need their mom, and a band to manage."

"Isn't there a list you can get on when other instructors have something come up?"

"Yes, there is a sub list."

"Well, why not the sub list? Why should Death Toll stop you from doing something you love?"

Evie thought about what Beau was saying, and she knew he was right. "All right, I will talk to Pam about it tomorrow."

"Good! So on tour, can we attend other classes in different cities?"

"Of course. I have been doing research on that for two weeks."

There was one thing that kept weighing on Beau's mind. "Okay. I am about to ask you some awkward questions, and I just hope you are okay with it," he said.

Evie grimaced a little. "Sure?" she said.

Beau cleared his throat. "Why did you get a divorce? You are such a great mom, colleague, and friend to everyone you meet. What happened? Was your ex a douche, were you unfaithful, was he unfaithful? I find it strange for a mom of two to suddenly take a job as a tour manager uprooting her family," he asked.

Evie was afraid of someone asking her that, but she had hoped that Luke or Kade would ask. She figured out how to explain what was going on, leaving out the abuse. "I really don't know what happened. The more he pushed himself into the corporate world, the more Jude became disinterested in me. That's all I can really say right now."

Beau felt like he only got half of his answer. *Why would he become disinterested in Evie? She's beautiful, kind, smart, ambitious, independent, a wonderful mom, the whole package. What the hell is wrong with Jude,* Beau thought to himself. He knew pressing would push her away, so he left the topic alone. "Well, thanks for letting me tag along. I had way more fun than I thought I would," Beau said.

"Thank you for coming with me today. You made class way more fun," Evie said back.

"You're welcome. So, is this a daily thing?"

"Yes, but Pam's schedule is changing, so I will let you know what's going to happen."

"Sounds good."

They drove to the Hansens' house and picked up Levi and Harper. Soon, they dropped off Beau at his home. "Bye, Beau!" the kids said. "Bye, guys," he responded back. Beau soon rubbed Evie's arm that was leaning on the window. "See ya tomorrow," he said. "Bye," Evie said.

Beau began attending Zumba classes with Evie every night at 6 for the rest of the week. Each class got more comfortable, and Beau's friendship with Evie grew stronger as they continued to talk more about their childhoods, high school, Evie's college experiences, Beau's early Death Toll days, and where they were on specific days.

"Favorite band?" Beau asked.

"Death Toll. Duh!" Evie said without hesitation.

"Besides Death Toll."

"Led Zeppelin, Black Sabbath, ACDC, Def Leppard, Red Hot Chili Peppers, Green Day, Motorhead, and Skynard."

Beau smiled, impressed, but asked, "You're not going to ask me mine?"

"I already know you love Aerosmith, King Diamond, Thin Lizzy, Diamond Head, Iron Maiden, and Motorhead."

She's a fangirl, Beau laughed to himself.

"Favorite car?" he asked again.

"1967 GT 500 Shelby Mustang," Evie responded with a big grin.

"Would not have pegged you for a muscle car girl," Beau said, thinking to himself, *Again, the hottest thing she could say.*

"Oh yeah. I went to car shows with my dad all the time growing up." *She is so cool*, Beau thought to himself.

"Well, what about you? What's your favorite car?" Evie asked.

"1967 Chevy Camaro. I drove that car in one of our music videos." Evie smiled at the response, remembering watching the music video.

"Favorite food?" she asked him.

"Steak. I am more carnivore than omnivore. What about you?" he asked back.

"Tacos, especially my brother-in-law's tacos." Beau nodded his head..

"So, what are you guys up to this weekend?" he asked.

"Oh, we know how to party. We are going to the park, visiting the children's museum, Pier 39 aquarium, and visiting the sea lions. Then when we get home and kids go to bed, I will get into my frumpy pajamas, eat a huge carton of ice cream, and watch an old movie," she said sarcastically. "Can I come with you guys? I really enjoyed going with you to the park. I'll even get my frumpy pajamas and watch the movie with you. Then I will go home," Beau said, trying to maintain boundaries. He didn't want Evie getting the wrong idea.

"Are you sure you don't have anything better to do? I'm just doing boring single mom stuff," Evie said. "Your life is not boring. Making memories with your kids is exciting. Watching their learning process is always exciting. Plus, taking time for yourself is good, too," Beau said. Evie needed to hear Beau's words as reassurance that she was doing a great job raising her kids. "Yes. We would love for you to come with us," she said. "All right. I will see you tomorrow. Bye, guys!" "Bye, Beau!" the kids said after dropping him off at his house again.

Chapter 7

Song Styles With Beau Halstead

Beau continued accompanying Evie and the kids to the gym as well as other outings. He really grew to love Zumba music and dancing, especially with Evie. Beau could not help but notice how happy dancing made her. He noticed how bright she smiled at Zumba. He sensed how passionate she was about dancing and fitness, and how that passion was being passed on to him. Beau noticed his energy levels had spiked. Writing songs wasn't as exhausting as it used to be. He soon found that he could keep up with the demands of his career, exercising, and even playing with Evie's kids. He also noticed that he had lost a little weight throughout his body and gained some muscle mass. He began to understand how Evie stayed so healthy and active.

The weather turned cooler as August transitioned into September. Beau and Evie were becoming better friends, but Beau's feelings for Evie grew each day he spent with her. He watched her at the studio as she performed her daily tasks and even kept up with her kids. Without being asked, she made sure band members had enough water, coffee, or matte in Beau's case. She would go down the street to Sprouts Farmers' Market to get lunch and snacks for everyone every day. When Death Toll felt like they had a song worthy of being played on the radio to help promote their new album, Evie would call Crazy Tony from ALT 107.6 to come into the studio to listen and ask him to play the song on his radio station. Beau knew how passionate she was about her jobs as a tour manager and mother.

Beau continued to notice more of Evie's characteristics. Even though she was stunning, she put minimal effort into getting ready for the day. Evie didn't wear as much makeup as he had seen a lot of women do. He noticed she liked wearing different colored wide-brimmed hats. Her hair had grown out about three inches since she moved to San Francisco, and he thought she looked sexy with it. Evie's hair stayed in beach waves most of the time, or she would throw it up into a high ponytail with no hat.

He noticed she was slender with lean cut muscles when she wore her gym clothes. Evie looked very alluring in them. While they were at the gym, Evie made the suggestion that they start lifting weights to help build up his muscle mass, which Beau thought was very considerate. Other guys would often walk up to the pair of them to talk to Beau and hit on Evie, which bothered him.

When she was working, Evie usually wore various button-up shirts, band tee shirts that he knew she listened to, large sweaters as it got colder, jeans, boots, and booties now that the weather was cooler. Evie often complained about being cold. He could tell Evie took more time for her children than herself. She was a very selfless person. She was very kind but spoke her mind when called upon.

Beau could tell she was super adventurous, but grounded. He believed taking care of her kids did that. She helped Levi with his reading and other homework assignments when not needed at the studio. Her sense of humor was very similar to his, considering he heard her quote all sorts of movies from Disney to *Friends* to *Sons of Anarchy* to *Monty Python's*

Flying Circus. One of his favorite times was when he watched Evie perform the "Silly Walk" sketch for Levi and Harper, and they began to imitate their mother. Plus, she cracked lame jokes just like he did all the time, and they laughed together.

He knew she had good taste in music because they would ride in her car on the way to the gym listening to the music on her phone. He also noticed she hated asking for help unless it was absolutely necessary. She loved helping others but hated letting others help her. Beau admired her independence and driven spirit.

However, her stubbornness irritated him. He had never met anyone so stubborn in his entire life, but Beau also knew that stubborn people got the job done, so he focused on learning to accept it, considering Evie was his friend.

Beau was a little afraid to admit he liked Evie considering it had only been six months since he lost his family. He would never forget Phoebe, Chloe, or Cordell. They were his world, especially Phoebe. In many ways, Evie reminded Beau of Phoebe a lot, which scared him at times because he wasn't sure if he was ready to open up his heart again. Evie spoke her mind and put everyone first before herself, and he admired that about Phoebe as well. Everyone loved Phoebe, just like everyone loved Evie. Beau was comfortable being in the Friend Zone with Evie for now.

Beau wasn't the only one developing feelings. Evie loved having Beau join her on various adventures with her children. When Evie took her kids to the Children's museum, Beau offered to come and played with both kids like he was a little kid. She loved the fact that Beau was a kid at heart. She remembered a time when Jude was like that, but as he entered the corporate world, he began to change more and more each day as he spent more and more time at his office. Evie always admired men who still acted like little boys at times. Another trait she loved about Beau was he would put his whole life on hold to help a friend, whether it was a small problem or a big problem. Evie witnessed this when Luke's son, Mason, fell from his chair and bumped his head at home. Beau, although out with Evie and the kids, found a way to Luke's house to take care of the other kids while Luke and Jetta took Mason to the hospital. His expressive blue eyes sparkled, even while screaming into the mic while recording lyrics.

Evie laughed at a lot of his jokes because they were very similar to her jokes. They often bantered back and forth with their lame jokes, laughing for ten minutes. She did not care for his occasional profanities, but she knew it was so ingrained into him that she accepted it. They didn't happen very often, which Evie was very thankful for. Evie hated how hard Beau was on himself sometimes, especially how he brought up going to rehab twice. She could see that Beau felt judged by others and himself for that, so she made it a point reminding him that getting help, even extra help, was a good thing. However, his smile lit up his entire face. Not to mention, he was very tall, she loved his blonde hair, and thought he was very cut. She also thought he had a nice butt. He was just an overall sweet, attractive, colorful, genuine guy who played guitar.

At the same time, she wasn't ready to open herself up in that way. Jude continued to tear her down, making her feel worthless that no man would ever want her again. She would often find herself very happy spending time with Beau and the kids, but deep down, she felt useless because of her insecurities. The pain she felt every day cut her to the very fiber of her well-being, and she had a hard time admitting to herself that she believed Jude.

Walls upon walls of skepticism and trust issues went up as Beau's laugh cheered her up, and Jude's words tore her down. *Seriously, why are you hanging out with a single mom and her kids? Do you feel sorry for her, or are you truly trying to be her friend,* she thought, directing her statements to Beau. Evie managed to hide her insecurities from everyone around her, especially Beau, Levi, and Harper.

One evening after a very productive day at the studio, Evie drove to the gym while Beau sat in the passenger seat. Jetta volunteered to watch the kids giving her a break for a while. Evie would have said no if Beau hadn't stepped in and said, "You take care of everyone here. Let someone take care of you." Evie's feelings for Beau swelled inside her, much to her dismay. She agreed to it, and Beau and Evie were soon on their way to the gym. They could take a little bit longer to lift weights without worrying about going over the time limit for Childcare.

Evie's phone played the song *Summer of '69* by Bryan Adams on their way to the gym. Beau began bobbing his head to the music. Evie looked at him for a few seconds and challenged him, "Sing." Beau stopped and looked at her in disbelief. "Really?" he asked. "Yeah, sing it how you would sing it," she said. Beau soon began singing the song in his style of voice distortion.

Evie laughed before saying, "All right, we are going to try something new. Have you ever watched Voice Impressions on the Tonight Show?"

Beau nodded his head but looked uncertain with what happened.

"Okay, the next song that comes on, you need to sing it the way that vocalist sings it," Evie said.

Beau hesitated. "I am not sure I can do that," he said.

"Try it. I will also sing a song you put on and imitate whomever you say," she said.

Beau looked less nervous. "Deal," he said.

The song changed, and Evie said, "There you go. *All Apologies* by Nirvana. Let's hear it … crap, what was his name?!" Evie freaked. *How could I forget the name of the Nirvana frontman,* she yelled at herself in her head. "You mean Kurt Cobain?" Beau asked. "Yes! Thank you! Man, my brain is not working right today," Evie replied, feeling relieved. "How could you forget Kurt Cobain's name? He's an icon for grunge," Beau said. "After you push two humans out of your body, graduate Cum Laude from college, teach high school students, teach fitness classes, and become a tour manager for a band, then you can ask me that question," Evie scolded sarcastically. Beau laughed. "Fine. So *All Apologies*?" "Yes, *All Apologies*," Evie said.

Beau tried very hard to imitate Kurt Cobain. Every now and then, Beau messed up, but he fixed it within seconds. He had fun singing differently than usual. Beau noticed that Evie provided backup vocals.

During a pause in between songs, Beau said, "Okay, *Heartbreaker* by Pat Benatar," he said. "Easy Peasy… Lemon Squeezy," Evie said, chuckling to herself. Beau laughed as well. When Beau found the song, Evie began singing it with ease. When the a cappella part came, Evie even let her voice fall just like Pat's. Beau could feel some hormones moving around inside of him and didn't stop them.

They kept going back and forth singing different songs by different bands and providing backup vocals for the other. They both hadn't laughed that hard in a long time. Evie's favorite part of the game was when Beau sang *Who's Crying Now* by Journey. Beau managed to pull it off, and Evie was even more impressed with his vocal abilities. Beau's favorite part of the game was when he asked Evie to sing a song by Adele, which he thought would surprise and throw her off. To his very own surprise, she sang *Rolling In the Deep* effortlessly. He liked that Evie's voice was low for a woman just like Adele's.

They went to another class that Evie told Beau about called Strong. Evie noticed that Beau was getting more and more comfortable at each class she took him to, but she was worried about this particular class because it was a HIIT class with lots of jumping, direction changes, and especially burpees. "So, what exactly is Strong Nation?" Beau asked, "Is it another dance class?"

"Not at all. It is a high-intensity interval training class. I attended this class twice a week in Baltimore before moving here. I noticed I was losing some muscle tone, so I started coming to this class about a couple of weeks ago. It has worked miracles," Evie said.

Beau thought back to the past couple of weeks to see if there was a difference in Evie. He remembered one time when Levi tried climbing in Evie's lap listening to her scream in pain and another time when she bent over to pick something up, and she kept exclaiming, "Ow, ow, ow, ow." She claimed sore muscles. "So, will I be sore after this class as well?" Beau asked.

"That depends on you. You can take it at any level you want," Evie said.

"What do you do in the class?"

"It's martial arts-based with a ton of lunges, squats, burpees, bear crawls, planks, and many other strength training moves."

Beau felt a little more intimidated. Beau recognized Pam at the front in a racerback tank, leggings, cross-training shoes, and her hair was pulled entirely out of her face. She looked completely different compared to when she taught Zumba. Beau realized that even Evie was dressed completely different than her regular gym clothes. Evie's hair was pulled completely out of her face, and she wore more form-fitting breathable gym clothes. He also noticed Evie grabbing two yoga mats from the closet and setting them down by Beau's and her stuff.

Soon, Pam began class with a three-song warm-up. Beau found the warm-up to be a little challenging, but he noticed it made him more limber. Pam began using strange lingo that went completely over Beau's head. He knew he would have to ask Evie or Pam about some of the moves and lingo after class so he could describe what they did to the band when they asked why he was sore.

The first section, or Quadrant 1 as Pam and Evie called it, started off with some jacks and knee lifts. Then it shifted to a side lunge and core rotation. Beau felt like he was very uncoordinated for this class. Soon, everyone transitioned into squats, followed by three side kicks to the right. Even though Pam wore a wireless mic to lead the class, Beau's brain couldn't think that fast. He looked at Evie for some guidance like he usually did during a Zumba class. During the scissor lunges and punch, Beau noticed how intense, accurate, and quick Evie's punches were. He also noticed her side kicks. They were incredibly quick. He thought he saw a hint of rage behind every punch and kick. He could not help but feel terrified about what would cause such a happy woman to have such anger.

Soon, the song morphed into a push-up challenge where you would alternate between wide-arm push-ups, tricep push-ups, and then traveling in the plank position left and right. In between each sequence, they would rest in a pike position, which didn't make it any easier for Beau. Again, he looked over at Evie, and still, each push-up and travel was intense with anger. *What is causing this girl to be so angry*, he thought to himself. Soon, his arms began to hurt, but he did his best to push through the pain. He followed the beat precisely and started counting out loud with the class to help take his mind off the pain. It helped a little, but his arms shook uncontrollably. Soon, the push-up challenge was over, and everyone stood up. Beau shook his arms out to release the tension.

After the third song in the section, which consisted of a ton of deadlifts, squats, and lunges, Beau's legs felt like they were going to fall off. Beau wondered how Evie was able to keep up, had martial arts training, or even a certification in this class. "Are you certified in this class, too?" he asked. "Yes," Evie said after swallowing a massive gulp of water. *Of course you are*, Beau thought to himself, *how else did you get those arms and that ass?*

Soon, Quadrant 2 began where it was a bit more intense with a section in it called gorillas. Beau decided to stay on Level 1, which was just shuffling. He looked over at Evie and watched her glide on her hands and feet, and then he had a come-apart when he watched her turn around in that position, get back up, and do the interior kick. *Oh my Hell! What did she just do*, he thought to himself. He decided to try Level 2, the gorilla move without the turn. He was amazed at how fast his entire body began to burn. The dance sequence, which Evie called the Recharge, began. Beau and Evie ran to get some water. He noticed how much he was sweating as well as how much she was sweating. He shook out his muscles as he watched Evie take deep breaths.

It was Quadrant 3 next, which Evie nicknamed the Death Quadrant. Beau began to wonder what he got himself into as he began following Pam as they class began doing sumo squats and alternating punches. This quadrant had way more intense moves in it. Evie, knowing she needed the extra push, added the tuck before the burpee, and she heard Beau gasp when she did it. She laughed for a split second before refocusing. The second song in Quadrant 3 had a movement where Beau realized he was swinging a sledgehammer, which was kind of fun, until his obliques started to hurt. Beau watched Evie and wondered who's jaw she broke in her mind because as each uppercut and cross punch grew in intensity. Soon, everyone was down on the floor doing plank jacks, which almost did Beau in. He was so relieved when this quadrant was over. His entire body felt like jelly. "Totally normal," Evie said, sounding out of breath herself. She wiped her sweat off her forehead before grabbing her mat. Beau grabbed his mat and laid it out next to Evie's.

Quadrant 4 took place on the floor, which Beau was very grateful for until Pam led the class in hip dips in a forearm plank position. Beau didn't realize his shoulders were also tired until he was in place. He pushed through his weaknesses, managing to make it through the entire class in spite of his weak muscles. He eventually had to go to his knees because his arms and shoulders couldn't hold himself up anymore.

The cooldown felt very good on his muscles and joints. He was so proud that he finished his first Strong Nation class. He chugged the last little bit of his water while Evie rolled up her mat. Beau pulled his mat off to the side by his stuff and rolled it up.

He and Evie walked out of the cross-training room where they ran into the same guys they always ran into who would often hit on Evie. "Hey,

Beau!" one guy said. Beau smiled. "Hey, guys. How ya' doing?" Beau responded, trying to be polite. "We're good. Can we get a picture?" said another guy. Beau nodded. "Here, I will take it for you," Evie said. Soon, the guys began drooling over Evie as she took the picture just like last time. It bothered Beau a lot because he liked her, but he tried to ignore it.

After Evie took the picture, she handed the phone back to the guy and said, "I need to use the restroom. I'll see you guys later." As she waved goodbye, all the guys and Beau watched as she walked towards the women's locker room. "Who is she again?" another guy asked. "That is my tour manager. She actually introduced me to this gym," Beau said. That same guy nodded his head. "So, are you guys dating also, or is she available?" the man asked Beau. He had no idea how to respond because Beau didn't want any other guy sniffing around Evie. "We aren.... are dating," Beau responded. "Oh, well, in that case, she's hot, Beau! I'm glad you're getting back out there!" the guy said. Beau, still lying through his teeth, said, "Thanks. We've been dating for a month now, and it's been going great. She's amazing." Beau knew that last little bit wasn't a lie. "Well, congrats. Good luck with everything!" the guy said before walking off with his friends. "Thank you. See you guys later!" Beau said. "Bye, man!" the guys all said before walking over to some other machines.

Beau could not believe he just lied to a group of guys just so he could keep Evie all to himself. However, when he saw her walking back towards him, he felt a sense of relief. "Want to go get tacos?" Beau asked after Evie got back from the bathroom. Her face lit up with excitement. "Sure, but I am paying for myself this time," Evie said. "You really are stubborn," he said. "It's my best and most annoying quality, I think," she said, laughing. Beau laughed, too.

Little did Beau know that Evie ran off to the bathroom with Jude's words screaming in her head, *Guys won't love you like I did because you gave birth to two kids. Your body is wrecked, and they will only see you as a mom.* She sat on a bench by the lockers and cried for a minute. *How can I be so happy and sad at the same time*, she thought to herself. Evie was truly happy to be at the gym with one of her favorite people in the world, but sad because she couldn't silence that voice inside her head telling her, *Those guys didn't even see you. Jude was the only one who saw who you used to be. Beau doesn't see it either, and he will never see it.*

Evie wiped the tears from her eyes, walked over to the sinks, and rinsed off her face trying to hide the puffiness. She looked at herself in the mirror. *Anxiety is a tricky thing*, she thought to herself. When she walked out of the bathroom and saw Beau standing there without the other guys, she felt calm. He had no idea how much she needed him. Then when he made the suggestion to go get tacos, Evie instantly cheered up. *The man gets me*, she joked in her head.

They walked outside of the gym to the parking lot and climbed into her car. Evie drove to El Burrito Taqueria and ordered food for her and Beau. Beau tried to get his money out, but Evie paid for both of them, and Beau scowled as she did it. She simply smiled as she grabbed the drink cups and sat down at a table.

As Beau went to grab salsa and guacamole, Evie's phone rang. She looked at her phone and saw Jude's name. She gulped, hoping this was finally the phone call that he was ready to come visit his kids, and answered. "Hey, Jude. What's up?" she asked, sounding as calm as she could. "I was thinking of taking Levi to go tour the White House when you come to Annapolis for Thanksgiving. Is that all right with you?" Jude said.

Not exactly what I was thinking, but hey, I'll take it, she thought to herself. "Yeah, that's fine. I think he would love that," Evie said, trying not to sound too excited.

"Awesome. I will make plans. How long will you be in Maryland for Thanksgiving?"

"Three days," she said.

"Okay. Will Friday work?"

"That's fine."

"So, what are you doing now?" Evie knew that Beau was a touchy subject for Jude, but she didn't want to lie. "I went to the gym with Beau, and we are just eating dinner real quick before picking the kids up at the Jeppsen's." Evie could hear the steam leaving Jude's nose, but he wasn't letting his anger get the best of him. "I would love to see that rocker at a Zumba class. Has anyone posted anything about it?" he asked. "Not that I am aware of." "Well, let's see," Jude said as Evie heard his various clicking.

Once Jude stopped clicking, Evie could hear some music playing in the background on Jude's phone. She recognized the music and soon realized that the song was *Tumbao*. Evie smiled, remembering how she felt after the class was over. After two minutes of the music, Jude's fumes resumed again. "Why are you dancing with him like that?!" he scolded. "Because it's Zumba. I dance like that with all my friends. You knew that."

"But he's a guy and plays guitar for the biggest metal band in the world. There's a hidden agenda there."

"I thought you said I would never be attractive again because of the whole mom thing."

"Don't change the subject. You need to start acting more like a mom."

"I thought you wanted me to be more sexy, which I'm still confused about because I dance like this all the time."

"Well, you never acted like that for me at home!"

Beau looked back at Evie and saw her on the verge of tears talking on her phone. He quickly rushed back and asked, "What's wrong?" Evie held back tears, but she couldn't answer the question. Beau knew it was Jude on the phone. Beau quickly took her phone out of her hands and held it up to his ear. Evie sat there, stunned and frozen, wondering what had just happened. "Jude Long?" Beau asked. Jude paused. "Beau Halstead?" Jude asked. "Yes, that's me. Stop harassing my manager and friend. She is putting up with a lot from you lately, and it's affecting her work."

Jude paused. "Why are you even with my ex-wife? Isn't there some other girl you could be with? Like those girls who hosed you down in the showers? You know, Evie could have been..."

"Are you seriously comparing your ex-wife to one of those shower girls? Do you even know her?" Beau interrupted, cutting Jude right off.

Jude paused again. "Um, yes, but…." Jude felt cornered.

"Okay, prick," Beau began, "I am going to say this loud and clear one time. If I see Evie's demeanor affected by you in any way, I will personally fly to Baltimore and kick your ass!" Beau heard Evie's phone beep, and he knew Jude hung upon him.

"He probably won't be bothering you for a while," Beau said, handing Evie her phone. When she grabbed it, she immediately threw her keys on the table and stormed out of the restaurant. Beau ran after her after he grabbed the keys.

"Evie!" he called, but she kept walking. "Evie! Stop! Please tell me what I did wrong," Beau shouted.

Evie stopped and turned around. "I don't need you to fight my battles for me," she said.

"I promise, that's not what I was doing. I was trying to get him to leave you alone."

"Please stay out of this! I can take care of myself."

"Really? I see you fight back the tears whenever he calls you. I saw your anger at him today in class. It's okay to ask for help, sometimes."

"You may have made things worse!" Evie scolded.

"What do you mean, 'made things worse?' Is he abusing you? Do I need to help you find a lawyer?" Beau immediately went into "fix-it" mode.

"I'm just feeling so overwhelmed right now with the first leg of the tour coming up in six months, all the venues that I still need to call, Levi's flag football game, finding a dance studio that takes two-year-olds...."

Beau could see how anxious this whole thing made her, so he decided to hug her. "Hey," he said as calmly as he could, trying to calm Evie down, "I'm sorry. I just hate what he does to you. It's like your entire demeanor changes when he calls, and I know he calls a lot. It takes some sort of a distraction to get that smile on your face again." Evie, shocked by the gesture, calmed down as she listened to Beau's soothing heartbeat as he rubbed her shoulders. They soon went back inside and sat back down at their table. Beau grabbed their food and brought it back to their table.

"Why do you let him talk to you like that anyways?" Beau asked as he sat down.

"Because I'm scared that he is right," Evie replied, unwilling to tell him she believed Jude.

"About what?"

"That no man will…" Evie couldn't bring herself to say the words. Unable to admit the truth, she continued, "that I am unable to raise my children in a stable environment because of the band."

"Do you think working for us is an unstable environment? It's not like we offer your children drugs and alcohol. We all have or have had children in the past."

"That's what I told him, but then he has a problem with you." Beau paused.

"What's his problem with me?"

"He hates that you're always around the kids and me when he thinks he should be the male figure around."

Beau processed Evie's statement. *Why would he have a problem with me*, he contemplated deeply.

Then he turned to Evie and watched her eat one of her tacos. She devoured it in three big bites, which Beau found really impressive and hot. Suddenly, Jude's insecurities about Beau made sense. Jude still had feelings for Evie in some twisted way. He didn't regret divorcing her, but he wasn't ready to let her go. Beau began piecing together the type of man Jude was.

"Well, why doesn't he come out here to visit? I'm not going to stand in the way of a father wanting to see his kids," Beau said.

"I've told him that, too. Jude's always been more bark, less bite. But he can be downright rude," Evie responded while inhaling another taco.

"I think Jude regrets divorcing you because he is missing out on this great adventure in the kids' lives as well as yours. I also believe he is trying to exercise some sort of control over you with his abuse."

"Why?"

"Because you're probably his cushion in case his plans backfire, whatever they are." Evie masticated Beau's words and her taco for a minute. She hadn't thought about that before.

Once they were finished with their meals, Beau and Evie drove back to the Jeppsens' to pick up Levi and Harper. "They've had dinner, so they should be ready to go to bed when you get home," Jetta said. "Thank you so much. Sometimes, it's a lot easier going to the gym childless," Evie said. "I understand. Anytime you need a day or night out, I can watch the kids. We have beds for them," Jetta said. "Thanks," Evie said, smiling at Jetta. Beau let Evie talk for a minute as he helped load the kids in her car. He soon climbed back in as well.

After hugging her friend, Evie walked back to the car, climbed in, and drove towards Novato to drop Beau off. "See you tomorrow!" Beau said, climbing out of the car. "Bye, Beau. Thank you," Evie said, referring to Beau's confrontation with Jude. "You're welcome," Beau said. "All right, can everyone say, 'Bye, Beau!'" "Bye, Beau!" the kids said, waving to Beau as he waved back at the little family.

At this point in his recovery, Beau hated and loved going home. He loved being home because it was his house with all of his restored cars and bikes he worked so hard on, he loved his comfortable bed, his TV, his kitchen where he loved to cook and bake, and how quiet it was. On the contrary, he hated it because the memories of his family still haunted him. He worked daily to try and remember all the good times and memories, but he hated that he had to move his comfortable bed into the mother-in-law suite to avoid memories of Phoebe and the wing he and his family used to live in. These memories caused a lot of sadness and anger Beau had all the time but amplified, and those emotions back in the day caused him to drive to a bar. But this time instead of driving to a bar, Beau pulled out his phone. There was only one person who could fix the urge.

"Hey! What's up?" Evie asked, "Is everything okay?"

"Yeah, I'm doing fine. I'm just... struggling," Beau stammered.

"Okay, what can I do to help you?"

"Just stay on the phone with me until the urge I'm having goes away."

"Okay. I'm warning you now, I need to bathe the kids and put them to bed, so things will get loud."

"I'm in a heavy metal band. Nothing is louder than that."

"Harper's screaming when Levi takes a toy away from her?"

Beau suddenly remembered a couple of times at the studio when that happened. "Fair point. She screams like a banshee. Although, Chloe was the queen of banshee screaming when she was two." The twinge in Beau's heart grew, and the pain got worse.

The statement surprised Evie. "I don't think I've ever heard you mention her up 'till now."

"I really don't like to talk much about her or Cordell. It causes me to have this urge and call the Death Toll Stabilizer."

"I'm assuming that's me?"

"You assumed correctly."

Evie lightly chuckled. "Well, you don't have to talk about them if you don't want to. Whenever you are ready is fine. Are you sure listening to my kids is a good idea?"

"Well, you guys help me focus on what's going on in my life now rather than reflecting on the trauma." Evie understood that.

Beau and Evie talked through the whole bath process as Evie got her kids ready for bed, sang the lullabye, and tucked them in bed. Finally, both of them were sitting in front of their own TV's, watching the same movie on Netflix. Beau let Evie pick, and she picked the movie, *Made of Honor*. Beau ate popcorn, cheese, and beef jerky while Evie ate popcorn as well, a chocolate protein shake, and some blueberries.

"Why do you like this movie again?" Beau asked with a mouth full of popcorn.

"Because it's a good story," Evie replied before taking a drink of her shake.

"It's so cliche, though. She was right there in front of him the entire time," Beau ranted.

"Sometimes the best things in our lives are right there with us, and we never take the time to notice. She even fell into the trap as well, see?" Evie pointed out. The main actress realized that her fiance shot and killed the animals they were eating at the rehearsal dinner. The look of disdain on the actress' face caught Beau's attention, and he thought about what Evie said. It made him think about all the people he was grateful for in his life at this moment; Luke, Kade, Rick, and even Evie and the kids.

"So, do you think she remembered what a nice guy her best friend was?" Beau asked.

"Just watch the movie," Evie bantered, eating popcorn.

Beau and Evie continued to watch the movie, and Beau realized that all of his urges and anxieties were gone. He hadn't felt relief like this in a while. Evie truly was the best medicine for him. Beau felt understood, which was huge for him. He wanted to make sure he took advantage of that every day.

Chapter 8

Music Lessons for Beau and Evie

Evie carried her violin and tenor saxophone into the equipment room, hoping it had the right conditions to store her instruments. San Rafael was way more humid than Annapolis this time of year, so she wanted to see what the room was like for all the guitars. As Evie walked into the equipment room, never had she seen so many guitars, bass guitars, amplifiers, and a bunch of other equipment. All of the guitars she had seen throughout the years sat on their racks or hung on the walls. Then she saw Beau's signature guitar, a white ESP EXplorer. She remembered seeing this guitar in college at a concert as well as in other videos. She believed it was one of his favorite guitars. Then she saw his collection of Flying V's. She knew the black one was his favorite. She wanted to pick one up to play, but she didn't want to get her fingerprints all over the guitar.

Beau walked into the equipment room and saw Evie staring at the Flying V's. He paused, watched her set an instrument case down on the ground, and reached out for his white Flying V. She hesitated to touch it, which made him smile. Then he saw that she had a violin case in her other hand. He smiled. "Do you know how to play guitar?" he asked. Evie jumped. "Only a little bit. I never had formal education on it. When I started teaching at the high school, they gave me a couple of guitar classes to fill my schedule, so that's how I learned. I've forgotten a lot, but I am sure if I looked at a book, I would remember," she said. Beau smiled, walked over to his chrome EXplorer, and picked it up. He grabbed two stools and motioned for Evie to sit down. She sat down on the stool, and Beau told her, "Pick up one of the V's." Evie hesitated again. "I don't want to get my skin oils all over your guitar," she said. "I have a guy who cleans them. It's okay," Beau said. Evie picked up the white V.

"All right, what do you know about playing guitar?" he asked her. "I know how to play the D Major scale," Evie said as she proceeded to play the scale two octaves up and down on the V. Beau was impressed. "Cool. Do you remember any chords?" he asked her. "It's been a few months. I don't," she said. "That's okay. What do you know about our music?" "I know you play a lot in E minor." "You really are a fangirl at heart, aren't you?" Beau joked. Evie scowled playfully. "Punk," she replied, drawing a blank on a witty comeback. "Lesson, please?" Evie was determined to just breeze over that. "Fine. So the E minor chord is open 1st, 4th, 5th, and 6th strings. The 2nd and 3rd strings have the 1st and 2nd fingers on the 2nd fret." Evie positioned her fingers into the E minor chord and strummed a couple of times. Pretty soon, she started playing the E natural minor, harmonic minor, and melodic minor scales.

Beau was amazed at the level and knowledge of musicality, technicality, and theory she possessed. He continued to go over some other chords with her, and once she figured out what note each string was, she played a scale. Beau decided to teach her the chord progression to *The Call of Ktulu* since he knew it was Evie's favorite instrumental song Death Toll wrote and played.

Once she figured it out, Evie began soloing much in Kade's style, and Beau accompanied her on his guitar. Noticing her left hand's form needed to be corrected, Beau set his guitar down, moved his stool behind Evie, and began manipulating the hand. Evie felt some butterflies in her stomach as Beau touched her hand. She could feel him breathing down her neck, which made it hard to focus. Beau rubbed her hand a little bit after he moved it, and he took a quick inhale of her hair. *Roses*, he thought. Without thinking, Beau wrapped his right arm around Evie's waist, and the tension between them grew as Beau's breathing grew heavier and Evie's heart rate grew faster. They felt the pull as they gazed into each other's eyes.

Evie finally asked, "Do I need to file a complaint against you with HR?" Beau stared back very confused, instantly letting go. "What?" he asked, feeling shocked. "Usually a teacher needs to ask for permission to touch a student before adjusting posture, form, technique, and embouchure," Evie said, trying so hard not to laugh. Beau stared back at Evie, not knowing what to say. He really had no explanation for what he just did. "Um... I..." Nothing would make sense. Finally, Evie burst into laughter. Beau pursed his lips, not sure what to do. "Sorry...?" "I'm just kidding. It's all good," she said, still chuckling a bit. Soon, Beau saw the humor in the situation. "That's funny," he finally said.

Beau moved the stool back to where it was, picking up his guitar and starting to play the chord progression to *The Call of Ktulu*. Evie began playing along again, and Beau watched her intently, trying to hold on to that tension he felt for her. *There's still something missing in her playing*, Beau thought. He became curious about her education in music. "I know you're a musician, but what are all the instruments you play, again?" Beau asked.

"Well, I play the violin, clarinet, and saxophone. That's what the big case is," Evie said, pointing to her tenor sax.

"Violin? Is that why everything is so technical?"

"What do you mean?"

"I just noticed you are a very technical musician. There wasn't much emotion."

Evie looked at Beau in disbelief. "I just started learning the song today. How can I play with emotion when I have yet to refine my skills on this song?"

"True, but you figured out everything super fast. I just thought you would add emotion rather than continue to work on your technique."

"I am a violinist. That's my job to have perfect technique. We need to have that technique before we add emotion to our playing."

"If you say so," Beau said, "I was always taught to know and understand the emotion you play."

"Classical music is a bit more complex."

"Prove it," Beau challenged.

Evie pulled out her violin, tuned it, and started playing an excerpt from Tchaikovsky's Violin Concerto in D Major. Never before had Beau seen a violinist play with so much emotion. The violin was like a detachable appendage to Evie's body. Beau watched and listened to every single intricate part of the first movement as well as her facial expressions, which kept changing depending on the riff, or run, as Beau remembered that's what long passages were in symphonic music. Evie's body swayed with each note on the violin. It was almost like watching her dance with her violin like that YouTube star. Beau couldn't remember her name. There was passion in her musicianship, too. *What wasn't she passionate about,* Beau thought to himself.

The joy on Evie's face exceeded the joy in a Zumba class. Beau was completely mesmerized and smitten with this girl as he continued to watch and listen. Once Evie finished her excerpt, Beau felt like he had to pick his jaw back up off the floor. "Well..." he began but couldn't find the words to describe what he saw and heard. "I learned and performed that concerto for my senior recital with the university's premier orchestra. I practiced 10 hours a week during college to keep up on my scholarships even when I followed you guys around. If you're not technical first, the violin will kick your ass," Evie concluded, realizing that Beau's cursing was rubbing off on her.

Beau's brain finally started working again. "Teach me the violin," he said. Evie looked at him in disbelief. "What?" "I want to learn the violin. And just maybe...." Beau brainstormed ideas in his head. "Maybe we could have you amped on your violin and play with us," he said. "What?" Evie asked again. "I need to get back to the recording room with Luke," Beau said before standing up and walking out of the equipment room. Evie had no idea what he was thinking. She remembered a few other songs from her senior recital, including an arrangement of *Stairway to Heaven* she arranged herself and the orchestra.

As she played and sang along, Evie didn't realize how much she missed her violin. She continued through her arrangement. Beau walked back into the equipment room to grab Evie, but he was stopped by her beautiful rendition of *Stairway to Heaven*. He leaned against the wall and listened. Finally, Beau had a crazy idea to plug in his EXplorer and play during the power section with her. When he started the guitar solo, Evie turned around, surprised by the familiar sound of Beau Halstead's signature guitar sound. They smiled at each other, and she continued her arrangement. Beau soon began accompanying her as she played and sang. They fed off of each other's emotions during the song. Beau would occasionally adjust his volume so he could hear the violin. At the end of the song, they both sang, "And she's buying her stairway to heaven," in unison. Adrenaline rushed through their veins, and hearts were pumping as silence filled the equipment room with the echo of guitar and violin. "We have got to do that again," Beau said when all was quiet. "Agreed." Evie smiled.

"So, would you teach me the basics for violin?" Beau asked. "Sure," Evie said, walking over to Beau. He sat back down on his stool. Evie turned her violin so that the fingerboard was facing Beau.

"So you know how there's an order of strings on the guitar?" Evie asked.

Beau nodded.

"Okay, well, the order of strings on a violin is different. Instead of starting on E, the lowest string and note on a violin is a G. The next string up is D followed by A and E," Evie taught.

"So instead of moving up in 4ths, it moves up in 5ths?" Beau asked.

"That is correct, but remember, on the guitar, we have one third from G to B," Evie said.

"Yep, got it. How do you tune a violin?" he asked, getting ready to move the pegs.

Evie quickly stopped him. "There are fine tuners that the strings are hooked into," Evie said, pointing to them, "If you move the pegs, the strings unravel."

Beau observed and began adjusting the fine tuners while plucking a string. "Okay, so just like a guitar," he said.

Evie smiled. "I figured you would pick up on that part pretty easily. The hardest basic part of the violin is arco," Evie said.

"What's arco?" he asked.

Evie handed Beau her violin bow. "Try playing with this," she said.

Beau positioned the violin under his chin and began trying to play each string, but the violin sounded like a dying cat.

Evie winced at the sound covering her ears. Beau stopped playing. "Is there some sort of a secret?" he asked, feeling embarrassed by his tone.

"The key to playing with the bow, or arco, is to move only at the elbow and not your shoulder. When you move your shoulder, you create that dying cat sound you produced on my violin," she said. Beau observed as Evie held her violin and played with the bow. He noticed her arm, wrist, and elbow would move, but the shoulder was stationary. Evie handed her violin and bow to Beau and walked behind him.

"May I?" she asked, holding up her hand over his right shoulder. Beau chuckled. "Yes," he said. Evie placed her hand on Beau's shoulder. "Okay, move your arm and bend your elbow, but focus on keeping your shoulder steady," she said. As Beau placed the bow on the E string, he could feel his shoulder staying in one spot, but the wrist did all the work as his arm moved up and down. The electricity came back, but for some reason, the atmosphere was more tender. The E string rang beautifully as Beau held his shoulder steady, adding some vibrato, which impressed Evie. Beau turned to look at Evie, inches from her face. "How's that?" he asked. Evie smiled, biting her bottom lip a bit. "Perfect," she said. As she felt her heart rate leap out of her chest again, she walked away from Beau, trying to regain some composure.

"So, do half steps and whole steps work the same on a violin as they do on a guitar?" he asked, trying to regather his faculties as well.

"Yep, but we don't have frets. Although, when I first started out, my teacher marked where the first four fingers were supposed to go on the fingerboard," she said.

"Cool. I think I can figure the rest out. So what's it called when you don't use the bow?" he asked.

"That is called pizzicato," Evie said as she grabbed her violin again, "You play each string with the thick, beefy part of your right index finger." Evie proceeded to play an excerpt from *Pizzicato Polka.*

Beau thoroughly enjoyed it. "That was cute," he said. "Pizzicato sounds cute, sometimes," Evie said, "It is also the first technique we learn in Orchestra." Beau absorbed all of the information Evie taught him. Evie knew it wouldn't be long before he would be dazzling audiences everywhere with his new skill.

Evie and Beau enjoyed learning from each other. Evie suddenly had a fantastic idea. "Have you thought about going to some of the schools around here to be a guest teacher in guitar classes? It would probably soften your image," Evie said. Beau thought about that idea. "I haven't, actually," he said. "I know it would appeal to teachers as well as students. Parents might even enjoy the thought of Beau Halstead teaching their kids guitar considering how talented you are, especially with the middle school across the street," Evie said. "If you make the arrangements, I will do it," he said. "Awesome! I will call around and see what I can do," she said. Just as Evie was walking out of the room, Beau asked, "Have you thought about becoming a guest artist for the San Francisco Symphony or any of the other orchestras around here?" Evie stopped, turned around, and looked at Beau. "Since when do I have time to do that?" she asked. "I don't know. You clearly love playing your violin. You are by far the most talented violinist I have ever seen, and that talent should be shared with the world, or at least the Bay area," Beau said. "It's not that simple," Evie said. "I do have a little pull with the Symphony. We played with them a few years ago," he said. Evie hesitated for a minute. "I don't know. I don't think I have time right now." "Okay, well, when you are ready, let me know," Beau said. He excused himself for a minute to go communicate with the band and use the bathroom.

Evie began playing the concerto again, trying to remember the arduous technique. She had to admit, playing Percival, the name she gave her violin, was by far the happiest she had felt in a long time. Evie used to practice every day for a half-hour while she was teaching, but since moving to San Francisco, Evie hadn't picked up the violin or even her saxophone. She quickly put Percival away and pulled out Dean, her tenor saxophone. Evie prepped the reed and put it on the mouthpiece. It took her a minute to produce a beautiful tone, but she adjusted quickly. Evie started playing a few licks she knew from Jazz standards. She soon began noodling some more and soloing. Jazz always brought joy into Evie's life. She decided to watch an old movie that night with some fun Jazz music.

As Beau walked back to the equipment room, he heard a different sound. He felt puzzled but followed the music back to the equipment room, where he found Evie playing her saxophone. Beau leaned against the wall and watched as she played all sorts of riffs, or runs. He wasn't sure what they were called on saxophones. Not only did her fingers move fast on the violin, but they were quick on the horn. He smiled and enjoyed every second of the music she produced. He decided to talk to Kade about letting Evie come jam with them the next time they start playing different Jazz chord progressions. Beau even thought about learning Rhythm changes for once. All of these thoughts popped into his head as he stood and watched Evie play her sax.

After about five minutes of playing, Evie stopped. She turned around and realized Beau was watching her, which made her jump again. Putting her hand over her heart as her sax dangled across her body, she asked, "How long have you been leaning there?" Beau shrugged. " I don't know. Not long. You seriously are a talented musician," he said. "Thanks. I appreciate the compliment," she said. She unhooked the sax and began putting it back in the case. "So, do you have any plans tonight?" Beau asked. "Just cooking dinner for my kids, Zumba, and going home, watching an older movie," Evie said. "May I...." "You are more than welcome to come with me anytime. Levi and Harper love having you around," Evie said.

"Well, what about you?" Beau asked.

Evie looked at Beau, trying not to give away her feelings. "I like it when you're around, too. You help me feel like I am not such a huge loser," she said.

"Why would you or I or anyone think that?" Beau asked.

"I feel so overwhelmed at times with work and juggling the kids," Evie said, choosing her words wisely.

"It's okay to be overwhelmed. They are great kids. Levi is progressing in his reading and behavior, and Harper knows her numbers and colors. You are doing better than you think. I remember when Chloe was learning how to read. It was awesome to watch. Cordell used to run through the house, counting backwards and forwards. He would even sing some of our songs. I absolutely loved watching them learn and grow. Those little things reminded me that maybe I was an okay dad," Beau said, feeling a little twinge of pain in his heart as he thought about his kids. It was still hard for him, but talking with Evie made it easier.

"Thanks," Evie said, smiling, "but I disagree with you." Beau looked puzzled. "On what?" he asked, feeling a little defensive. "From my observation with my kids, you were an amazing father," Evie said. Beau smiled, realizing he needed to hear that. "Thanks. That means a lot to me."

Chapter 9

Beau Bonds With the Kids

Evie, Harper, and Levi were at the Gerstle Park for the late afternoon. They had about an hour and a half before Evie really had to go grocery shopping. Levi held a football occasionally throwing it in the air, and Harper was busy crushing leaves underneath her boots. She giggled every time the leaves made crunching noises. "Can we play catch now, Mom?" Levi asked. "Sure, why not?" Evie said. She stood up off the bench to walk toward Levi. Harper saw her mom walking towards the field, so she followed her mom.

"Okay, Levi. Do you see the lace on the football?" Evie asked.

Levi nodded.

"Okay, put this finger," Evie said, wiggling her right middle finger, "in the first lace." Evie demonstrated for Levi as he watched intently.

Levi followed the steps exactly. "Good job. Now, when you throw, let the ball roll off your fingers," she said. "Can you show me?" Levi asked. He handed the football back to his mom, and she did her best to show him how the ball was supposed to roll off the fingers. Even though the ball didn't go precisely straight, it still spiraled in the air. She wished Jude was there at that point because he was really good at throwing a football.

Suddenly, she heard a deep voice call Levi's name. She turned around and saw Beau running towards them. She smiled instantly and looked at her watch. *They must have ended early*, she thought to herself noticing the time was 3:50. "Hey, guys! May I join you?" he asked. "Yes. Mom is showing me how to throw a football," Levi said. "Your mom can throw a football?" Beau asked, looking over at Evie. "She was a huge tomboy growing up. Grandpa took her hunting, camping, fishing, and she played all sorts of sports including flag football, but kickball was her specialty," Levi said.

A woman of many talents, Beau thought to himself. Evie blushed a little and said, "I'm not very good at throwing a football, and I'm not a fan of camping anymore." "Whatever , Mom. You still outfish Grandpa when we go visit," Levi said. He truly believed his mother was the coolest and most perfect mom ever.

"Cool. So, Levi, go down the field a little bit and throw the football," Beau said. Levi did what he was told and threw the football. It didn't spin as well as he had hoped. The ball also went left instead of straight at Beau, but Beau ran and caught the ball. Levi slumped down on the ground, pouting and crying. Evie face-palmed losing her patience with her son. He had been acting out all day.

Beau walked over to Levi carrying the football. He sat down on the ground next to Levi. "What's wrong, Buddy?" Beau asked. "All of my other friends have a dad who can teach them this stuff, but I don't have a dad," Levi sobbed.

Beau put his arm around Levi to hug him. "Guess what, Buddy?" Beau asked.

"What?"

"My parents divorced when I was 14 years old. I didn't really have a dad either because he traveled so much for work. My mom died when I was 17 of cancer, so I had to go live with my older brother. He was the one who taught me all this stuff, and I can teach you if you let me. I even played football in high school until my coach gave me an ultimatum to either cut my hair or quit football," Beau said.

Levi wiped his eyes. "You didn't have a dad, either?" Levi asked.

"Not really, no," Beau said, "but I had an amazing mom just like you do."

"She is pretty awesome," Levi said.

Beau turned around to see Evie with tears in her eyes. "Yes, she is, Buddy."

"You played football?" Levi asked.

"Yes, I did. I was pretty good, too; A wide receiver. I could catch footballs all day long," Beau said.

Levi wiped his eyes. "Could you teach me how to catch as well?" Levi asked, wiping the rest of the tears away from his eyes.

Beau smiled. "Of course."

With that, Beau stood up, grabbed Levi's arms, and pulled him up to standing. Beau proceeded to show Levi different techniques of throwing and catching a football that Evie didn't know about. When Beau kneeled down, Levi wrapped his little arms around Beau's neck.

Evie continued to observe Beau and Levi as Beau wrapped his arms around Levi. Levi's smaller arms squeezed Beau's neck as they hugged it out. She then saw Beau explain a little trick to Levi about how to get the ball to spin faster than before. After the lesson, Evie thought about asking Beau to teach her the method.

"All right, Buddy, go long!" Beau said. Levi ran a few yards away from Beau before stopping. Beau threw the football directly at Levi. Levi tried catching the ball, but the gap between his arms was too big. "Good try, Levi. How about bringing your arms closer like this?" Beau asked, demonstrating with his arms as Levi observed. Levi quickly practiced. "Good, now try throwing the ball to me exactly how I showed you, and then when I throw it back, catch it like that," Beau said. Levi nodded his head before picking the ball back up. "Okay, Levi. Throw it!" Beau shouted with encouragement.

Levi remembered the technique Beau showed him and threw the ball directly at him. The ball spiraled a lot better and straighter than it had before Beau showed him the method. Beau caught the ball. "That was awesome, Buddy! Okay, I'm going to throw it at you, now. Remember to keep your arms closer together and bring the football into your chest," Beau said, demonstrating. Levi nodded.

Beau threw the ball at Levi, and Levi caught it. "Yes!" Levi shouted and began jumping up and down with excitement. Beau immediately ran to Levi, picked him up by the waist, and swung him around. Evie was thrilled to witness that moment. She eventually took videos of Beau and Levi throwing the football back and forth before playing with Harper on the playground, the slide, and the swings.

Beau's heart began to hurt a little bit, realizing he wouldn't have this moment with Cordell. One of Beau's memories began playing in his head of his son. Beau had been out of rehab the first time for about two years, and he was jamming with the band as Cordell sat in his dad's lap as Beau held his guitar. Every now and then, Cordell would smack the guitar, and everyone would laugh. Soon, Phoebe walked in with Chloe. They had just gotten back from Chloe's ballet class. Beau suddenly felt this darkness cloud his mind, and the itch for his drink of choice started coming back.

Snap out of it, Beau quickly thought to himself. He looked around him and saw Harper walking around and Evie sitting on the grass. Harper wore a cute mint oversize sweater with dark jeggings, and Evie wore an oversized leopard print sweater, black jeans with holes in the knees, and black booties. Evie's hair was curly today. Harper picked up a feather and brought it to Evie, who proceeded to blow on it. Harper squealed for joy before blowing on the feather herself, taking turns with her mom.

As Evie smiled at her daughter, the sunlight hit her hair just right. Beau's urges changed, filling his chest with warmth. *She really is beautiful inside and out*, Beau thought to himself, staring at Evie. Suddenly, Beau heard Levi shout, "I'm gonna get you, Beau!" Beau smirked. "Not if I get you first," Beau responded before chasing Levi. Levi screamed and bolted the other direction, but Beau caught up to him and pulled him down. The boys began laughing as Beau gave Levi a noogie. *You know what*, Beau thought to himself, *today is a good day*.

After about an hour, Evie looked at her smartwatch. "Time to go! We have stuff to do tonight!" Evie said in Levi's direction. Beau, holding the football, walked with Levi to where Evie and Harper were. "What kind of stuff?" Beau asked, walking with the family back to Evie's car. "I have to make some more phone calls to secure the Central and South American portion of the world tour, go grocery shopping, cook dinner, clean my apartment, the list is just never-ending," Evie said. "Mommy, what 'bout our tea party?" Harper asked, sounding sad. "I'm sorry, Baby, but we don't have time today. We can try tomorrow," Evie said with a melancholy tone.

This was the second time Evie had to say no to the tea party. Beau could see that Harper was getting tears in her eyes. Evie watched Beau pick up her little girl. "Maybe you should ask your mom if I can come with you guys, help your mom shop, and I can have a tea party with you while your mom cooks dinner and works," Beau suggested. Harper and Levi looked up at their mom with such excitement and awe, and Beau looked at Evie.

All Evie could do was smile, but there was still sadness in saying yes. She wasn't ready to admit she couldn't do everything by herself, yet, but she knew her kids would be even sadder if she said no. "Yes, Beau may come with us," Evie said caving. "Yay!" both kids shouted. Beau smiled. Evie glanced at Beau with a dejected look in her eyes. "I knew you wouldn't say no if the kids asked you," Beau said, chuckling. Evie smiled and shook her head in disbelief. Beau helped put Harper in the car seat while Evie proceeded to help Levi buckle up.

The four of them drove to Sprouts, where Evie did the majority of her grocery shopping. She tried to buy organic and non-filler foods for herself and her children. Beau noticed some of the items Evie bought including lactose-free milk, kale, the bread, pasta, the different broths, and a bunch of other stuff. Once they were done, they drove across the Golden Gate Bridge to Costco where she bought the typical bulk items. Beau did his best to entertain Levi while Evie picked out the items and Harper rode in the cart basket. Beau helped Evie load the groceries into the car before driving back to Evie's townhouse.

They unloaded the groceries before Evie started prepping dinner. "What's on the menu?" Beau asked. "Meatloaf cakes, scalloped potatoes, and a salad for those who want one," Evie replied. Beau salivated, thinking about the last time he had a good meatloaf. "Beau! We need to have tea party!" Harper cried, tugging on Beau's hand. "All right, Princess, let's go," Beau said laughing. Levi plopped on the sectional and turned on the TV as Evie began making dinner.

After she set the oven timer for 35 minutes, Evie began making the phone calls she needed to make to the Latin American countries. Once she was off the phone, she noticed it was very quiet in her house besides the occasional noise from the TV. She checked her living room and saw Levi watching *Batman. Where are Beau and Harper*, she thought to herself. Evie quickly gave her son a kiss on the cheek before going up the stairs and down the hallway to Harper's room.

The door was closed, and she could hear Harper talking mostly with occasional agreeance from Beau who was speaking with a distorted high-pitched voice. Evie lightly knocked on the door before opening it. Inside, she saw Harper wearing an assortment of costume jewelry Evie got her daughter for her 2nd birthday, and Beau wearing one of Evie's floppy hats she gave to Harper, a pink boa that usually hung on Harper's wall, and fuschia nail polish on his fingernails. Neither Beau or Harper heard Evie open the door because they continued to clink teacups and sip.

Evie quietly pulled her phone out of her back pocket and snapped a picture. Beau froze and looked towards the door after he heard the phone. Evie held back her laugh, but it was the hardest thing she had done so far. Beau stuck out his pinky and drank out of the cup before setting it down and standing up. Evie cracked up, took another picture of Beau and the pinky, and slipped out of the doorway and into the kitchen. "Will you excuse me, Harper? I need to go defend my honor," Beau said politely and calmly. Harper nodded her head before turning to one of her dolls.

Beau took off the hat and boa before walking out of Harper's room. He heard the commotion coming from the kitchen. Evie hid her phone in one of the secret cabinets so that Beau wouldn't find it. She then turned around just as Beau entered the kitchen.

"I believe you have something that I need," he said calmly.

"Sorry, I will never delete that picture," Evie said.

"Well, then. It looks like I need to fight for my honor," he teased.

"Good luck finding my phone."

"I have my ways," Beau responded. He proceeded to look through the kitchen but had no luck.

"All right, Missy. I guess I will need to interrogate you."

"How?" Evie teased.

"I believe you are ticklish. Am I right?"

"Good luck catching me," Evie taunted.

Beau proceeded to come towards Evie, but she quickly pushed him away.

"Remember, one of my classes is martial arts based."

"So is one of mine," Beau responded, trying to be witty.

Beau still grimaced hoping Evie wouldn't punch him in the face as he cornered her against the fridge tickling her ribs. Evie tickled him back before her back hit the refrigerator.

They looked at each other for what seemed like a long time before Beau rubbed Evie's left cheek with his right hand. Beau really wanted to kiss her, and Evie was taken aback by the gesture. However, if Beau kissed her, she would not try to stop him. He leaned in closer to where their noses brushed against each other, but the oven alarm went off breaking the trance.

Beau swore under his breath as Evie walked past him to the oven to turn it off and pull out the meatloaf. She went back to the fridge and pulled out some scalloped potatoes she had bought at Costco. Beau just watched Evie as she continued to put the potatoes in the microwave as well as prep the salad looking for some sort of a response, but he saw nothing. He started to doubt himself. *Maybe she's not interested,* he thought to himself as he went into the living room. "What are we watching, little man?" Beau asked Levi. "*Batman,*" Levi responded.

Beau sat on the big sectional with Levi and watched his show wondering what Evie must have been thinking. They had known each other for five months and were friends for four of those months. He spent every spare minute he had with her and the kids since that first outing in the park clear back in August. It was now the end of September. It started out as a way to help him with his recovery, but this little family had become more to him with each Zumba class, park outing, aquarium visit, carousel ride, and now each tea party. He felt like he had waited long enough, but Beau wished he knew where Evie stood.

Beau Halstead tried to kiss me, Beau Halstead tried to kiss me, Evie kept thinking over and over again. Sure, she liked him and would not have stopped him from kissing her, but after it happened, Evie wasn't sure she was ready for the next step in their relationship. She mulled over the events that transpired thinking about what would have happened if the alarm hadn't gone off. The thoughts made her happy and scared all at the same time.

Fear soon ruled her emotions as Jude's words filled her brain from one of the previous nights he called. "Do you honestly think that rockstar would date you now? It doesn't matter how many gym classes you go to or what you eat. No man, especially Beau Halstead, will look at you the same way again." Tears filled Evie's eyes as those poignant words played over and over again in her head.

Evie continued to set the table, pull the potatoes out of the microwave, prep the salad, and get drinks ready. She walked into Harper's room and said, "Dinner's ready, Baby." Harper smiled and bounded out of her room to the kitchen table. Evie walked into the living room, finding Levi and Beau sprawled out on the sectional watching *Batman*. Evie smiled. "Dinner's ready," she said. Beau quickly got up and helped Levi up before turning off the TV.

Everyone sat down at the table and began eating. Never before had Beau tasted such delicious meatloaf. "This is wonderful," he said to her. "Thank you," she said, smiling. After they looked at each other for a while, they stared back down at their plates. Evie wasn't sure if they were going to talk about the incident. Evie felt herself putting the wall back up, and she sat quietly and ate her food. Beau knew that look very well since he tried helping Evie find the townhouse. She was going to stonewall like never before. He decided to just let it go and continue like nothing happened.

Finally, when everyone was done, Beau volunteered to clean the kitchen while Evie got the kids ready for bed. After the kids were bathed and lying down in their beds, Beau peeked into each of their rooms watching Evie sing their lullaby and tucking them in bed. He smiled. Finally, Evie closed Levi's door, met Beau in the hallway. His gaze was so intense Evie felt like she was going to blush. Soon she just walked past him down the stairs into the living room. Beau followed her and sat down on the sectional next to her.

They both felt very uncomfortable. To break the ice, Beau requested a specific show to watch, and Evie turned it on. About ten minutes into the show, Beau finally said, "So, are we going to talk about what happened in the kitchen?"

"I don't know."

"Did I just make things completely awkward between us?"

Evie turned to Beau. "I don't know."

"If I did, I'm sorry."

"Do you believe in do-overs?" Evie asked.

"What do you mean?" Beau asked.

"I mean, whenever Levi yells, is impolite, or does something socially unacceptable, I tell him to do it again. When he does it right, I praise him. So, do you want a do-over on the whole situation?" Evie asked.

"Yes. Let's just continue our friendship the way it is," Beau said.

Evie smiled. "Agreed. Nothing has changed except maybe you are my best friend."

Beau paused. "I am?"

"Of course. Who else do you know that goes out of their way to spend time with my family and me?"

"Good point. Well, you are probably my best friend right now, too. You've helped me out a lot."

"Good."

"And as for the picture," Beau began. "I was only going to keep it for myself. It would pop up when you called me," Evie said with a chuckle. Beau blushed but laughed.

Beau watched his show as Evie went into her room to change into her pajamas, brush her teeth, and wash her face. When bare-faced Evie walked back into the living room, Beau realized he hadn't seen Evie without makeup on before, but she was still stunning. She didn't wear too much makeup; just enough to highlight her features, especially those eyes. Evie sat back down on the couch and leaned her head against Beau's shoulder. Eventually, she fell asleep on the sectional as well as Beau. They stayed there all night where Evie occasionally cried or whimpered, startling Beau. Out of habit from his days of helping Cordell fall asleep again, Beau would rock Evie to sleep.

Evie woke up with Beau's arms around her on the couch. She looked around her to make sure nothing happened, remembering the almost kiss. Evie snuck away to go make a special breakfast for everyone and shower before the kids woke up. She got dressed, put makeup on, and put more curl in her hair. She went back into the kitchen and began making breakfast for everyone. She washed some fruit and set the table.

Beau woke up to the smell of French toast, bacon, sausage, and hash browns. He soon realized where he was and what happened the night before. Beau looked at his watch and realized that Evie would need to take Levi to school in about an hour. Beau salivated. He stood up, stretched, and proceeded to walk to the kitchen to see Evie all bright-eyed and bushy-tailed ready to tackle the day.

"Good morning, Bestie," he said.

Evie jumped. "Oh, you scared me," Evie said, putting her hand over her heart.

"Sorry," Beau said.

"It's fine. I, myself, sneak up on people and make them jump."

"What do you need help with?"

"Could you go wake Levi and ask him to change his clothes? I will go get Harper," Evie said.

"Sure thing."

Beau proceeded upstairs to wake Levi up. As Beau opened the door, Levi rolled out of bed and proceeded to get dressed.

Levi?" Beau asked. "What?" the boy responded. "Does your mom often cry in her sleep?" Levi's countenance suddenly changed from happy to sad. "Every night since my dad divorced her." Beau's heart suddenly sank. "Do you know what happened?" Beau asked. "He started being mean to her more and more after Harper was born. Soon, he decided to love someone else because he thought my mom was ugly. She's been really sad since. She cries a lot when she's alone."

Never before had Beau's blood boiled like it did when he heard those words. More than ever did Beau want to fly to Baltimore to pummel Jude into the ground.

"Thanks, Buddy. Finish getting ready for school. Your mom made French toast." Levi's face lit up with excitement. Beau figured Evie didn't make French toast very often, but when she did, it was absolutely delicious. Beau salivated some more. Once Levi was dressed, Beau walked with him to the table and sat down. Harper was sitting in her booster seat, ready to eat with a big smile on her face as well. Soon, everyone was enjoying breakfast together. "Thank you for feeding me," Beau said. "You're welcome. It's the least I can do for my best friend," Evie said. Beau and Evie smiled at each other. "So, can we do this all again tonight?" Beau asked. "Why not?" Evie said, smiling.

Chapter 10

Nole Bradshaw Day

Beau stayed at Evie's townhouse every night for a month. He paid close attention to Evie's behavior to see what he could do to help her. Sure enough, he could see a woman who had been deeply hurt, abused, and betrayed, but to what extent, he had no idea. Too scared to ask, Beau stayed silent on the matter. Beau noticed that Jude called Evie every day for a week. First, Jude would talk to the kids for about five minutes, and then he would spend the next fifteen yelling at Evie for whatever reason. She usually locked herself in her room during that time. After what happened at the Mexican restaurant, Beau decided to stay out of it out of respect for Evie. He hated it. He hated the fact that Evie let Jude do this to her. Once Evie was off the phone, Beau always suggested going somewhere fun to cheer her up. The kids loved the idea, as well, so they would load up in Evie's car and head out.

As September proceeded to October, Beau realized what day it was; October 10, a significant day in Death Toll's history for Luke, Kade, and him. That day in 2008, their fellow bandmate, bassist, and best friend, Nolan Jay Bradshaw, or as the guys called him, Nole, died while they were on tour in Europe. The bus rolled and threw him out the window, but as it kept going, it landed on him.

Beau remembered how devastated, sad, angry, disoriented, and confused he was. After that event, his behavior and alcoholism started to spin out of control. He never realized that he had substantial abandonment issues, but when Nole died, that's when they manifested. The anniversary of Nole's death always brought out emotions Beau had a hard time dealing with, especially now that Phoebe, Chloe, and Cordell were gone.

While they were at the studio writing songs, Beau began noodling with the B Minor scales on his acoustic guitar. He quickly wrote that riff down before he forgot it. Luke walked into the room and said, "Hey, we're going to go to Castro Valley to pay tribute to Nole. Want to come?" Beau shook his head. "No, I want to work on this song a bit more if that's okay with you guys."

"You know, man, one of these days, you need to go visit him," Luke said. Beau swallowed a lump in his throat. "It's too hard. One minute, we're all sleeping, and the next, we're rolling around like clothes in a dryer. I turn around and see Nole's legs underneath the bus. I can't get the image out of my head," Beau said with a crack in his voice. "It's been 12 years. When are you going to face it?" Luke asked, a little annoyed. Beau just shook his head. "I don't know. Maybe next year?" Beau said. "Okay. Just know the longer you put it off, the harder it's going to be. See ya later!" Luke said. "Bye!" Beau went back to playing his guitar.

Soon, lyrics and poetry started flowing through Beau, and he quickly grabbed a notepad and a pen and began writing about how fragile life is, and it can be taken from anyone at any given time. He wrote about how he often felt sitting in his house by himself, wishing he could join his family. He wrote about how much longer he would live before Beau had given all he needed to offer to Death Toll.

Beau suddenly had a vision of an explosive guitar riff after the first verse. He started noodling again until his fingers found the riff he heard in his head. Beau wrote it down. As he repeated it over and over again, he thought about the good old days when everyone he truly loved and cared about was still alive. Fast forward to the present day, and they were all gone. Nothing would ever be the same again.

More lyrics flowed to Beau's mind about how much can change within a short amount of time. He wrote about how much he missed Phoebe and the out-of-body experience Beau had when he received the news of her death. He remembered the hole he felt inside of him and relapsing into bad habits, but he didn't know how to stop them on his own until a few months prior. Everything seemed pretty repetitive. He played through both verses and solos a few times, and he made sure to write them down.

Suddenly, Beau heard little people's voices, and he knew Evie and the kids just got to the studio. Levi ran into the equipment room where Beau was sitting. "Hi, Beau!" Levi exclaimed before running off to the second living room. Soon, a flash of blonde curliness rushed by the door, but then it reversed. "Hi Beau!" littler Harper said, smiling. Beau smiled back. Soon, Evie walked to the door, waved her hand towards the kids as if to give up, and walked into the audio room.

"Hey!" she said out of breath. "Hey! Where did you go this morning?" Beau asked. "Parent/Teacher Conference for Levi. His teachers commented on how much his behavior has improved and rewrite some other goals," Evie said. "That's wonderful news to hear," Beau said. Evie smiled. "So, isn't today Nole Bradshaw...?" Beau quickly interrupted her.

"Yes. The guys went to Castro Valley to see him," Beau said quietly. "Oh, well, why didn't you go with them?" Evie asked. "I started working on this song about feelings of losing a loved one." "May I hear it?" Evie asked. "Sure."

Beau soon began playing the opening riffs, transition, first verse, solo interludes, second verse, and solo interludes again. He sang the lyrics during each verse. Evie was always amazed with Beau's ability to sing with his heart even with brand new songs.

When he was done, Evie had tears in her eyes. Finally, she said, "I think you need to go see him." "Why?" Beau asked. "Because it's a critical year for you. You lost Nole, Phoebe, Chloe, Cordell, and your mom. Your dad was absent from your life before he eventually passed on, and you keep feeling like everyone is going to leave you. I think you need to face this fear."

Beau could feel a lump in his throat as he held back his emotions. "I can't," Beau said. "Why?" Evie asked, pushing the subject. "Because! It's just too hard! Why do you always have to push, push, push!?! Your stubbornness is so damn frustrating!" Beau snapped, raising his fists in frustration. Watching Evie's eyes become watery, Beau immediately regretted that decision. "Evie, I'm…" "Don't," Evie cracked, holding up a hand and walking out of the recording room. He saw her wiping the tears away.

Shit, what did I just do, Beau contemplated, *why did I yell at her? She's just trying to help. Why can't I go see the plaque? It's just a plaque.* Beau dug deeper into his interior to figure out why this was so hard. Then he knew the answers. No one knew what caused the bus to swerve out of control, so Beau had no one to blame. Nole's death was a true tragedy, and it always bothered Beau. Plus, Beau had bad abandonment issues. Dr. Bennett had addressed those issues in therapy many times before, but Beau never applied it to Nole's death.

Suddenly, Dr. Bennett's words came to his head from two weeks prior. "Who do you trust the most in your life right now?" "Evie, Luke, Kade, Rick, and you," Beau said. "All right. A few years ago, I told you to surround yourself with your family, which you did. Phoebe was the perfect medication for you, and being involved in your kids' lives reversed all those issues. Now that they're gone, surround yourself with your new family," Dr. Bennett concluded.

Beau immediately ran through the studio, looking for Evie. "Evie?" he called, trying to listen for her. Thinking of all the places she would go, he finally realized she was in the second living room, the farthest she could get away from him. Sure enough, he found her sitting on the couch with her arms folded. She still had tears coming down her cheeks, which she wiped. The one person she had grown to trust yelled at her, shaking her confidence. *Are they all like this*, she asked herself, wondering if all guys were jerks.

Beau ran to the couch and knelt down. "Evie, I'm so so so sorry. This issue I'm having has nothing to do with you."

"Are you sure? I'm a very stubborn human." Evie's voice was strained from crying. She hated crying and noticed she had cried more and more since her divorce. She could not remember a time in her life when she cried this much.

"I promise. This is a problem I've had for years that I need to get control over."

"And that's okay. I understand if you're not ready to face this yet."

"You were right before. I need to go this year because it's a critical one."

Evie smiled, sitting up and wiping her tears off her face. She was super happy that Beau decided to go. As Beau stood up off the floor, he turned to look at Evie. "Would you be able to come with me?" he asked, wanting someone he cared about with him for comfort. "Absolutely. Let me go get the kids," Evie said. Beau suddenly remembered Laila was at the studio in the toy room with her kids. "Actually, I will go ask Laila to watch them while she is here; that way we can be more respectful and focused on what I need to do," he said. Evie paused and knew he meant facing his fear. "Okay. If that's what you want. I will say goodbye to them," she said as she stood up off the couch.

They walked into the toy room where Beau explained what was going on. Laila was very understanding about the whole situation and willing to watch Levi and Harper. Evie kissed her kids and hugged Laila. "Thank you!" Evie said. "You're welcome. Take all the time you need," Laila said.

Evie followed Beau out of the studio to where the cars were parked. "Want to take yours?" Evie asked since she wouldn't need car seats. Beau hesitated. "I brought one of my choppers today. I have a second helmet in the seat," Beau said. "Oh, okay. That's fine," Evie said, wondering when the last time she had been on a motorcycle was.

Beau opened the seat, pulling out the second helmet and handed it to Evie. It was a very light pink, so she assumed it was Phoebe's. Figuring out how to run the strap through the rings, Evie attempted to secure the helmet. "Here," Beau said, approaching Evie and feeding the strap through. His right index finger stroked her jawline, which caused both of them to gaze into each other's eyes. The pull they felt to each other came back, but Evie turned away, trying to keep her head straight. Beau, snapping out of the trance, straddled the chopper and fired it up. He balanced it with his legs before Evie climbed on. She was very thankful she wore a leather jacket and boots that day to protect her just in case they crashed. Once Evie was on the bike, she wrapped her arms around his waist. As they both ignored the pull again, Beau sped off towards Nole's elementary school where his plaque was.

The drive was beautiful to Castro Valley. All the leaves on the trees had changed colors, and it was overcast outside. Evie could smell the salt in the air from the bay as Beau zoomed down the I-80.

Beau exited the freeway sooner than anticipated. She believed they were in El Cerrito. When they got to the bottom of the ramp, Beau turned around and asked, "Want to see the house we lived in during our second and third albums?" "Yes!" Evie said with a little too much excitement.

Beau smiled and joked, "You've been there before, haven't you? Are you sure you're not a stalker?"

Evie jabbed Beau's ribs and answered, "Hey! Didn't you beg your mom to paint you in an Aerosmith poster where Joe Perry was over your bed?"

"You are a stalker!" Beau teased some more.

"And yet, you hired me. So who can truly be trusted here?" Evie whimsically said.

Beau pursed his lips. "So that's a no?" he asked her, ignoring the question. Evie laughed. "Nope, I haven't. I've only seen pictures," Evie said.

When the light turned green, he zoomed towards the house. "Do people live in it now?" Evie asked. "I think so. The owners still rent it out, but the garage we used to rehearse and write songs in is gone," Beau said.

When they arrived, Beau parked the chopper. He balanced it so Evie could get off. He put the kickstand down and climbed off himself. Both of them took their helmets off and stared at the small house. "The words 'Death Toll Mansion' really deceive people, don't they?" Evie asked with a little laugh. Beau chuckled himself. "Yeah. Even though we were making money, we still lived dirt cheap to save money for equipment, booze, hook...." Beau stopped talking. Evie laughed again. "My, how all of you have come such a long way from crazy kids messing around to husbands and dads," she said. Beau smiled.

A crazy thought entered Evie's head as she began walking towards the front door. "Are you seriously going to knock on their door?" Beau asked, feeling a little embarrassed. Evie turned around after she walked up the stoop. "Yes, I am," she said, facing Beau and knocking on the door. Beau ran up the steps where he proceeded to listen for footsteps inside the house. The footsteps grew louder as they heard a hand reach for the doorknob and turned it.

When the door opened, there was a guy with curly, dark hair and thick-framed glasses wearing a Death Toll T-shirt. He first looked at Evie followed by Beau. The man smiled once he recognized Beau. "Hey, how are you?" Beau said, holding out his hand. The man, in shock, shook Beau's hand. Evie smiled at the interaction. "Did you know you live in my old house?" Beau asked. The man stammered through his sentence, but said, "Yeah, I do. Um, would you like to come in?" Beau smiled. "No, thank you.

I just wanted to say 'hi,' and I hope you like the house. It holds sentimental value to all of us," Beau said.

The man smiled. "It's a good house," he said.

"It is. Which room do you have?" Beau asked.

"The one farthest from the street," the man said.

"Hey, that was my room!" Beau said.

"I know!" the man said with a huge grin.

"Well, hey, how about I come in, sign something, and you can hang it on our door. That way people will know for sure," Beau said.

The man looked like he was going to wet himself. "Yes, please! Let me go find a piece of paper!" He soon disappeared into his house and found paper and a pen. Beau signed it.

"All right, it was nice to meet you. What's your name?" Beau said.

"Dave, and who is this hot thing with you?"

Evie turned about thirty shades of red. "Evie. I'm the Death Toll tour manager," she said.

"A woman tour manager? That is so cool!"

"Well, Dave, I hope to see you soon. Are you coming to any shows?"

"Hell yes! I will be at all of the California shows."

"Awesome. Well, bye, Dave."

"Bye, Beau! Bye, Evie! If you're single, call me!" *Seriously*, Evie thought to herself, laughing. "Will do. Bye, Dave. Thank you!"

"All right, that was fun. You really are bold, aren't you?" Beau asked as he walked back to the chopper. Evie, following him, flashed a cheesy smile. "A bit."

"Well, thank you for being you. Yes, I get annoyed with your stubbornness, but overall, it has helped me grow."

Evie smiled. "All part of the plan, and thank you."

Beau and Evie began their drive to Castro Valley again. Once they arrived at Nole's elementary school, Beau parked the bike. Evie followed him to the exact spot Nole's plaque was; behind the playground near the trees. Beau walked ahead of Evie since he knew where they were going. She could see the plaques from the other side of the playground. Suddenly, Beau stopped dead in his tracks, and Evie bumped into him a little bit but quickly recovered. She moved to Beau's right side, where she saw him look down. When she looked down, there on a plaque, it read:

> Nolan Jay Bradshaw
> January 8, 1980 - October 10, 2008
> "Thank you for your music."

Near the plaque were some flowers and guitar picks in the corners. Beau rummaged through his pockets and found a guitar pick that he placed next to Nole's name. Evie rummaged through her purse, looking for anything she had that would be appropriate to lay on the plaque. Other than diapers, wipes, mints, a hair tie, and chapstick, there was nothing. Beau walked a little bit to the left where there was another plaque. There on that plaque read:

> Todd Lee Bradshaw
> May 12, 1977 - June 6, 1993
> "We love you, Todd!"

The plaque looked a little dirty, so Evie pulled out a couple of baby wipes and began wiping it off. Beau knelt down and started helping as well. "When Nole was alive, we came here a couple of times to make sure his brother was taken care of. I'm glad you started to clean it," Beau said, sounding a little choked up. Evie smiled at Beau. Soon, they went back to Nole's and stared at it for what seemed like a half-hour without saying a word. Evie kept looking at Beau to see if he was doing all right emotionally and ready to talk. Evie knew the story well about how Nole died. She remembered when the news went all over the Internet.

Death Toll couldn't afford to fly on airplanes yet, so they used cheap tour buses. On the drive to Copenhagen, Luke's hometown, Nole and Kade drew straws for Kade's bunk because it was the best. Since Nole got the longer straw, he got to sleep in the bunk. Kade went towards the front of the bus and fell asleep.

Suddenly, the bus began skidding and went off the road rolling. Nole was thrown from the bus where it eventually landed on him. Beau recalled that he wasn't sure if he was still alive at that point because EMT's brought a crane to pull the bus off of Nole, but it malfunctioned, and the bus landed on Nole again. Soon, the bus driver staggered to Nole's legs and tried to tug on them. Beau yelled, cursed, and punched the driver in the nose, telling him to leave Nole alone.

The band was angry and devastated all at the same time because there was no black ice on the road. Beau walked two miles each way to be sure. Kade even related stories of Beau being so hammered after the funeral that he would often wander the streets calling Nole's name.

Evie wrapped her left arm around his waist to offer some form of comfort. When Beau felt the arm, he put his hand over Evie's trying to hold back tears. Beau missed his friend terribly. He knew it wasn't anyone's fault for Nole's death but still struggled with the idea; Beau figured God needed him for something. Nole had way more living experiences than most people did at 28.

Beau felt a tear running by his nose, and he quickly wiped it. How he missed his friend! The best guy from Death Toll not only as a musician, but as a friend and overall human tragically died. Some old thoughts and emotions came back to Beau's brain that he directed to Nole. *Why did you have to leave me!? You could have shaped the metal world even more! You were supposed to move in with your girlfriend! Your parents didn't deserve another son to be taken away from them so soon! I needed you! Your girlfriend needed you! Your parents needed you!*

After a half-hour, Beau finally said something. "Want to go get a soda or something?" he asked. Evie smiled. "Sure. My treat," she said as she led Beau back to the chopper. They put their helmets on and got back on the motorcycle. Beau drove down Castro Valley Blvd where he pulled into a parking lot of a diner called Norman's Grill. The restaurant was in the shape of an old barn, which Evie thought was a cool feature, included with outdoor seating.

They went inside the building where a friendly host seated them at a table outside. Beau decided to order a strawberry milkshake and a side of fries while Evie ordered a chocolate milkshake and bacon cheese fries. After their orders went in, they sat in silence for a few minutes before Evie asked, "Beau, was it a mistake encouraging you to go visit Nole's plaque?" Beau shook his head. "No, it wasn't. I'm glad you did," he said. "Are you sure? You've been awfully quiet, which is unusual for you," Evie chuckled.

Beau laughed as well. "No, this has been good for me. I was able to process some thoughts I've been having lately." "Like what? If you don't mind me asking." "He was the best one out of all of us. He paced himself in the lifestyle, and he figured out what he wanted a lot earlier than we did. He set the tone for the band. Then when he died, it destroyed me. First my dad left, then my mom, then Nole, then Cordell, and Chloe, and Phoebe. I don't know why everyone keeps leaving me." Evie knew Beau's personal life all too well.

Evie suddenly felt the urge to tell Beau something a bit more personal about her that she never talked about with anyone. She hated how vulnerable it made her feel and all the crying it had caused. "Want to hear a story that might give you some perspective?" she asked. "Sure," Beau responded, sounding a bit hopeful. "Well, my mom had cancer way back when I was in seventh grade, also," Evie said. "Didn't know that," Beau responded, looking at Evie with some concern. "I don't tell anyone about it. My kids don't even know. During that time when I heard the word, 'cancer,' I thought it meant death, but my parents reassured me that the treatments would make it go away.

"Now, I didn't watch cancer suck the life out of my mom like you did, but I saw the damage the treatments caused her as she had surgery, began chemotherapy, lose her hair, slowly lose her appetite, start radiation, and watch her body become puffy from the steroids inside the chemo drugs. It was awful; truly awful because I was also enduring a lot of bullying and ridicule as well because we all know how fun Jr. High can be," Evie said sarcastically as Beau let out a chuckle, "and I didn't want to tell my parents or my sister these things because our family had bigger problems like whether my mom was going to survive or not. My dad reassured me she would be fine because they caught the cancer early, but again," Evie pointed at herself, "13-year-old girl who didn't fully understand cancer at that time.

"Probably one of the reasons why I don't ask for help very much because other people have bigger problems than me. I know how blessed I am because I got to keep my mom, but sometimes I contemplate how different my life would be if my mom did die. Yes, I would have been very sad and tried to hide it somehow, but I think I would have come to terms with it.

"Now, you have a problem with abandonment, but you also have the choice whether or not to let this define who you are. Are you going to keep going to those dark places, or will you treasure the people you have in your life now like the band, your brothers, your sister, Levi, Harper... me?

"And maybe, just maybe, one of the reasons you have survived so many accidents is because your mom and Nole are watching out for you to ensure you are around to share your talent and passion with the world, because that's what you were born to do," Evie finally concluded.

Beau soon remembered a couple of sessions he had with Pete about treasuring those he lost as well as treasuring the people in his life now. He also couldn't believe what Evie went through at such a hard time in her life. "Your mom had cancer?"

"Yes, and she even developed a tumor in her brain just before Jude and I moved to Baltimore for his big promotion. That was a hard thing to do because I wanted to be with my mom while she recovered from surgery," Evie responded.

"Twice? Wow, your family has been through Hell," Beau said.

Evie nodded. "Yep, but we overcame it, and so can you. We all love you and will be there for you, I hope you know."

Soon, the waitress brought the orders of fries and milkshakes to Beau and Evie. "Have you thought about writing any songs?" he asked her. Evie laughed. "No. I'll leave that up to you," she teased as they each took a bite of their fries. "Thank you for coming with me today and telling me a little bit more about your life. I think I understand you just a little bit more," Beau said. Evie smiled, "Anytime you need me, I'm here for you."

Suddenly without warning, words flowed into Beau's head about how he was feeling. "I need a pen," he said as he grabbed a napkin.

Evie reached into her purse again and found a pen.

"Which song?" Evie asked.

"*Frantic.*"

"Oh, cool! Care to share, or should I...?" Evie decided to let Beau finish his thought.

Once he put the pen down, Beau scooted the napkin over to Evie. She read about how Beau was done being scared of his abandonment and anxiety. He was ready to embrace his fears and vulnerability, letting go of his abandonment issues altogether. "Whoa," Evie gasped. "Thank you," Beau grinned, feeling proud of himself. He grabbed the napkin, folding it up, and putting it in his pocket.

Back at the studio two hours later, Beau excitedly walked in and said, "I have another verse for Frantic." Everyone froze. "Great! Let's hear them!" Luke exclaimed. Beau pulled out the folded napkin from the diner. Beau unfolded it and handed it to Kade. Rick looked over his shoulder and began reading them as well.

Kade looked utterly blown away by the words, whereas Rick looked a little confused. "They're awesome, but what do they mean?" he asked.

"I'm done being afraid of abandonment as well as the grandiose rock star lifestyle we've lived in the past. Plus, you guys, we've been playing together for so long with so many memories. The three of you are my family, and I am thankful I have each of you in my life. Sorry if it's sappy, but it's the truth," Beau concluded.

Luke lightly smiled, walked up to Beau, and put his hand on Beau's shoulder. "I'm thankful you answered my ad in the newspaper all those years ago because I would not have gained a brother like you," Luke said before turning to Kade, "or you," and turning to Rick, "or you." The four of them huddled together just like they always did before a show. "Let's do this! Let's finish this record!" Luke shouted as well as adding some profanity. "YEAH!" Beau shouted his signature battle cry.

Chapter 11

Halloween

Halloween approached extremely fast. Beau knew it was Kade's favorite time of year with his annual Halloween party whether they were on tour or not. Beau remembered how much Kade loved all things horror, and how big Halloween night was to him. Beau RSVP'd yes to the party, but was still clueless as to what to be. He decided to be a SWAT guy with a skull mask like the previous year. He liked to call himself the "Creeping Death" after their song. He really liked that costume. Plus, it reminded him of the last Halloween when Phoebe and the kids were alive. Two days before Halloween, Beau went to the garage where Phoebe kept past Halloween costumes and found his costume from last year. He pulled it out and took it up to his room.

That same day, Evie took her kids over to Kade and Laila's house so that they could play, and Evie and Laila sat and talked. "Are you coming to the party?" Laila asked. "I've been working so much, I haven't had time to look for a costume," Evie said. "Well, you've come to the right place. I have so many Halloween costumes. You can borrow one," Laila said, smiling.

"Thanks, but I don't know who would watch the kids," Evie said again. "Luke, Rick, and Beau trade off watching the kids each year. It's

Luke and Jetta's turn this year," Laila said. "I guess I'm not getting out of this?" Evie asked. Laila smiled. "It's your first year with us. Of course not. We need you here," Laila said.

Evie sighed, feeling defeated, but smiled. Laila always pushed Evie out of her comfort zone. "Fine. What do you suggest I wear?" Evie asked. "Well, follow me. Let's see what we have," Laila said, standing up off of the couch and walking downstairs to the basement. Evie followed her into a huge media room overlooking a huge backyard with a view of the bay.

Horror memorabilia hung all over the walls and sat on the shelves. "Wow, I knew Kade was obsessed with horror movies, but his collection is massive," Evie said, looking around the room. "Yeah. It creeps me out a little that his mom put him in front of all these movies, but I can understand why he likes them so much," Laila said, opening a door, looking inside, and closing the door. "Why?" Evie asked, still not understanding. "Well, look at the artwork and intricacy of the Creature statue," Laila said. Evie glanced over at the bust of the Creature from the Black Lagoon. She looked at it more closely, and indeed, the bust was very intricate. "Ah, I see it now," Evie said.

Laila walked into another room as Evie continued to walk around the basement, looking at Kade's collection. "So, what do you like to dress up for on Halloween?" Laila shouted from the room. "I don't know. The last time I dressed up for Halloween was before Levi was born. After that, Jude began going to company Halloween parties while I stayed home with Levi and Harper when she was born. I took them Trick-or-Treating last year dressed in normal clothes. My Halloweens consisted of large Toblerone bars and watching *Jaws*. I'm lame," Evie said.

Laila laughed. "Why would your ex-husband leave you alone with the kids?"

"He said he had company events he needed to go to, but I think that was code for sleeping with other girls. I'm seeing a pattern in his behavior, now as well as bank account history," Evie said.

Laila pitied the poor girl. "Well, let's get you back into the swing of things. Come on in. I think I have some good contenders," she shouted back to Evie. Evie followed Laila's voice into the room.

There were racks and racks of Halloween costumes all over the place. There were scary costumes, provocative costumes, furry costumes, masquerade costumes, and just about all the costumes a person could imagine for men and women. Evie picked her jaw up off the floor. "All right, so I am thinking something sexy but understated for you," Laila said. "Like what?" Evie asked. Laila walked over to one of the sexy costume racks and began digging. Finally, she pulled out a red strapless dress with a high slit and a deep v-neckline.

"So, you want me to be Jessica Rabbit?" Evie asked. Laila smiled and nodded. "Not only 'no,' but 'hell no,'" Evie said. Laila put it back on the rack. "Fine. I just want you to feel confident, maybe attract some handsome men," Laila said. "Not in that thing. I don't want to attract douchebags. A dress like that got me into the situation I'm in now. Not a chance," Evie said.

Laila began digging again. "What about this?" Laila said, pulling out a blue plaid skirt with a white oxford shirt, a silver ribbon, and a black cardigan.

"A Catholic schoolgirl?" Evie asked.

"No, a Ravenclaw," Laila said, "there is no crucifix. The skirt comes to just above the knees, and the cardigan has the Ravenclaw seal on it. Plus, the whole Britney Spears thing," Laila said with a chuckle.

"I was thinking about saying yes until you referenced Britney Spears," Evie said.

"C'mon. I believe this will get the right reaction," Laila said.

"What do you mean?" Evie asked.

"From a potential gentleman caller," Laila said.

"I'm not looking to get any attention from any guy. I would much rather wear one of those furry onesies that blend into your couch."

"Oh, come on! It's been months since you had any attention from a guy. Live a little," Laila said.

More like years, Evie thought to herself before saying, "Who's attention are you hoping I grab anyways?"

"Just a couple of guys," Laila said with only one in mind. She knew something was going on between Beau and Evie, and she was hoping to give a little push with a fantasy she knew Beau and the rest of the band had at some point in their lives.

Evie rolled her eyes. "Fine, I will wear it, but never mention Britney to me again," Evie said. "Won't happen," Laila said, holding up the costume. Evie grabbed the hanger.

"We actually have a fitting room over there," Laila pointed to the corner. Evie walked into the fitting room and began to try on the costume. The costume ended up fitting pretty well. Evie had some black knee-highs she could wear as well as some Dr. Martens. Evie walked out of the fitting room to show Laila. "Yep, it does do the trick," Laila said, smiling. "Oh, goody," Evie said, rolling her eyes.

The day of the Halloween Party arrived. Evie dropped her kids off at the Jeppsen's'. "Thank you again for watching my kids," Evie said to Jetta and Luke. "No problem. We have done this for years," Luke said. He was looking at Evie's costume. "Catholic schoolgirl?" he asked, pointing at Evie. "No, a Ravenclaw. Watch *Harry Potter*," Evie said.

"That will get his attention," Jetta said, walking back to the foyer.

"Whose attention?" Evie asked.

"B…." Jetta stopped before finishing Beau's name. "Just this guy we know who will be at the party," Jetta said. She was in on the plan with Laila.

"His name starts with a B…?" Evie felt very confused.

"Yes, B-ryan," Jetta finished.

"Who is Bryan?" Evie asked. "Yeah, who is Bryan?" Luke asked.

Jetta rolled her eyes at Luke. "A guy Laila and I know who we thought would like to meet you. I think you would like him."

Luke looked at his wife with a confused look. Jetta looked at him, smiled, and looked back at Evie, still smiling. "Okay, I will keep my eyes open for a Bryan," Evie said, "you guys are creeping me out. Please don't give them too much candy or anything French, please." Jetta sighed and looked flabbergasted.

As Evie walked out the door, Jetta grabbed her phone. "Great, now I need to text Laila," she said.

"Why?"

"To introduce Evie to a Bryan. I don't know a Bryan. Do you?" Jetta asked.

"Brian Johnson, but Evie might be a little out of his league," Luke said, "She can do way better than the lead singer of AC/DC."

"I meant another Bryan who is possibly some sort of an intellect,'" Jetta said.

"What about Beau?" Luke said.

"We can't tell Evie that.... You know what? Just leave it to the women to meddle in their friend's life," Jetta concluded.

"Whatever you say, Babe," Luke agreed.

At the party, Beau avoided the booze table. Kade made sure there was sparkling water, soda, sparkling cider, and plenty of bottled water to help Beau feel like he had options. Kade also invited other straight-edge musicians to ensure all of his drinks were consumed. "Your costume is pretty awesome," Beau said to Kade, who was dressed like an undead version of himself. "Thanks. I like that you wore last year's costume. It's a good one," Kade said. "Thanks," Beau smiled.

Beau mingled with other musicians he hadn't seen in a while including Don. They got along pretty well now since Don started his own metal band and became very successful with it. He soon ran into Axl, Brian, Slash, Tom, Ian, and his friend, Jon, the comedian. Every now and then, he would look around the room and backyard, hoping to see Evie, but she was not there yet. They had talked the day before, and both were going to the party.

It was an hour into the event, and Beau was standing by the pool talking with Brian Johnson about upcoming studio albums when Evie walked outside. Her costume was just how Beau pictured her when she was in high school because he knew she was a beautiful honor student with a wicked girl edge, much like the Catholic School Girl stereotype she was portraying.

Beau watched as she walked up to Laila, who was dressed as Morticia from the *Addams' Family*. They admired each other's costumes and continued to talk. Soon, Laila grabbed a guy dressed as the snobby king of France during the sixteenth century by the sleeve and pulled him to Evie. Laila introduced them and walked away.

Beau began living another Hell he hoped never to see. The two of them started talking and laughing as the snobby French king sipped his booze, and she chugged on a bottle of water. Beau so badly wanted to find a Jagermeister to help him cope, but he resisted. He finally walked inside the house into the basement bathroom.

Beau splashed water on his face. *She's not yours*, he thought to himself. *Really*, he asked himself, *who else has been spending the night on her couch, talking about life, and helping her take care of her kids?* The behemoth part inside of him was awakened without the Jagermeister, and he soon stormed out of the bathroom. Rick and Kade saw Beau walking towards someone huffing and puffing and stopped him. They knew him well enough to know what that behavior meant. "What are you doing, man?" Kade said, trying to push Beau back. "A snotty guy is talking to Evie," Beau huffed. "Have you had a drink?" Kade asked, trying to smell Beau's breath. "What?! No! I've been drinking water all night," Beau said in disbelief.

"So, you're mad because a girl you like and employ but aren't dating is talking to another guy?" Rick asked.

"She's not just a girl I like. She's way more than that," Beau huffed again.

"Dude, tread lightly," Rick said.

"What are you saying?" Beau asked.

"Yes, we're all rooting for you two, but she needs you to be a friend first, and if she starts dating another guy, don't get all huffy and puffy about it," Kade said, "this could be a good thing for her considering all she's been through."

"You don't know what she's been through. I don't even know all of what she's been through, but I certainly want to be around to find out," Beau said, beginning to push against Kade.

Even though Beau was four inches taller than him, Rick was stronger, and he began to restrain Beau as well. "Dude, let her be. Don't ruin this. She's the best manager we've ever had. If you are truly her best friend, she will come find you," Rick concluded. Beau stopped and began scanning the crowd looking for Evie again. She was nowhere to be found or the snobby French king. Beau felt defeated, walked back inside, and sat down on the sectional facing the open doors to the basement. He began sipping on a soda.

Evie soon walked in through the doors spotting Beau on the couch. "Hey! I've been looking for you! What kind of a SWAT guy are you supposed to be?" she asked. Hearing her voice surprised Beau. "I'm supposed to be 'Creeping Death.' You know, like our song," Beau said, smiling. Evie sat down on the couch next to Beau. "I like it," she said, smiling. Beau lightly smiled back after drinking his soda. "Catholic schoolgirl?" he asked, pointing at her. "A Ravenclaw," she said, showing the eagle crest from the movie. "Oh, didn't know you were a Harry Potter fan," Beau said. "I am. I dressed up as Professor McGonagal during the premier of the last movie," she said. *Hot nerd*, Beau thought to himself.

"So, who was that guy dressed like that sixteenth-century king of France you were talking to?" Beau asked.

"Are you talking about the guy dressed like Louis XIV?" Evie asked.

"I knew his name would be snotty."

"Well, his actual name is Bryan."

"So, did he ask you out, or…?" Beau asked.

"He tried, but I started talking about my kids. I had taken them Trick-or-Treating earlier, and I wondered if Luke and Jetta let them have too much candy because I knew everyone would be cranky tomorrow. He soon lost interest and walked away looking for the girl dressed like Lady Godiva, but that's okay. He wasn't really my type anyway," Evie said.

Beau let out a massive sigh of relief. Now he felt like he could be the best friend. He hated being the jealous guy. It got him in trouble a lot during the early days of Death Toll. "Sorry to hear that," he said. "It's okay. He kept going on and on about his Harley collection, anyways. I mean, I'm a girl who loves motorcycles and classic cars, but if that's all you're going to talk about, then bye-bye. The right guy will be willing to listen to my stories, worries, and complaints about my kids," Evie said. Beau smiled.

"Yes, he will," he said. *He already does*, Beau thought to himself, *because I'M THE GUY!* "Plus, I can just show you mine," he said, not realizing the alluring tone in his voice.

"Are you hitting on me?" Evie asked, grabbing his soda and taking a sniff.

"No," Beau responded quickly, grabbing his drink from her, "I'm just simply stating a fact."

"By far, yours is the best collection I have seen. It's better than going to a car show with my dad," Evie said, smiling.

"So," Beau said, trying to change the subject, "what do you normally do on Halloween?" he asked.

"Eat a ton of Toblerone and watch *Jaws*," Evie said.

"Really? *Jaws*?" Beau asked.

"It's a classic thriller," Evie said.

"I know that, but it's not that scary," Beau said.

"I'm not one for horror movies. I will only ever watch *Young Frankenstein*, *Dark Shadows*, or even *The Mummy* movies besides the *Jaws* series," Evie finished.

"Did Jude ever watch the movies with you?" he asked.

"No. He was too busy with company parties, or as I've discovered, cheating on me with various secretaries," Evie said.

"How does he still have a job?" Beau asked.

"He is highly respected in Baltimore, paid people off to keep quiet, that sort of thing," Evie said.

"How did you find all this out?" he asked again.

"Looking at past bank statements and my excellent problem-solving skills," Evie said.

"Would he at least come home and want to...?" Beau paused, thinking about what it would be like himself with Evie.

"No. He always claimed to be tired. I wore a very slutty bustier one year, and nothing. After that, I quit trying. I would fall asleep in bed wearing a huge tee shirt surrounded by Toblerone wrappers before he got home," Evie said.

"Sorry Halloween has been lame for you in the past," he said, picturing Evie in that bustier. *There's always tonight*, he thought to himself.

"It's okay. I enjoy watching *Jaws* and eating enormous amounts of Swiss chocolate," Evie giggled. Beau laughed, *Witty, smart, and sexy. You really are the whole package.*

"So, what did you do last year for Halloween? Were you here or was it your turn to watch all the kids?" Evie asked.

"I was here," Beau said, "I wore this costume, and Phoebe was a sexy cop."

"Did you guys always match?" Evie asked.

"Most of the time. Sometimes, we would do our own thing, but not often."

"Did you take the kids Trick-or-Treating?"

"Yes we did, and we were in our costumes as well," Beau chuckled.

"I bet that was a sight having you show up on the doorstep of your neighbors with your family," Evie giggled.

"I don't know what they thought. Even though we bought a huge house for my collection, we still tried to live as normally as possible. Phoebe cooked all our meals, cleaned all the bathrooms we used, made our bed, and did the laundry most of the time. She took our kids to the library, arcade, the park, children's museum, taught them how to clean their rooms and do the laundry, and a bunch of other stuff. We wanted our kids to have as normal of a life as possible," Beau concluded.

"So, she was preparing them to be adults…?" Evie tapered off when she realized what she was saying. Beau winced when he thought about his children never getting that opportunity.

"Beau, I am so sorry," she apologized.

"It's not your fault. It's no one's fault really," he said with a cracked voice.

"But I am sorry if I triggered anything," she said.

"It's all right. I can handle it," he said, looking into Evie's intense blue eyes he adored.

"Do you want me to go?" she asked.

"No! Don't do that. In fact, how about we go? I'll give *Jaws* another try. You can eat Toblerone, and I'll eat whatever fruit you have in your fridge," Beau said, smiling, finally feeling ready for what could happen.

Evie smiled back. "I didn't buy Toblerone this year, but I have a bunch of grapes, apples, oranges, pineapple, and popcorn," she said. "That sounds perfect," Beau said. Evie and Beau said goodbye to Kade and Laila before walking to their cars.

"I need to go get my kids," Evie said.

"Actually, they are probably in bed by now. They are really good about following bedtime," Beau said, feeling lucky, "so why ruin a good thing?"

"All right, I will go get them in the morning," Evie said.

Evie and Beau climbed into their cars and headed to Evie's townhome. Evie went to her kitchen and immediately began popping the popcorn. Beau started pulling out all of the fruit he could find. Beau found the little foldable table Evie kept behind her sectional that she set food on when she was eating while watching TV. He set it up and began taking bowls to it. Evie soon followed with the popcorn.

They found the movie on Netflix and selected it. They often joked about what happened in the film, such as the cause and effect situations. Beau noticed Evie would not put her feet on the floor or even close to the edge of the sectional. "Are you afraid the shark is going to get you?" Beau teased as he grabbed Evie's leg trying to tickle her. "Maybe," Evie laughed, kicking Beau's leg. They continued to watch the movie. Even though Evie had seen the movie a million times, certain parts still made her jump. Beau jumped himself when the dead guy in the boat appeared, when the shark surfaced out of the water when Brody was chumming, and when the shark leaped onto the "Orca" before eating Quint.

When the movie was over, Beau was frozen to the couch. Evie suddenly had a crazy idea. "Want to go jump into my complex pool?" she asked.

"You are nuts," Beau said.

"My friends in college and I used to do it after watching any of the *Jaws* movies," Evie said.

"Well, I don't exactly have a swimming suit here," Beau said.

"That didn't stop us," Evie said. Beau looked at her in disbelief. "Are you suggesting skinny dipping?" he asked, swallowing a lump in his throat, feeling like he was going to back out of his decision.

"You have some sort of undergarments on, right... I hope?" she asked him.

"Yeah."

"Use those," she said.

"What about you?" Beau said, getting choked up.

"I've got it covered," Evie said.

Beau hesitated, wondering if he was ready to see Evie in her underwear. However, the idea of jumping into a pool after watching a shark movie sounded crazy and fun. "All right. Let's do this!"

They got up off the couch and ran outside to her complex pool. It was after hours, so they hopped the locked fence. Beau proceeded to get undressed until he was down to his boxers. Evie did the same until she was down to her bra and underwear.

They moved to either side of the pool and stared at each other. Evie noticed more tattoos on the right side of his torso that looked like words to a children's book. *Okay, he is hot, and I just want to have a nibble on his abs, shoulders, pecs,* Evie thought to herself, drooling. Beau's imagination didn't do it justice as he stared at Evie's body, memorizing every curve, muscle, and the underwear. He tried to think about the crazy thing they were about to do. "On the count of three?" Evie asked, trying so hard to keep her head straight. "Okay, one…." "Two…." "THREE!" they both said before jumping into the pool.

Evie swam to the top, but Beau was still underwater. Since it was dark, she couldn't see where he was. Suddenly, Evie felt a tug on her ankle before submerging in the water again. She broke free of Beau's grip and swam to the surface. He swam up and started laughing. "Did I scare you?" "Didn't phase me. You're not the first one to do that," she said before splashing Beau's face with water. He immediately grabbed her arm and pulled her close. Evie soon dunked Beau, which surprised him. However, he grabbed her and pulled her under.

Out of breath, Beau and Evie grabbed onto each other once they broke the surface. Beau could still touch the bottom of the pool, but Evie was too short, so she wrapped her arms around Beau's shoulders. They looked into each other's eyes, and the atmosphere became electric. Beau soon wrapped his arms around Evie's waist, rubbing her left side. *Feels better than I thought,* Beau sighed to himself. *Okay, Evie. Just let it happen,* she coached herself as she wrapped her legs around Beau's waist.

They leaned in to kiss each other before all of the lights around the pool turned on.

"Hey! What are you guys doing!?" Evie's building manager shouted. Faster than the manager could get down to the pool and see their faces, Beau and Evie jumped out, grabbed their costumes, and hopped the fence. They ran back to Evie's townhouse. Luckily, she lived far enough away that the footprints they left would be gone before the manager figured out who they belonged to. When they got inside, they began leaning against the wall laughing so hard. Eventually, they slumped onto the ground, rolling with laughter.

Finally, after laughing for what seemed like twenty minutes, Evie regained some composure. "I'll go get towels," she said as she began standing up. Beau grabbed her hand, intertwining his fingers through hers. Those thoughts and feelings lingered in his brain as he imagined pulling Evie down into his lap, kissing her finally, kissing every single ounce of her body, pleasuring her, and making love to her. He revelled in his thoughts for a while.

"Beau?" Evie asked. His staring was making her feel a little vulnerable considering she was wearing a wet bra and underwear. *I know I don't have stretch marks, but do I look that awful? I'm still trying. At least I wax*, Evie told Beau in her head. Beau snapped out of it. Finally, he said, "Thank you for suggesting we jump in the pool. Not the craziest thing I've done, but it was still lots of fun." Evie smiled. "I haven't done that in years, so thank you for doing it with me," she said.

Beau let her hand go, and Evie went and grabbed towels as well as warm pajamas for herself. After changing, she rummaged through her loungewear and pajamas, finally finding one pair of men's gym shorts that would probably fit Beau as well as a large T-shirt. She took the towel and clothes to Beau. He went into the bathroom and put on dry clothes. When he walked out, Evie was bundled up on the sectional underneath a plushy turquoise blanket watching one of her favorite shows.

"May I climb in, too?" he asked. "Yes," Evie said. Beau sat back down, and she soon covered him up. Her hands and feet were freezing, causing Beau to shiver, but they soon warmed up as they snuggled closer to get warm. She leaned her head against Beau's shoulder, and he put his arm around her. Evie fell asleep first, so Beau pulled her a little closer, stroked her cheek, kissed her forehead. He positioned himself on the sectional so he could pull Evie under his chin. He rested his head on top of hers, and closed his eyes, feeling at peace. *My girl*, he thought before falling asleep.

Chapter 12

Evie Gets Help

"I am pleased with the progress you have made, Beau," Peter said, "You are living an active lifestyle and spending lots of time with Ms. Long and her kids. I truly believe her family was sent to you to help you cope with your loss even more."

Beau smiled. "I have grown to care for those kids like they were my own. Chloe was a little older than Levi, but he has the same energy and spirit that she did. Cordell and Harper would be the same age, so seeing her reach certain milestones reminds me of where he would be. I still miss my kids, but the wounds are healing," Beau responded.

"What about spending time with Ms. Long? What has that been doing for you?" Peter asked. Beau hesitated to answer because he knew Pete suspected Beau's feelings for her. "What do you mean?" Beau finally asked. "I think we've all seen the way you look at her, like she's the only woman who existed in the world. The chemistry between you two is unreal," Peter said.

"Evie reminds me of Phoebe a lot. She says things I can only imagine Phoebe saying to me when I step out of line, but Evie has some other qualities that I love. Evie has more knowledge about music than anyone else I know. She plays the violin, she dances, she's kind, and she's selfless. If you're wanting me to say I like her, then I will say it. Yes, I like Evie," Beau concluded. Peter smiled. "That's good. It's been nice watching your heart open up. Being with the Longs has been the best medicine for you."

Evie heard the last bit of Dr. Bennett's statement as she walked towards the first living room. Her heart rate began to increase as she listened to the one and only Beau Halstead admit his feelings for her. Evie was super happy that Beau chose to spend time with her and her family to help him recover faster. She knew how much he struggled, not going back to drinking.

Evie's feelings for Beau had grown exponentially since that first park outing, but they freaked her out still because she didn't want to get hurt again by another man she liked. Then Evie reminded herself that Beau was a completely different guy not only from the time she met him but from Jude. He chose to spend his days with a single mother and her two kids doing regular everyday activities. One of her favorite moments of Beau was watching this rockstar have a tea party with her daughter wearing a huge floppy hat and pretending to sip a little teacup with his pinky up.

She loved listening to his singing in the car when they invented the game, Song Styles With Beau Halstead. She cherished the moment that Beau taught Levi how to throw a football. Beau adopted himself into their family and became one of Evie's best friends since moving to San Francisco, but Jude…. Jude's ever present abuse held Evie back, *No man will love you like I did. They will never know how adventurous, fun, and sexy you were before you had kids. You're just a mom.*

Trying to brush off Jude's words, Evie peaked her head inside the living room and watched Beau and Dr. Bennett conclude the session. She leaned up against the door frame, watching Beau intently. Suddenly, Evie felt the urge to sneeze. She tried to make it go away, but then she sneezed, causing Dr. Bennett and Beau to jump. "Sorry, guys. I came to say that the rest of the band wants to have a meeting real quick," Evie said, wiping and scratching her nose. "No problem. We were finishing up. I will see you next week, Pete," Beau said. Beau and Dr. Bennett shook hands. "See ya, man. Keep up the good work!"

As he walked past her, Beau paused by Evie and rubbed her shoulder a bit before running his fingers through her hair, causing Evie to smile. Dr. Bennett watched the interaction as he packed up his briefcase. Beau walked out of the living room to the band meeting. When Evie entered the room, Dr. Bennet looked up at her. "How are you this evening, Ms. Long?" Dr. Bennett asked. Evie smiled a little and began fidgeting with her smart watch. "Doing all right, I guess," she responded, still fidgeting with her watch. "Are you sure? You keep coming here as sessions are ending, and you always look like you have something you need to say," he said.

Evie pursed her lips. *Okay, Evie. You can do this. You can ask for help*, she encouraged herself. "Well, I think I am finally ready to face my demons. I overheard the last bit of your conversation with Beau, and I feel like I need to get this off of my chest so I can begin to heal and … possibly… ," Evie said, looking towards the hallway Beau walked down. "Have a seat. Let's talk about it," he said, motioning towards the couch. Evie sat down.

"So, what seems to be the trouble?" he asked her. Evie spilled her guts. "When I found out Jude cheated on me and had cheated on me for the last four years of our marriage, I felt like this huge hole had been punched through my chest leaving me hollow inside. Soon," Evie's tears began flowing, "Jude told me that no man would ever love me again because I gave birth to two babies. No man wants to be with a mom who has lost her sense of adventure and leaves her sex appeal in a Zumba class. I felt so betrayed, and it was almost like I became a robot whose sole purpose was to keep two little kids alive.

"Once we moved here, I never realized how awful Jude had been to me for the last eight years of our marriage. He is constantly putting me down and building himself up, never owning up to his mistakes, blaming me for his problems, that I will beg him to take me back, tells me he's the better parent when it comes to dealing with Levi's behavioral problems, and the worst one that no one will love me the way he loved me because he knew me back when I was the adventurous one.

"I began to have awful thoughts that I wouldn't be able to have peace unless I ended my life; that my kids would be better off with their dad. It doesn't help that Jude calls every week not just to talk to the kids, but to remind me of everything I have told you. The only things that have been keeping me going are Levi and Harper," Evie concluded.

Dr. Bennett listened intently taking notes and handed her a box of tissues that sat on an end table. Evie grabbed one and wiped her eyes. She had never entirely told anyone how she truly felt. "I don't know what to do to cope with his words or how to brush it off. What suggestions do you have, Doc?" Evie asked. "Well," Dr. Bennett began, "what was he like when you first met him? And how did you meet him?" "I met him in the library during my sophomore year at University of Maryland. It was a quick, intense, and passionate romance. He was so charming.

"Once we were married, I noticed little things and put-downs towards me, but I knew my sister and her husband had to go through some adjustments as well, so I ignored them. However, they never went away, even after four years of marriage. Once Levi was born, they progressively got worse and worse. Once I called Jude at 11:00 PM to see if he was coming home, and he told me I knew better than to call him at work since he would lose his job if he didn't get back to his meeting. I later found out he was with a call girl. As the years progressed, his rudeness and inconsideration for everyone else besides him grew exponentially," Evie said.

"Well, I've only heard one side of the story, but it sounds like Jude may be a narcissist. They are difficult to get along with," Dr. Bennett said, "They tend to gaslight. He sees himself way differently than how he truly is."

"How can I stop his words from affecting me? I have cried myself to sleep just about every night since I moved here because of his words. What can I do?"

"Take everything he says with a grain of salt. When he tries to manipulate you, remember all you have accomplished so far. Be mentally strong, remember your self-worth, and let his words brush off your shoulders. I would also recommend setting up boundaries. I will let you think of those boundaries whether it's co-parenting, personal lives, that sort of thing."

"Thank you, Dr. Bennett."

"You're welcome. Now, do you feel like you need some validation and positive affirmations about yourself?"

Evie thought about that and responded, "Not all the time. It's nice to hear now and then."

"All right. I will make sure you get it occasionally from myself, the band, other employees, and especially Beau."

"Why 'especially' Beau?" Evie asked.

"I know you guys are really close, and usually, people need to hear words of affirmation from those they trust."

"We are close. I've never had a friend like him before."

Dr. Bennett could tell Evie would not admit her own feelings right away. "What makes him so different?"

"He's always there for me and my kids. We just make each other happy."

"Why does he make you happy?" Dr. Bennett probed.

"Because my feelings for him are deeper than just a friendship." Evie's voice became super mousy as she spoke.

"Indeed, they are."

"Are you still my therapist or a nosy coworker?" Evie joked.

"Both, I guess. Sorry if that is too personal."

Evie shrugged. "Well, we're all family now, anyways. The truth is, I'm afraid of getting hurt again. Also, I know that if Beau and I dated, I would be all in; no going back, and that terrifies me because I'm still trying to deal with a narcissistic ex-husband. So I'm not ready to open myself up that way again no matter how kind, funny, handsome, dorky, strong, and protective he is. I've told people I don't have time to date, but it's my fear. I don't want another guy telling me the same things Jude tells me already, so why ruin my friendship with Beau?" Evie asked.

"Do you honestly think Beau would ever tell you that you've lost your sex appeal and sense of adventure?" Dr. Bennett asked. Evie paused before shaking her head. "Not in a million years would he do that," Evie said, "so the problem lies with me. I'm the freaked out one here who shuts people out the first sign of conflict."

"Don't be so hard on yourself. You are a very independent woman who likes to do everything herself. Maybe when you feel that urge to push Beau away, let your guard down, and let him help you. Accepting help does not make you weak. It makes you smart."

"I will try, but it's complicated. I've just bottled up my emotions and shoved them down since I was a teenager dealing with my mom's fight with cancer. I always felt like we had bigger problems at home, and I didn't want to stress my mom out with my stupid adolescent things because she was already sick from cancer treatments."

"Well, start practicing. Maybe if you opened up and communicated a bit more, Beau would be able to help you."

"Scary thing for me to do. When I tried communicating with Jude, he made it all about him because… well, narcissist."

"Indeed, but Beau isn't one, so it's okay to talk to him. I bet he will be open to your thoughts, ideas, and feelings."

"I will do my best to recognize when I start to close off."

"Sounds good. You are one of my best patients willing to take counsel. Also, may I suggest changing your goal from not getting hurt to something else?"

"What do you mean?"

"What I mean is, what kind of relationships do you want your children to have? Do you want Harper to be in an abusive relationship like you were, or do you want to see her married for years and years to a man who loves her unconditionally?" Dr. Bennett asked Evie.

"Definitely the latter. So, what goal would you suggest?" Evie asked.

"Well, what kind of a relationship do you think a strong, independent woman has?"

"Probably one where her man supports her in all of her endeavors, loves her no matter what, and lets her be herself," Evie responded.

"Well, who do you know right now who can give you that?" Dr. Bennett asked rhetorically because he already knew the answer. So did Evie, and she thought to herself, *Beau.*

"You are good. Thank you."

"That's why they pay me the big bucks. And you're welcome. If you need any more therapy, we will consider it as part of your benefits," Dr. Bennett chuckled. Evie chuckled as well.

Beau walked back into the living room and saw Evie sitting down on the couch across from Pete. "What's going on?" he asked suspiciously. Evie smiled at him. "I just needed to talk to Dr. Bennett for a few minutes," Evie responded. "You okay?" he asked her. She nodded. Beau looked at Dr. Bennett to get reassurance. "Nothing some talking can't fix," Dr. Bennett said with a little smile on the emphasis. He soon picked up his briefcase and walked down the hallway.

Evie stood up to follow, but Beau lightly grabbed her arm. Evie, feeling herself close off, fought the urge as Beau's wise almond-shaped hooded blue eyes bore into her soul, but it was harder than she thought.

"What's wrong? Why were you talking to Pete? You have black running down your cheek," Beau said, tracing the mascara and eyeliner line going down Evie's cheek. She tried shrugging it off as she wiped the mascara runoff. *Too hard. Not ready*, she thought to herself. "I just needed some advice on how to handle some stuff."

"Like what? Please tell me."

"It's difficult for me to tell you because... I'm...." The urge got harder.

Beau finally had enough of the walls Evie kept putting up. As calmly as he could, he said, "It's okay. Nothing you can say or do will scare me. Evie, come on. What's going on?"

Evie surrendered, finally letting her guard down. "Jude tells me constantly I am an unattractive woman because he watched me push two humans out of my body. No man will ever love me the way he did, and I'm no longer adventurous and sexy." At first, Beau started to chuckle and said, "And you believe him?" Evie began sobbing and covered her face because Beau's reaction was not what she was hoping.

Beau's heart sank as he realized he said the wrong thing. Evie tried to wipe her tears away, but she kept crying harder. Beau wrapped his arms around her shoulders, and Evie wrapped her arms around his waist. "I'm so sorry. I didn't mean to be so insensitive," Beau said, trying to calm Evie down. "Jude's right," she said sniffling. "He is NOT right. Far from the truth," Beau reassured.

"Where are the kids?" "Shh, they are fine. Laila's got them. They are eating snacks in the kitchen," he said, rubbing her shoulders. "I should go get them," Evie said sobbing, getting ready to walk away, trying to put another wall up. "Don't you dare get away from me," Beau said, holding her tighter. "They'd be better off without me, anyway," Evie said, still sobbing. "Shh, don't say that," Beau said, holding her tighter. Evie buried her face into Beau's chest sobbing harder. The pain she had felt for the past six months had erupted, but as painful as it was to admit the abuse out loud, Evie was very thankful Beau was there to comfort her.

How can she believe that asshole, Beau thought to himself, *she is everything Jude says she isn't.* Beau was tempted to fly to Baltimore, punch Jude in the face, and fly back home. However, given individual life experiences, Beau knew that wouldn't fix the situation. He began to feel helpless as he held Evie. Beau rubbed her shoulders occasionally but wasn't sure if his presence was helping at all. Suddenly, they heard little footsteps down the hallway. "Mommy?" Evie heard Levi said. "Mommy?" Harper said. Both kids walked into the living room and saw Beau hugging their mom. Levi ran to his mom and hugged her leg. "What's wrong?" he asked. "Your mom is sad. Should we go to the couch to cheer her up?" Beau asked. Levi and Harper nodded their heads. Beau led Evie to the couch, sat down, helped her sit down, wrapped his arms around her again, and helped Levi and Harper climb onto the couch. Both kids wrapped their arms around their mom. Beau kept rubbing her shoulder with his right hand.

Evie had never felt so much support before except from her parents when she lived at home. Jude would never comfort her like this. Her children showed their love for their mom by hugging her and laying their heads against her. "Are you happy yet, Mommy?" Levi asked. "I am getting there, Bub," Evie said, starting to wheeze. Harper leaned in and kissed her mom on the cheek. "Hey guys, why don't we sleep here tonight. Let's go get you ready for bed," Beau said as he laid Evie down on the couch gently.

He helped the kids get ready for bed and put them up in the bedroom where Evie and the kids lived when they first moved to the Bay area.

Afterward, Beau went back to the living room. Evie was asleep, but still catching her breath. He lifted her head off the couch, slid behind her, wrapped an arm around her, and proceeded to fall asleep. Throughout the night, Evie would occasionally cry in her sleep, waking Beau up, but he was there for her. Even though he felt a little disturbed by her behavior, Beau knew that Evie needed the support that she provided for him. He eventually decided to lay down on the floor. Beau didn't know if it was sleeping on the floor, Evie's frequent cries, or a combination of the two, but Beau slept horribly throughout that night, but all he cared about was making sure Evie knew he cared about her.

The next morning, Evie awoke in the living room, lying down on the couch. When she sat up, the pounding in her head started, and the slits in her eyes became super thin as she looked around the room and realized Beau was fast asleep on the floor by the couch. There was a blanket draped over her to keep her warm. She felt like a complete idiot because Beau finally saw the vulnerable side she hid from people, including her parents. Everyone always looked to her for support, but that night she crumbled.

Evie stood up quietly to go to the bathroom. She took a good look at herself in the mirror. Her eyes were as bloodshot and swollen as they felt. Her makeup was smeared all over her face from crying. She washed it off in the sink. Taking the day off sounded like an excellent idea to her so that she could rest some more.

She walked out of the bathroom. Beau stirred when she walked past him and climbed on the couch. He woke up and reached for his back. His back hurt so bad from the hard floor, but he couldn't think about that right now. "Morning, Beautiful. How are you feeling?" Beau asked. "Fine, I guess," Evie said, rubbing her head and eyes, "I didn't mean to wake you up." "No, it's fine," Beau said, trying to stretch and ignore his pain. They looked at each other. "Why don't we take the day off?" he asked her. "I know I can, but can you take the day off? The tour starts in 5 months, and the album needs to hit the deadline in a few weeks for promotion," she said. "I will tell the guys that my best friend needs me today," he said. "That will make them happy," Evie said sarcastically. "They can work on some stuff without me today," Beau said. "That means you will have to relinquish control, and we all know how much you love that," Evie said sarcastically but winced in pain because laughing hurt her head. Beau smiled. "This takes precedence. You need more sleep so that your migraine can go away."

"All right. Where's Levi and Harper?"

"In the spare bedroom you stayed in by the bathroom.""Okay. Who put them to bed?"

"I did."

Evie rubbed her head as she and Beau talked. "You were here the whole night?"

"Yes."

"Sorry if I kept you up."

"You've been dealing with some stuff for a while. I just wanted to make sure you were okay, and I didn't want you to be alone."

Evie lightly smiled. "Thanks."

"Mommy, are you awake?" Levi said, peeking his head around the corner.

Evie smiled. "Yes, Bub. Come here," she said.

Levi and Harper came running into the living room and gave Evie the biggest hug. She kissed both of them on the cheek. "Mommy, you still sad?" Harper asked. "Not after seeing your faces," Evie said, kissing her sweet daughter. Harper laid her head underneath her mom's chin. Levi rested his head on his mom's shoulder. "I love you, Mommy," Levi said. "I love you, too." Evie held back tears again. "Love you, Mommy," Harper said. "Love you, sweet girl."

Evie wrapped her arms around her children, hugging them tightly and kissing their cheeks. Beau watched this sweet moment and smiled. He checked his smartwatch, which read 7:45. "Luke should be here by now, so I will go tell him we are taking the day off, and then I will take you guys home," Beau said. "Thank you," Evie said.

Beau walked into the recording room, finding Luke sitting at the drum set. He tapped his friend on the shoulder. "Hey, what's up?" Luke asked. "I need to take today off. Evie and the kids need me," Beau said. Luke grimaced a little. "All right, but we will need to work twice as long tomorrow, and we will make certain decisions without you," Luke said. "I am okay with that for now," Beau said.

They bumped fists, and Beau walked back to the living room. He helped Evie stand up, picked up Harper, and they walked out to Evie's car. Beau helped Evie sit down in the passenger seat, put Harper in her car seat, and secured Levi in his booster seat. Once he knew the kids would be safe, he climbed into the driver's side and proceeded to drive to Evie's townhouse.

Beau pulled up into the carport, climbed out, and pulled Harper out of her car seat. Evie climbed out of the car and helped Levi get out of the vehicle. "We need to get you off to school," Evie said to Levi before grabbing her head. Her migraine was getting worse. "I will help with that and take him," Beau chimed in, "You need to rest."

"Really, Beau, I can handle this," she said wincing in pain as the migraine disagreed with her. "I know, but you don't have to do everything by yourself. You let me into your life last night. Would you be willing to do it again?" he asked. Evie remembered the commitment she made to Dr. Bennet about letting her guard down when she felt like it was going up. "All right. They need to eat breakfast," Evie said, feeling uncomfortable with the help. "On it. You go to your room and rest. I will take care of them," Beau said. Evie smiled, walked into her room, changed into a racerback tank with pajama bottoms, and laid down in her soft, comfy bed and fell back asleep.

Beau quickly got Levi and Harper their breakfast. "Okay, cheerios?" Beau asked. "I want pancakes," Levi said. "I wan' pa'cakes," Harper imitated. "Not today, guys. Maybe tomorrow when your mom is feeling better," Beau said, opening the fridge to get the milk out and looking at the lactose-free milk carton. "Who cannot have milk?" "Mom can't," Levi said. *Good to know*, Beau thought, remembering grocery shopping with the Long's.

Once the kids finished their breakfast, Beau sent Levi to his room to change his clothes. Beau was extremely thankful that Harper could dress herself. He helped her pick out her clothes and left her room so she could change. Once both of them changed clothes, Beau loaded them back up in Evie's car and took Levi to school. He came back, pulled Harper out of the car, and asked, "What would you like to do?"

"Uuuuuummmm, watch the circus," she said as they walked back inside the townhouse.

Beau froze, not fully understanding what the toddler wanted. "What's the circus?" he asked her.

"With elephants," Harper perfectly pronounced.

Beau had to pull out his phone and do a search on elephants and the circus movies. A sappy movie first appeared, but after doing some scrolling, Beau realized Harper meant *Dumbo*. He quickly found the movie while Harper went to go get her blankie and a baby. After sitting with Harper for 10 minutes, Beau fell asleep, himself. He slept through the whole movie before Harper started poking his stomach.

"Beau, i's done," Harper said. Beau grunted. "Beau! Wake up!" Harper demanded as she began shaking Beau. Even though the shakes weren't strong, Beau finally opened his eyes. "Okay, what do you want to go do, now?" Beau asked. "Pway wit' my babies and kitchen," Harper said. "Is it okay if I go make your mom and me some breakfast?" he asked. "Yeah," she said, super sweetly. Beau loved how much spunk, sass, and sweetness Harper had. She was a lot like her mother. "All right. If you need me, I will be in the kitchen," Beau said. "Okay, bye!" she said before hugging Beau. He squeezed her extra tight and watched her climb the stairs.

Beau walked to the kitchen and began searching through the fridge. He found eggs, cheese, bacon, ground sausage, tomatoes, cilantro, and some spinach. Beau decided to make Evie and himself omelets as well as bring her protein shake. He whipped everything up as quickly as he could. Miraculously, Beau found a tray with foldable legs in one of the cupboards. He put both plates of food, glasses of water, and Evie's protein shake on the tray. Beau found a little vase, remembering a peony bush outside. He filled it with water, grabbed some scissors, and cut a peony off and put it in the vase. After setting the vase on the tray, Beau carried it into Evie's room.

Evie was fast asleep in her bed, burritoed up in her covers lying down in the fetal position. That was the first time Beau saw her sleep peacefully. Beau considered coming back in about another half hour to let her sleep some more because it had only been an hour and a half since she went back to bed. However, Evie smelled the food that entered her room and woke up. Beau propped the legs of the tray up, took his shoes off, and sat down on Evie's bed. She sat up as well. Beau noticed she had changed into a tank and jogger pants. Once she was propped up, they began eating.

"Feel any better?" Beau asked.

"Much better. Thanks," Evie said.

"Good. How's the food?"

"Delicious. Where's Harper?"

"In her room playing. She gets more like you every day," Beau said, laughing.

Evie also laughed. "Yeah, she does that."

They proceeded to eat their food. "Sorry if I scared you last night. That is not exactly my proudest moment."

"It's fine. I often forget that I am not the only one with problems. I am sorry I made you tell me."

"It's okay. I tend to keep everything to myself, so my parents don't know the full situation, my sister doesn't know, not even some of my other friends here in San Francisco or Annapolis know. Only you and Dr. Bennett know the abuse I've been putting up with. I rarely ask for help unless I am sure I need it. It was a bit of a relief telling you."

"I hope you know you can talk to me about anything, too."

"I know that."

They smiled at each other. "I know you said last night that you thought your kids would be better off without you, but please don't think like that. Sometimes we feel inadequate for what comes our way, and that voice that tells us we are is tumultuous. You need to learn to ignore that voice. It's one of the hardest things I've ever had to do to learn and keep on learning."

"I know. I'm going to talk to Dr. Bennett about once a week to help with more positive affirmations about myself," Evie said.

"Would it help if they also came from me?" Beau asked.

Evie smiled. "Yes, it would. Dr. Bennett made the suggestion last night as well." They smiled at each other again.

Beau decided to unpin the conversation that needed to take place with Evie. "You know you don't have to put up with Jude's shit, right?" Beau said.

Evie hesitated. "This is all I know from him," she responded. "I know you can put a stop to this. Start by not answering his phone calls. If you need a good lawyer to rewrite certain clauses in your divorce agreement, we have good ones. Take a stand. I know he will react like a child, but I can help you get through it. What do you say?" Beau asked.

Evie thought about what Beau said. "I think you are right. I will consider talking to the lawyers, and take that stand," she said. Beau nodded.

Beau stayed at Evie's for the rest of the day, picking Levi up from school, helping her with Harper and around the house. Later, Beau and Evie watched a comedy on Netflix in the living room. Beau knew they needed a good laugh. Levi came out of his room a couple of times to try prolonging the process of going to bed. Beau did his best to give Evie a chance to rest some more.

Beau's arms wrapped around Evie while she laid her head against his chest. The sound of his heart had become one of her favorite sounds. Beau's real laugh was even becoming one of her favorite sounds. They lingered in that position for about two minutes before Evie sat up. "Thank you for spending the day with us," she said. "You're welcome. I stayed to be with you, though. I always stay for you," Beau responded.

Evie blushed before Beau asked the question, "Do you believe him?" "What do you mean?" "Do you believe what Jude said about you is true?" Evie looked down at the floor. "I don't want to." "Well, you shouldn't because you are beautiful." Evie still looked at the ground. *He says that because I'm the only woman working for them,* she thought, putting herself down. Beau could sense her self-doubt, so he lightly lifted her chin softly and gazed into those beautiful blue intense eyes that knew him so well. "How could he not fall in love with those eyes? Your smile? Sense of humor? Selfless nature?" Beau said softly before leaning in. Evie could feel all the blood rushing to her head and ears as their noses touched. They both leaned in further finding each other's lips.

The kiss was very tender. Beau and Evie felt each other's emotions in that kiss, whether it was sadness, happiness, excitement, and fear as Beau gently caressed her jawline. Evie pulled away for a minute to look at Beau's facial expression. He looked at her like she was the only thing that mattered to him. She kissed Beau again with a bit more fire. Beau's arms wrapped around her waist as he pulled her closer, and Evie's arms wrapped around his neck, pulling him closer to her. As Beau laid down on top of Evie rubbing her leg, she could sense where the kiss was going, and immediately pulled away and jumped up off the sectional.

"What's wrong?" he asked out of breath, calming himself. Evie wasn't sure how to respond pacing the room. "Um… I can sense where this is going, and I'm just not ready for that yet. I am so scared right now. If we continue, that's it. There's no going back. I also don't know if this is all brought on by my freakout last night. I'm scared of getting hurt, I'm scared of myself, and I don't… know…."

Beau quickly stood up and wrapped his arms around hugging her tightly. Evie began to calm down and wrapped her arms around his waist. "I'm sorry if I jumped the gun," Beau began, "Maybe this is all brought on by what happened." Evie could feel the comfort zone returning as she listened to Beau's heartbeat.

As he held her in his arms, Beau made a bold move with his words. "What if it wasn't?" he asked. The words pierced Evie's core. "What?"

Beau adjusted to make sure Evie was looking in his eyes. "What if the kiss wasn't brought on by your meltdown? What if I've had feelings for you since the first park outing when we talked about music?" Beau asked.

"Really? My speech about *Bohemian Rhapsody*?"

"Yes, it was that effective."

Evie lightly chuckled.

"So, am I the only one who has detected chemistry between us, or…?" Beau tapered.

"No, you haven't imagined it. For me, it started when this tainted rockstar took time out of his day to go for a walk with a single mother and her two kids explaining the meaning of his tattoos to her little boy."

Beau rubbed his thumb against Evie's cheek. They kissed each other passionately again wrapping arms tighter. *Is this the greenlight,* Beau thought to himself. *It's happening... It's actually happening.... No, not ready,* Evie thought to herself as Beau backed Evie up against the wall. "Wait," Evie said out of breath. "What?" Beau whispered as he kissed her neck, playing those thoughts he had since Halloween. "One of us needs to think straight," Evie said, pushing Beau away.

Beau felt confused and a little rejected. "What does that mean?"

"It means nothing more is going to happen tonight," Evie said.

"So, where does that leave us?" Beau asked still not satisfied, "Do you want me to leave?"

"No," Evie responded.

"No?"

"No."

"I'm confused."

"Me too, but all I know is that we…"

Evie tried to explain what she wanted, but every word sounded like she was all in or stringing him along, and she didn't want to do that to him. "Okay, so what do you want?" Beau asked. "I don't want you to leave tonight, or any night until I leave to visit my family next week for Thanksgiving," Evie said, grabbing his hand.

"Okay, can you help me understand what all this means? Are we friends, more than friends, in a relationship? Help me out here."

"We are two very close unplatonic friends spending more time together, watching a movie together, and falling asleep on my bed," Evie said.

"So an old married couple?" Beau teased.

"Laugh all you want," Evie teased back before saying, "but this is what I'm comfortable with right now. After my trip, we can discuss what this is." Beau nodded and understood. "I can live with that," he said.

Chapter 13

Nothing Else Matters

The next morning, Beau woke up first and watched Evie sleep for a few minutes. She began to stir a little, so he kissed her on the cheek and said, "Good morning, Beautiful." Evie smiled sleepily. "Good morning," she said, remembering the events from the night before. They kissed, finally. Beau told her how he felt, and she reciprocated the feelings. As Beau kissed Evie's cheek again, Evie found Beau's lips and kissed him. It was a tender kiss. Despite both of them having morning breath, Beau and Evie did not mind one bit.

Beau spent the night every night at Evie's house for the rest of the week. He enjoyed waking up every morning to Evie sleeping soundly, making breakfast for her, playing with the kids in pajamas, and holding Evie as she fell asleep in his arms while watching a movie in her room.

For the first time in nine months, Evie stopped crying herself to sleep. Beau's presence, as well as the displays of affection, helped with the healing process she had been going through. More often than not, Beau would wake up before everyone, make Levi and Harper their breakfast, and bring breakfast in bed to Evie. He always made sure his first words to her were, "Good morning, Beautiful," making sure Dr. Bennett's prescription for Evie was being utilized. As Beau continued to stay the night, Evie realized how effortless their relationship would be, and her anxiety of it all eventually went away.

The day before Thanksgiving, Beau drove Evie and the kids to the airport. The weather was extremely brisk outside, but everyone was bundled up nice and warm. Beau found a beanie for little boys that Levi was wearing with Death Toll's logo on it, and Harper's ears were covered by ear muffs that Evie had in her stash. Evie's brown hair, which had grown six inches since moving to the Bay area, was topped with a loose beanie with waves going down. She wore a loose colorblock grey, pink and cream sweater underneath a grey moto-jacket with dark skinny jeggings and booties. Beau was wearing a plaid shirt underneath a black moto-jacket with fitted jeans and work boots. It was a long flight from San Francisco to Annapolis. The weather was cold in San Francisco, and Evie knew it would be colder in Annapolis.

Beau walked Evie's family to security carrying Harper. He set her down and helped Evie get kids ready to walk through security, and began setting carry-ons on the conveyor belt. Evie took off her jacket, hat, shoes, and pulled all metal objects and her phone out of her pockets. She put them into the little baskets to be scanned. Beau helped Levi take off his jacket and hat. Just as he began reaching for Harper's jacket, Evie said, "She doesn't have to take anything off. I checked." Beau stopped and watched Harper walk towards her mom. He couldn't help but notice how beautiful Evie was.

"I will miss you guys," he said. "I will miss you, Beau," Levi said as he wrapped his little arms around Beau's leg. Beau grabbed Levi's arms and lifted him up into a big hug. Levi squeezed his arms very tightly around

Beau's neck. He put Levi back down, and Harper lept into Beau's arms. Beau hugged her extra tight and gave her a kiss on the cheek. He put Harper back down and turned to look at Evie. "So, I will see you in three days," Evie said. Beau nodded his head. "I know, but it's still going to be hard having you away," he replied. "Well, work extra hard on your album. Plus, we can always do Facetime," Evie reminded him.

Beau wrapped his arms around Evie. She wrapped her arms around him. His cologne was very potent, and she soaked up every ounce of it so she could recall it on her trip. Beau inhaled the scent of Evie's hair, which always smelled like roses. He contemplated kissing her but wasn't sure how Levi would react since they never kissed in front of the kids.

"Beau, you can kiss my mom if you want. I don't care," Levi said. The grown-ups laughed. "Thanks, Buddy," Beau replied before wrapping an arm around Evie, pulling her in, and kissing her sweetly. Evie kissed him back before wrapping her arms around his neck to give him a hug. Beau wrapped his arms around her waist, not wanting to let her go. Finally, they let go of each other. Beau smiled at Evie, and she smiled back.

Evie picked Harper up and asked Levi, "Will you grab my sweater so that we can walk through the big rectangle?" Levi did just what he was asked to do, and they walked through the metal detector. Once they got to the other side, Evie turned back around and waved to Beau telling the kids to wave at him as well. He waved back and watched the cute little family he had grown to care about gather their belongings.

Beau walked through the terminal to the parking garage. He found his black Range Rover, climbed in, and pulled out of the parking garage. His mind kept wandering back to Evie. He reflected on the past few months getting to know her. He loved going to do all the mundane outings, Evie would say, with her and the kids, playing Song Styles in the car, and going to Zumba and Strong classes with Evie. He loved watching her dance.

Beau loved Evie's spunk, determination, compassionate nature, and firmness. He remembered the first meeting he had with her and what she said. "Clean up your act, or else I will replace you with any idiot who can sing. If I have to do the singing, I will. You have been through too much already to back-peddle now. Don't let your family die in vain. You cleaned up for them. Now it's time to clean up for yourself and your bandmates. They all love and support you. Take care of yourself again." Those words motivated him.

Since then, he tried so hard to focus on the music that made him happy. He really worked harder than ever to maintain his friendships with Luke, Kade, and Richard. He did not expect to fall in love with his tour manager.

Suddenly, his phone rang, causing him to jump. He read his dashboard, noticing that Luke was calling him. Beau answered, "Hey, man. What's up?" "Hey, can you head back to the studio? Rick has this cool bass riff you need to hear," Luke said. "Yep. I just dropped the Longs off at the airport. I should be back in 20 minutes," Beau said. "Cool. See ya, man!" Luke said. "Bye," Beau ended the call.

Beau headed to the studio as quickly as possible. Despite his longing to see Evie again, he knew he had to work. Beau was also interested in what Rick came up with. He loved improvising with his bandmates because it was their writing style. Beau pulled into the parking lot, climbed out of the Rover, and walked inside the studio.

Beau walked through the doors into the recording area and sat down among his guitars, amps, headphones, and notepads. He put the headphones on so he could hear what Rick came up with. "Okay, let's hear it," Luke said. Rick went on to play this riff on the bass that was very Van Halen-esque with more of their style. Eventually, Beau started messing around on his guitar, and eventually came up with a riff that complimented the bass. Luke immediately began a thrash metal drum beat. Kade listened to everything and finally started soloing. "Okay, pause!" Beau shouted and signaled, "Everyone write down what they just did. Rick, what notes did you play?" Rick responded, and everyone wrote it down. After about one hour, they had a song written and ready to record for the next day. "Okay, guys. Let's take a break," Luke said. Everybody set their guitars down.

Everybody got up to go get a drink, but Beau stayed sitting. He picked up his custom Gibson guitar and began noodling around with some arpeggios, which reminded him of Evie, her eyes, her smile, her selfless nature, her talents as a violinist, and her dazzling body. Beau began playing the E minor arpeggio but very legato. He soon improvised playing a solo that went along with the chord changes in the same style. Beau liked what he heard and quickly wrote it down repeating the riff over and over again. Then Beau began to embellish the theme even more.

The song was unusual for the band's style, but Beau wanted this song to be different from the others. He hadn't written a love song in years since he met Phoebe. None of the songs ever made it onto an album because they were too sappy, but Beau had a feeling about this song.

After the Intro was written, he decided to pause and write lyrics while he was on a role. He thought about his and Evie's current circumstances. They were, as Evie put it, unplatonic friends, but there were a lot of unspoken words Beau wanted to say to her.

His phone started ringing, causing him to jump. He pulled it out of his pocket and saw that Evie was video-calling. He smiled and immediately picked it up. "Hey!" he said. "Hi, Beau!" Levi shouted as their faces appeared on his screen. Levi was sitting in the window seat while Evie sat in the next chair with Harper on her lap. "Hi, Beau!" Harper said in her broken up toddler language. Evie smiled at her kids. "We just got in our seats. We will be taking off in about 15 minutes," she said.

"That's good. Everything going alright?" he asked.

"As good as they can be in my position, but I will be pulling out iPads soon to watch movies."

"All right. I am just at the studio. We have one new song to record."

"Already? That is awesome! I can't wait to hear it."

"It's a blend of our old stuff and new stuff more on the thrash side. I know you prefer a different style… "

"Hey, I have an open mind about music. I once listened to a concerto for orchestra and a florist. Nothing surprises me."

"A concerto for orchestra and florist?" Beau said, wondering how that would go.

"My reaction exactly. Went completely over my head."

Beau laughed. "I will have to look that up."

"Not without me. Maybe there is something I missed about it." They both laughed.

"Evie," Beau began. "Yeah?" she responded. "I miss you. I miss all of you, but I especially miss you," he said. Beau watched Evie do that girly thing she always did whenever Beau gave her a compliment; blush, smile, and bite her bottom lip.

"I miss you, too. Do you miss Beau?" she asked her kids. "Yeah!" they both said very enthusiastically. Beau smiled even bigger, but Evie could see his eyes weren't sparkling as much as they normally do.

"Want me to cut my trip short?" she asked. Beau shook his head.

"No. I know you've missed your parents, your sister, and you need to meet your niece. Levi and Harper need to see everyone as well. Besides, I have to work anyway. We are a couple songs away from completing our album."

"True," Evie agreed.

"So, I better get back to work. I started working on this melodic ballad that I want to show you when you get back. It's in 6/8 time," Beau said.

"That's different. I can't wait to hear it!" They both smiled at each other. "Okay, say bye-bye to Beau." "Bye-bye!" all three said, waving. "Bye!" Beau said, waving back. He pushed the end button, and his phone went dark.

He sat for a moment thinking about the distance that would soon be between them, and how easy it was to talk to Evie in person, over the phone, text, and video calls. *Distance won't change our relationship*, he thought to himself. He suddenly wrote down the first line about how close their friendship and hopefully their relationship would be once they talked about it. Beau also wrote about how heartfelt, vulnerable, and open he had been with Evie. He knew just how much she mattered to him.

A melody came into his head that went along with the guitar. He sang the words along with it, picked up his guitar, and sang it again while playing the accompaniment. He started to reflect on the past couple of months. He remembered his first Zumba class with Evie, watching her dance, going to the park with her and the kids, giving her a refresh on how to play the guitar, learning how to play the violin, and watching her take care of the kids.

He remembered his talks with Evie about his underlying issues as well as hers the past few days. He remembered the trust they built with each other and how much he trusted her. He quickly wrote the words down about their many "mundane," as Evie would put it, adventures. However, the various trips never bored Beau.

On the contrary, he loved every single outing with the Longs whether it was storytime at the library or trips to the pier watching the kids play on the playground next door to the aquarium. He remembered holding Evie's hand extra tight that day. Beau knew they had a strong relationship and bond. He also mentioned in his lyrics about how he doesn't say these sorts of things to anyone. He realized he needed to tell Evie how he truly felt about her whether by listening to this song or just a simple conversation.

Beau began contemplating what the repercussions of dating Evie would be since she was Death Toll's tour manager. What would the band think? What would her parents think? Would Jude fight extra harder to take the kids away if he found out his ex-wife was dating an addict? Suddenly, two thoughts came to his head. He didn't care; He loved her. *I love this girl*, he thought for the first time, *and I love those kids*.

Beau included not caring about what anyone thought in the lyrics. He felt like the lyrics were pretty complete. Beau would just repeat the verse again because the words had a particular emphasis on them.

However, he felt the final chorus needed an extra punch. Beau wanted to really emphasize that he didn't care what anyone thought whether it was Evie's parents, the band, or Jude; especially Jude. Beau knew all the trouble, pain, heartache, and drama he caused for Evie, and he wrote them down. Beau played around with the phrases a bit to make it as poetic as possible. He soon started writing a melody for the chorus that complimented the verse. He kept going with melodic lines and harmonies for the guitar solo and interludes.

Luke was the first one to walk back into the studio to his drums. He heard the opening melody and noticed the 6/8 time. Luke sat down on his stool and listened to Beau play the melodic riff. He hadn't heard this much passion come from Beau's playing in about 8 years.

Luke decided to compliment the guitar with a simple downbeat on his bass drum, and snare drum with the typical cymbal hit on counts 2, 3, 5, and 6. He occasionally played on the bass drum on other counts.

They played together through half of the song before Beau realized what Luke was doing and stopped. They both stared at each other for what seemed like forever. "Did you not want me to come in?" Luke asked.

"I wasn't expecting you. I was in the zone. You played the kit just the way I heard it in my head. I got caught up in the moment, but soon realized it was real. I think this is why we work so well together, man," Beau concluded.

Luke pointed at Beau with a drumstick. "Twenty-two years and counting!" Luke said.

"Can you write down what you just did so that we don't forget?" Beau asked.

"Yep," Luke responded as he grabbed a notepad and pen.

"What is this song called anyways?" Luke asked.

Beau examined the lyrics, and a phrase jumped out at him. "*Nothing Else Matters*," Beau responded. "*Nothing Else Matters*," Luke said, writing the title on top of his paper.

"I am curious. Did Evie inspire the song?" he asked. Beau hesitated to answer because he dreaded the reaction. "Yeah, she did."

"I should have known since you started going to the gym with her and talking about Zumba, whatever that is." Beau laughed. So did Luke.

"Beau, this is good."

"Really?"

"Yeah. We were all rooting for you two. She has helped you so much, and we have seen a drastic change in the way she carries herself because of you. You compliment each other very well; very compatible," Luke said.

Soon, Kade and Rick came back and heard what Beau and Luke were putting together. "What the…," Rick began, "is that 6/8 time?" Beau nodded his head. Rick quickly picked up his bass. "This needs a few good down beats and embellishments. What key?" Rick responded. "E minor," Beau said as he started from the beginning.

Rick looked down at Beau's notes to follow the chord changes. Rick soon had his own part written down on his notepad. When Beau said E minor, Kade quickly picked up his guitar and started noodling himself with some arpeggios and chord changes. Beau stopped. "Hey, Kade, I love your enthusiasm, but I actually wrote the lead guitar part. Sorry, man."

Kade was always a humble guy. "Not a problem. How does it go?"

"Well, you weren't off by much. I played with some arpeggios and came up with this." Beau showed him how to play it as well as his notes.

Kade caught a glimpse of the title of the song. "Really? Now that Evie is in the picture, we don't matter?" Kade said, teasing. Luke, Richard, and Kade began laughing. Beau just stared at the ground. He wasn't sure how to respond to the joke. Beau stood.

"No, wait!" Kade said. "We think it's great. She adds an element to the band and to you that we like. Plus, Levi and Harper are super cute and fun. We need their energy, and you need Evie," Kade concluded.

Beau observed the band's facial expressions, which were supportive. "She just does something to me, you know," Beau said. "Makes you a better man," Rick said, "as Phoebe did." Beau nodded.

"Well," Luke said, "Rick, I know we were working on your song, but let's get *Nothing Else Matters* recorded. This is definitely going on our next album. Kade, can Beau play both lead and rhythm while recording?" Kade nodded. "Yes, how about I go listen to you guys and help mix the sound?" Kade said as he stood up and walked to the audio room. Death Toll agreed.

It took two hours to record, but soon Beau's song was recorded and ready to be added to their new album besides the vocals. Beau suddenly had an idea. "Hey, Luke, when the Longs get back, could you watch the kids? I want to take Evie out on our official first date," Beau said. "Sure. I will double-check with Jetta." "Thanks," Beau said.

Chapter 14

The First Date

Evie and Beau talked every night through video calls. He would sing the lullaby Evie would sing to the kids before she tucked them into bed at her parents' house. Then Evie and Beau would end up talking for four hours. "So, anything new happen today?" Beau asked. "Nothing really. We went to the Smithsonian and the White House today to see the Christmas lights," Evie responded. "That's cool. Has Jude tried to make contact?" "He called once, but I ignored it. Eventually, he started texting me the same old stuff, so I blocked his number. I'm going to need the number to Death Toll's lawyer," Evie said.

Beau nodded his head, very pleased with her decision. "I will send it to you when we end the call."

"Thank you."

"Hey, Evie?"

"Yeah, Beau?"

"The suspense is killing me. Have you thought about us at all during your trip?" he asked. "I have, actually," she said, smiling, trying to add to the suspense.

"Well, what did you decide?"

Evie took a deep breath before saying, "Having you around even before you kissed me felt so natural. It was almost like you should have been with us the entire time; Like you are a part of our family."

"Okay, but how do you feel about me?" Beau asked.

"If I said it out loud, it might sound stupid."

"Evie, like you, I am dense, what's the verdict?"

"Okay, fine. I like you. I like the frontman of Death Toll," Evie said, blushing.

Beau realized why Evie was afraid to say it aloud and laughed. "Now I understand why you wanted to keep it to yourself," Beau said, "but you know me better than most of those fans or roadies, so I think it makes it less stupid."

Evie smiled. "Very true. I cannot speak for many girls my age, but along with a few of them throughout the world, I have seen you in your underwear," she chuckled. Beau laughed, too.

"So, does that mean you're ready for us to start dating?" he asked.

"I think so," Evie said.

"Are you sure?" Beau asked for reassurance.

"I'm still terrified, but throughout the whole week, it felt so effortless and natural as you stayed with us," Evie said.

Beau smirked and said, "All right, then. I guess there is nothing more to discuss. You and I are going out tomorrow night after you and the kids get back."

"Really? I have some unpacking to do. The kids will be cranky, laundry, the kids will need dinner, I need to go grocery shopping ...."

"Evie, I can help take care of all that. I can come pick you up from the airport like we planned, take you back to your townhouse, help clean up, feed the kids, and take them to the Jeppsen's'. I will make sure they have stuff for bedtime as well just in case..."

"In case what?" Evie asked.

Beau suddenly became very nervous. "Well, I think we've gotten close a few times to take our relationship to a more... intimate level," Beau said as delicately as possible, "and maybe tomorrow night could finally be that step?" Beau questioned.

Evie smiled faintly with a chuckle, but Beau still couldn't get a read on her. "I can't tell if that's a 'yes' or a 'no.' Give me something," he said

"Okay, fine. Definitely that first time you kissed me, I wanted to, but, again, I chickened out. When we were in the pool Halloween night, I thought about it then. And then that first night you stayed the night, we were in the kitchen, we almost kissed. I thought about it then, too. I've also been thinking about it more this past week, and I think I'm ready," Evie concluded.

"Are you sure?"

"Positive."

"Okay, so I am taking you out on our official first date. The flight gets in at 5, right?"

"Right."

"Okay. While you get ready, I will take the kids out for dinner and drop them off at Luke's. After I drop the kids off, I will pick you up at 7."

"Okay, what are we doing?"

"We will go to a pub, play pinball or pool, eat food, and listen to some live bands. Plus, I have a surprise for you."

"Seriously, you don't have to do more than that. Plus, will you be okay with going to a pub?" Evie asked.

"No, it's band-related, but it's about you. Yes, I should be fine. I've resisted the urge many times," Beau said.

"Okay, that sounds fun. Just so you know, I hate surprises. If you're going to surprise me, don't even tell me about it. The anticipation kills me."

"I want the anticipation to kill you," Beau smirked. *Turd face*, Evie joked to herself wondering what he was planning. "All right, I will see you tomorrow around five at the airport." "Okay, bye, Beau!" "Bye, Evie."

They hung up the video call and went to bed. The next morning, Beau realized he had a little more to do to prepare for the day. He wasn't sure how Evie would feel about it, but Beau decided to call one of the cleaning companies who would often come clean his house, pick up his laundry, pick up groceries to come to wash Evie's laundry that evening. Beau made the arrangements for someone to be at her townhouse around 5:30 when they would be walking through the door. Evie had given a key to him since he cosigned the lease, so he decided to go to her townhouse and see what needed cleaning.

Beau washed everybody's bedding and towels to make sure they were clean and fresh when they got home. He swept and mopped the floors, spot vacuumed, dusted, and he even decided he would have dinner ready for them the day after they got home. Beau quickly went through the pantry and fridge to see what to throw together and freeze in the freezer, remembering what Phoebe used to make in a slow-cooker. He found some chicken still frozen and some salsa left with two days left before it expired. Beau suddenly remembered the chicken tacos Phoebe used to make. He knew there were gallon freezer bags somewhere in the kitchen since he had been cooking in it all week last week. Beau found the bags, dumped the chicken, salsa, and some taco seasoning in one, and put the bag in the freezer for chicken tacos.

Beau looked in Evie's fridge again to see if there were a few things from the grocery store she needed. He knew Evie was lactose intolerant, and the carton felt empty. There were about two eggs left as well as a little bit of whole milk. Beau also noticed that cereal was running low as well as Evie's protein powder. So Beau ran to Sprout's and Costco to pick up those items as well as a few things he might need for the night for the kids as well as himself.

Beau decided to get his Camaro washed for the date and took it to the closest do-it-yourself car wash, bringing some towels with him to dry it off. He got a haircut since his hair was getting long again. He got it cut and styled where it was really short on the bottom, but the top was long with a shaved part on his right side.

He called Luke to make sure everything was all set for him and Jetta to watch Levi and Harper. "So, will the kids be staying the night, or are you going to pick them up?" Luke asked. "They will probably stay the night," Beau said. "Ah, finally taking that plunge. What else are you guys doing tonight?" Luke asked. "We are going to dinner at Gallager's. We will listen to live bands, play pool, pinball, that sort of thing. Then afterward, I am going to take her to the studio and show her *Nothing Else Matters*."

"You still need to finish the vocals."

"I know. That's why I'm going there."

"But you'll be on your date."

"I know."

"So, are you trying to work on your date? I don't understand what you are trying to do."

"I want the vocals to be raw and real. What better way than to bring the woman who inspired the song to listen in on the recording?" Beau asked.

"Bruh, nice touch," Luke said.

"Thanks." Beau felt both invigorated and terrified at the same time.

Beau looked at the time on his phone and realized it was 4:30. "I gotta go pick them up now. I will drop Harper and Levi off in about an hour and a half," Beau said. "Okay, see ya later, man!" Luke said. "Bye, brotha," Beau said before hanging up and climbing into his Range Rover.

He drove to the airport, parked the car, and climbed out. Beau walked inside and waited on a bench in the baggage claim. He even checked to make sure the flight was on time. The flight from Annapolis said it had arrived, so he waited.

"Beau!"

Beau smiled as an enthusiastic Levi ran through the baggage claim. Beau wrapped his arms around Levi. Beau missed Levi so much it hurt. Soon, he heard little footprints approach him and saw Harper's incredible curly blonde hair in his peripheral vision. She gave him the biggest hug, too. He held the kids tightly in his arms before setting them down. "You both grew. You need to stop!" he teased. Both kids giggled.

Suddenly, the woman he wanted to see for three days came into his view. Evie wore a beanie with a Death Toll logo over her long brown hair, which made Beau smile. Evie wore an oversized grey sweater, skinny jeans, and booties with a duffle bag around her shoulder and her backpack on. She looked positively radiant. "Hi," she said. "Hey," he said. He hugged her and inhaled the rose smell of her hair.

When Evie heard him breathe in, her heart began racing. She missed Beau more than she realized. She wrapped her arms around Beau's waist. He had more of a musky smell that day, but he was always clean. Levi and Harper were each hugging Beau's legs. "So, let's get the bags," Beau said as the carousel began to turn. Beau immediately grabbed the bags and picked Harper up. She felt denser than three days ago.

"How was visiting your grandparents?" he asked the kids. "Super fun! We had Thanksgiving dinner there, I got to play with my cousins, we went for a ride in Grandpa's boat, and we saw the White House Christmas lights," Levi said.

Beau was impressed. "That sounds like a lot of fun. You forgot to tell me in some of your videos, dude!" Beau said, teasing Levi. "Oh, I'm sorry. We were always just so tired," Levi said.

Beau smiled. "It's okay, Buddy. Well, guess what we're doing tonight?" Beau asked. "What?!" both kids said. "I am going to take your mom to dinner, and you are going to go play at the Jeppsen's' and have a sleepover. What do you say?" Beau asked the kids.

"Can you play with us, first?" Harper said in her cute broken toddler talk. Beau missed this little girl so much his heart was going to burst. "Absolutely. We could give your mom some alone time, and we get pizza for you if that's okay with her." Beau, Levi, and Harper looked at Evie. She smiled. "All of this sounds fine to me," she said. "Yay!" the kids cheered.

By then, they had reached Beau's car. He loaded Harper into her car seat, put the bags in the car, and walked to the passenger's side. Evie helped Levi climb in and buckle himself. Beau opened the door for her. "You are quite the gentleman today," she said, feeling extra happy. "I missed you," he whispered. "I missed you, too." Evie and Beau stared at each other for a while. "You can kiss her if you want. She likes it," Levi said from inside the car. "Levi!" Evie turned to her son and scolded. "Well, you do! That's what you told Aunt Jennifer," Levi said. She felt very embarrassed.

Beau watched Evie's cheeks turn pink. He softly caressed her cheek and jawline before leaning in and kissing her. They kissed for a few seconds before both of their heads began spinning. Once they stopped, Evie climbed into the car, Beau climbed into the driver's seat, and they all pulled out of the garage heading towards Evie's townhouse.

Evie missed driving over the Golden Gate Bridge. She missed the smell of the West Coast, the ornate architecture, the bumps, hills, all of the Redwood trees, and the man driving her home. She thought about what would happen on the date and contemplated the surprise he had planned. It was driving her nuts. When she saw Beau sitting on the bench in the airport and Levi and Harper run to him, Evie knew she was ready for the next step in their relationship. She missed his kind smile and beautiful eyes. Evie missed his personality, dorkiness, and watching him play with her kids.

When they got to Annapolis, Jude showed up the day after Thanksgiving to take Levi to tour the White House. After what Evie thought was a successful outing, Jude dropped Levi off, fuming. "All he did was talk about Beau. Beau this. Beau that. Why is my son talking about that low-life? Are you guys dating now? Do you honestly think he likes you? Just look at you! He won't replace me as our children's father!" Jude yelled. The conversation did not improve, but at least Evie, remembering Beau's words and Dr. Bennett's words, held her own when she said, "I will not be spoken to this way. If you want to see your children again, this behavior will stop. You will be hearing from my lawyer on

Monday." "You have a lawyer. It's the same one I use," Jude said. "I have new representation. Goodbye, Jude," Evie said before closing the door on him. She felt elated, but the kids saw the whole conversation, so she knew Levi and Harper needed to see the man who had become a father figure for them.

Beau pulled in front of the townhouse where the cleaning lady was standing outside the door. Evie stared at her. "Who is that?" she asked Beau. "This is Greta. She works for MaidPro. While you get ready for tonight, she will be doing the laundry. I cleaned the apartment for you, and you have a meal for tomorrow night in the freezer. I will take the kids after I bring in your bags, and we will get pizza while you get ready. Does that work for you?" Beau asked.

Evie looked at him in disbelief, but she wasn't angry. She tried working on being grateful for any type of help since talking to Dr. Bennett. "You are amazing. Thank you!" she said. Beau smiled. "You're welcome." They climbed out of the car, and Beau took Evie's bags inside. Greta followed them inside. "Where is the laundry room?" Greta asked. "The first door in the hallway upstairs on your right. There are hampers with sorted laundry in it already. I will bring you the rest in a second," Evie said. "Thank you," Greta said as she walked into the hallway.

Beau and Evie looked at each other while standing in the small living room. She wrapped both arms around Beau's waist. He wrapped his arms around her shoulders. "You okay?" he asked. "Yeah, I'm fine. I'm just looking forward to tonight," she said. "Me, too. Okay, I will get the kids fed and take them to Luke's. I will pick you up in an hour," Beau said.

Once everyone left, Evie hopped in the shower to make sure she got the awful smell of plane off of her. She recently purchased a pair of faux leather pants and a black leather moto-jacket to wear to concerts that she thought she could try out for her date. Evie paired them with a beaded racerback chiffon tank and some black knee-length boots with a chunky heel. Once she was dressed, she took the dirty clothes from the bags into the laundry room where Greta was.

When it came time to do her hair and makeup, she hadn't realized how long her hair had gotten since she moved to San Francisco. Her hair used to sit on the shoulders, but now it was way past them almost to the middle of her back. She decided to wear her hair straight, sweeping her long bangs across her face. She applied a full face of makeup for the first time in months, making her eyes pop even more. She put her moto-jacket on and a blush pink scarf with some fringe.

Since she had about twenty minutes to spare, she sat down and turned on Netflix. She watched an episode of *Friends* to help her relax. Her nerves were acting up for many reasons. It was her first date since her divorce, and it was with her best friend and love interest who happened to be the frontman of Death Toll. She knew that if any press got wind of their outing, they would be all over that, especially since she was Death Toll's tour manager. She tried so hard not to think about any repercussions, but it was super hard. Finally, her doorbell rang. Her heart began to beat a million miles an hour. She stood up and went to answer it.

Beau cleaned up very nicely. His hair was spiked coming to a point in front, and he wore a nice dress shirt, a leather jacket, dark indigo jeans, and to her surprise, loafers. She looked outside her door and saw his Camaro. Her heart started to calm down when she saw him smile at her. "You are perfect," he said. Evie blushed. "You are, too. I had no idea you owned a pair of loafers," she said. Beau laughed. He held up his hand. Evie grabbed her black purse before grabbing Beau's hand. He opened the passenger side door for Evie before she climbed in. Beau climbed in the car on the driver's side and pulled out of the driveway, driving towards the city.

Evie watched as Beau drove across the Golden Gate Bridge. She had never ridden inside a Camaro before, and it had a lot of horsepower. It had an updated stereo with Bluetooth installed so that a phone could connect to the car. Beau turned his music on, which was playing *Walk This Way* by Aerosmith. *Of course*, Evie thought to herself. She knew how much Beau admired Aerosmith. They were the reason he picked up the guitar in the first place. Her mind began wandering to when Beau played Percival, her violin. Then her mind wandered to how he named all of his guitars including his chrome guitar, which she called Chromy even though Beau called it Chrome.

They were quiet for a while, so she decided to ask, "What did you and Phoebe like to do on dates?" Beau looked at Evie for a second. "We did a lot of stuff. We loved watching movies, going for rides on my motorcycles or roadsters, trying out new restaurants, shopping, walking at Fisherman's Wharf, Pier 39, going to concerts, and we went dancing a lot when we started dating," he responded.

"She sounds like she was lots of fun."

"She was. She helped me grow up back when the band started, and we were crazy. She was really kind."

"I think I would have liked her," Evie said.

"Everyone did, but I think you guys would have been the best of friends." Evie smiled at that thought. Beau paused before reaching for Evie's hand. "You remind me of her quite a bit."

Evie smiled bigger. "I'm glad. I'm not exactly like her, am I?"

"No, I don't think so. She was very on point about everything whereas you are a bit more laid back. You dance way more than she did, but you guys dance very similarly. You have a broader interest in music. She was from Argentina, and you are American. She sewed, designed, and made her clothes."

Evie laughed because she shared a lot of similarities with Phoebe. "Well, actually, I made my kids' bedding since I didn't like any of the bedding in stores. Also, my brother-in-law is from Mexico," she said with a big smile on her face.

Beau looked at her. "Wow, I have a type," he said jokingly. They continued laughing. "What other similarities do I have with her?" Evie asked. "You are both very selfless people who do whatever they can for their kids. You both are extremely determined and stubborn. Everyone loves you, too," Beau said winking. Evie smiled. "Thanks," she said. "You're welcome," Beau said, rubbing his thumb against Evie's hand.

Beau pulled into a parking garage in Downtown San Francisco. He climbed out, walked over to the passenger side, and helped Evie climb out of the car. Holding hands, they walked to the street towards a pub called Gallager's. When they walked inside, the song *Paranoid* blared through the room. Evie instantly liked the place and smiled trying to see where the local band playing a Black Sabbath cover was.

"Beau, hey, man!" said the host. Beau shook his hand. "Who is this?" the host said, turning to Evie. "Evie Long," she said, holding out her hand. "Nice to meet you. Follow me, and I will get you guys a table by the band." "Thanks, man," Beau said.

They followed the host to a table relatively close to the band who all looked like they were in their early 20s. The host pulled out Evie's chair for her before she sat down. She proceeded to take off her scarf and jacket. Beau sat down across from her before taking his jacket off as well. Evie looked around the place and saw a pool table and a pinball machine. The bar had that underground thrash vibe from the early days, which Evie loved. "Hey, Beau! Where have you been, man?" an older gentleman said as he walked up to the table. Beau stood up and hugged the man. "Hey, Carl," Beau said. Carl then turned to Evie.

"And who is this hot, young, thing?" Carl asked as Evie began turning fifteen shades of purple. "This is my date and tour manager, Evie Long," Beau said to Carl, "Evie, this is Carl Gallager. He owns the place." "Oh, hello. It's nice to meet you," Evie said, shaking Carl's hand. Carl smiled at Evie. "The tour manager, huh? She is by far the hottest one I have seen to date," Carl said candidly. Evie blushed again. She couldn't recall a time in her life when she had blushed so much in one day. Beau smiled at Evie, knowing that Carl was right because she was the only woman to take on the task, but he had seen other women before and knew Carl was right.

"So," Carl said to Evie, "how do you like my bar?" "I love it," she said. "Cool. My bar is where Death Toll got started," Carl said. "Really? You guys played here, too?" Evie asked Beau. "Yes. We used to help him clear out all the tables, chairs, pool table, and pinball machine so that there was room for everyone to stand. Also, fans broke a lot of stuff during those days," Beau said. Evie lauged. "Well, guys, enjoy your meals. I will make sure your server takes good care of you," Carl said before walking away. "Thanks, man. See ya!" Beau said.

The server stopped by their table, took drink orders, and food orders. Beau ordered a Coke and a double bacon cheeseburger wrapped in lettuce. Evie ordered water with lime and a single bacon cheeseburger wrapped in lettuce. "While we wait for our food, want to play some pinball?" Beau asked. "Absolutely," Evie said.

They stood up and went over to the pinball machine. Beau pulled out two quarters and put them in the machine. "You go first," he said. Evie pulled back to release the ball. She kept everything going for a while and ended up with a pretty high score before her game ended. Evie noticed that Beau kept an arm around her at all times rubbing her shoulder now and then, which she enjoyed. Beau pulled out a couple more quarters and had his turn. He kept the ball going for a long time as well, eventually ending up with the highest score. The band played some sick covers of AC/DC, Black Sabbath, Ozzy, Aerosmith, Thin Lizzy, Motorhead, and of course Death Toll. Evie was having a lot of fun. Beau and Evie sat back down before their food got to the table. Just as they were diving into their food, the band took their break.

"Hi, are you Beau Halstead?" the bassist asked Beau as he approached their table. Beau swallowed his bite of burger and nodded. "Awesome! Could we get a picture with you?" he asked. Beau smiled. "Of course! Death Toll got started here, so I am happy to take pictures with the bands playing here," he said. "Would you mind?" the bassist asked Evie handing her his phone. "Sure," Evie said. The band and Beau huddled together, and she took a couple of pictures of them. "All right, there you go, boys. Good luck!" Beau said. "Thank you, Mr. Halstead!" they all shouted. He chuckled to himself. "You are super nice," Evie said. "So are you," Beau responded.

They continued to finish their meals. Beau snarfed down his burger, and Evie inhaled her burger and fries. She didn't realize how hungry she was until she saw the burger. "Shall we go?" Beau asked as Evie wiped her face with a napkin. Evie suddenly felt very nervous, and her hands became clammy. Beau stood up from his chair and helped Evie stand up. Beau left the money plus a tip on the table. He threw a $100 bill into the guitar case of the bassist before they walked out the door.

Beau and Evie walked back to the Camaro, climbed in, and began driving towards San Rafael. They held hands again, but this time there was a bit more electricity in their touches. Beau rubbed his thumb against Evie's hand. Soon, Evie started moving their hands up Beau's thigh where it rested. She wanted to make sure he knew she was ready for what was ahead.

"What are we doing here?" Evie asked as Beau pulled up in front of the studio. "It's now time for your surprise," he said. He climbed out of the Camaro and opened Evie's door.

"It's nothing sappy, is it?" she asked.

"Since when am I a sappy guy?"

"I don't know. I've never seen 'dating Beau' before. 'Dating Beau' could be sappy," Evie said wittily.

Beau laughed. "'Dating Beau' is pretty much like 'friend Beau,' just a bit more thoughtful. I don't buy the cheesy gifts like candy and roses. I go for the personable gifts and gestures," Beau said.

"Okay. I'm a little more curious now what you've got cooked up," Evie concluded.

They walked inside the studio while Beau wrapped his right arm around Evie's shoulders, and Evie wrapped her left arm around Beau's waist. They walked through the kitchen and into the audio room. There was a microphone set up in front with headphones on a stool in the recording room. The flag with Nole Bradshaw's picture and dates hung behind the mic.

"What's going on?" Evie asked. "I started working on something while you were gone. I wanted to show it to you tonight," Beau said, "plus, I still need to record the vocals."

Evie watched Beau walk into the recording room, put the headphones on, and got close to the mic. He had everything rigged where he could hit record from inside. Evie took off her jacket, gently threw it on the couch behind her, sat down on the stool, and began to listen in the audio room.

She listened to the arpeggio at the beginning and elaboration. It pierced her soul to the very center. It was the most beautiful guitar intro she had ever heard as the riff continued to progress. Beau looked at his muse very intently watching every reaction she made to the song. Evie met his gaze. Evie felt chills. Then Beau started singing the simplest, yet most heartfelt, lyrics she had ever heard.

There were not enough words in the English dictionary to describe Evie's thoughts about what she was feeling or thinking. *Beau wrote a song about me, a beautiful song*, she began. Every word he sang was real. Their relationship and friendship were so strong no matter how far they were apart. After last week, Evie knew she trusted Beau and could count on him. There was an interlude giving Evie a chance to process the lyrics. Their relationship had blossomed from an amazing friendship to commitment. She thought back to all their adventures; the gym, going to the park, teaching Levi how to throw a football, his tea party with Harper, and those late nights on her couch watching their favorite movies.

Beau, never doing something like this before, was willing to risk his comfort and pride for Evie. The last words of the song were what touched Evie the most. She knew he was referencing what Jude might do and say if he found out about Beau. There was a lot of emotional baggage Evie had to carry, but he found a way to let her know he was okay with it and wanted to help her.

The guitar solo exploded much like Evie's inability to contain her feelings for Beau. No one had ever done something like this for her in her entire life. The solo expressed the magnetic pull Evie felt to Beau as well as his pull to her. Evie was very impressed with musicality. Soon, the music began to fade, and Evie heard that E minor arpeggio again as well as the opening melody fade out as Beau repeated the first four lines of the song.

Beau paused the audio before taking off the headphones. He grabbed the equipment and carried it back into the audio room. Once everything was cleaned up, Beau walked up behind Evie, wrapped his arms around her, and asked, "So, what did you think of the song?" Evie smiled. "That was beautiful. The level of musicality displayed in this song was sensational. It's almost like that arpeggio represented an individual rather than just a motif. Plus, you sang your heart out," she said. "What did you think of the words I sang?" Beau asked, hoping Evie got the message. "They were very beautiful and genuine," Evie said as her cheeks turned pink. Beau smiled lightly.

"Did you write all of the parts? Drums, both guitars, and bass?" Evie asked. "I wrote the guitar parts and helped Luke and Rick tweak their parts to match what I heard in my head," Beau said. "Who played the solo? It almost sounded like Kade, but there wasn't enough Wah," Evie said, joking about Kade's stereotypical playing. "That was me you heard playing the solo," Beau said. "That song is... us," Evie finally said, figuring out what she wanted to say. "I know," Beau said as he began kissing Evie's neck and rubbing her shoulders. Instantly, Evie's eyes rolled to the back of her head as Beau brushed Evie's hair to her right shoulder and kissed her left. "Was this also part of the plan?" she asked, feeling aroused. "Turn around and find out," Beau said, sounding just as out of breath. Evie turned around where Beau's lips were waiting for hers. They kissed, feeling the tension that had built up. Beau thought about this moment on and off for the past month and a half, so he indulged in it. Evie sensed Beau's assertiveness and matched it, ready to succumb. No man had ever made her feel safe, accepted, sexy, and loved.

Chapter 15

We Are Death Toll; Nothing Else

Kade and Rick drove up to the studio. Beau's Camaro was parked in front already. They figured he wanted to record the vocals to his song before anyone else got there. They climbed out of Kade's car and walked into the studio. They noticed a men's leather jacket on the floor and a women's leather jacket on the couch. They saw a black purse sitting on the floor by the controls. "Did... Beau and Evie...?" Rick couldn't finish the question. "They must have. I'll go look in Beau's room," Kade said. Sure enough, laying in his bed were Beau and Evie bare-shouldered, fingers intertwined, laying down, sound asleep. Evie had nestled up against Beau while his right arm rested over her. Kade quietly closed the door and turned to look at Rick. "Yep, they hooked up," he said. "We knew this was going to happen," Rick said, "should we wake them up?" "Probably before the kids wake up... if they're here," Kade said. "They could be at Luke's," Rick said.

Kade quietly approached Beau's door. He knocked lightly but continued to hear steady breathing. Kade knocked a little louder and heard some movement, but no one got up. He finally cracked the door and slipped his head inside. He loudly cleared his throat. Beau stirred and opened his eyes. He looked straight across at Kade. Beau froze, not sure how to proceed. "Evie," he whispered in her ear. She groaned and opened her eyes. "Hi," she said sleepily. When she saw the look on Beau's face, she realized something was wrong. She saw him look across the room, so she looked over as well and saw Kade's head peering in the room. Evie slowly grabbed the covers and pulled them over her head, burrowing down in bed.

"Good morning," Kade said, opening the door wider. "Morning," Beau said, sitting up and rubbing his eyes. "I would ask how your date went last night, but I can already see that it went well," Kade said. Evie blushed. "Did anyone else see?" Beau asked. "Just Rick and me," Kade said. "Rick's here, too?!" Evie said underneath the sheet, sounding embarrassed. Beau reached under the covers to touch Evie's shoulder for reassurance that it was okay. "Let's face it. This isn't the worst thing you guys have caught me doing," Beau said. "Not helping," Evie said again, feeling more embarrassed. By that time, they could all hear Rick laughing in the hallway. Kade began to snicker as well before closing the door and walking away from the room.

Beau sat up, keeping Evie covered. He reached for his boxers, which he found lying on the floor. He slipped them on as he stood up. Evie poked her head out of the covers just as Beau began rummaging through his dresser. "What are you doing?" Evie asked while sitting up. She managed to keep the flat sheet over her chest. "Finding clothes for us to wear today," Beau said. He found some jeans and a tee-shirt for him to wear. He then started going through some of his old clothes he had held on to since Death Toll started. He figured one of those shirts would fit since he was a lot smaller back in the day.

In his peripheral vision, Beau saw Evie climb out of bed, keeping a sheet over her as she looked for her clothes. He walked over to her and began kissing her again. "What's this for?" she asked in between breaths. "Just prolonging the moment," Beau said. "It was a perfect night," Evie said. "It was," Beau told Evie before kissing her.

Beau laid her back down on the bed, pulling the sheet off of Evie. Just as Evie began to shimmy Beau's boxers off again, there was a pounding at the door. "Luke's here with Levi and Harper. Get dressed so we can go to work," they heard Kade's voice. Evie realized they needed to stop. "We should get dressed," she said as Beau nuzzled her neck. He stopped and said, "Fine." They kissed one more time before Beau went back to his dresser.

Beau looked in his dresser for a shirt as Evie proceeded to slip her bra, underwear and pants back on. Beau found an old gray muscle tee shirt with a Death Toll log that looked like it would fit Evie. "Would you wear this?" he asked. Evie looked at the shirt and said, "Yeah, I'll wear it."

After handing her the shirt, Beau proceeded to get dressed while Evie put the shirt on. She tucked her shirt inside the front of her pants. Evie then put her boots back on. Luckily, there was a full-length mirror in Beau's closet that she was able to see herself. She grabbed the hair-tie on her wrist and proceeded to throw her hair up into a high ponytail. After Evie went into the bathroom to make sure she still had makeup in place, she and Beau were ready to go to work.

Evie walked to the kitchen, figuring that's where her kids would be. Sure enough, they were sitting at the table eating applesauce out of pouches. "Hey, guys," Evie said. "Mommy!" they said, jumping out of their chairs and hugging their mom.

"How was your night?" she asked. "It was so much fun. Beau took us to get pizza and dropped us off at Uncle Luke's," Levi said. Evie smiled.

"What did you do at Uncle Luke's?" Evie asked. "I played with Eli," Harper said. "And I played with Mason," Levi said. "Sounds like lots of fun. Did you guys go to bed at bedtime?" Evie asked. "Aunt Jetta made sure we went to bed at the same time as we always do," Levi said. Evie knew she would need to thank Jetta later. "How was your date with Beau?" Levi asked. Evie had to think about how to answer the question. She just kept it simple. "It was perfect," she said. "Is he going to be our daddy now?" Harper asked. Her question stumped her mom. "Let's just say he will be more involved in our lives now," Evie finally answered. "So, is he our new dad?" Levi asked, still searching for the answer he wanted to hear. "Beau and I are going to be dating for now, and if everything continues to go well, he might be," Evie responded. "Okay. I hope so," Levi said. Evie smiled. "Me too," she said. She hugged her kids super tight.

Beau walked into the kitchen and found the three people he loved more than anyone else in the world. When Levi heard Beau's footsteps, he looked up. "Beau!" he shouted before running into Beau's arms. Harper followed her brother's lead giving her new fatherly figure a huge hug. Beau held them very tightly. As he hugged the kids, Beau looked up at Evie. They smiled at each other. Beau wanted so badly to be a part of this family, and so did Evie. They were both determined to make this work.

Suddenly, Levi grabbed Beau's face. "I need to talk to you," he said, grabbing Beau's hand and walking out of the kitchen. Harper tried to follow, but Levi said as nicely as possible, "This is a boy talk, Harper. I need you to stay with Mommy." "Okay," Harper said, sounding sad. Evie walked over to her daughter and picked her up. "It's okay. You can be with me while I make a few phone calls," Evie said. "Can you put on speakerphone?"

Harper asked. "Yes, but you have to be quiet, or I will have to take you in the other room," Evie said. "Okay," Harper said.

Levi and Beau walked into the living room just outside the audio room. They both sat down on the couch. "Do you like my mom?" Levi asked. Beau smiled. "Yes, I do. I love her, actually," Beau responded. "Okay. Please don't hurt her over and over again like my dad does. He always played with me when I was a baby, but then he stopped. He treated my mom the way you treat her now, but then he stopped when he got another girlfriend. I don't want to see her cry again," Levi said.

Beau looked Levi square in the eye with confidence. "The last thing I ever want to do is hurt your mom..." Beau paused and realized what Levi was doing. "Are you giving me the talk that fathers are supposed to give?" Beau asked. Levi smiled. "Yes," he said, "so, I think you know what will happen if you hurt my mom." "You'll kick my butt?" Beau joked. "No, I will hunt you down and gut you like a fish," Levi said, sounding a bit sinister. Beau felt a little intimidated, but he figured Levi was quoting a movie. "I promise not to hurt your mom," Beau said. "Good," Levi replied. "I am so glad you are looking out for your mom," Beau said. Levi smiled. "I want her to be happy, and she is happiest when you are around," Levi said. Beau smiled.

"Hey, can I show you something?" Beau asked. "Sure," Levi said as he watched Beau stand up and walk to the sound board. Beau turned on the recording he made last night. "I wrote this song for your mom," Beau said as they heard the beginning to *Nothing Else Matters*. Levi listened to the song very intently. "Is it about my mom and you?" Levi asked. "It sure is," Beau said, smiling. Levi soon smiled also.

Soon, the other band members walked into the audio room. Beau stood up and hugged Luke. "Thanks again for watching the kids last night," Beau said. "You're welcome," Luke said, "Please tell me you finished the song." Beau nodded. "I was just showing Levi the song, right, Buddy?" Levi nodded. "You were such a big help last night. Thank you, Levi," Luke said, holding up his hand for a high five. "You're welcome, Uncle Luke," Levi responded, hitting Luke's hand. "All right, let's hear it," Rick said. Beau started the song over again.

All five of them listened super intently. As the song progressed, they all had a smile on their faces. "By far, this is the best love song in heavy metal I've heard, possibly ever," Kade said.

Rick and Luke nodded. "The vocals sound very raw. Like there was a lot more emotion behind the lyrics than any other song we have written," Luke said.

"All a part of the planning process," Beau said, smiling. "So, she watched you?" Luke asked. "Yes, and she understood what the musical theme represented. It was…" Beau looked at Levi to try and figure out how to explain this to the band and Levi, "the best night ever."

"Awesome. This song is going on our album. Let's finish up Rick's song and maybe work on some others," Luke said. The four members of Death Toll went into the recording room while Levi sat down on the couch and listened to the guys jam.

Meanwhile, Evie had to put Harper in the toy room because she was too disruptive. Evie worked on securing venues and stadiums for the East Coast part of their trip. She even made sure they stopped at her alma mater's stadium to put on a concert. Evie secured stadiums in Buffalo, Albany,

Madison Square Garden, Pittsburgh, Philadelphia, University Park, and Raleigh.

When she was on the phone with the booking agent in Raleigh, he asked her a question that stumped her. "What are we calling this tour?" Evie hadn't given it a whole lot of thought. She told the agent that she would talk to the band and get back to him. Evie also made sure to speak with PR and the group to figure out how they would advertise the tour. When Evie got off the phone, she walked to the recording room. She waved to Levi, who was still watching the band intently inside the audio room.

"Hey guys, sorry to interrupt," Evie began as the boys quit playing for a minute, "we need to figure out what to call this tour and how to advertise it." Beau looked at Luke, Kade, and Rick, trying to see if they had any ideas. "Huh, okay. Well, what has been the main theme of this album?" Beau asked the collective. "We've been talking mostly about what we always talk about," Luke said. "True, war, addiction, and abuse of power are always our main themes," Beau said. "But what about *Nothing Else Matters*?" Luke said. Beau shrugged. "We can't open the concert with a ballad," he said.

"Okay, what if we call it the Nothing Else Tour. Because we are Death Toll, nothing else," Luke said.

"How about the We Are Death Toll, Nothing Else Tour?" Evie asked.

"Simple, yet strong," Luke said.

Everyone else nodded. "All right. I will talk to Marketing. When will the album be finished so that we can start promoting it, releasing more songs to radio stations, that sort of thing?" Evie asked the band.

"We should be done by the end of the week or as early as today. You can call Crazy Tony and have him come listen to *Frantic* and *Nothing Else Matters*," Beau said.

"Perfect. I will take care of everything before then, hopefully, today, if Harper behaves," Evie said with a chuckle. The band smiled. "All right, play pretty," Evie said before walking out the door. Everyone laughed at that joke.

Beau watched Evie as she sauched out of the studio. Luke caught him in the act, wadded up a piece of paper, and threw it at his head. "Focus, man! We are just two songs away from finishing our album," Luke said firmly. Beau shook his head. "All right, who has some other ideas?" Beau asked.

"Well, I have this riff I wrote after listening to a Soundgarden record, if you don't mind hearing it," Kade said to the group. "Let's hear it," Beau said. Kade, surprised at how open-minded Beau had become, started in the key of E minor but progressed to an A minor chord, sounding almost like a metallic version of Rhythm changes. Kade ended the riff on E minor. Beau liked it, but Luke suggested, "Repeat that first bar again." Kade followed Luke's suggestion, and the entire band went, "Whoah!" at the same time. The band continued to work on that song as Beau soon spat out the lyrics.

After Death Toll listened to their entire set, Evie walked into the audio room again. "So I was able to contact Crazy Tony, and he wants to come in sometime tomorrow to hear your songs, choose some to promote on the radio, that sort of thing. Would 10:00 in the morning work for everyone?" she asked. Everyone nodded. "Cool, I will go confirm with him. I will be in the living room helping Levi with his reading, calling other radio stations, and doing a craft with Harper if anyone needs me," Evie said. "Okay, bye, Babe," Beau said. Evie smiled and blushed. "Bye."

She walked back towards the living room where her kids were. Levi, who went into the living room to play with his sister, was now reading silently, and Harper was at a little kids' table coloring in a princess coloring book next to a turkey with googly eyes that Evie helped put together. While they were preoccupied, Evie made a few other phone calls to radio stations seeing if they could come in within the week to listen to Death Toll's new album and even put some of the songs on their radio station. Sure enough, all of them were very interested, suggested times, and Evie scheduled everything out.

Evie listened to him read out loud, helped him with any words he had a hard time pronouncing, and praised him when he finished the book. When she told him to read silently again, Evie pulled out some playdough for Harper from the shelves in the living room and monitored her as she made different things with the dough.

Harper began to get a little cranky and started screaming at her mother when it was time to clean up the playdough. "Okay, Miss Sassy Pants, nap time for you!" Evie said, feeling frustrated.

"No, no! Wha' 'bout 'tory time?" Harper begged, crying.

"Will you take a nap after I read you a story?" Evie asked.

"Yes," Harper agreed.

"Will you stop screaming at me?"

"Yes."

"Okay. Let's go to the extra bedroom, and we will find a book, okay?" Evie negotiated.

"Okay," Harper said.

"Mom, I'm bored! I'm hungry. Can I have a snack?" Levi yelled as he dropped the book.

Evie felt a little strained. She looked at her watch, realizing it was lunch time and calmly replied, "There are some grapes, goldfish, and fruit snacks in the kitchen. I will make a lunch run here soon after your sister goes down for her nap," Evie turned to Harper, "Do you want a peanut butter and jelly sandwich while I read the story?" Evie tried to compromise.

"Yes, and a drink," Harper said, rubbing her tears away.

"Of course," Evie said, still trying to remain calm, "let's go to the kitchen, first."

The kids followed their mom into the kitchen. Levi grabbed his snacks while Evie made a sandwich for Harper. *Good Evie. Just keep your cool. Get Harper down for a nap, and then go get food for everyone*, she coached herself, *the kids are hangry, and so are you. Just keep going.*

Once Harper had her sandwich and story, she fell asleep. Evie tucked her in and gave her a kiss. *How can someone so little have such big emotions and ideas*, Evie contemplated as she closed Harper's door.

"All right, Bub," Evie said quietly to Levi, "shall we go get lunch for the band?"

"Yes!" Levi said rather loudly.

"Hey," Evie snapped quietly, "should you be yelling?"

Levi hated when his mother did the scary quiet voice. It was worse than yelling. He slowly and shamefully shook his head.

"All right. Let's run to Sprouts and get food for everyone. When we get back, I think you need to take a nap," Evie said, seeing Levi's tired eyes.

"No! Levi yelled. Evie grabbed Levi's arm and dragged him away from the extra bedroom. "Do you want to take a nap now or after lunch?! Levi, you need to be quiet or you will wake up your sister. Do you want to take care of the whining and screaming?"

Levi paused. "No," he shamefully responded.

"All right. So let's go. If you can show me you are happy, then you can stay up and watch a movie. Does that work?" Evie tried to compromise.

"Yeah."

"Okay, let's go get in the car. Now, I need you to be obedient. Can you do that for me?"

"Yeah."

"Okay, good."

Evie, praying that Levi would behave while at Sprouts, went to the prepared food section and grabbed everyone's usual lunch orders. She gave Levi's lunch to him in the car, but he fell asleep before he finished it. Struggling to lift him up, Evie managed to carry Levi into another room with a futon and laid him down. She set the kitchen table with the band's lunches before making a green smoothie and a steak burrito bowl for herself.

"Want to eat lunch with us?" Beau asked as Death Toll entered the kitchen. "I think I want to eat by myself. The last hour has been hard, and I just need some alone time," Evie said. "That's fine. I could hear Harper screaming a while ago," Beau said before kissing Evie's cheek. She smiled. "Thank you for understanding," Evie said, wrapping her arms around Beau. Evie soon went into the second living room, turned on Netflix, and ate her lunch. She ended up falling asleep on the couch.

After taking a nap for about an hour and a half, Evie woke up and looked at her smartwatch to check the time, which said 3:30 pm. The day would be ending soon with dinner prepping, gym time, and going to bed. Evie, feeling groggy, also wondered what Beau's plans were in the evening if he would want to go to the gym with her, eat dinner with her and the kids, and spend time with them.

Just as she was about to stand up, Beau walked into the living room. He sat on the couch next to Evie and put his arms around her. She smiled and leaned against him, and Beau kissed her cheek. "Did you take a nap?" he asked. "Yeah, I didn't think I needed it, but I guess I didn't sleep as much as I thought," Evie laughed. Beau chuckled himself. "Me either, honestly. So, what are your plans this evening?"

"I was going to head home, eat dinner, load everyone back up in the car, and head to the gym," Evie responded. "May I tag along?" Beau asked.

"Yes, please. I would love that, and I know the hoodlums would love it, too." Evie said.

"Where are they?"

"Taking naps. Shall we go wake them up?"

"Yes."

Beau went into Harper's room and woke her up. She slept in a similar way to her mom, which made Beau laugh. When she opened her eyes and saw Beau, Harper threw her arms around Beau's neck and sweetly said, "Hi, Beau." How he missed being a father!

Once 4:00 hit, Luke loaded Levi and Harper back into his car and drove to Evie's townhouse. Beau and Evie followed in Beau's Camaro. Once they got to the apartment, Evie walked inside and immediately began preparing dinner. She soon realized that her crockpot was on with what looked like chicken and some salsa in it. "Did you…?" Evie asked, turning to Beau. "Yes, I did. I remember Phoebe making this a ton on busy days. I had Greta come and pour that this morning," Beau said. "I like 'Dating Beau,'" Evie said. Beau hugged Evie. "'Dating Beau' likes Evie."

Once dinner was ready, Harper ate whatever Evie ate, and Evie was always grateful for that. Levi decided to eat whatever Beau ate. Beau became Levi's role model and wanted to do everything Beau did. When everyone finished eating, Beau and Levi cleaned up the kitchen while Evie went to her room to get ready to go to the gym.

She forgot Beau would need some clothes, but then she remembered the large tee shirt and basketball shorts he wore when he stayed the night. Evie quickly changed into black leggings, a light pink high neck tank, and her black high-top Nikes. When she came out of her room, Evie immediately told Beau, "I have the tee-shirt and gym shorts for you in my room. Oh, no, shoes…" Evie tapered off before looking at Beau's feet. He was already wearing tennis shoes. "Changed before we left," Beau said. "Cool. I will load kids in the car while you go change," Evie said. Beau nodded.

Evie looked around her kitchen and noticed it was clean and tidy. "Thank you for cleaning," Evie said as Beau walked towards her room. He smiled. "You're welcome. I had some help," he said, looking down at Levi. Evie gave her son a hug. "Thank you, Bub," she said. Beau quickly rushed into Evie's room and changed into the gym clothes. He rushed to the car to make sure Levi had buckled himself.

They all drove to the gym, playing "Song Styles." Each of them took turns singing a song on the radio either in Beau's singing style or trying to imitate the actual singer. They all laughed. When Beau would sing, he had back-up vocals by Evie and the kids. Despite the kids singing off-key, he loved the game.

After the Zumba class, Beau and Evie went and lifted some weights for about 20 minutes. A couple of guys walked up to Beau and Evie, trying to talk to Beau before hitting on Evie. "Thank you guys, but I believe my girlfriend and I need to finish lifting before picking up the kids," Beau said, wrapping his arm around Evie. She could not help but hold in a laugh trying to smile gracefully. *Smooth*, she thought to herself sarcastically. "Bye, guys," Evie said as Beau led them to another machine. She watched the guys stand there looking stunned and deflated. Beau and Evie soon went and picked up Levi and Harper in childcare, and then they drove back to Evie's townhouse. Evie gave the kids baths and helped them get dressed. Beau read them a bedtime story. When Evie was getting ready to tuck her children in bed, they both asked if Beau could do it. She smiled, told Beau what they wanted, and he soon went to tuck them in bed and sang their lullaby to each of them.

Once they were in bed, Beau and Evie sat down on the couch for a second. "So," Beau started wrapping an arm around Evie's shoulders, "should I go home or...?" Evie took in a deep breath and sighed. "I don't know if it will be weird for them or not because sometimes they come into my room at night. I mean, they saw you in my room last week, but I don't know about...," she said.

Just as Beau was about to say goodnight to Evie, Levi came out of his room. "Bub, what are you doing? You need to go back to your room," Evie said sternly, but lovingly, before standing up. "I just wanted to tell Beau something," he said, walking towards Beau, "If you want to sleep over, you can. I know my mom loves it when you do. We like seeing you in the morning."

Beau and Evie smiled. "All right. I will even sleep on the couch if you want me to," Beau said. "My mom's bed is way comfier. She likes to cuddle at night with you," Levi said. Evie was laughing so hard internally. Beau struggled himself. "Thank you, Levi. I will talk to your mom about it. Now, it's time for you to go to bed," Beau said, pointing to his room. "Okay, goodnight, Beau," Levi said, hugging Beau. "Goodnight, Mommy," Levi said, hugging his mom after that. Evie smiled. "Goodnight, Bub. Sleep well. I love you," Evie said. "Love you, too," Levi said as he walked back up the stairs to his room and closed the door.

Still sweaty from the gym, Beau and Evie sat on the couch. Beau put his arm around Evie and asked, "So, what should we do now?" he asked. "Well, I need a shower," she said before standing up off the couch, walking towards her room. Beau smiled and watched her walk up the stairs as Evie proceeded to take off her tank top and sports bra, throwing them on the floor. Beau swallowed a massive lump in his throat, remembering what she looked like last night. Beau followed her up the stairs into her room. He closed and locked her door.

Evie washed her face, brushed her teeth, turned on the hot shower, and climbed in, waiting for Beau to join her. Evie heard the faucet turn on, assuming Beau found the toothbrush she left for him, followed by his shoes landing on the floor. Soon, the shower curtain opened, and Beau climbed in. He stood behind her, wrapping his arms around her and began nuzzling her neck. She cozied up to him. Never had she felt so safe in her life.

Chapter 16

On the Road

Four months passed since Beau and Evie began dating. Many holidays were celebrated including Evie's birthday the first week of December, Christmas, and New Years'. These were the best holidays that Evie and the kids had in a really long time. Jude always spent those days away from his family, claiming he had to work late to get his Christmas bonus.

On the morning of Evie's thirty-first birthday, Beau snuck out of bed into Evie's kitchen and began making special breakfast crepes filled with scrambled eggs, spicy sausage, mushrooms, spinach and peppers. He made sure there was plenty of Evie's favorite fruit including grapes, kiwi, pineapple, strawberries, blackberries, and blueberries. He managed to book a massage and facial for Evie while he baked her cake, a triple layer chocolate cake. The kids went over to the Hansens and played while Beau made the cake. Later that evening, Beau made a reservation at Gary Danko's for Evie's birthday dinner before taking her and the kids back to his house for the evening and night. Never before had Evie's birthday been the best day ever.

Evie and the kids spent Christmas with Beau since his brother's plans fell through. Luckily, Evie's parents understood. It turned out to be the best Christmas ever, according to Levi. Beau was super excited to be Santa again, and went all out for the kids. Taking Evie's advice from the first date, Beau held back a huge surprise for Evie; a trip to London to go see her best friend, Abella. Since the album was done, Beau could watch the kids while Evie spent the first full weekend of January with Abella. Evie cried when she saw the tickets.

It was the best New Years' for Evie and the kids since Beau made plans to stay home, have a special dinner, play all sorts of games with Evie and the kids, put the kids to bed, and spend the rest of the night with Evie, ending the night with a kiss. Evie loved how simple and personable Beau was when it came to planning dates. He wasn't a gift-giving guy, but he put a lot of thought into each date and outing with the kids.

When it came time to go to work, Evie and Beau maintained professionalism. Every now and then when Evie passed Beau in a hallway, he would pull her into a room and kiss her when no one was looking.

They dated all while promoting Death Toll's new album, Death Toll. Eventually, the press caught wind that Beau was dating the band's tour manager. The media tried to do everything they could to interview Evie, but she always found ways to evade the press. During certain events, Beau invited Evie to come along as his date. The media became harder and harder to avoid after they found out where she lived, so she arranged for them to come in and interview band members as well as her mainly to promote the Death Toll album.

The day of the interview arrived, and Evie sat down on a stool in front of a couple of reporters for MTV, VH1, Metalhead Zone, and a bunch of other rock news channels and podcasts with cameras. "What is your full name, beautiful?" one reporter asked. "Genevieve Willa Long, but my parents started calling me Evie from the day I was born," Evie responded. "Where are you from, honey?" one asked. "What is your family like?" another reporter asked. "What other jobs have you had?" "How long have you and Beau been dating?" "Where did you guys meet?"

One reporter asked an uncomfortable question. "How does Death Toll feel about your relationship, and how do you set boundaries between your relationship and work?"

Evie froze, caught off guard. "Well, if you mean what Luke, Kade, and Rick's thoughts are, you need to ask them. As for our boundaries, we know when it is time to work and when it is time to clock out. We both work extremely hard, and we have mutual respect for one another's career," Evie responded with class.

"Are those two cute blonde kids yours from your previous marriage?"

"Yes. Their names are Levi and Harper."

"How long were you married to your ex-husband?" the TMZ reporter asked.

"For the record, I refuse to answer questions about my ex-husband for his protection, my protection, and my children's." The press quit prying after that.

There was one comment and question that surprised Evie. "We have been watching and interviewing Beau for years, and we have never seen him do so well. Sure, he did well with his wife and kids, but you have done something to him that is hard to explain. What is it that you're doing to help him?"

Evie shrugged. "Well, I'm just trying to be supportive of Beau. Before we dated, there were a couple of times he called me to talk him out of drinking. His therapist has been a huge help as well; encouraging Beau to replace unhealthy choices with healthy ones. We started going to the gym together, and Zumba seems to be a key factor," Evie said with a laugh. Everyone else laughed as well.

Radio stations played Death Toll's new songs regularly. The instant favorite was *Nothing Else Matters*. Radio DJ's began to speculate if Evie inspired the song. Many stations invited Death Toll for interviews about the album. They asked each band member questions about specific songs they contributed including Rick's song, Kade's song, and *Nothing Else Matters*.

As everyone was getting ready to go on tour, Evie had to give her month's notice at her townhouse. She put all of the big furniture into storage again. Even though Evie wouldn't be living there when her lease ended, Evie hired Greta to clean her townhouse again to make sure she would get her security deposit back. Evie made sure she had adequate supplies to homeschool Levi while they went on tour. To ensure that everything was accurate, Evie made a spreadsheet for each bandmate of their equipment for insurance purposes as well as to make sure it got packed.

As she was packing up the kids' clothes, her phone rang. Her dad was calling. "Hi, Daddy!" Evie said, answering her phone. "Hey, Evs! We've been listening to the radio, and we want to say congratulations on the band's success," her dad said. "Thanks, Daddy!" Evie said.

"Now, when will we get to meet Beau?" he asked, "Do you think we could meet up when you guys stop in Baltimore?" Evie quickly looked at her calendar when they would be in Maryland. "I think we could arrange something, especially since that's around Harper's birthday. I will talk with Beau and see what works best for us," Evie said. "All right. We are proud of you. By the way, Jude tried to visit us about two weeks ago, but we haven't let him come over. He shouts through our front door that he is not liking the environment you are putting the kids in," Mr. West concluded.

Surprise surprise, Evie thought to herself. "Well, I amended the terms of our divorce, and I guess that's why he's showing up at your house to throw his temper tantrum since he cannot call me anymore unless he's with his lawyer or Death Toll's lawyer," Evie said. "I reminded him to follow the agreement, but Jude gave up about two weeks ago. We just wanted you to be aware in case he shows up," Mr. West concluded.

"Thanks, Dad. I will keep my eyes out. He has our address, and I've been updating him on our locations and hotel rooms we will be staying at all via email so he can see the kids, but no response. Still, knowing him, he will show up and expect to be accommodated without any regard to others in direct violation of what we agreed," Evie said.

"Sorry he's been treating you this way since Levi was born," Evie's dad said.

"I'm over it. My life is way more fulfilling now than it has been in the past. I feel like I have accomplished more with my life professionally and as a mom," Evie said.

"I cannot wait to see how big your kids are getting."

"I am excited to see all of you, too," Evie said.

After she got off the phone with her dad, she finished packing her kids' clothes. She then proceeded to her clothes. She stocked up on rolls of quarters to ensure she could do laundry at the hotels they would be staying. Evie also made sure that there would be plenty of stops for everyone to get out, stretch their legs, and give Levi and Harper a chance to burn some energy. She put all of the suitcases in her car. She and the kids would be staying the night at the studio with the band so they could all get up bright and early to hop on an airplane. They had a long trip ahead of them to the East Coast.

Evie, with the kids loaded up in her car, began driving towards the studio. She turned the radio onto the station that would be interviewing Death Toll and listened. "I hear Uncle Rick!" Levi shouted. "Bub, I need you to say that in a quieter voice. That was too loud," Evie said. "I hear Uncle Rick!" Levi said, quieter but just as excited. "Much better. Thank you. I hear him, too! Shall we listen to what he has to say?" Evie asked. "Yeah," both kids said. They listened to the DJ ask Rick all sorts of questions about the song he wrote. Then the DJ began asking Beau questions, and that's when Evie heard the interview about *Nothing Else Matters*.

Everyone working with Death Toll had no idea what a hit the song would be. The DJ proceeded to ask Beau about Evie. "I wrote this song during Thanksgiving when she was visiting her family in Maryland. I knew I was in love with her, and I knew she had some emotional baggage from her previous marriage. I also wondered what her parents would think if they found out their baby girl… oh, she is the youngest of two daughters, caught the attention of an addict, but then I focused on everything she had done for me and her kind heart. I realized I didn't care about her baggage or what her parents thought. All I knew was that I loved her, and I wanted to take care of her," Beau concluded.

Evie's heart melted, but then there was something that bothered her. Beau had told the radio DJ plus the majority of the Bay area that he loved her before he told her. She tried very hard not to let it bother her, but it was hard considering Jude used to display how he felt about Evie and the kids publicly, but when it was just the family, Jude would ignore them. It's not that Beau ignored the kids or her, but Beau's words triggered some of Evie's insecurities.

She knew her relationship with Beau was more in-depth, kinder, caring, and more intimate than any relationship she had ever had with any man. When they would wake up in the morning with bad breath, messy hair, no make-up at least on Evie's part, and baggy pajamas, Beau would always kiss Evie on the cheek and wrap his arms around her. He always made time for Evie after he got home from work, which was essential to her.

Evie pulled into the driveway of the studio and parked next to Kade's car. She planned to cook baked ziti for dinner for those who were staying at the studio, go for a walk to the park so her kids could burn some energy, put them to bed, and talk with Beau about what he said on the radio station. Evie sent the kids into the playroom while she put suitcases in the two kids' bedroom they stayed in previously, put her bag in Beau's room, and began pulling out the groceries she had bought for the evening to make dinner. After throwing everything together, Evie set the large table that sat twelve, and then she decided to sit down in the second living room, turn on the TV, and put her feet up.

After watching an episode of *Friends*, Beau walked inside the second living room. Evie stood up to greet him. "Hey, Beautiful," Beau always said when he saw Evie. "Hi, Honey," Evie always responded and blushed. They kissed and embraced each other. Beau held her tight. "How was your day?" he asked. "Pretty good. I got my townhouse packed, and I arranged for movers to put my belongings in a storage unit while we are gone. I also gathered Levi's homeschooling materials so that he wouldn't fall behind, I made dinner, and I was relaxing for a minute," she said.

"Wow, busy day," Beau said, "Where are the kids?"

"In the playroom."

"I was always glad we had a playroom for our kids."

"Me, too, honestly."

They walked over to the large sectional and sat down. "Dinner smells good. What are we having?" Beau asked. "Baked ziti and salad. I made enough for everyone, including some vegetarian options for Luke and Kade."

"You are amazing. What will you do with leftovers?"

"Take them with us to save some money on my part."

"Babe, I can take care of the food."

"I know, but just because I'm dating a rockstar doesn't mean I have to give up everything about myself, does it?"

"Good point. I am glad you are way more grounded than I have ever been."

"Someone has to be." They both smiled and laughed at each other.

"Beau, can I talk to you about something important?" Evie asked, feeling a little nervous about what she was about to say. "Sure. Should I be worried?" he asked. "No. I am just because it is so silly, but yet I still have insecurities I am trying to overcome," she replied.

"Like what?" he asked, looking concerned.

"Well," Evie began with hesitation, "I heard your interview on the radio station today." "What did you think?" he asked, looking more intensely at Evie. "I loved every word that came out of your mouth, but..."

"But? There's a but?" Beau looked even more concerned. He had insecurities he faced, as well. "I just figured the first time you would say you were in love with me would be to my face. Not on a radio station," Evie said, feeling extremely scared. "Oh, I see," Beau said, "Sorry. I was trying to tell the truth."

"I know. It shouldn't bother me, but this is something Jude would proclaim to his coworkers at the office all the time, but when he got home..." Evie couldn't finish the sentence.

"His follow-through sucked. Got it," Beau said. "I know you aren't Jude, but it's just my insecurities," she said. "You are right. I should have told you upfront on the first date rather than let the song speak around Thanksgiving."

"See, and I am a very dense woman compared to most. I should have put that together."

"But I have learned you are very literal and denotative, which is fine. Not to mention, it's nice because you don't play mind games like some other women I have known. I will do better."

"Thanks."

They hugged each other while sitting on the couch after resolving the issue. *Well, that was painless*, Evie thought.

That's when Beau decided to be bold. "Evie?"

"Yeah?" "Since we are on the subject," Beau began, taking a deep breath, "I love you."

Evie smiled. "I love you, too."

Beau stroked Evie's cheek before he leaned in. They kissed very passionately, and Beau laid down on the couch, pulling Evie on top of him. Soon the oven timer went off. Beau swore at the oven, and Evie laughed as she stood up to turn it off. She pulled the two pans of baked ziti out of the oven and set it on top to cool off. Beau followed her into the kitchen as Evie walked to the stove.

Beau walked behind her and nuzzled her neck after she set the pans down. Evie had a hard time focusing. "Keep it in your pants, man. People might see," she teased as she snuggled into Beau's chest. He chuckled, kissed her cheek, and turned Evie around. "Fine, but you owe me," he teased back. "Really?" Evie bantered while folding her arms, "who made dinner for everyone without leaving a mess and arranged your biggest tour to date?" Beau scowled again. "So, that means I owe you?" Evie nodded. "What do I owe you?" Beau asked.

Just as she was about to say it out loud, the kids walked inside. Levi immediately washed his hands and helped Harper as well. Evie then walked over to Beau and whispered what she had in mind after the kids went to bed. Beau's hormones flared, and for a moment, he thought about pushing all the dishes off of the dining table and laying on top of it with Evie. Then he remembered the kids were there and quickly stopped his thought process.

The four of them sat down to eat dinner, which was delicious. Beau hated comparing Evie to Phoebe because they were two different people, but he was only human. Phoebe was a good cook, but lots of times, she ordered take out or hired a chef. Evie was an excellent cook and preferred preparing the meals herself. He began to be thankful Evie chose to live the lifestyle of preparing meals and exercising because it helped Beau's lifestyle as well. All four talked about their day, plans for the tour, meeting Grandma and Grandpa West, being in Baltimore for Harper's birthday, visiting cousins and Evie's sister, and revisiting the White House and Smithsonian.

Beau felt nervous about meeting Evie's parents. He heard lots of positive stories about them, but he was still wary about meeting them. Beau always considered himself one of those guys a girl hid in her closet or pushed out the window instead of introducing him to her parents.

Soon, the rest of the band, spouses, and kids joined them and began eating. After clearing their dishes, the four of them went on a walk to the park where the kids played while Beau and Evie sat and watched. Occasionally, Beau would get up and chase the kids, causing lots of laughter on everyone's part. At one point, Beau and the kids ran to where Evie sat and tackled her. She got up and ran away from them. Soon, it was time to walk back to the studio so that the kids could get ready for bed. Once they were in bed, Beau read the kids a story, and Evie tucked them in bed. Beau and Evie proceeded to do what she talked about earlier that evening and slept in Beau's room.

Evie's alarm went off at 4 AM. Beau groaned as Evie turned it off and proceeded to put comfy casual clothes on. Beau pulled the covers over his head as Evie turned on the light in his closet. "Come on, Hon, it's time to get up," Evie said as she walked back to the bed to help wake Beau up. She kissed him tenderly on the cheek. "I hate waking up this early," Beau grumbled. "But you have no problem staying up this late?" Evie teased. "I haven't stayed up late in months," Beau argued, still feeling grumpy. "You can sleep on the plane," Evie whispered.

Beau gave up and sat up, rubbing his eyes. Evie stood up, but before she could walk away, Beau grabbed her and pulled her down on the bed. He began kissing her cheek and neck mainly to tease. They both laughed. "C'mon, Beau. We need to leave the studio at 4:30. Our flight leaves at 7," Evie said.

"We don't have two minutes?"

"Not unless you want to be late," Evie said.

"What's rock n' roll if we aren't late now and then?"

"What's rock n' roll about only taking two minutes?" Evie teased. Beau just kissed her to ignore her comment. Two minutes later, both got out of bed and got dressed.

After getting ready and loading sleeping kids in the car, Beau and Evie drove towards the airport while all the other vehicles followed them. There were town cars waiting for them in New York that would take them through the East Coast after their show in New York the following two days. The kids slept for three of the five hours on the flight. Beau and Evie managed to sleep during some of the trip, as well.

When the kids woke up, it was breakfast time, so Evie pulled out the kids' breakfast. Beau didn't realize that Evie had bought him and her some breakfast as well. They all ate as the kids watched a movie provided by the airlines. When they touched down, it was lunchtime.

The town cars picked them up and took them to the nearest Wendy's, where the band and crew all ate. A few fans noticed them and asked to get their pictures taken with the group. A couple of fans introduced themselves to Evie and told her how impressed with the work she did for promoting the tour, the new album, and helping Beau in his recovery. She felt very humbled and honored.

Once they were done eating lunch, they loaded back up on the tour bus and headed to the hotel they were staying at for that night. Evie felt that all four of them sharing a room would be very overwhelming for Beau, so she got her own room with the kids. The rooms were adjoining so that they could still be close. Evie snuck out of her room into Beau's at night, and she snuck back in before the kids woke up each morning, even getting a run on the treadmill in the hotel's gym.

The band and crew loaded up in the town cars late the next morning and headed over to Madison Square Garden. Evie oversaw the set up to make sure everything was in the right place. She advised Levi and Harper to help the crew as much as they could and to stay out of the way when it came time to move the big stuff. Evie was able to find a place in one of the locker rooms to set up a pack 'n play for Harper to take a nap while Levi had quiet time on one of the couches the crew brought. She hoped and prayed that Harper and Levi would be bright-eyed and bushy-tailed for the concert. Beau talked about hiring a nanny to take care of the kids while everyone had to work, but Evie didn't want to let someone else raise her kids.

It was a half-hour before the kick-off concert for their tour. Beau had on headphones warming up his voice with his tape he got a while back. Crew members were tuning guitars, and everyone else stood in silence, taking deep breaths.

Evie felt tense because she hoped everything would run smoothly. She wore the faux leather pants, and a rose gold flowy tank with embellishment around the neckline. She wore knee-high boots with a one-inch sole.

Beau was wearing his signature leather vest with Death Toll's logo on it as well as various bands and influences, a black tee-shirt, black jeans, and black boots. Kade's long, curly black hair sat on his shoulders. He wore a black silk shirt, a black leather vest, black jeans, and black boots as well. Kade painted his fingernails black. Rick wore a black Death Toll tee shirt and shorts with flip flops. His hair carried his signature four braids with a backward snapback. Luke dressed in layers like always wearing black because he still ended up shirtless by the end of the show. Evie encouraged him to get a haircut, which he did.

The lights soon went dark, and the hundreds of fans screamed at the top of their lungs as their pre-show song began. Adrenaline pumped through everyone's veins. The band took their places on stage, and soon the whole place lit up in a spectacular display of pyrotechnics and lights. The concert opener was *Wherever I May Roam*, which was a blend of the old and the new. Everyone cheered, sang along, clapped, and looked happy. Evie grinned from ear to ear as she heard each song on the playlist and the crowd cheering.

Death Toll played three songs before they decided to take a little talking break. Evie hadn't written the script for the concert, so she had no idea what was coming up next. One of the crew members grabbed Beau's white ESP EXplorer from him and handed him his black EXplorer. Kade and Rick had an instrument change as well, while Luke got out from behind the drumset to interact with the crowd. Once everyone had a new instrument, Luke went back and sat on his throne.

The crowd cheered louder as Beau approached the mic. "Wow, thank you!" Beau shouted into the mic. He noodled a little bit on the guitar, and the crowd got louder. Evie smiled at the showmanship.

"Okay," Beau said, trying to get the crowd to hush, which they did. "This next song is very special to me," he said, "It's about one of the best humans I have come to know. It is a very different song than any other we have done. Now, almost a year ago to the day, I lost my family in a terrible car accident, and I relapsed. I ended up back in rehab, a place I had no desire to go back to face my demons. A month later, I met this stubborn and independent woman with hurricane blue eyes who turned my whole life around. Six months later, she became the most important woman in my life, and I wrote this song for her. Evie, will you come out here, please?"

Beau turned to where Evie was standing, which was where they entered the arena. Her eyes widened, and she shook her head in terror very slowly. Beau's smile changed from showman to the man she was in love with as he saw the gesture. The crowd cheered louder, trying to get her to come on stage. She continued shaking her head very slowly. "Please, Babe?" he said in the mic. "What about the kids?" she shouted, pointing to backstage. Beau could see her lips move and her finger gesturing towards the locker rooms, and he figured she was talking about Levi and Harper. "Someone is taking care of them. They will be fine. Come on out," he said very compassionately into the mic. "Who's taking care of them?!" she shouted. Beau squinted, trying to read her lips. "I hired a nanny. Please come up here," Beau begged a final time.

Evie slowly started walking towards the stage. When she got on stage, the bright spotlights blurred her vision, and the crowd was the loudest it had ever been. Evie continued to walk to where Beau was not sure what he was planning.

When she got to him, Beau wrapped an arm around her, and they kissed tenderly. She waved to the cheering crowd, immediately regretting it. *This isn't concerto night in college, Evie. Just be cool*, she said to herself. Beau started talking in her ear, "I have a surprise for you." Suddenly, she felt a tap on her shoulder. She turned around, and a crew member she didn't know was holding her violin. Beau said again, "I've been hearing you play our song for weeks now. I think it is time you played with us."

She was scared, but also grateful because she wanted to perform so bad. When she grabbed her violin, she started tuning it. The crew member shouted, "I tuned it for you. You are amped up and ready to go." He slipped the monitor into her back pocket for her. She nodded at him. Beau motioned to Kade that Evie would be playing the solo, and Kade nodded. Evie took the violin, and the crowd cheered.

Kade started playing the opening arpeggio to *Nothing Else Matters*, and Evie soon came in on the opening solo. She played every guitar riff on her violin. When Beau started to sing, Evie often played with Rick on his bass lines. She occasionally added harmony and embellishments to Beau's singing. The crowd was surprisingly quiet throughout the whole song as they listened to all the excellent musicians. When the actual "guitar" solo came about, Evie played the solo with double stops and distortion as she imitated Beau's style. That's when the crowd went wild. When the song began fading, the crowd went quiet as Beau finished singing the song.

When the song finally faded, Beau and Evie kissed much more passionately. The crowd loved every minute of it. "I love you," Beau said tenderly. "I love you," Evie said. They kissed again before Evie bowed to the crowd. Beau walked off stage with her. "Do you think you could do an encore when we finish our setlist?" he asked. "Which song?" she asked. "*Enter Sandman*. I know you've been practicing that one, too," Beau said, winking. Evie smiled. "Yes, I can." He kissed her a final time before he went back on stage. "Oh, by the way, I made arrangements for you to play that concerto you know so well as part of this tour with many premier symphonies here on the East Coast," Beau said to her. Evie smiled and gave Beau an even bigger hug and kiss.

The concert continued, and Evie played the encore with Death Toll. When the song was over, Death Toll did their signature bow while Evie clapped. They then motioned toward her, and she bowed. The rest of the East Coast tour ran just as smoothly as that first night, including Evie's guest appearances with various symphonies and rehearsals.

Chapter 17

Harper's 3rd Birthday Party

Baltimore is a beautiful city, Beau thought to himself as he stood by the window wearing only sweatpants he slipped on when he got out of bed, peering through the drapes at the view from his hotel room. Watching the sunrise, he sipped his mug of hot cider with some supplements inside of it that Evie recommended. She laid in bed, sound asleep wearing only Beau's Death Toll tee shirt from the previous night.

He looked over at her. He knew today was a big day for both of them. Today was the day he would meet Evie's parents, her sister, her brother-in-law, nieces, and nephews. He also knew the chances of running into Jude were higher, considering he tried calling her last night after the show when they had gone to bed. He remembered why this was all happening; it was Harper's birthday. The sassy toddler was finally 3. They would be driving an hour away to Evie's hometown for a special birthday party for Harper at Evie's parents' house.

As the sun peered through the drapes, Evie began to stir. Beau turned around again and walked to her. He kissed her cheek. "Good morning, Beautiful," he said. Evie smiled. "Hey," she said sleepily. They kissed tenderly before Evie sat up. "What time is it?" she asked. "About 7:30," Beau said. "Crap, I need to get back to my room. The kids will be waking up," Evie said, grabbing her pajama bottoms. She slipped them on quickly and hurried towards the adjoining door. Beau smiled and grabbed Evie's arm.

He pulled her back in for a kiss. They kissed for a few seconds before she said, "Beau, I really need to go. I need to give Harper her birthday speech."

"What's a birthday speech?" he asked. "Come and see," she said, grabbing Beau's hand and leading him to her room. He grabbed the tee-shirt he threw on the table from last night and put it on.

They walked through the adjoining door to Evie's room. Evie slowly opened the door to ensure she didn't wake her kids up. Sure enough, they were still laying down in their beds, fast asleep. Evie and Beau walked into her room. Beau sat down on a chair and watched Evie walk over to Harper's bed. Evie bent over Harper and kissed her. "Happy Birthday, Baby Girl," she said quietly. Harper stirred before waking up. "Hi, Mommy," she said, scooting over so Evie could climb into bed with her.

"I can't believe how fast you're growing up," Evie said.

"But I'm still so little," Harper said.

"Trust me, it's going by so fast," Evie replied, "So, what do you think of your life so far?"

"I like it," Harper said.

"That's good. Any complaints?" Evie asked.

"I'd like to see Grandma and Grandpa a bit more," Harper said.

"We will today, and I will work on it more," Evie said.

"Do I look older?" Harper asked.

"Very much so. You'll have to start paying for your movie tickets soon," Evie teased, but continued, "Guess what I think?"

"What?" Harper asked.

"I think you are the sweetest, sassiest, prettiest little girl I know, and the best daughter a girl could hope for," Evie said.

"Thanks, Mommy," Harper said.

"And it is so hard to believe that at exactly this time on this day, I was lying in the same position with a fat stomach, fat face, and fat ankles pushing this sweet little girl out...."

Evie proceeded to tell the graphic story of how Harper was born, including a comparison to the pain using anecdotes from Carol Burnett, Bill Cosby, and even Loralai Gilmore. Beau only knew Loralai Gilmore because Phoebe loved watching Gilmore Girls. Evie also mentioned the funny story of how Jude threw up just before he cut the umbilical cord. Despite the graphic detail Evie went into, Beau smiled. He treasured this moment he got to watch. Evie was, indeed, a great mother. He only assumed she did the same thing with Levi. He hoped to witness that one in a couple of months when Levi would be seven.

"Guess what time it is?" Evie said to Harper. "What!?" Harper exclaimed. "It's time to get ready to go see Grandma and Grandpa!" Evie exclaimed. Harper gasped enthusiastically. She immediately jumped out of bed and onto Levi's bed, where she proceeded to dance to wake Levi up. "Wake up! Wake Up!" Harper said over and over again, jumping up and down. Levi sat up complaining, but when he heard the words, Grandma and Grandpa, he jumped up as well. "Happy Birthday, Harper!" he shouted. "Thank you!" she said back. "Shh! Guys, other guests are probably asleep, so we need to be quiet."

The kids quickly but quietly grabbed their clothes and began changing. Beau slipped into his room to change as well. He put on a charcoal Oxford shirt hiding his tattoos besides the ones on his hands and the one that poked out around his collarbone. Beau also slipped on some nice jeans and his loafers.

After getting dressed, Beau knocked on the door, and Levi answered. "Good morning!" Levi said, smiling. Beau gave him a big hug before looking over at Harper, who was staring right at Beau, wearing a light pink lace dress. "Is it someone's birthday today?" Beau asked mischievously. Harper grinned from ear to ear. "It's Harper's birthday!" Levi shouted. Both kids giggled. "Happy Birthday, Miss Harper!" Beau said, hugging her before kissing her cheek. "Thank you," Harper said, still grinning.

Evie then walked out of the bathroom wearing a bell-sleeved striped shirt with blush-colored pants. Her hair was straight and tucked behind her ears. She wore her black sunglasses on her head like a headband for the moment, and she had a black purse with a gold chain strap over her shoulder. She wore black strap sandals. When she saw what Beau was wearing, Evie was caught off guard by his appearance. He dressed very similarly to when they went on their first date minus the jacket. She knew he was nervous about meeting her family, so she didn't say a word.

All four of them went down to the hotel lobby for breakfast. Beau had found the hotel with the best breakfast in the morning because he knew how important that was to Evie's kids. Luke, Kade, and Rick were already sitting in the dining room, eating. The kids ran over to them to give hugs. "Happy Birthday, Harper!" the three of them each said. She grinned back at them. They each reached into their pockets and pulled out necklaces. Harper squealed and said, "Thank you!" She hugged each of them again before she and Levi made their way back to the table.

Evie and Beau grabbed food for everyone and chose a table while Levi and Harper were talking to the other band members. As Beau walked past Luke, Luke said, "You're pretty fancy today. What's the occasion besides Harper's birthday?" Before Beau could answer, Evie said, "He's meeting my parents today." "That's right. Well, good luck," Luke said, raising his glass of mimosa before taking a drink.

When the kids sat down, they began to eat the food that was in front of them. Evie pulled out a baggy of her protein powder and supplements, poured each of them into her water cup, and stirred. She began drinking it as well as picking at the eggs on her plate. Beau ate the sausage and bacon that was in front of him while Harper ate everything on her plate, and Levi ate bacon, eggs, and sausages. After everyone finished, Beau asked Levi to help him carry the dishes, empty them in the garbage, and put them on top of the garbage cans to be collected later. Evie and Harper stood up afterwards and followed Beau and Levi out to the rental car that Beau acquired the previous day for the trip.

The drive was beautiful as they looked out at the coast. Harper fell asleep in her car seat while Levi colored in a coloring book. Beau and Evie held hands. She gave Beau directions on where to go to get to her parents' house. Evie's parents lived in the Highland Beach district of Annapolis. Harper requested to go for a ride on the family boat while they were staying there.

Beau played out every single scenario of how the trip could go. He knew Evie came from a good family just like Phoebe did, and he always felt intimidated by that. He felt like he was sweating bullets as he pulled in front of a rambler with a huge yard surrounded by trees with a minivan parked in the driveway. Evie could sense he was tense, so she squeezed his hand and said, "My parents are going to love you." "Are you sure? I'm not exactly the picture-perfect guy parents expect to bring home to Mom and Dad," he said. Evie smiled lightly. "They will love you because I love you," she said calmly. Beau calmed down a little as he climbed out of the car and helped Harper get out of the vehicle. Evie climbed out and grabbed Levi's hand as he closed his door.

The walk up the driveway felt very long, but bearable as Beau squeezed Evie's hand. Eventually, Levi and Harper bolted for the front door and rang the bell. By the time the grown-ups got to the door, a middle-aged woman with dark hair and green eyes opened it. When she smiled, Beau saw Evie. He knew instantly that this was Karen West, Evie's mom. She was a little shorter than Evie and was more voluptuous than her daughter. "Hello!" Mrs. West said. "Grandma!" the kids shouted as they gave her a huge hug. Mrs. West looked up at her daughter and smiled even more.

The women hugged very tightly. "Hello, my pretty girl! Your hair has gotten so long," Mrs. West said. "You look good, too, Mommy," Evie said. Beau smiled. *She calls her mother Mommy*, he thought, *that's sweet*. The women separated, and Mrs. West turned to Beau. "This must be Beau," Mrs. West said, holding her hand out. Beau grabbed her hand and shook it. He watched his tattooed hand shake this woman's hand for a split second, and he could not help but wonder what she was thinking.

However, Mrs. West looked directly at Beau's eyes with the same kindness in them that Evie possessed. Rather than intense blue, Mrs. West's eyes were intense green. "Nice to meet you, Mrs. West," Beau said, trying to hide his nerves. "Please, call me Karen," she said, smiling. Beau could see why Evie was so warm and friendly. Her mom was like that. "Well, let's go inside. Everyone is here," Karen said.

Everyone walked inside. Levi and Harper were already running around outside with three other kids with brown hair and brown eyes. Beau looked around the hallway to see various pictures of her parents' adventures, Evie and her family, and another woman's family. She had red hair, green eyes, and was very fair-skinned in contrast to Evie's more medium complexion. Beau assumed that was Evie's sister, Jennifer.

They walked through the large foyer and into the living room with a huge sectional. Two men and the red-headed woman were sitting on it. The older man had dark hair that was going grey. He was average height and average weight with a more olive complexion. That explained why Evie's skin was darker than her sister's. He stood up, walked towards Beau and Evie, and hugged his youngest daughter. "How are you, Evs?" he asked. "Excellent," she said to her dad. Mr. West then turned to Beau, held out his hand, and said, "Richard West." Beau grabbed his hand and shook it. Both of them noticed that they each had a firm handshake.

As they shook hands, Evie and Jennifer were already hugging. Beau knew how close the girls were growing up since it was only them. Beau thought he saw Jennifer mouth the words, "He's cute." He smiled, feeling a little smug. "Jennifer, Evie's favorite and only sister," she said, holding out her hand. Beau smiled as he shook Jennifer's hand. The other man, Hispanic with dark brown hair and light brown eyes, stood up. "Andres Martinez, Evie's brother-in-law," the man said with a Spanish accent. "Beau Halstead," Beau said as he reached for Andres' hand. He also had a firm handshake.

Once all of the adults sat down, five children, including Levi and Harper, came running through the living room to go to the playroom. "Freeze!" Jennifer shouted. All five froze and turned to look at her. "Martin, Alicia, Matteo, we have a visitor," she said. The oldest boy, who was about seven or eight, noticed Evie sitting on the couch. "Hi, Evie!" he said. "Hey, Marty! How are you?" Evie said as she stood up to hug her oldest nephew. The little girl who looked about Levi's age walked up to Evie and hugged her. The three-year-old boy followed. He assumed the girl was Alicia, and the little boy was Mateo. All three kids looked very similar, but the youngest boy looked the most like his dad. Alicia looked a lot like her grandmother and similar to Evie. Beau could feel how warm and welcoming the household was.

Beau found out that Harper requested her uncle's famous tacos for dinner as well as the family's guacamole. Beau watched the family gather together to make the food. While Andres was cooking the taco meat, Evie and Jennifer were making the guacamole. Karen and Richard were busy adding in the extra leaf to the table and setting it up.

Beau also knew that once they were done eating their early dinner, they were going to go out on Richard's boat, have snacks, and eat birthday cake. Beau found Richard to be a little intimidating because he was the head of the household. He also seemed very protective of his family, especially his youngest daughter. Beau knew that Evie was her dad's little hunting and fishing buddy while she was a child.

Before dinner started, Richard asked Beau to follow him outside where the kids were playing. Beau knew the talk was coming. "I am pretty sure you know what my question is," Richard West said. "I think so. Mr. West, I love your daughter. She is the most selfless, kind, caring, and nurturing woman I have ever met. She has so much talent and spunk," Beau said. Richard nodded his head and smiled. "I've never seen Evie so happy. About a year into her marriage, she started to lose a lot of her spunk and personality. Thank you for bringing her back." "She saved me way before I saved her, I assure you. She puts everyone else first before herself," Beau said. "Ah, a family trait. Evie takes after her mother, but she inherited my temper. Be warned," Richard said. "Noted," Beau said, remembering the Strong Nation class.

The men continued to talk about common interests, including hunting and fishing. Richard told Beau about the time he took Evie to Alaska to hunt for moose when she was about 15. Richard then told stories of Evie when she was a child. Beau laughed because he now had confirmation that Levi was more like his mother than Harper was, but Harper was still incredibly sweet just like her mom.

The men went back inside after calling the kids inside for dinner. The three oldest wanted to sit by Grandpa, which they all did on a bench next to Richard. Matteo and Harper were in high chairs. Suddenly, Beau heard a baby cry. "I will go get her," Evie said as she stood up and walked out of the dining room. Beau remembered that Jennifer had another baby around Halloween. Evie often showed pictures of Baby Andrea to Beau.

After a couple of minutes, Evie soon walked back into the room, carrying a baby with chubby cheeks. Just like her older brother, she had dark hair, light eyes, and fair skin. Andrea was a beautiful chunky baby. Evie sat back down at the table, ready to eat, holding her sweet niece. Beau could not help but smile while watching Evie hold the baby. He wondered if there would be a baby in their future.

Everyone ate in peace for the most part. Levi ate his version of tacos, Marty ate the fruit on the table, and the rest of the kids ate everything else. Beau could not believe how delicious the tacos were. The meat, guacamole, and salsa had such flavor. He now understood why Evie's favorite food was tacos. Beau ended up eating about five tacos while everyone else had about 2-3 and snacked on the chips, salsa, and guacamole. Soon, everyone assisted Karen in cleaning up the table so that they could head out to the marina. Harper's excitement burst through the seams.

While everyone cleaned up, Karen took Harper into the other room for her birthday surprise. Richard went into the garage to gather the lifejackets. Jennifer and Andres were sitting on the couch cuddling with their baby while Evie continued to put dishes in the dishwasher and put food into containers. Beau walked behind Evie and put his arms around her. He kissed her cheek, tenderly. "Want help?" he asked. "Yeah, thanks." Beau went to the counter and began scooping the guacamole. "Remember to keep some of the pits in the container as well. That's what keeps it fresh," Evie said. "Didn't know that. Thanks," Beau said, fascinated.

Suddenly, the doorbell rang. Karen walked to the front door to answer it. "Oh, Jude!" Karen exclaimed from the foyer. Evie froze. Beau suddenly felt the hairs on the back of his neck stand up. "I came to see my daughter," Jude said. Karen hated confrontation, and Evie knew that. Evie quickly came to her mother's rescue. Before the trip, Evie talked to her parents about not letting Jude in the house. Her dad was nowhere in sight, so she went to her mom's aid.

"Hi," Evie said, "Mommy, could you go help Jennifer with Andrea, please?" "Yes," Karen said before walking back inside. Just as Karen walked inside, she nearly bumped into Beau. "I wouldn't go out there. Might make things worse," Karen said. "I'm just going to watch unless he starts yelling at her," Beau said. Karen nodded. Beau listened carefully to their conversation.

"You look... just... wow," Jude said. "Yeah, yeah. I got my body back. What brings you here?" Evie said. "Our daughter is three today," Jude said. "You missed her birthday last year even when we lived with you. Why this year?" Evie asked. Jude stared down at the ground. "I don't know. No comment on how I look?" Jude asked, hoping for acknowledgment of some affection. "You still look like a lying, cheating schmuck to me," Evie said without any emotion.

"So, can I see our girl?" Jude asked, ignoring the comment. "No," Evie said firmly. "Why not?" Jude asked, starting to fume. "Because you came here unannounced without checking with me first. I believe there is a clause under Visitation that states there needs to be open communication with both parties for visits, and by coming here without communicating with me, you are in direct violation. If you want to see her, you will need to call later and make the arrangements," Evie said, not letting up on the firmness.

Jude's temper began to flare. "I tried calling yesterday to make the arrangements," he hissed. "At 3 AM when we are in bed? You broke the agreement, so I have every right to say 'no' right now," Evie said.

"She's my daughter, though. Not that neander...."

"This has nothing to do with Beau! Leave him out of this!" Evie scolded.

"I'm the one who makes sure she and Levi get fed, attend good schools, have a roof over their head, clothes..." Jude snapped.

"Keep letting your ideal world tell you that when you send me that money, which only covers my rent," she responded to him.

"So what? Is Beau her 'father' now? I helped create that girl!" Jude yelled.

"Yes, you provided 23 chromosomes to make her, but you're not her dad. Any douche can father a child," Evie said with a little chagrin.

Burn, Beau thought to himself as he watched his girlfriend confront her ex. He suddenly saw Jude raise his hand towards Evie's face. Before it made contact, Beau ran outside and punched Jude in the nose knocking him down. Beau wrapped his arms around Evie as they watched Jude roll on the ground gripping his nose gushing out blood. "Are you okay?" Beau asked, turning to look at Evie. "Yeah, I'm fine," she replied. "Were you seriously going to let him hit you?" he asked, sounding concerned. "No, I had it under control," Evie said. Beau realized that if he had waited longer, Jude would have received an uppercut to the chin.

Jude finally regained some composure to stand up, wiping his nose. Some blood had gotten on his shirt. Beau stared Jude down, and Jude scowled at Beau. "Evie, I need you to go inside, please," Beau said. "Um… no. You guys aren't going to fight," she said. "We're not going to fight, are we?" Beau said to Jude. "No, we're not. It will be civilized," Jude noted, wiping his nose some more. Evie slowly turned around and walked back inside.

"Wow, you have some nerve," Beau said. "You're the one who punched me. I'd say you have nerve getting involved." "Getting involved? I have done nothing but trying to get Evie uninvolved with you from the beginning because all you want to do is control her. I know you regret letting her go, especially after seeing how happy she is without you in her life trying to control everything she does."

"She was happy with me."

"Keep telling yourself that," Beau said with a little arrogance.

"Why do you think Evie chose to be with you? Because she wants those feelings back when she was with me."

"No, she doesn't. Evie was miserable with you because all you do is think about yourself. You let her go, and you realized what an idiotic move that was on your part because she is the most selfless person you know, and you liked that ego boost every day. She chose me because we make each other happy. It's not a one-sided relationship," Beau concluded.

Just then, the front door opened again. Richard walked outside onto the lawn. "Jude, I need to ask you to leave. You are not welcome here anymore," Richard said. "My family is in there!" Jude yelled. "I have called the police. If you're not off my property in two minutes, they will escort you off," Richard said calmly but firmly. Jude slowly walked to his car, climbed in, and drove away.

As Jude pulled out of the driveway, Richard said to Beau, "Don't play his game. Don't argue with him, and keep loving and protecting my daughter like you did today." Richard walked back inside his house. Beau stared at the street again, making sure Jude was truly gone. Sure enough, he never came back, and Beau walked inside into the living room, sat down by Evie, and wrapped his arms around her holding her a little tighter than before.

Soon, everyone loaded up into cars and headed towards the marina, where Richard parked his boat. Before they left, Jennifer and Evie helped their mom pack the snacks. Jennifer asked, "So, are you guys going to get married, do you think?"

Evie blushed. "We've only been dating for six months. I think it's a little early to be thinking about that," Evie responded.

"True, but you both fit so well together, it's creepy. He's very charismatic and just lets you be you," Jennifer said.

"I know. That's why I love him," Evie said.

"He has such a wonderful smile and eyes only for you."

Evie blushed again. "Thanks. Even with his rough exterior?" Evie asked. "Did you think we would all have a problem with the tattoos and his past?"

"Maybe a little considering the last guy I was in a serious relationship was a narcissist, so my judgment on men might be compromised."

"We were a little surprised to see you with him on TV, but we noticed the way he looked at you, and we quickly got over that. Plus, it's ironic that the clean-cut guy turned out to be a complete douche, whereas the rough rocker turned out to be the loving and supportive man you always deserved."

"I've often pondered the irony myself."

Soon, everyone was on the boat. Richard pulled out of the marina and drove towards the open ocean. Soon, they were going fast. Beau held on tightly to Harper and Evie as she held onto Levi. Richard drove his boat very fast as they pulled out of the harbor. He soon pulled up to the West Secret fishing spot, as Evie called it, and soon started pulling out fishing poles. "Want some help?" Beau asked. "Sure," Richard responded.

Beau handed Harper to Evie before standing up to assemble fishing poles. In about ten minutes, everyone had a fishing pole in the water. Within fifteen minutes, Levi and Marty had hooked some fish. Harper soon followed as well as the other kids. Beau watched the kids reel up the fish. Evie and Jennifer took pictures of the kids with their fish. Soon, Karen pulled out the birthday cake and candles. Everyone sang to Harper, and her grin was the biggest as her mother took her picture. Evie was so thankful that Harper was having fun.

After about two hours on the water, everyone reeled in, and they drove back to the harbor. Soon, Beau, Evie, Levi, and Harper were back in the rental car heading towards Baltimore. The kids were sound asleep, and Beau held Evie's hand. "That was lots of fun," Beau said. "Yes, it was. What did you think of my family?" Evie asked. "Everyone is so kind, especially your mom," Beau responded. "She is the most selfless person I know," Evie said, thinking about her sweet mother. "I'm glad you take mostly after her." Beau squeezed Evie's hand. "Me too." Evie smiled.

Chapter 18

Evie Moves In

The first leg of the tour was over. Evie felt super relieved as she crashed on the first living room couch, where she talked with Dr. Bennett. She and the kids would be living at the studio for a while until she could find another place to live. Beau walked into the living room and sat down next to her just as Dr. Bennett walked out with his briefcase.

"So," Beau said, "it was good meeting your family."

Evie smiled. "It was. Fishing was a lot of fun," she said.

"I keep forgetting to take you and the kids fishing."

"Since when do we have time?"

"The next couple of months before we go back on tour."

"Maybe I need to see what the schedule will be like after I hire a tutor for Levi to keep him caught up with school during the summer."

"What if I helped out with that expense?"

Evie considered it for a minute, but ultimately, she thought it wouldn't be a good idea because Levi was her responsibility, not Beau's. "I appreciate the offer, but I can educate my own son," she said.

Beau knew how relentless, stubborn, and independent she was, but he also knew how to get past the walls. "What if I was around more to ensure Levi got the right education, and Harper got into a good preschool?"

"How?"

"The three of you move in with me."

Evie paused. "Sorry, what?"

"Move in with me." Beau grabbed both of Evie's hands, feeling like he was pleading.

"What...? Are you...? Have you...?" Evie was having a hard time forming a sentence. "How long have you been thinking about this?" she finally said.

"Since I saw you holding Andrea."

"Why didn't you mention anything all those months ago?"

"Because it was just an idea, but think about it. You need a roof over your head. You guys stay at my house about four days a week, and my house is in a good school district where they can accommodate Levi's behavior issues."

"What would that mean for our relationship?" Evie asked. "Well, I think that means it's progressing," Beau joked. Evie could feel herself start to hyperventilate. The thought of living with Beau was both exciting and terrifying because she loved Beau and wanted to be with him, but Evie was afraid that living with Beau would change their relationship in a negative way like it did before with Jude.

Beau realized his joke triggered Evie's anxiety, so he pulled her next to him, hugging her tightly. He noticed this move instantly calmed her down. Evie closed her eyes listening to Beau's soothing heartbeat again. "I understand you're freaking out," Beau said, trying to comfort Evie, "but I haven't been able to get your words out of my head since before we started dating."

"Which ones? I talk a lot," Evie said.

Beau chuckled. "I know. That's one of the reasons I love you. It was after we kissed for the first time. You said that if we continued, there was no going back. That would be it for you. Well, I'm all in, Babe. I want you, all three of you. I'm not saying we have to get married tomorrow or within the next month, but I do see us moving forward toward that. I see us getting married maybe in a couple of years, me adopting the kids, and having our own. The question is, has your mind changed since we started dating? Have you thought about our future?"

Evie looked into Beau's eyes; those lidded, blue, almond-shaped eyes she knew so well and who knew her. Beau was the love of her life, but commitment scared her still.

"Babe, you've been quiet for a while. I'm a little worried now," Beau said.

Evie chuckled. "Sorry. I was thinking. The answer is I'm on the same page as you with our relationship. I can see us getting married within that time frame as well, maybe another kid with a huge emphasis on maybe, and you adopting Levi and Harper, but you know how commitment scares me."

"I know. That's another reason I haven't brought it up because I didn't want to freak you out."

Evie continued to process the conversation. She knew how committed, loving, protective, and caring Beau was to her and the kids. Harper called Beau "Daddy" once, and no one corrected her. She called him that ever since. Levi always asked when Beau would be his dad. As Evie continued processing everything that was said, she looked up into Beau's eyes, and serenity swept through her frame. He was the love of her life.

"Okay," she said. Beau's eyes grew wide.

"Okay?" he asked for reassurance.

"Okay. Let's move in together," Evie said.

Beau kissed her. They hugged for a while. "So, when should we move in?" Evie asked. "Why not today?" Beau asked. Evie laughed. "Don't we need to figure out what to keep of mine and what to keep of yours?" Beau paused.

He didn't realize all the stuff there was to go through. "Well, what do you want to keep of yours?" Beau asked. Evie thought for a moment about the stuff she wanted to keep and what she wanted to give away. "Well," she began, "I really like my sectional, and I think you do, too." Beau nodded his head in agreement. "I want to keep the TV in my room and put it in your room, keep my bed and bedding, all of the kids' belongings, my crockpot, and that's about it," Evie concluded. "So, what are we keeping of mine?" Beau asked. "Your TV in the living room, your dishes, cookware, your Instapot, and pretty much everything I didn't mention," Evie said.

"Works for me. So do you want me to hire movers to arrange everything?" Beau asked. Evie nodded. "All right. I will call them. I can oversee what they put in the house and take out. What should we do with the stuff we don't want?" "What about The Struggle Ends charity Death Toll is doing?" Evie asked.

"Oh yeah! I forgot about that. Sure, I will take care of everything." Beau grabbed his phone and looked up movers. He called the best ones and made all the arrangements while Evie went to Beau's room and the kids' rooms to gather all their stuff to take over to Beau's house.

Evie was excited to be living in a house again. She loved his home. It was huge, but she loved the location, which was near a bunch of hiking trails. It was far away from all of the noise of San Francisco, but very close to the studio. She loved the vaulted ceilings and the kitchen. She noticed that her style was a bit more modern, considering Phoebe had decorated it more cabin chic. Evie liked contemporary farmhouse chic, but she knew Beau wouldn't care about the house decor.

Evie loaded the stuff and the kids in the car and drove to Beau's house. She couldn't believe it was her house now. On the way, Levi asked, "Mommy, have you found a house yet?" Evie smiled. "Yes, we are on our way now. It's a surprise," she said, hoping her kids would be excited about their new house. "Are we living by Beau?" Harper asked in broken toddler language. Evie smiled again. "You will see," she responded.

Evie pulled up into the available slot in Beau's big garage with his hot rods and car collection. "Mom, I don't get it. We are at Beau's house," Levi said as Evie opened the door for him. "Well, I told you we were going to our new home, and we are at Beau's house," Evie said, trying to help Levi solve the puzzle. Levi thought for a moment. "So, is Beau's house our home?" he asked. Evie nodded her head. "Where will Beau live?" Harper asked. "We are living with him since we needed a place to live," Evie replied, smiling.

It took a couple more minutes, but the kids eventually grinned. "Is Beau finally going to be my dad?" Levi asked, very excited. Evie hesitated. "Do you want him to be?" Evie asked. "Yes, I do," Levi said. "Then ask him tonight. I know he would love that," Evie said.

Meanwhile, Beau was at Evie's storage unit, pointing at all the things he and Evie discussed they would give to Death Toll's charity. Beau gave a list of furniture and items from his house for the movers to take to the charity. He was very excited to begin this new chapter in his life with Evie and the kids.

Suddenly, a gut-wrenching thought came to his mind; Chloe and Cordell's rooms were untouched since they passed, and Beau knew their rooms would be way better for Levi and Harper since they were in the same wing as his room. When he got home from the tour, Beau was finally able to sleep in the master bedroom again, but he wasn't sure if he could go through his kids' belongings after all these months. He quickly pulled out his phone and called Evie.

"Hey, Hon! What's up?" Evie answered.

"The movers have everything under control. I'm on my way home. Could you meet me outside Chloe's room?" he asked.

Evie paused. "Are you sure?" she asked.

"Yeah, I'm sure," he said.

"All right. I will see you in about fifteen minutes?" Evie asked.

"Yeah. Love you! Bye," Beau said.

"Love you! Bye," Evie said.

Beau put his phone back in his pocket. He gave the list to the man in charge, climbed into his brand new Tesla that he bought after the first leg of the tour was over, and began driving. His thoughts wandered to Phoebe and his kids. He tried to remember the happy times instead of the pain their deaths had caused him. As he drove home, Evie made a simple dinner, put it in the oven, and set the kids up with a movie. She began walking up the stairs into the wing Beau lived in with his family. Evie could feel their presence there, and she knew this whole thing would be hard for Beau.

Soon, she heard Beau walking up the stairs. He looked very melancholy, and Evie hugged and kissed him. He was so grateful she was there to make this whole experience bearable for him. "You ready?" she asked. Beau nodded as he reached for Chloe's door and opened it.

Inside was a white twin bed with all sorts of pink and lace on it. The white dresser had all kinds of ballet decor on top lying down next to some hair accessories. Her ballet shoes hung over the bed. Dolls and toys were overflowing the bins. Her pajamas were still on her bed from the last night she slept in the room. Beau walked over to Chloe's bed, grabbed her pajamas, hugged them, and sat down on the bed. Tears filled his eyes as he buried his face into the pajama shirt. Tears filled Evie's eyes as she watched Beau mourn his daughter. Evie walked into the room, sat down on the bed next to him, and put her arm around him.

Beau laid his head down in Evie's lap, holding the shirt against his face. It still smelled like his sweet Chloe. He remembered how happy, kind, and smart she was. He remembered going with Phoebe to Chloe's ballet classes. He loved watching her dance. He missed his little girl so much.

"Beau," Evie began not knowing what to say. She rubbed his shoulder. Beau cleared his sniffles. "What?" he said. "Why did you want to come in here?" she asked. "Because it's time to move on with life. I need to deal with these emotions so I can move on with life," Beau concluded. "Are you saying you want to give Levi or Harper Chloe's room?" she asked. Beau nodded. "We can continue living in the other wing," Evie said.

Beau shook his head. "No, it's time," he said with tears and a raspy voice. "I just wish I knew what to do to help you," Evie said, trying not to start sobbing herself. Beau quickly sat up, looked Evie in the eyes, and caressed her face. "You have done more than you know," Beau said, "I am so grateful that you let me into your life and the kids' lives. All three of you have been the best therapy for me. Yes, I am sad, but look up at those," Beau said, pointing to Chloe's ballet shoes. Evie turned around to look at the point shoes on the wall. "Things like these are filled with so many wonderful memories. I think Chloe understands that two other little kids need a father to watch them grow up and teach them how to live their best lives," Beau concluded.

Evie, with tears in her eyes, smiled and hugged Beau. She turned back to look at the ballet shoes. "I think we should keep those," she said, pointing at the point shoes, "and these." Evie touched the pajamas Beau held. "I agree," Beau said, smiling with watery eyes, "what do you think about the bed frame and dresser? Do you think Harper would like this room?"

"I think she will love the room, the bed frame, and the dresser," Evie said. Beau and Evie hugged again. Evie stood up and grabbed the ballet shoes off the wall, and gave them to Beau. "Where would you like those?" she asked. "I have a special box of items I keep that remind me of Phoebe and my kids. I will put these in it," Beau said. "That's awesome. I will make sure we never get rid of that box," Evie said.

After deciding more thoroughly about what to keep of Chloe's, Beau and Evie moved onto Cordell's room. The process wasn't any easier for Beau as he sorted through Cordell's belongings. There were a lot of balls, trucks, and giant Lego blocks in the various toy bins. His bedding followed the theme of the room, as well. Beau decided to keep Cordell's baby blanket because Cordell walked around with it everywhere. Since the room was the same size as Chloe's, Beau and Evie decided to keep the espresso bed frame and matching dresser inside for Levi.

As the movers came through and boxed up everything to take it to The Struggle Ends Foundation, Evie pondered a question she had had for a while now, but couldn't find herself to ask Beau. *Are we the replacements*, she thought to herself. She shrugged it off, and continued comforting Beau. After everyone moved in, ate dinner, and the kids were in bed, Evie finally mustered enough courage to ask Beau the question. They were sitting on Evie's massive sectional watching Beau's show when Evie decided it was the right time.

"Beau?"

"Yeah?"

Evie hesitated, but finally went on, "I've often wondered if the kids and I replaced your family. Is this what it is?"

Beau turned off the TV and faced Evie. "No, not at all," he replied, "I wasn't expecting my life to go this way at all. I consider you and the kids blessings. I think God and even Phoebe knew how much I needed you. I don't think you realize what an angel you have been to me in my life."

"I just took a job originally and tried to work as hard as I could, but I didn't think I helped you at all with those early months. I was just a huge nag," Evie said.

"Even when you were the 'huge nag,' as you called yourself," Beau said with a chuckle, "you said a lot of things that made me rethink my life choices. I remember when we went to Nole's plaque, you said something interesting that I've never forgotten. There are lots of those, by the way," Beau said, laughing again.

"What was that?" Evie asked, smiling.

"That my mom and Nole were watching over me during all those accidents I had during the early years. I now believe Phoebe joined the team when she died, and all three of them sent you and the kids to me because they knew I needed an angel with me," Beau said.

Evie digested his words and smiled. "I've had a lot of those thoughts as well," she said, "and I believe it was no coincidence that I moved here." Beau smiled, feeling happy that Evie agreed with him. They hugged each other. "Sorry, your first night home was an intense one," Beau said. "It's okay. I am glad I was here to help you, and I'm glad I'm here with you," Evie said. Beau wrapped his arms around Evie, pulling her back down on the couch before he turned the movie back on. They fell asleep ten minutes later, where they stayed the night.

Chapter 19

The AMA's and No Roadblocks

The album, <u>Death Toll</u>, was up for Best Metal Performance AMA. It wasn't just one song that stood out in the record, but the whole album itself. Beau, Luke, Kade, and Rick were all ecstatic about this accomplishment. Death Toll, or the "Dark Album" as fans and band members began to call it because of the dark artwork on the cover, had sold well over 500,000 copies in the opening week, and now had sold almost two million copies since the first leg of the tour ended. When Evie got the phone call that Death Toll was up for an AMA, she ran into the studio where the guys were and put the phone on speaker so they could all hear the conversation. They were all so happy. They were even asked to perform at the award show.

The AMA's would mark almost one year since Beau and Evie began dating. She and the kids had been living with Beau for five months. Levi was at the top of his class in first grade, and Harper was thriving at preschool. Beau thought about proposing to Evie as their first anniversary approached. Still, he hesitated to do so because every time he made a suggestion to take their relationship to the next step, Evie freaked out. Sure, they talked about the future, but not enough to get the ball rolling.

The night of the AMA's arrived, and all of the producers rode in one limo. Kade and Laila rode in another limo, Rick and Kaylee rode in another limo, Luke and Jetta rode in another limo, and Beau and Evie rode in the last limo. Evie made sure they all had on their best suits. Beau even made arrangements for a designer to come and design a gown for Evie. She wore a blush-colored mermaid strapless dress with a subtle sweetheart neckline, sequins across the neckline, and sequins speckled all over the dress. Her hair was pulled up into a low updo. She had been hounded by paparazzi before, but she was more nervous than she had ever been.

The limousine pulled up to the red carpet, and cameras began going off. A doorman opened the car door. Beau scooted out first, waved to the people, and turned back to the car to help Evie get out. She did not know how a woman gracefully climbed out of limos at award shows in ballgowns. Feeling like a monkey crawling on the ground, she climbed out of the car. Every single camera caught her ungraceful moment. She waved at the crowd and smiled, trying to be gracious.

Beau and Evie proceeded to walk up the red carpet. Eventually, they came to Nancy O'Dell of Entertainment Tonight. "And here we have Beau Halstead of Death Toll and his lovely partner and tour manager, Evie Long. Beau, what are you anticipating for tonight?" she asked. "Well, we are performing, and someone will take home the AMA for Best Metal Performance. We are just happy to be here, that our artistry is being celebrated, and I get to share this moment with Evie," Beau said, turning to look at Evie. She blushed.

"And Evie," Nancy shifted the conversation. Evie froze. "You are absolutely glamorous in that dress. Who are you wearing tonight?" Nancy asked. "I honestly have no idea. A guy came, took measurements and coloring, and then made me this dress. Two weeks later, it was dropped off at the house," Evie said, looking up at Beau to see if he knew the designer. "Valentino," he whispered in her ear. "Oh, Valentino," Evie said before turning back to Beau and whispered, "Really?" Nancy looked underwhelmed by Evie's speech. Evie felt a little deflated.

"So, you're living together now?" Nancy asked, trying to make things interesting again. Beau smiled and put his arm around Evie's shoulders. "Happily, I might add. And may I just say to her ex...." Evie covered his mouth before he could finish. "You know, Nancy, we are thrilled to be here. The band, especially Beau, has come a long way since those dark days. I am sure they will not disappoint the audience and viewers from all over the country," Evie said. "All right, thank you both for being here. We look forward to your performance," Nancy concluded. Evie grabbed Beau's hand and pulled him along.

"Why wouldn't you let me finish...?" Beau started.

"Because you're a grown-ass man, and the kids are watching this," Evie interrupted, "I don't want to give Jude any more fire, power, or control than what he already has."

Oops, Beau realized. "Sorry, I wasn't thinking."

"Good thing you're dating your tour manager," Evie joked, "and you're forgiven."

There were cameras all over the place as they proceeded across the red carpet into the Staples Center in Los Angeles. Evie wasn't sure how many people took pictures of the spat, but she didn't really care. *That's real life*, she thought to herself. She recognized a few reporters from MTV and VH1. She saw cameramen from all national broadcasting stations. She tried to stay calm and be gracious. The dress pinched around her chest, and she questioned whether or not she would be able to wear it all night. Her feet were beginning to hurt, but she bore it well. She knew she would spend the majority of the night sitting in the arena.

Evie saw all sorts of performers, entertainers, and musicians she never dreamed or thought she would meet. She saw Axl Rose, Jon Bon Jovi, Paul McCartney, Slash, Brian Johnson, Flea, Robert Plant, and many others she was excited to see. Then there were a few others who were more mainstream that she didn't really care for.

Former lead guitarist of Death Toll, Daniel, approached Beau and Evie. "Beau! Hey!" Daniel said. The men shook hands before Daniel turned to Evie. "It is nice to meet you," he said, holding out his hand. She took it, and they shook hands.

Evie knew that he was undergoing cancer treatments for his throat, so she graciously asked, "How are you feeling, Daniel?"

"Oh, you know, taking one day at a time. I haven't lost my hair yet, and my doctors reassure me I am going to make a full recovery," he said.

"That's good. You actually look terrific," Evie said.

Daniel smiled. "Hold on to this one before one of these other stock guys swipe her up," Daniel said to Beau.

Evie blushed while the men smiled.

"All right, we better go find our seats," Beau said.

"Sounds good. See you later!" Daniel said, walking and waving. Evie waved back while Beau wrapped his arm around her shoulders and continued to walk towards their seats. He said hello and introduced Evie to all sorts of hard rock musicians Evie dreamed of meeting someday.

Eventually, Beau and Evie made it to their seats next to the rest of Death Toll and spouses. Talk show host and personality, James Corden, was hosting the AMA's again. He started off by telling some jokes, which made Evie laugh hard. Soon, Bruno Mars was on stage performing the song, *Chunky*. Evie really wanted to stand up and begin dancing the Zumba choreo she knew for that song, but she was afraid of what other people would do around her. Much to her surprise, she looked to the left and saw Jennifer Lopez doing the same choreo Evie knew. Beau saw the twinkle in Evie's eyes, and said, "Go. I know you want to."

Evie kissed his cheek, took off her shoes, stood up, and danced her way over to J-Lo. Beau watched the two women dance, and he knew the girls would be friends forever. He smiled and shook his head. Luke, Kade, and Rick watched Evie dance. All three had this pensive look on their faces. Beau shrugged and said, "That's what Zumba is." They continued to watch the girls dance in a trance as other women stood up and began dancing with them.

"That's what you do?" Luke asked. Beau hesitated and nodded. "Are the women there that beautiful, too?" Luke asked. Jetta slapped Luke, and all three men broke free from the trance. "Do you want me to do Zumba, now?" she asked Luke. "It couldn't hurt," Luke said, feeling cornered.

Soon, Jetta, Kaylee, and Laila stood up and joined the massive group of women now dancing. Evie began directing the moves since the crowd was so large. When the song was done, the entire crowd cheered and yelled as loud as they could. Bruno looked super pleased with what had happened since he even started dancing along. After a while, everyone retook their seats. "She is so nice!" Evie said about J-Lo. Beau smiled. James Corden invited different artists up to read various categories of music. Various musicians performed as well.

Finally, Death Toll's category came up, and James invited the legend, Paul McCartney, up to read the nominees, which were Death Toll, Slayer, and Daniel's band, Matador. Paul placed the AMA and the envelope on the podium. Beau, Luke, Kade, and Rick held their breaths as Paul opened the envelope. When he read the winner, he smiled. "And the winner is… Death Toll… for their self-titled album, <u>Death Toll</u>." Everyone jumped up in celebration before Paul could finish reading. All four members of the band stood up and gave each other a group hug before walking on stage. To Evie's surprise, there was a lot of cheering for them. She realized that even the mainstream artists appreciated exceptional talent.

Luke was the first to touch the AMA and speak once they made their way to the podium. "This is truly amazing, considering how far we have come. I would like to thank my wife, Jetta, and my children for being so supportive during all of those long nights. Huge shout-out to our producers and sound guys for helping us with our album, and an even louder shout-out to our amazing tour manager, Evie Long." Evie smiled and clapped as she watched Jetta blow a kiss to Luke on stage.

Soon, Kade walked up to the podium to speak. "Thank you, Laila, for always showing your love and support, and our amazing crew for this wonderful album you produced."

Rick spoke next. "I love you, Kaylee! Thank you for always believing in me. Thank you, guys," Rick said, looking around him at the band, "for hiring me. I am forever grateful for this opportunity to be a part of Death Toll."

When Beau walked up to the mic, the crowd cheered even louder. "This is truly a humbling experience to stand among the greatest artists in the world, and hold this award in my hand." Beau started tearing up. "This year has been an interesting one for me. I went from rock bottom to flying in a matter of months all thanks to the most wonderful woman I have come to know and love." Beau looked at Evie. "I love you, Sweetheart," he said, looking at her from the podium. Evie's eyes welled up with tears as she said the words, "I love you, too."

"The last time I stood on this podium, I thanked my Phoebe for saving me more than once. Evie, I extend that gratitude to you and the kids. All three of you saved me, especially you. Thank you for sharing this moment with me. And thank you, all, for continuing to show your love and support for us. Nothing will separate us, except death." The crowd cheered louder than ever as the band walked backstage. "C'mon. Let's meet the boys backstage," Jetta said, nudging Evie.

All four women stood up and began walking backstage to join the band. Luke was the one holding the AMA as photographers took pictures of all of the men in their handsome suits. Beau stood a head taller than the rest of the band, which made Evie laugh. Soon, the photographer asked to get a picture of each band member with their spouse or significant other holding the AMA. Each couple cozied up. Beau and Evie, however, could not stop kissing. "If you're going to copulate, at least wait until after the after-party," the photographer said. Everyone laughed.

After pictures, the band had to change fast because they were performing *Nothing Else Matters* really soon. Crew members went to work to set the stage up to Death Toll's specifications while the curtain was down. Evie also ensured everything was going according to plan. Beau and Evie kissed before he put his black EXplorer over his shoulder and walked on stage. Luke kissed Jetta, Kade kissed Leila, and Rick kissed Kaylee all before taking their places on stage.

The curtain went up, and Kade began playing the opening arpeggio to *Nothing Else Matters*. He started playing the solo, which morphed into a trio between Beau, Kade, and Rick, with Luke hitting the occasional cymbal. This was by far Beau's most emotional performance as he sang his heart out and played his guitar. When they were done, the crowd cheered very loudly. The band was very gracious and bowed. The curtain soon went down, and Beau went into a dressing room to change back into his suit. He wanted to make sure he matched what Evie was wearing, and he insisted they be formal that night.

The band and girls proceeded to the outside canopy where the after-party was. Bruno, Paul, Slash, and a few other people were already drinking cocktails, talking, and dancing. Everyone with Death Toll claimed a table and sat down. Beau walked over to the bar and grabbed two bottles of water. Evie glanced around the room, and she soon realized that the after-party was very clique-ish, just like her high school. She soon saw Kanye West was working the crowd with a martini in his hand. He approached the band's table.

"Beau!" Kanye exclaimed. "Hey, Kanye, how are you doing?" Beau calmly said, standing up. The two men embraced. Evie was a little surprised by this interaction. "Pretty good. I just came over to congratulate you and meet your little girlfriend," Kanye said, turning towards Evie. She stood up and held out her hand shaking Kanye's hand. He simply smiled. "You are beautiful. I hope your ex regrets his decision," Kanye said candidly. Beau soon put his arm around her. Evie's cheeks turned pink. "Thank you, Mr. West," Evie said, trying to be polite. Kanye laughed. "Please, call me Ye. I know my wife would love to meet you," he responded.

Evie froze. If she was frank with herself, meeting a woman who only became famous because of a sex tape was not on her priority list, but Kanye led Evie over to his table and pulled out a chair for her. Next thing Evie knew, she was face to face with Kim Kardashian West, who turned out to be a really kind person with a taste for luxury. "I love your Valentino gown," Kim said. Evie smiled. "Thank you! I honestly had no idea who made it until Beau whispered the name in my ear," she responded. "I also loved how you led everyone in dancing during Bruno's song. Are you a dancer?" Kim asked again. Evie explained she was a Zumba instructor. A lot of other female artists and actresses overheard their conversation, sat down, and began talking with Evie.

Beau watched Evie and Kim talk as many other musicians and artists approached him to offer their congratulations. He watched as other musicians sat down next to Evie and began chatting with her and Kim. People would often ask where Evie was, and he pointed in her direction. Beau and Evie would occasionally glance at each other. They mouthed, "I love you,' to each other quite a bit throughout the night.

In the background, all of the award-winning songs were playing as well as some of the performance songs. Evie led a large group of people in the Zumba choreo of *Chunky*, and this time, Bruno came to dance with her. Beau knew the choreography to *Chunky* pretty well, so he came to dance on the other side of Evie. Everyone continued dancing, chatting, and drinking. Evie felt like she and Beau were the only sober ones at the party. People kept crowding around Evie to talk to her and ask questions, which became obnoxious to Beau.

However, when *Nothing Else Matters* came on twice, Beau excused himself from the crowds and stole Evie away for dancing. To Evie's surprise, Beau began leading her in a waltz. "Since when do you know how to waltz?" she asked. "I think you will find I am full of all sorts of surprises tonight," he said, leading her in a spin. When the song was over a second time, Beau dipped Evie and kissed her.

Beau brought Evie upright again. "Let's get out of here. I've made a reservation," Beau said. Evie, feeling light-headed for more than one reason, nodded. Beau and Evie held hands and walked to the various people to excuse themselves. They said goodbye to the group and turned to the door. As they were walking out, they saw multiple artists throwing up on the hedge outside the arena. Evie just laughed. Beau snickered himself quietly. They eventually found their limo and climbed in. It was a lot easier climbing into the limo than climbing out. Beau slid in behind her. "Where to?" the limo driver asked. "The Fairmont, please," Beau said.

Evie and Beau walked into the penthouse. The view of LA overlooking the ocean was spectacular. Evie went out on the balcony to take everything in. Beau made arrangements for sparkling cider and water to be delivered to their room so he would not be tempted. After throwing his coat onto an armchair, he poured two glasses and admired Evie on the balcony. He soon joined her. They clinked their glasses and drank. "Beau, we could have just stayed at an inexpensive hotel tonight. You didn't have to go all out for this," Evie said. "I have always admired your simplicity, modesty, and humility. You are right, I didn't have to do this, but how often does one win an AMA, and they get to share it with the woman they love?" Beau asked.

"You have two others plus eight Grammys. Also, you won the majority of them with Phoebe," Evie said.

"True, but this award is the first one we are together, plus I just wanted tonight to be perfect," Beau said.

"Why is that?" Evie asked.

Beau reached into his pants pocket, clutching a box with a ring inside it. "Well," Beau began, but suddenly he chickened out and let go of the box, taking his hand out his pocket and holding Evie's free hand. "Because it's our first trip together without the kids. That's something special," he said, recovering. Evie smiled. "It is. Thank you. This really is beautiful," she said.

Beau pulled Evie in and wrapped his around her waist. They began kissing before hugging. "Look behind you," Beau said. Evie turned around and saw that they had a private swimming pool a little bit bigger than a hot tub. It was large enough to swim laps in but smaller as not to overpower the balcony. Evie was too distracted by the view to see the pool when she walked outside.

"Wow, who knew a high school band teacher could become a tour manager, date the frontman of the band she works with, and end up in a penthouse with its own private pool!?" Evie said.

Beau laughed. "And who knew a shy kid from LA would become a frontman, experience Hell many times, and be up here in this penthouse with the most amazing woman he's ever met?!" he responded. Beau sat his drink down on a little table on the balcony before wrapping his other arm around Evie's waist. She soon set her glass down, melting into Beau's embrace.

****

As the sun began to rise, Evie woke up, realizing she was lying on her right side with Beau spooning and holding her. She slowly tried climbing out of bed, trying not to wake Beau up. She walked past her dress on the floor and into the bathroom, hoping there was some sort of bathrobe. Sure enough, hanging on the back of the bathroom door were two bathrobes. Evie proceeded to put one on before walking over to her bag. She grabbed her cosmetics bag to look for her toothbrush.

Suddenly Evie realized she forgot to pack something essential; her contraceptives. She also knew Beau hadn't packed any of his either. Panic entered. She quietly ran to her phone to check her fitness app for her ovulation days. A massive sigh of relief was heard as she read her phone; two days left until ovulation would start. Her heart began to slow down as Evie continued to take deep breaths. There soon came a knock on the door. "Room Service?" Evie heard a male voice say outside the door. Making sure the bathrobe was secure, Evie walked to the door and opened it. "Here is your breakfast order," the man said. "Thank you," Evie said, grabbing the cart and pulling it inside the room.

The food smelled delicious. There were eggs, bacon, sausage, hash browns, ham steak, and various fruits, including blueberries. Evie's mouth salivated. As the smell filled the room, Beau began to stir. Evie brought the cart over to Beau's side. He opened his eyes and smiled at his girlfriend. "Morning, Beautiful," he said. "Good morning," Evie said back, smiling.

They kissed. "They brought the order?" he asked as he sat up and stretched. "Yep. It all smells delicious," Evie said as she started grabbing plates and setting them on the bed. They proceeded to eat everything. "So, last night, did we forget...?" Beau began. "Yep," Evie said. "So, does that mean...?" Beau began asking. "We should be fine," Evie reassured, hoping it wasn't one of those weird months where she ovulated early.

Chapter 20

The Incidents

It had been three weeks since the AMA's when Evie woke up one morning with the sudden urge to vomit. She ran to the bathroom and hung her head over the toilet. *Great*, she thought to herself, *Levi got me sick*. When Evie and Beau got home, Harper had a stomach bug, and Evie quarantined her toddler in Harper's bedroom despite protests. A week later, Levi caught the bug, so he spent the next few days quarantined in his room to ensure the bug was out of his system. Evie spent the next week doing a Spring Cleaning to ensure every bit of that virus was killed. She knew Beau couldn't afford to be sick, considering the next leg of the tour would be starting, and Evie couldn't be sick either. But it looked like all of Evie's work was in vain as she laid on the bathroom floor. The tile was soothing to her forehead.

Evie carefully thought about how she felt. She wasn't cold, and her head wasn't hot. Her stomach and abdomen didn't feel like there was anything that needed to come out. All she felt was nausea and exhaustion. *Uh oh*, she thought to herself. The last time she felt like this was when she found out she was pregnant with Harper. She didn't have time to run to the store because everyone was getting ready to leave for the second leg of the tour. The maid Beau hired to clean the house and pick up the groceries already left to run the errands. Evie thought about when she could sneak away and buy a pregnancy test. She knew she couldn't send anyone because then they would know her secret. *I'll take one tomorrow when we get to the arena*, Evie thought to herself.

She slowly stood up, changed into grey jeggings and an oversized white sweater. Nausea grew stronger, and she ran back to the bathroom to throw up. Soon, she heard large footsteps running up the stairs into the master bedroom. Beau heard Evie all the way in the kitchen. "Hey, Babe, you okay?" he asked, kneeling down next to her. He rubbed her shoulders and moved her hair away from her face. Vomit didn't bother Beau at all because of all his intoxicated nights throwing up after shows back when Death Toll started out. "Yeah," Evie said, trying to mask how she really felt.

"Did you finally get it?" Beau asked, referring to the stomach bug. "Most likely," Evie lied. "Do you think you'll be better by tomorrow?" he asked. Evie hadn't thought that far ahead. "Let's get through today, and we'll see. If I'm sick, then I'm sick," she replied. "All right, well, how about I make you some ramen, you curl up on the bed with your blanket, and watch movies. I'll take care of the kids today while you rest," Beau said.

Evie giggled. "You have top ramen?" she asked. Beau looked at Evie in disbelief. "Yeah. That's what I eat when I am sick," Beau said. Evie giggled again. "All right. Hopefully, I can keep it down," she said. "Hopefully," Beau said with a chuckle. He went into the closet to pull out Evie's favorite blanket. Beau helped her stand up, walked with her to the bed, helped her lay down, and covered her up. He kissed her forehead before proceeding downstairs to the kitchen to boil the water.

Evie turned the TV on and immediately opened Netflix. She started watching a cheesy, sappy series that Hallmark produced when she and Beau got home from LA, and she loved it. After about ten minutes, Beau brought out a massive bowl with top ramen in it with lots of broth. Evie smiled because that is just how she liked it. It actually smelled really good to her. *Great, this baby wants carbs*, she thought to herself as she scooped up some noodles. Beau sat down next to her and watched the sappy series with her for an episode. He soon stood up to go check on the kids, who were playing outside.

Evie soon fell asleep on the bed even with her kids running through the house. She would occasionally hear her kids ask Beau, "Is Mommy sick?" Beau would shush and reassure them that she was sick. "Aren't we supposed to leave for Omaha tomorrow?" Levi asked. "Yes, and if we let her rest, she'll be fine by then. How about we go to the park? That way, your mom can rest," Evie heard Beau say. Even though things were dream-like, Evie loved hearing her kids get excited. Soon, the house was quiet, and the garage door closed. She soon fell asleep again.

She was on the stage in front of thousands of people. Metal music blared from the speakers, but no one was on stage with her. Suddenly, the scene changed, and she was in the hallway of a hotel. She could hear a man and woman moaning from inside the door she was standing by. She soon realized it was Beau's voice she heard. Suddenly, a room key appeared in her hand, and she opened the door. To her surprise, it was Jude in bed with the woman. He sneered at her. The woman was blonde and looked trashy. "Carrying my baby?" Jude said, but with Beau's voice. Jude climbed out of bed, suddenly wearing clothes. He walked towards Evie as she backed up out of the room. The scene changed again to a dark alley just outside of the studio. Jude spoke again, still with Beau's voice. "That baby should be mine. You should be mine. I will do whatever it takes to make that happen." Jude then pushed Evie against a wall and began kissing her neck. Evie started to scream.

She jolted awake, screaming herself. She looked around and saw she was home safe in her bed. "Evie!" she heard Beau shout from downstairs before running up to the master bedroom. "What's wrong? What happened?" he asked, sounding worried. "Sorry, bad dream," she said. "You okay? You haven't done that in a while," he said, remembering the nights he stayed at her house on the couch, listening to her whimperings and screams. "Yeah, sorry. Didn't mean to scare anyone," Evie said. Beau wrapped his arms around Evie.

Ah man, she thought to herself, *already with the vivid dreams*. Evie knew she needed to take a pregnancy test soon and tell Beau about the situation. She made the decision to tell him tomorrow after the show if the test was positive.

Because Evie still wasn't feeling her best, Beau made dinner; spaghetti with meat sauce. It smelled really good to Evie, but she felt frustrated because all she wanted was carbs. The special meat sauce even smelled delicious. Beau had a unique recipe for his meat sauce as well as a secret ingredient: ground elk meat that Beau personally shot and ground up himself. Evie had elk meat a couple of times as a teenager while she was out hunting with her dad, and she loved it.

Beau even had a salad ready to go for Evie, which she ate, trying not to throw it back up so as not to raise suspicions. Evie did her best to give the kids a bath, but her exhaustion fought against her gumption. Luckily, Levi was able to wash his hair and body by himself, but Harper still needed help. When bath time was over, the kids went into their rooms to get dressed in their pajamas. Beau read them a story, sang their lullaby to them, and tucked them in.

Beau walked down the hallway and found Evie fast asleep on their bed underneath her favorite blanket. The TV was on, so Beau took off his shoes, slid underneath the blanket behind Evie, and turned on one of his shows. Evie stirred and woke up. "Sorry, Babe. I didn't mean to wake you," Beau said. "It's all good," Evie said sleepily. "Are you feeling any better? I noticed you were able to keep dinner down," Beau observed. "Yeah, I'm just exhausted, I guess," Evie said. "You've been tired all day today. Normally, you are Miss Energizer Bunny," Beau said with a smile. Evie smiled. "Maybe this illness is taking more out of me than I thought," Evie said. "Are you sure you'll be better by tomorrow?" Beau asked.

"What choice do we have if I can't go tomorrow? I still have to take care of the kids, so I might as well go."

"I'm just worried you'll get others sick."

"I didn't throw up dinner, so I don't think I'm contagious anymore."

"Okay. But if you get me sick…"

"I doubt I will. I'm feeling better-ish." Beau and Evie laughed.

They fell asleep on the bed, watching Beau's show underneath the blanket until Beau's phone rang. "Bruh, where are you?" Evie could hear Luke yelling on Beau's phone. "What time is it?" Beau asked groggily. "It's 5! Our flight leaves in two hours!" "Shit! Evie, we need to go!" Beau shouted, leaping off the bed.

Evie stirred, and that's when nausea came back with a vengeance. She ran to the bathroom closest to the living room and threw up. "Evie, are you still sick?" Beau asked. "I'm fine. You go wake up the kids. I'll gather our stuff," Evie said. "But you threw up again!" "Beau, just get the kids. We need to get to the airport ASAP!" Evie shouted.

Beau grumbled but got the kids loaded in the car. Evie brought down their suitcases and put them in the back of the Range Rover. Once she climbed in the car, Beau sped to the airport. They got to the airport with an hour to spare. They were able to get the bags checked in. They breezed through security as fast as they could and ran to the terminal. They were able to sit down by boarding with a half-hour to spare before TSA would let passengers on the plane.

Evie was very proud that her nausea was gone. *Again*, she thought to herself, *it goes away with exercising, eating, and sleeping.* She facepalmed. "How are you feeling? I was surprised you were able to run through the terminal keeping Harper by you," Beau said. "I'm doing okay, right now," Evie said. Beau put his arm around Evie and kissed her cheek. Evie leaned into him.

Suddenly, she realized she had a pregnancy test to get. "Beau, I need to go get something real quick. Will you stay with the kids, please?" she asked. "Absolutely. Just hurry," he said. "I will." She ran to the nearest gift shop and found the cheapest test she could see. She knew she wouldn't have time to take it right now, so she ran back just as Beau and the kids were ready to board the plane. They tucked the kids into their first-class seats so that they could go back to sleep. Beau and Evie sat across the aisle from the kids. They soon fell asleep and slept all the way to Omaha.

They got into various cars that took them to the arena. Evie was going over schedules and on the phone with multiple security companies to make sure security would be provided. There had been a few attempted break-ins in previous cities, so Evie was trying to prevent future robberies.

They arrived at the arena where crew members immediately went to work setting up the stadium. Evie went into one of the locker rooms to find a place to put Harper's pack n play. She also found a place to put a couch for Levi to sit, watch his tablet, and sleep when the time came during the concert to say goodnight to him.

Meanwhile, a crew member named Preston handed out the concert clipboards Evie put together for the band members. "It looks like Evie set up an interview with a reporter about the progress of the tour so far at 4," said Preston, handing Beau his clipboard. Beau glanced at it to make sure it was legitimate, and everything checked out. He was to have the interview in his dressing room, which he thought was strange since all of them were usually in the tuning room. However, Beau trusted Evie.

He looked at his watch and realized it was almost 4, so he ran to his dressing room. Sure enough, standing outside was a female reporter wearing a form-fitting pink dress and a blazer with high heels. She had long blonde hair and was very curvy. She was attractive, but she was no Evie.

"Hello," Beau said as he approached the reporter. The reporter faced him. "Hello! Rachel Wilson," she said, holding out her hand. Beau shook it. "How are you today?" Rachel, the reporter asked. "Doing well, thanks. How about yourself?" he asked back. "Pretty good. So, shall we?" Rachel asked, motioning to the door. "Yes, here," Beau said, opening the door and holding it for Rachel. She walked in.

Meanwhile, Evie was helping crew members set up the stage and equipment areas for Beau, Kade, and Rick. Everything was accounted for. After someone tried to break into their storage unit a few concerts ago, Evie wanted to take extra precautions to keep all the guitars and amps safe. Her violin was among the collection of guitars as well as old tee shirts, retired guitars, and props from previous tours that were put on display for the VIP ticket holders were also in the storage unit. She knew that crazy obsessed fans would do anything to get their hands on Death Toll memorabilia.

Since soundcheck was about to start, Evie decided to escape to the bathroom to take the pregnancy test. After she was done, she waited for the appropriate time before reading the test. She looked down at it. Sure enough, it was positive. She smiled. She had to go tell Beau and the kids. She put the test in her back pocket as she washed her hands and walked out of the bathroom.

She looked around, but couldn't see Beau. "Where's Beau?" Evie asked Brian, the guy who tuned Beau's guitars as she walked past him. "He's in that interview you set up for him in his dressing room," said Brian. "He doesn't have any more interviews until we play in Fresno. Who said I set it up?" Evie asked. "Preston did," Brian said, pointing to the guy who told Beau about the interview.

While Evie was going to interrogate Preston, Rachel proceeded to ask Beau questions. "How do you feel the Dark album is being received?" Rachel asked. "I think the fans love it. It is a bit more mainstream than what we have done in the past, but there are still lots of metal elements in it," Beau said. "What do you think is your most popular song on the album?" Rachel was writing down responses on a notepad. "Probably *Nothing Else Matters*. *Enter Sandman* is pretty popular, and so is *Frantic*. *Wherever I May...*" "*Nothing Else Matters*, you say? The song inspired by your girlfriend?" Rachel interrupted. "Yeah. I think that the song shows a softer side to..."

Rachel suddenly stood up from her chair, climbed into Beau's lap and kissed him. Beau immediately pulled away, pushed Rachel out of his lap and stood up. "What the hell are you doing?" he shouted. "We're just getting started," Rachel said as she walked towards Beau. "Are you even a real reporter, lady?" Beau asked. "What do you think?" the woman said again, reaching behind her dress. To Beau's surprise, she unzipped her dress, and it fell down to her ankles.

Before Beau could see anything, he closed his eyes. "Okay, lady, you need to get out now," Beau said, trying to find a button in his room to page security. "We're not done yet," said Rachel in a sultry voice as she approached Beau. He soon realized he was cornered. His phone was on the other side of the room, so he couldn't send a text to anyone. Rachel leaned against Beau. He felt so helpless. He didn't want to hurt the woman, but he couldn't think of any other way to make her stop. She started running her hands all over his body. She began nibbling on his ear and neck. That's when Beau struck. He found a way to pin the lingerie-wearing woman down on the ground.

Just then, the door opened. "Beau, that interview…" Evie looked down at the ground only to see the love of her life pinning a woman wearing the skimpiest lingerie down. Beau looked up in horror. Evie, Levi, and Harper were in the doorway. Evie froze before she covered her children's eyes. "Babe, I can explain," Beau tried to say. "Don't," Evie said before walking out from his view. Beau let go of Rachel and ran after Evie. "Security!" he shouted once he saw a bodyguard and pointed to his dressing room.

Evie walked outside of the arena holding her children's hands. "What was Beau doing with that naked lady?" Levi kept on asking. Evie tried to ignore his questions, but he was persistent. "I don't know, Bub. All I know is that we can't stay here," Evie said, trying not to hyperventilate. "Where are we going?" Harper asked. "I don't know, Sweet girl. I'm working on it," Evie said.

Just as she was pulling out her phone, Evie heard a familiar voice calling her name. "Jude?" Evie said, looking to her left. Sure enough, Jude was walking towards her and the kids. "Dad?" Levi said. "That's not Daddy," Harper said loudly. Those words stung Jude as he walked to Evie.

"What are you guys doing out here? Isn't the show going to start in about a few hours?" Jude asked. "What are you doing here in Omaha?" Evie asked, puzzled. "I had a business meeting, and I thought I should see the success my ex-wife has inspired. I also wanted to ask your permission to see the kids tomorrow before you head out."

"Why Omaha?" Evie asked. "We're opening an office here, and I am overseeing the project," Jude responded. Evie shrugged it off, too emotional to care. "You still need to answer my question. Why are you guys outside?" Jude asked. "Oh, we are actually leaving. Not sure where. Probably hotel first to get our things," Evie said. "Where after that?" Jude asked. Evie started crying because her life crumbled before her. "Honey, what's wrong?" Jude asked as he wrapped his arms around her.

Beau searched all over the arena, trying to find Evie. "Brian, where's Evie?" Beau asked, grabbing Brian. "I thought I saw her go outside with the kids," Brian said. Beau let him go and ran outside. His eyes skimmed everything, trying to find Evie.

Suddenly a dark figure caught his eye; Jude. He was hugging a crying Evie while the kids held onto her legs. *Dude, get your hands off my girl*, Beau thought, continuing to run towards them. Soon, a cab pulled up by them, and all four climbed into it just as Beau got to the curb. "No, no, no... NO!!!!" Beau yelled, placing his hands on top of his head. Jude's smug face stared back at him as the cab faded from Beau's view.

Chapter 21

Jude Wins

Evie packed her belongings in the hotel room, as well as Levi and Harper's things. Jude waited in the chair. "Where to after this?" Jude asked. Evie, still holding back tears, responded, "Probably back to Annapolis." "Right. Want me to accompany you back?" Jude asked. "Sure. I don't care," Evie said. "Okay," Jude said.

Evie stopped gathering her things. "You want to come back with us?"

"Yes. I've just missed you guys so much."

"You have a phone. You could have called to come and visit at any time."

"I know, but I thought showing up here would show you guys how serious I am about seeing you, especially to Levi."

"Fine, whatever you want to do is fine," Evie said, trying to process all that had happened in the past 30 minutes. *Pregnancy, ex-boyfriend/father of your child pinning a slut down, ex-husband showing up out of the blue to see you and the kids. Man, could this day get any worse*, Evie thought to herself.

Once Evie packed everything, she left her room key on the dresser by the TV. Jude asked his son, "Can I hold your hand, Bub?" Levi hesitated. "You haven't called me Bub in a long time," he said. "I know. I just missed my little boy, but you're not so little anymore. You are becoming quite the young man." Jude smiled.

Levi hesitated again, but he grabbed his father's hand while Evie carried Harper. "Mommy, is that my real daddy?" Harper asked. "Yes, Sweety, that's your real daddy," Evie said. Jude smiled. With that, he put his arm around his ex-wife and daughter. "Hey, how's my pretty girl?" Jude asked Harper. "You are my daddy," Harper said, remembering Jude.

They climbed back into the cab, where they proceeded to the airport. When they got there, Evie asked for three tickets to Annapolis. "Four, actually," said Jude handing the TSA agent his credit card, "make them first-class, also." Evie looked at him in disbelief. "You don't have to do that." "I know, but I can tell you are very anxious, and I want to help you out," Jude said.

Okay, weird, Evie thought, but she brushed it off still processing what happened. "Thank you," Evie responded. Jude paid for the first-class tickets, and all four of them proceeded to security.

They sat in the first-class waiting room. Jude pulled out his phone to give to Levi to watch Netflix since Evie left the tablet at the stadium. Harper was asleep in Evie's arms.

"So, are you ready to tell me why you are leaving your job? The biggest tour to date? Your boyfriend?" Jude asked, hoping everything had worked according to his plan. Tears began flowing down Evie's cheeks again. "Beau cheated on me just like you did," Evie cried. Jude did his best to act remorseful. "Seriously? Why would a guy want to do that to such an incredible woman?"

Evie looked at Jude in disbelief, and he soon realized he was the pot calling the kettle black. "Yeah, you're right. I did that." Jude was still trying to figure out his next move. "Well, maybe it was a misunderstanding," Jude said, feeling disgusted that he defended the behemoth. "He was pinning a practically naked woman down on the ground when I opened the door to his dressing room. How could I misunderstand that?" Evie asked. *Nice touch*, Jude thought. He would need to call the Omaha Police Station to bail Rachel out of jail because she needed to be back to work on Monday.

Much to Jude's relief and pleasure, Evie buried her face into his shoulder. He wrapped his arms around her, trying to comfort her. Soon, Jude, Evie, and the kids were called to board the plane. Once they were in, Evie tucked Levi under his blanket in his comfy first-class seat while Jude laid Harper down in her place. He covered her with the blanket he remembered Evie making for her. So many happy memories filled his mind of his wife and children as he watched them.

Jude and Evie sat down in their first-class seats. "Again, Honey, I'm so sorry this happened to you… again," Jude said. "Please stop calling me Honey," Evie said, a little annoyed. "Why?" "Because you are acting like we're still together like nothing happened. You are being super nice to the kids and me, and it's freaking me out. This entire time, you've been looking at me like I'm the only woman in the world, and I am so confused and vulnerable…." Evie soon began crying again.

Jude wrapped his arms around his ex-wife. "I didn't realize how much pain you were in," Jude said quietly, and he truly meant it. "For months, all I got were mind games from you. I felt worthless, unwanted, like trash," Evie shrieked. "Again, I'm so sorry, Honey. I'm here, now," he whispered, trying to calm her down, but then Evie threw his arms away. "With all due respect, you're the last person I want to comfort me right now." "You're right. I seem to have lost that trust," Jude agreed, "so, what can I do to make it up to you?" As she wiped tears away, Evie thought about Jude's question. "I don't know. I need to see a major change from your behavior," Evie said. Jude understood what she meant. "As in, you want me to focus more on the kids and you before you can trust me again?" he asked. "Yes, but I know that's going to be impossible with your job and affairs, so after dropping me off in Annapolis, I don't want to see you unless you are committed to putting us first. No more late nights, affairs, yelling, mind games, passive aggressive statements, and narcissism. If you commit to all of these conditions, you can see us on a regular basis," Evie said.

Jude, willing to say anything to keep Evie around, agreed. "Yes, I can do those things, even if it takes months to gain your trust," he said. "All right. I'm holding you to that. If I see you break these commitments at all, we're done," Evie said, issuing the ultimatum. Jude nodded. "I understand."

"You're willing to do these? No arguments? No put-downs? Who are you?!" Evie asked. "Well, I did some soul-searching after Harper's birthday, and I realized that I truly missed the three of you. I never fully appreciated all you did for me and for the amazing mom you are to our children.

"I got some counseling, started looking back at the photos of you when you were pregnant with both kids, and you looked radiant. I made a promise to myself that if I ever got a second chance with you, and we had another baby, I wasn't going to screw it up." Evie smiled a little. "I really want to believe you, Jude, but again, I need to trust you again." "I understand. I'm willing to meet your conditions if you'll have me. You can work, not work, teach Zumba again, teach Strong, music… I don't really care what you do as long as you're with me and happy," Jude said.

Evie's vulnerability got the best of her. She knew the baby was growing inside of her, and Jude was offering her his heart again, but she couldn't lie to him after his full disclosure. "Jude, I'm pregnant," Evie said, feeling scared. Jude froze not sure how to proceed. "Are you sure?" he asked. Evie reached for her back pocket and pulled the test out. Jude looked at it, and sure enough, the test read positive. "Wow, um, when did this…?" Jude stammered. "About three weeks ago at the AMA's. I guess I ovulated early, and…" Evie said, feeling like the whole situation could turn on her any second.

Jude began kissing Evie, which surprised her. "Whoa, really?" Evie asked. "Really. I love you, and I will love that baby. Hell, he loved our kids and took care of them. I can take care of his kid. As for our relationship, we can take this as fast or slow as you want," Jude said. Evie smiled lightly before kissing Jude. Jude enjoyed every minute of it, and Evie could not help but feel happy that her husband wanted her back, but she felt dead inside because ultimately, she still wanted Beau. Jude wrapped his arms around Evie as she leaned into him and closed her eyes, wishing she would wake up from this alternate universe.

****

One month later, Beau stormed through the sliding glass doors of Jude's brokerage office building. He walked straight past security to the elevator.

He quickly looked to see which floor Jude's office was on, and pushed that button.

Beau threw open Jude's office door. "You lying son of a bitch!"

"Nice to see you, too," Jude said, trying to keep calm.

"You set me up!" Beau shouted, "The timing was too perfect. Why else would you be in Omaha?"

"Because I'm in charge of..."

"That's bullshit, and you know it. Your company is nowhere near Omaha. I did some research and digging. You sent the fake reporter, and you were waiting outside the arena for Evie and the kids to come out!" Beau shouted. Jude's smile looked like a cat's who swallowed a canary. "So, I guess I won. They are back here in Baltimore where they belong. Children really should have both of their biological parents," Jude sneered.

"I am having a hard time believing you know what a true family is. Death Toll is my family. All four of us have been through so much together, make each other better, encourage each other to work harder, and support each other.

"Before your ex-wife came into the picture, I had another perfect woman in my life and two wonderful kids. We all worked together and encouraged each other to be our best authentic selves. After they died, I lost sight of that until your ex-wife came along. Evie and I made each other better, supported each other, and loved each other. Those things never happened when you guys were married. I don't believe you know how to do any of those things. I think you lied through your teeth to get her back here. Typical Jude being selfish all over again," Beau sneered back. Jude glared at Beau.

"You don't know anything about me," Jude growled. "Evie talked more about you than you know. Plus, I used to be just like you, wanting what you can't have. That's why I cheated on Phoebe at the beginning of our relationship. I thought my life needed excitement. Still, I realized it was already exciting watching my kids grow up, my wife taking care of them, and caring for them myself. I went to rehab to help with my problems, but instead, you schemed.

"I have evidence that you paid off one of my roadies. I also have a bank statement of one of your employees, Rachel Wilson, where you paid her off to pretend to be a reporter as well. This scheme must have cost you a fortune."

Beau pulled out the bank statement to Preston's bank account, showing a deposit into his bank account of $5,000 from Jude's bank account. He then pulled out another bank statement with Rachel's name on it with $10,000 directly from Jude's bank account. For the first time during this whole interaction, Jude squirmed. "Why couldn't you just leave her alone? There are plenty of other women who can validate your ego. Why Evie? Why do you feel the need to control everything she does? Do you think she's that weak? Because you are wrong," Beau snapped back.

Jude stood up from his desk, knocking some papers over, winding up his fist. He swung at Beau, but Beau was quicker as he dodged the punch. "You don't want to fight me," Beau said, catching Jude's fist. "Why's that?" "Because I will kill you! If we fight, Evie will know I was here. I think I will just wait for this whole thing to blow up in your face, and let her punch you." "Evie is too sweet to punch anyone." Beau laughed. "That's how you would see it. You never saw the rage you caused her. She will punch you, and punch you good once she finds out what a giant selfish bastard you are. Wait and see," Beau said before walking out the door.

Beau stormed out of the office building and called an Uber. The driver took him to Jude's house. Beau had hired a PI to try and find out how Rachel got into the arena, as well as everything he could find about Jude. Apparently, Jude paid Preston off to change Beau's schedule and let Rachel in the arena unnoticed. The PI also found the deposit from Jude's bank account into Rachel's as well as a history of Jude and Rachel hooking up for a while right before Jude pulled off this scheme. As the driver pulled up in front of Jude's house, Beau climbed out of the car.

He looked in the front window of the house. He saw Evie sitting at the dining room table reading a book. He couldn't see the kids anywhere, so he figured Levi was at school, and Harper was taking a nap or at a friend's house, considering the time. He stood there and watched Evie read her book for about five minutes.

Rather quickly, Evie set the book down, stood up, and ran into the bathroom. After about two minutes, she came out crying. He so badly wanted to storm into the house and wrap his arms around her, show her the evidence he found to prove himself faithful to her, and take her back home. However, he knew that Evie wouldn't listen to him at this point, so Beau decided to patiently and painfully wait for Evie to put the puzzle together. Finally, Beau walked away from the house and back into the car. "Where to now?" the driver asked. "The airport, please," Beau said.

****
***

Jude walked into his house, and the smell of sweet pork burritos filled his nose. Evie was asleep on the sectional. He knew how tired pregnancy made her, so he assumed she was really exhausted. He walked over to her, kneeled down, and kissed her cheek. She stirred and opened her eyes.

"Hey, you," she said sleepily.

"Hey, how are you feeling?" Jude asked.

"All right. I've been tired lately," Evie said.

"Are you feeling any better at all?" Jude asked.

"I'm fine. The first trimester is always the hardest," Evie said while standing up and stretching.

"Did you make a doctor's appointment?" Jude asked.

"Yes, but I have to wait two weeks. Apparently, there are hundreds of other knocked-up women this year," Evie joked.

Jude laughed. "That's funny. Want me to go with you?" he asked. "No, that's okay. You stay home with the kids," Evie said, really wanting to be alone during the appointments. "Okay, if you say so," Jude agreed.

Jude inhaled the delicious smell of sweet pork burritos, and he salivated. "Dinner smells good," he said. Evie smiled a little bit. "Thanks. I know it's one of your favorites," Evie said. "It is. Thank you. You are extremely thoughtful," Jude stated, thinking again about how fortunate he was to have pulled off his biggest scheme.

"Thanks," Evie said, smiling back.

"Want me to shred it?" Jude asked.

"Seriously?" Evie asked in disbelief.

"Sure. That way, you can go herd the kids. Where are they?" Jude asked.

"Harper is at our neighbor's house, and Levi is upstairs working on his reading," Evie said.

"How did we get such a smart kid?" Jude asked.

"I have no idea. He came out that way," Evie said.

"He gets his brain from his mother." Jude wrapped his arms around her in the kitchen. "Seriously, since when did you become so thoughtful?" Evie said with a giggle. They kissed tenderly. "All right, I will go get Harper while you shred," Evie said. "Sounds good." Jude grabbed two forks and pulled the pork out of the crockpot and began shredding it while Evie walked next door to get Harper.

The four of them proceeded to have dinner. Jude suggested the four of them go to one of the gyms where Evie used to teach Zumba to see if she could get her job back, Evie could attend a class, Jude would lift, and the kids would go to Child Care.

Evie was shocked again. Ever since they arrived back in Baltimore, Jude really made an effort to try and make Evie, Levi, and Harper a priority in his life, and Evie noticed. She really liked it, but she was still very skeptical.

They soon got ready to go to the gym. Evie ended up on the sub list at that gym. She attended her old Zumba class, where the current instructor asked her to teach a song. Jude lifted weights. He tried really hard not to look at other women working out. Jude occasionally walked by the aerobics room where Evie was to watch her dance. He noticed her smile was bigger in class than it had been at home. Jude knew the adjustment would take time and that the trust would be rebuilt.

When the four of them got back home, Evie bathed the kids while Jude got them ready for bed. He sat in on storytime and kissed his children goodnight. Evie was pleasantly surprised by Jude's efforts. As Evie tucked Levi into bed, he looked up at his mom and said, "I miss Beau. I want to go home." Evie's heart sank, but she still kept a brave face. "Bub, you have no idea how much I miss him, but this is our home again. Good night," she said, kissing his forehead. Evie held the tears in as she walked to Harper's room to tuck her in. "Mommy?" "Yes, sweet girl?" "I miss Daddy." "I can go get him." "No, not my real daddy. My daddy." Evie could barely hold herself together, hearing her daughter tell her this. Evie kissed her daughter on the forehead. "I miss him, too. Goodnight, my sweet girl. I love you," Evie said, holding in tears.

After she closed the door, she ran into her room, laid down on the bed, and began crying the hardest since that night of confession with Beau. *Wake up*, Evie thought to herself, *wake up*. She took some deep breaths and wiped away her tears.

She decided to face her new demons. She played her last image of Beau in her head and what she was doing before. Before she walked in on Beau, she was yelling at Preston, one of the roadies who changed Beau's schedule without consulting her. She told Preston he was on thin ice, considering he had been slacking at his job for two weeks. She realized she never asked him who changed the schedule, whether it was Beau, Preston trying to take matters into his own hands, or if the slutty reporter paid him off to sleep with Beau. Evie pulled out her phone, opened her contacts, and stared at Beau's name, considering calling him because she never gave him a chance to explain himself. *Did I act too rashly*, Evie thought to herself. Maybe she did, maybe she didn't. All she knew was that she was back in Baltimore, pregnant with his baby, and Jude seemed committed to his family. That was good enough for her.

"Honey?" Jude called. Evie wiped tears away. "Yeah?" Evie answered. He found her on the bed. "Are you okay?" he asked. "Yeah. I'm happy to be here, but when I saw Beau pinning that woman down, I had horrible flashbacks and deja vu experiences. I just ran away because I didn't want to deal with them again. I guess now I'm grieving," Evie said. Jude listened, hoping this would gain her trust. "Want me to start playing the guitar again?" Jude joked. Evie laughed while sniffling. "Only if you want to," Evie said, wiping her nose.

Jude caressed his hand on Evie's cheek. "I love you," he said. Evie smiled with tears in her eyes. "A part of me wants to say it back to you, but I'm still not ready," she said. "I understand," Jude said, "but I hope this will help you see how serious I am about us." He pulled out a little box from his pocket and opened it. Inside was her old engagement ring. Evie forgot how much she loved that ring, but her head began to spin. "I know to ask you to marry me is a big step right now, but we can wait as long as you want," Jude said, "What do you say?"

Evie smiled a little bit, but Jude knew it would take more time for her smile that lit up an entire room to return. "I say yes," Evie said after sniffling again. Jude slipped that ring on her before kissing her. He was thrilled she said yes. Evie could see the glimmer in her life again, but was this what she really wanted?

Chapter 22

Douche-y Douche Douche Douche-bag

The two weeks went by super slow, considering Evie's nausea became constant. It wasn't easy hiding the pregnancy from the kids, but somehow, Evie managed to conceal her frail state. Jude had suggested she apply at a few more gyms she used to work at to try and get some classes again or at least on the sub list as a Zumba instructor. She was able to get one class back and on the sub list of a few other gyms. Her trust issues with him were slowly repairing themselves. Jude was more invested in her and the kids, but she often thought how long that would last, even with him being extremely supportive of her through the pregnancy.

Levi was back at his old school, and Harper stayed home with Evie unless other parents arranged to have their kids come over. Finally, the day of her doctor's appointment arrived, and Evie felt relieved.

Evie sat in the OB's office, waiting for her turn. She saw a bunch of young mothers with their significant others in the waiting room. Evie began contemplating the night this baby was conceived. Before she and Beau broke up, they had an incredible night where all roadblocks were down after the AMA's. Three weeks later, a pregnancy test read positive, but she was betrayed again by the love of her life and the father of her baby.

Even though she was content that she and Jude got back together, Evie could not help but miss Beau. She missed his smile, his eyes, his jokes, his personality, his charisma, his intimacy, his stability, his warm embrace, and his affection. Beau made Evie feel like she was flying with little to no turbulence. Even though Jude did his best to ensure that kind of security for Evie, she still felt like the air pockets were taller and bumpier than they should be. She hoped the feeling would go away.

"Evie?" the nurse called. Evie stood up and walked through the door. The nurse took Evie's weight, blood pressure, and temperature. All were very normal, and the nurse was impressed with how well Evie took care of herself. The nurse handed a cup for Evie to take into the bathroom. Then Evie went back to the exam room and changed into the gown. She sat on the exam table, waiting for the OB to come in.

Two minutes later, the doctor that delivered both Levi and Harper came in with a big smile. "Nice to see you again, Evie. How are we today?" he asked. "Pretty good. It looks like I'm pregnant with number three," Evie said. "Great! Let's look at the sonogram," he said as he pulled out the ultrasound. Evie laid down and opened the gown a little exposing her stomach. Sure enough, a little baby was growing inside her abdomen. She smiled as she heard the fast heartbeat. "Wow, the fetus is very strong," he said. He began measuring how big to predict a due date. "Well, it looks like that confirms the due date; July 20 of next year," he said. *Yep, Beau's the father*, she thought. "So, that puts you at about 9 weeks. I have a few questions for you," he said, grabbing his clipboard.

"Are you living with the father of this baby now?" he asked. Evie hesitated to answer. Should I lie, she thought. "Um… no, the father lives in San Francisco," she responded.

"Oh, did Jude move out...?" he began asking.

"No, Jude and I divorced and I moved out there for a job," she said.

"Oh, what brought you back here?" the doctor asked.

Evie winced in pain. "I just felt the need to be closer to my family," she quickly thought up and said.

"Any symptoms?" the doctor asked.

"Constant nausea again that goes away with sleep, exercise, and eating," Evie responded.

"Shall I write that prescription for your nausea medication again?" he asked.

"Yeah, that would be great," Evie said, feeling relief.

"Any signs of depression and anxiety again?" he asked.

"Not yet, but I will call the second I feel something," she said.

"Will you want the same birth plan as last time?" he asked.

"Yes, and I would like to be induced a week early, as well," Evie said, remembering how comfortable she was when Harper was born.

"All right, well I'm glad you're back. We will take care of you and your baby," the OB concluded.

"Thank you, Doctor," Evie said, smiling.

Two weeks went by, and Jude's office Christmas party was approaching. Evie did everything she could to help the assistants and various wives of the colleagues plan the event. She called the caterers and arranged for hors d'oeuvres to be passed around as well as cocktails. Evie made arrangements with her own money to have a couple of specialized servers serve her sparkling cider to hide the pregnancy from the other corporate wives and Jude's colleagues.

Despite trying to be as involved as she could be in the event, Evie felt a massive hole in her life. Still, she knew her kids needed her, and Jude seemed extremely dedicated to making their relationship work. He was even okay with waiting on the intimacy part of their relationship until Evie felt ready.

Evie wore a red sleeveless sheath dress with an asymmetrical neckline with black pumps to the Christmas party. Her hair was pulled back elegantly. She wore a band around her stomach to ensure suspicions wouldn't arise since it began to pooch a little. Jude wore a dark grey suit, a red tie that matched Evie's dress, and black loafers. Evie stood around a tall round table, talking to a few of the wives of the other brokers, sipping on sparkling cider. She glanced over at Jude occasionally. He spoke to a lot of his colleagues. Now and then, an attractive woman would approach him flirting. Instead, he looked up at Evie and smiled. She blushed. His flirting days were over hopefully. The glances looked very similar to the way Beau looked at her. That twinged a little.

Evie missed Beau so much, but after watching him pin down a crazed blonde on the ground, she didn't want to put herself in that situation again. That flashback suddenly made her have another flashback to when she walked into Jude's office, carrying Harper and holding Levi's hand. Jude and Carmen were having sex in his office chair. *How long is this going to last,* she thought to herself, *when is this nightmare going to end? Why am I here with the guy who cheated on me?* More insecurities and doubts filled her head as her nausea began to surface.

"Excuse me," Evie said to the other wives as she excused herself to go to the restroom. Evie knew she was going to vomit, but she tried acting calm even though the urge was strong. When Evie walked inside the bathroom, she ran to a stall, closed it, and leaned over the toilet. Evie was very thankful her hair was pulled back. When she finished, she grabbed some toilet paper and wiped her face. Evie came out of the stall, washed her hands, and checked to make sure her makeup was still in place. She knew she had to get over Beau, but she didn't know where to start.

At that moment, another woman walked into the bathroom with long wavy blonde hair and blue eyes. She looked like a supermodel wearing a bright pink sheath dress with a sweetheart neckline with thick shoulder straps. She stumbled a little, so Evie assumed she was a bit tipsy. She looked a little familiar, but she figured she was just another wife of a broker. "Oh, sorry, Miss Long. I didn't see you there," the woman said as she almost stumbled into Evie, slurring her speech. "It's all good," Evie said, trying to be polite. As the woman fluffed her hair, Evie suddenly got this weird feeling about the woman. *How does she know who I am? I've only been here for a month*, Evie thought, *I've had to reintroduce myself to at least ten people tonight, and this woman knows me.* Evie knew she had seen the blonde before, but not in this setting.

"Do I know you? Where are you from?" Evie asked the woman. The woman laughed. "I'm the fake reporter from Nebraska," she said, slurring her speech. "Excuse me?" Evie asked. Suddenly, Evie's memory came back to her. The woman Beau had pinned down on the floor was standing next to Evie at her fiance's Christmas party.

Evie felt the urge to punch the girl in her perfect nose that probably had plastic surgery a few years ago. "Well, then. What brought you here?"

Evie asked, trying to stay calm. "Your fiancé found me on Tinder and met up with me. We boned for an entire weekend..." The woman continued to explain in gruesome detail that after she and Jude hooked up, he hired her at his office as well as paid her to ruin his ex-wife's relationship with rockstar, Beau Halstead. "Oops, I was supposed to keep quiet," the woman said, laughing.

Evie's blood boiled, and she knew who she wanted to punch instead. She soon grabbed the woman's arm and dragged her out of the bathroom. She began marching right up to Jude and his fellow colleagues. Jude saw the look of fire in Evie's eyes as well as the woman she was dragging behind her. His demeanor went rigid because he remembered Beau's words. Jude saw that rage Beau mentioned.

As Evie got closer, she let go of the woman, moved her old wedding ring to her right ring finger, grabbed the woman again, and proceeded towards Jude. Evie punched Jude right in the eye, making sure he felt every ounce of the ring he gave her 10 years ago. She kneed him in the groin and drove her heel into his foot.

Jude collapsed onto the floor in pain. Everyone witnessed this event, and all of their faces looked mortified for Jude. "You hired this whore to sabotage my relationship with Beau!?" Evie shouted at Jude. Everyone's glance went from Evie to Jude. "You're fired, Rachel," Jude said in pain to the woman. The woman, Rachel, just laughed and drank another cocktail. "Don't make her the fall woman! You sent her to sabotage my relationship with Beau!" Evie shouted. "It was the only way to convince you that Beau was not the man for you or the right father for my children," Jude said, still in pain. Evie grimaced at him.

"You just couldn't let me be happy, could you? You just proved to everyone here what a giant, narcissistic ass wipe you are," Evie said. She took off the wedding ring, threw it on the ground, and stomped on it. The setting shattered on the ground, and the diamond laid next to Jude. A few women started racing for the diamond.

"Screw you, Jude," Evie said, flipping Jude off in true metalhead fashion. Everyone was appalled with Evie's behavior, but she didn't care. "Are you going back to him? I love you more than that bastard does. I loved you enough to pull this off," Jude yelled. Evie said nothing as she walked to the coat check and out of the building.

Evie called an Uber to come pick her up. She planned to pack her clothes and the kids' clothes. Everything else would stay in Jude's house. After she called in an Uber, she quickly called Luke.

"Hello?" he said, sounding very perplexed.

"I want my job back," she said.

Even though Evie couldn't see it, she knew Luke was ecstatic that she called. "Absolutely. When can you start?" he asked.

"Immediately. I am catching the red-eye with Levi and Harper tonight," she said.

"All right. We will see you back tomorrow. Should I tell...?" "No, that's fine. I will surprise him," Evie said.

"Evs, you know he was set up, right?" Luke asked.

"Yes, I do. Jude and the little tart in Beau's dressing room confirmed it all," she said.

"Wait, what?!" Luke asked.

"I'll explain later. I need to book flights," she said.

"Wait! Hold off on buying tickets until you get home."

"Why?"

"Do you trust me?"

"Yeah."

"Just do it. I'll see ya later!" Luke said.

"Bye, Luke," Evie concluded, wondering what that was all about.

Little did Evie know there was a surprise waiting for her at Jude's house, which Luke was a part of. Beau caught an earlier flight to convince Evie to come back. He wasn't sure what he was doing, but the only thing Beau knew was that he loved Evie and had to get her out of Jude's poisonous trap.

He sat down on the sectional in the living room that looked a lot like Evie's couch. Beau assumed Jude went and repurchased the couch to cope with Evie being gone. Beau had parked the car down the street, paid the babysitter, and took over watching the kids.

At first, the babysitter questioned whether or not to call the police until Levi and Harper ran to Beau and hugged him so tightly. "I missed you, Daddy," Harper said. "I missed you, too, Princess," he said. "I missed you, Dad," Levi said. "Bub," Beau said, knowing that pet name meant more to Levi than anything, "you have no idea. I'm never letting you guys leave me again," Beau said with tears in his eyes. When the babysitter saw the reaction, she decided it was okay to leave.

"Where's your mom?" Beau asked the kids. "She went to a party with my other daddy, but he's not my daddy," Harper said. Beau was super impressed with how well the sassy almost three-and-a-half year old was talking. "All right, shall we pack your clothes and blankets?" Beau asked. "Yes," both kids said.

Beau, Levi, and Harper packed clothes and some favorite toys. The kids were sound asleep in their beds, waiting for their mother to come home. Beau sat down on the couch, thinking about what he would say to Evie, and what would happen if she said no. His heart broke at the thought, but he wasn't sure if she could forgive him, although he did nothing wrong. While he sat on the couch, he received a text from Luke saying:

EVIE FOUND OUT. SHE'S COMING BACK. ARE YOU AT HER HOUSE?

Beau texted:

YES. I'M WAITING FOR HER NOW ON THE COUCH.

Luke sent a thumbs-up emoji. Beau put his phone back in his pocket, feeling excited and relieved. Beau looked out the window and saw Evie climbing out of a car with an Uber sticker. She was dressed in a trench coat, a beautiful red pencil dress with her hair pulled back in a bun. He never thought he would see Corporate Wife Evie. However, he thought she was beautiful no matter what she wore or didn't wear. He laughed at the last part of his thought.

Evie walked into Jude's house and began saying, "Lucy, you can go. I'm... home." Evie saw Beau sitting on the couch. Her heart stopped as she froze. He slowly stood and began walking towards her. When they stood two feet away from each other, Beau and Evie looked at each other before she leaned into him, wrapping her arms around his waist. Beau wrapped his arms around her shoulders, resting his left hand on the crown of her head. Tears began flowing down her face. Beau's eyes were a little watery as well.

"I'm so sorry about everything," he finally whispered.

"I'm sorry I left," Evie cried.

They kissed, pulling themselves closer to the other. "We need to get back to San Francisco," Evie said while still kissing Beau. "We have time.

Our flight doesn't leave for four hours," he said, kissing her in between words. Ah, Luke, Evie thought to herself. Beau took off Evie's trench coat, feeling for the zipper on her dress. After finding the zipper, Beau unzipped her dress and folded it down, not caring about the band wrapped around her waist. Evie removed his coat and shirt. Beau lifted Evie up, wrapping her legs around him, and carried her to the kitchen counter as Evie pulled off his belt, and Beau pulled Evie closer and closer to him.

****

They laid down on the living room floor covered with a plush throw. Evie's hair was down out of the bun, and their clothes were all over the room. Beau rubbed Evie's bare back as she laid beside him, resting her head on his bare chest. She listened to his steady heartbeat and smiled, inhaling his scent.

"Beau?"

"Yeah?"

"I have some news. Like big news," Evie said.

Beau looked at her perplexed. Evie propped herself up higher to where she could see his face. "I'm pregnant, and you're the father," she said slowly. Beau looked flabbergasted at first but then softened to utter joy.

"Are you sure it's mine?" he asked.

"Positive. Jude and I were never intimate. Plus, I'm due in July, which if we do the math..."

Beau was filled with joy. "That's... that's wonderful! I'm just so sorry all of this led you back here."

"In a way, I am glad all this happened. I got to sucker-punch Jude, flip him off in front of his company, and make love to you in his house after I found out he sabotaged our relationship."

Beau laughed. "I rubbed off on you, and it's made you even hotter. How did you find out?"

"Miss Slutty Reporter was at the party tonight telling me all about it, and Jude confirmed it as well."

"Wow, that's quite the night for you." Beau felt very proud of Evie going full metalhead on her ex-husband.

They both smiled at each other and kissed again. Beau looked at his watch. "We have about two hours before our flight leaves," he said. "Okay. I will get dressed and pack my stuff. Will you go help the kids…"

"Their stuff is packed and in the rental car. We just need to put them inside," Beau said.

Evie smiled. "I love you more, and more every day, Beau William Halstead," she said.

"And I love you," Beau said, reaching for his pants and pulling a little box out from the pocket. Evie's eyes widened. "Genevieve Willa West Long, will you marry me?" Beau asked, opening the box to reveal the most beautiful double claw-set oval opal halo ring with tiny diamonds forming around a rose gold band. Evie's heart raced. "Yes," she said. They kissed again, and he slipped the ring on her finger.

After two minutes, they both got up. Beau put his jeans, tee-shirt, and jacket back on. Evie put her bra and underwear back on before she went upstairs to the master suite into the walk-in closet. Evie put on jeggings, a Death Toll tee shirt she kept hidden from Jude, a sweatshirt she kept of

Beau's, and her favorite maroon hat with the wide-brim. Evie put her tall beige boots on.

She grabbed the largest duffle bag she could find and shoved all of her clothes, shoes, and accessories inside. Evie left the red dress and black pumps she wore that night laying on the living room floor. She then went to the bathroom and shoved all of her cosmetics she would need inside.

Beau walked outside and pulled the rental car into the driveway. He went back inside, grabbed Levi, walked back to the car, and put him inside. Once Levi was buckled, Beau got out of the car, went back upstairs inside the house to grab Harper, but stopped when he saw Evie carrying her. Beau then grabbed all the bags, blankets, and pillows. He followed Evie outside to the car and put everything in the trunk. He climbed back into the driver's side and waited for Evie to finish buckling Harper up. As Beau pulled out of the driveway, Evie watched as Jude's house grew smaller and smaller, feeling liberated.

Once they got on the plane, Evie and Beau cuddled on a first-class seat, Beau talked to Evie's stomach and slept. The kids slept in their own individual seats. Once the plane landed, they grabbed their luggage and walked through the terminal to Beau's car. He still had all the car seats installed in his Range Rover. It was 3:00 AM in San Francisco, so when they got back to Beau's house, they all went back to sleep. He had kept all of their rooms the same.

Everyone finally woke up at about 10:00 AM. Beau made a late breakfast while Evie helped the kids get ready for the day. "Guys, we have something big to tell you," Beau said after everyone sat down at the dining room table. Levi and Harper looked up from their plates. "I asked your mother to marry me, and she said yes," Beau concluded. The kids cheered and gave Beau and their mother a hug. "So, you will really be my dad?" Levi asked. "Yes," Beau said, remembering conversations he had with Evie about adopting the kids. They ran to where Beau was sitting and hugged him. Evie watched, smiled, and held back tears. She would tell them about the baby later.

Evie spent the rest of the morning and early afternoon calling her family and friends as Beau went to the studio to rehearse and informed the band of the events that transpired. Everyone was thrilled to hear the news, but some had concerns considering all that had happened to Evie.

"I thought you were engaged to..." Jennifer began asking her sister.

"Jude fooled us all," Evie said.

"Are you sure?"

"Yes. Why else would I move back here?"

"Fair point. It's just you've been through so much already, and we're just worried about you."

"You will always worry about me because I'm your baby sister, but I promise. The issues have been resolved," Evie reassured. Jennifer couldn't remember the last time she heard this much resilience from her sister.

Evie and the kids stayed home to play outside as well as rest, considering she was always fighting nausea. Evie began looking ahead in the calendar to see when the best time to set a date for the wedding would be. She thought about waiting a year after the baby was born to get married. She wanted to discuss everything with Beau to make sure he was okay with planning a wedding in 18 months.

After playing outside for three hours, Evie put Harper down for a nap, and put a movie on for Levi. She re-enrolled him in school for the next day. Evie planned to stay home for the duration of the tour to help Levi with school, providing consistency in her children's lives, taking care of herself during her pregnancy. Still, she planned to stay on top of tour updates, scheduling with the band as well as attending the concerts in the Bay area. Levi eventually fell asleep watching TV, and Evie carried him upstairs to his room. She made her way to the master, where she laid down on the bed and dozed off.

Beau walked in through the garage door to discover his house a little too quiet, which was unusual even before all Hell broke loose. Still, Beau remembered everyone was trying to catch up on sleep. He quietly went upstairs to check on everyone.

Sure enough, the kids were sound asleep in their rooms. Peace and calm entered Beau as he closed each door and walked towards his room. Looking through the door, Beau saw Evie lying down on her left side, sound asleep. Quietly, he walked in, took off his shoes, and snuggled up next to her, wrapping his right arm around her making sure to rub her stomach with his baby inside. Beau dozed off for a minute as well. Never had he been so happy.

www.ingramcontent.com/pod-product-compliance
Lightning Source LLC
Chambersburg PA
CBHW070915260626
47162CB00007B/2683